Aktal and the
Five Planets of Han

By

John Charles Harman

Prologue

I began writing this book in 1985. I heard that if you wanted to become an author it was a pretty good idea to start with a science fiction book. Why that is I do not really know! It took about 8 years to finish the book and it was all typed on an old electronic typewriter. I printed it out and there it sat on a shelf gathering dust. I never even looked at the manuscript for at least ten years!

Soon enough I had a computer and started writing on the computer. I wrote other novels. "Blood and Butterflies" being my most popular to date. It was much easier to write on a computer, but don't let anyone fool you, editing tools are not yet perfected!

Many years later I pulled the typewritten manuscript off the shelf and began the arduous process of typing it into the computer. This proved to be a lot more difficult than I imagined so I often only did a few pages a week.

I have always been a big fan of science and new technologies. My degree is a Bachelor of Science in Kinesiology from UCLA. I have always enjoyed writing but it has never been a career. Writers do not often make decent livings or get paid very well. Here in 2017, the average length of a novel has shrunk from 80,000 words twenty years ago to now under 50,000 words. People read and purchase fewer hardcover books than anytime in modern history. Some feel that online digital media has brought this lack of reading about. Others think that our educational institutions have lowered their standards and not emphasized the importance of reading for both education and enjoyment. I won't express my opinion at this time. I think a good story is a good story no matter the time period. I write because I have stories to tell.

Most science fiction, be it literature or media, is far beyond scientific probability. This seems to be an ongoing trend. I like to call it the "Toy Story" phenomena. The common saying,

"To Infinity and Beyond", is an oxymoron. We have so much computing power nowadays that it is possible to show that, "anything" is possible. Our Universe is just so large that really anything is possible! The reality is that we would be much better off to focus on what is probable not what is possible, because the massive amounts of energy required to make a lot of what we see in Science Fiction into reality is highly improbable. Actually for the betterment of our own future on our small green blue/green planet we would be a lot better off to eliminate the word, "impossible" and replace it with "improbable" so that we can focus more of our education and research money on projects that benefit humanity other than concepts that deceive humanity. The tremendous amount of computing power we have today has led governments and private industries to fund way too many worthless projects.

This book was mainly creating out of a dream I had when I was 12 years old. It is worthy to note that I predicted WIFI when I wrote this book over 20 years ago. What I believe and what you believe in regards to alien life forms, visits from aliens, aliens influence on human culture may differ and that is probably good for all of us. I'm a scientist, so I write to hopefully make you think, not to convince you of a theory either with or without evidence.

In all my literature I try to teach with analogies, plots and interactions to show the value of morality, devotion and open mindedness. I think those are good qualities to have!

My other novels can be found at www.JohnCharlesHarman.com

THERE WAS NEVER A BEGINNING ONLY THE FLUX OF TIME AND MATTER. LIFE EVOLVED THROUGHOUT OUR PULSATING AND ENDLESS UNIVERSE IN A MYRIAD OF FORMS. NATURALLY COMMUNICATION EXPANDED BEYOND INDIVIDUAL PLANETS. TRAVEL AND EXPLORATION TOUCHED REALMS OF WHAT WAS PERCIEVED AS MYSTICAL. IN REALITY MOST OF THOSE PERCEPTIONS WERE SUBJECTIVE AND OFTEN UNEXPLAINABLE.

Chapter 1
Mr. Kyn

Five planets orbited the waning sun called Han. All of the planets were of more or less the same age and the same size. They circled their mother sun at nearly equal distances yet miraculously their orbits never collided. Even more mathematically rare and visually odd was that each planet had two moons. Now some had bigger moons others smaller but they all had two. The odds of that happening have to be just outrageous yet taking odd to another level is also the fact that even with all the similarities, the five planets had very different environments. Their geographical paths differed and life evolved only on the planet Mara. The other four planets remained barren until the migrations began.

The people of Mara lived in a lush green paradise. The planet was overall slightly warmer than our earth. There were warm sub-tropical forests and huge snowcapped mountains. Clear streams flowed into numerous sparkling lakes. In actual size Mara was about three quarters the size of our Earth. Mara became overpopulated early in its evolution. In spite of the overcrowded conditions the Marans lived in relative peace.

The other four planets, Yih, Misa, Tyijo, and Kulo were thought of as the homes of strange and mystical spirits for as long as the Marans could remember. As modernization and technology developed the myths faded and it was learned that all four of the planets had potential for migrations. It was discovered that no other life-forms had originated on the other four planets and therefore each planet would require unique methods to create environments that were habitable.

Tyijo Kyn almost felt like a great warrior at times. This was not a common feeling for a Maran. As a matter of fact it was not normal feeling for Mr. Kyn and he didn't feel this way too often. He had been alone way too long for any civilized creature either of this earth or of an alien planet so he spent a lot of time thinking. Now as he was getting older he did a lot more than just think he also fantasized about being a great warrior. He imagined himself as a great warrior of the past, old tales of how the Marans fought off their rival to take control of the planet. Unfortunately he knew too well that the past was long gone and that the fantasy was just a whim of his mind to kill time; time alone. He let his mind go back to his plans for the future. It was hard to concentrate though because he didn't want to ponder his dilemma, so, back to the great warrior. Mr. Kyn smiled and ate some more of the sacred fruit.

Mr. Kyn came to the planet called, Tyijo, when he was a young child. He was named after the planet because his Father wanted to be one of the first immigrants to the new planet. The Father was one of many workers who helped transform the toxic gasses of the planet into breathable oxygen, an atmosphere similar to Earth. It had taken decades, with the aid of robotic machines, to transform the atmosphere so that it could sustain life. Tyijo Kyn's Father came on to the project in the later stages and his wife had become pregnant during this time so they decided if the child was a boy they would name him after the planet. Now that the once barren planet had become suitable for migrations it also became the home of Tyijo, the child.

Mr. Kyn was quite different from his Father. He was very reserved, thoughtful and often lonely. The biggest difference between Tyijo Kyn and his Father was that even though Tyijo was lonely he was never bored. Tyijo saw his Father when he retired and his Father did nothing, just sit around and go to entertainment venues, nothing creative, nothing thoughtful, and nothing that had a lasting value. Still, Tyijo remembered his Father the day before he died when Tyijo was only 17 years old. It was a sad day. Accidents happen and even though he was aware of that he never thought about it happening to anyone he knew, especially not his Father. The transport vehicle malfunctioned and crashed. The Universe was perfect because it was flawed and random, Tyijo knew this and he knew his relationship with his Father had never been that perfect. Still he honored his Father, and he loved his Father.

Years passed and now the main reason Tyijo was never bored was because he was just way to wealthy. He was middle aged for a Maran and at the peak of his success. The times had changed and he knew this was a crossroad, maybe a historical one.

He had duties with his various corporations. He enjoyed his hobbies and a few close friends. The truth is that Mr. Kyn was by far the wealthiest of all Marans and it all happened by good thinking and opportune luck. Because of his wealth and some outcries from certain aspects of Maran culture he had to maintain a low profile so he was almost never seen anywhere in public. His wealth enabled him to now be almost a complete recluse and he was starting to like it. Mr. Kyn had inherited the foundation of his wealth from his Father. After the death of his Father, Tyijo acquired old land contracts his Father had won in a big card game before he left his company. At first Tyijo thought the land was far too remote and uninhabitable so Tyijo just held onto the contracts for the first year. The second year the Federation started contacting him asking for higher tax payments and Tyijo guessed the land must be worth more than what he thought it was worth so he had it investigated. The results of the investigation were more than fruitful. Tyijo found out that the Federation knew the land had vast deposits of precious minerals and one rare mineral used in energy technology. The Federation had been trying to repurchase the land contracts for the past 5 years but Tyijo's Father held out and said nothing to anyone. Tyijo didn't like that he had to find out on his own but he started to understand why.

30 years later and the mining operations were almost completely automated with the aid of state of the art robotics. One month after Mr. Kyn had found out that the Federation wanted his land he formed a mining company. One of the mining company's first acquisitions was a Federation robotic company that was outdated. Mr. Kyn's mining company grew exponentially with the aid of the best mining robotics. It was thirty years ago that Mr. Kyn started his hobby and passion for personal robots just as his wealth began to grow with the mining company.

A his wealth grew he purchased more and more land adjacent to his until eventually he owned almost all the land as far as one could see from the highest mountain. The operation was small compared to the surrounding land but the operation headquarters was very large. The support staff was around a hundred and they had state of the art living quarters so many of them rarely left. Not many of them ever saw Mr. Kyn though and when they did it was for brief discussions in small groups always about certain aspects of the various operations. The vast majority of the operations were run by robots. The staff had multiple personal robots that controlled the automated mining operations. The personal robots at Mr. Kyn's lavish palace were rumored to have been modified in various ways but this was mainly just due to his reputation for reclusiveness. Because Mr. Kyn was so far removed now from Maran culture he really had become somewhat of a legend that most Maran's were not sure really existed.

Mr. Kyn's palace was also a highly rumored and ongoing legend in Maran culture. Back on the home planet in the largest cities where most of the wealthier Marans lived new rumors about the palace would surface at least twice a year.

Of course there were a number of older pictures that were taken more than ten years ago and the satellite photos of the palace that showed it was there but then again many Marans believed this was just propaganda from the Federation and that the Federation actually ran the mining operations. Still the old photos were impressive with the ornate walls of solid gold and silver. A somewhat endless mixture of alloys and colors splattered with various finishes to the surfaces in conjunction with the lighting. A glimmering maze of halls and passage's that only one who lived there would know led to quaint yet functional rooms. There were artful designs everywhere one's eyes looked. Etched metal walls and various forms of backlighting lent a feeling that time was slowing down. It was a peaceful place. You could not help but stand and stare at wall after wall. The palace was so large that it would take at least one day to see all the various rooms and workshops. The most interesting rumor to the Marans was a rumor that was actually true. There were no doors or gates. 20 years ago when Mr. Kyn designed the palace. He had already experienced over ten years of nearly constant isolation as the mining operation was being set up. It was a very remote area. He realized from staying with his workers at the main base that they would all have to have the best comforts if his operations were to thrive and he realized that the concept of security needed to be changed. In such an isolated area there was no need for so many doors and gates; they were isolated and they had personal robots. The spiraling entries were designed to keep out the elements. Visitors that came on space vehicles from the home planet or others and the Marans that worked at the mining operation had to take an underground magnetic subway to Mr. Kyn's place that was nearly twenty miles from the main mining operation. It was nearly impossible to get to the palace on foot because the terrain was scattered with large boulders and extremely arid landscape. The migrations were focusing on the other side of the planet where the climate was much milder.

Almost every day there was a small group of Marans that came to visit Mr. Kyn; well actually they came mainly to visit the palace because rarely did any of them meet with Mr. Kyn. The most interesting part was that these Marans that came were exclusively at the invitation of the corporation and only rarely was any Federation official allowed to visit. There were both men and women that came to visit the palace and the robots that were showcased there. The visitors that came knew the main reason they were coming and almost always were more than happy they had visited. The palace was lavish and ornate in its own right similar to a large museum on their home planet. It was worth saying you had seen the palace but the robots Mr. Kyn displayed for sale were mainly why Marans came to visit. They usually ended up purchasing one or more of the new prototypes.

Chapter 2
Aktal

Kyn's sexual robots were the top brand amongst Marans. Marans had migrated from their home planet and were enjoying an unprecedented surge in their personal comfort and wealth. It was just how the society had evolved. Maran culture had always been a highly sexual culture. They had early on become the dominate species throughout their planet. When the planet had reached a stage of ecological imbalances and environmental degradation the Marans had not yet developed advanced technologies or space travel. They knew the other planets were habitable if the environments were modified. Yet even though they knew the theory and science of how to do it the full effort was not committed until almost the turning point of destroying their home planet. The Federation was forced to finance private green industries and technologies. It was at this phase that birth control was mandated. Philosophies changed and leisure became dominated with sex. The Maran's sexual urges only increased and now that the migrations were underway it seemed that the need to experience adventures had enhanced the Marans sexual desires all over again. Recreation was easy, artificial wombs were becoming popular and the populous enjoyed more leisure time as robots did more and more of the work.

The Marans were small creatures about half the size of humans. They had larger hands and feet in proportion to humans. Some of their features were similar to ours but the main difference was that they had only one eye with two larger than normal pupils in the middle of their bulging forehead. They originally had hair, and in a way seemed ape like, but evolution had rid them of any hair other than on the backs of their hands and feet. They were slow moving and peaceful creatures. They often stopped to pause and think before they continued walking.

Almost all of their aggressive traits had disappeared over the 150, 000 years of their evolution, yet, they were still evolving. At least Mr. Kyn knew he was still evolving! With the continued phase of migrations Marans were becoming increasingly independent and open minded especially the ones living on the outlying planets. From a lack of space to too much space the Marans were changing their belief systems. The amount of Marans acquiring and creating wealth was on an unparalleled rise and this also strengthened the Federation because of taxes they could take in. It was the beginning of a golden age for Marans and most could feel the excitement of the times.

It had been rumored for quite a while now that Mr. Kyn preferred the company of his robots to that of other Marans. Now, Mr. Kyn's closest friend, Kafta, new the rumor was even truer than anyone even could imagine. This was only recent though and one hundred percent due to the new prototype. This prototype was far beyond any technologies most could ever imagine. It had been over 5 years in development and re-development. By far it was one of the most secretive projects that Mr. Kyn had ever undertaken.

Mr. Kyn always woke up early. He liked to walk out to his patio and watch the sun rise early in the morning. He usually wore a purple or dark blue robe, the colors of his company and the only two colors he wore. He was alone in the morning and he liked it that way. His personal robots were at his beck and call but he liked to have plenty of time to himself. He liked to think and he liked to plan. When he looked at his communicator he saw he had a note from his friend Kafta.

"To my dearest friend, Mr. Kyn, thank you ever so much for graciously letting me be the first of your friends to spend time with your newest prototype. Aktal is an appropriate and lovely name for her. I compliment you on selecting the name. Believe it or not I have found myself becoming very much attached to her on more than one level. I think you would agree this may not be appropriate behavior for us Marans but under the circumstance and due to the fact that you asked me to evaluate the prototype to the best of my ability I have to let you know my feeling. I am not sure this is a good or bad factor should this prototype go to market but I think it is an important subject to discuss at a later time. She is indeed an incredible woman if I may call her a woman and not a robot. Actually, if I may be frank I could almost end the evaluation on that statement and I am sure you understand why. Her movements, behaviors, and communication skills are far beyond anything I have ever seen. You did diligent work in keeping this project secret until now and I am honored to be working with you on this project. We must meet in person soon. I know there must be other things you have to tell me."

After reading the communication Mr. Kyn sat at a small black marble table and looked out at the desolate horizon. He could see one of the air transport vehicles taking off from the mines in the far distance. The processed metal was being exported to the home planet of Mara. He thought to himself, "The mines will create wealth for centuries, but, what will that mean to me long after I am gone?"

Robots had been in use in Maran culture long before Mr. Kyn was born but it is only after Mr. Kyn purchased the robot company for his mining operations that his experimenting with robots became a hobby. His hobby became almost as lucrative as the mines. He was constantly experimenting with various models and refining them for his own needs. When he entered the lucrative market of personal and sexual robots it was right at the height of the migrations. The advanced crews, the immigrants and vast amount of new space increased the demand for robotic labor and company. As the robots become more advanced they also became more responsive but still lacked true emotions. Eventually they had advanced to the level of basic servant with talents and skills.

Aktal exhibited a new generation in robotic technology at least a generation ahead of anything else that had been built and Mr. Kyn knew it. He had planned it that way and had brought in the best of the best to work on the project. He spared no expense and made sure the planning for each phase included breakthroughs in technologies that he directed. The memory capacity alone was unprecedented for a personal robot. What was most incredible was that Aktal was a smart machine. She was able to pick up, compartmentalize, store, analyze and discard data that she constantly scanned from radio and Wi-Fi frequencies. Even more advanced was that Aktal could pick up complex waves emitted from emotional responses including, heat, eye movements, body movements and other sensors. Data was continuously absorbed from the environment and was discriminately stored, discarded or ignored no matter what situation she encountered.

In reality, as Mr. Kyn stared out over the horizon from his small patio he felt uneasy about what the future would hold for him. He knew he had to be scared but at the same time he knew his resolve had to be strengthened. He knew that the robot he had spent so much time in developing was indeed not a robot at all, not a Maran, but a unique, tender, compassionate and continually changing being. It was the first time this had been done in Maran culture. Everyone was under the belief it was at least a century away before the issue of robots gaining rights would have to be legislated.

Aktal looked much different physically from Mr. Kyn's other personal and sexual robots. For reasons only know to Mr. Kyn he had modified her to have two eyes instead of the large single Maran eye. It was one of the main points Mr. Kyn had insisted on when he instructed his development team. When asked by the other scientists why he was making her appear in this way Mr. Kyn always responded that it would be needed to have the two eyes apart to increase her visual capabilities and other sensory functions. Some of the scientists told Mr. Kyn that this would not be good from a standpoint of marketing and Mr. Kyn always responded that the new prototype would break into new yet undiscovered markets. No one thought of doubting Mr. Kyn and his logic, as he had proved time and again his genius. As the process evolved and the prototype started to come together the team could see that Aktal broke all the regulations and limits that were allowed by the Federation. Everyone knew if any of them broke the code of secrecy with Mr. Kyn that they would never work for him again.

Now that Aktal was nearly complete the actual final product was not totally know by the people that had worked on the project. The final stages of the project were covered in even more confidentiality and known only to a few. The small groups that were aware of what this prototype had become knew they had entered a new realm of technology that most likely would change Maran culture forever. Aktal could be a teacher, a companion, and a highly skilled operator of all kinds of equipment. She also had the capacity to lead and control the other robots around her. She was the perfect sexual companion and mate, either male or female. Mr. Kyn knew once the prototype was mass produced it would sell millions and all other personal robots would become antiquated. He also knew he would have to have her approved by the Federation with very strict terms and this is not something Mr. Kyn liked to think about. The good thing was that all the years of solitude had honed Mr. Kyn's senses to think and feel far into the future so he was in no hurry to mass produce his new prototype. He was well aware of the many problems that could arise within Maran culture if the prototype was able to pass Federation guidelines and be sold into the society. What Mr. Kyn knew that no one else knew, not even the scientists that were closest to the project, was that Aktal was being developed by him for a specific purpose. Yes, her so called intelligence was unique but she had other qualities that to him made him think of her as a precious and rare jewel, a gem that you liked to fondle and admire, yet too valuable to reveal to others. The only reason he had sent her to Kafta for the short time he did was because it had scared him how fast he had become attached to her. She had become the perfect friend and companion in a very short time. He liked the feeling but it also overwhelmed him like nothing before in his life. He wanted to see if she had the same effect on Kafta. Now he could tell she had. Mr. Kyn was excited to sit down and talk face to face with Kafta. It would be an interesting conversation.

Chapter 3
Kafta

Even though Kafta was one of Mr. Kyn's best friends there was an element of the friendship that Mr. Kyn kept personal. He had learned over the years that even the closet of friends had the ability to break the high standard of trust that he demanded in all his relationships. Trust had been a key element in his development of Aktal and the fact that this was an underlying theme in all the technology that went into her creation shows how much he honored the trait. Actually Kafta was very much like Tyijo Kyn in that he was highly intelligent and also reclusive.

Kafta lived on the planet Kulo which was the closet planet to Tyijo where Mr. Kyn lived. Many Marans that migrated to one of the outlying planets used the name of the planet or some variation of it in their name. Kafta had no first name as did many Marans. Kulo was the last planet to be settled and still was in effect a lot less habitable than the other planets because of the lack of water. The Federation had almost decided to not try and change the environment on Kulo because of the complexity and cost but in the end Marans wanted to be able to know that they had completed their plan of migrating to all the planets. The Federation had installed series of nuclear reactors at each of the poles of the planet to melt the miles of thick ice so that the planet would warm and have liquid water. The process was well underway but not completed. For the few Marans that lived on Kulo it was a harsh and difficult life because of the harsh conditions. Each day there were strong winds and fierce electrical storms as an effect of melting the ice at the poles. To Kafta though, the storms were magnificent and exciting. He very much enjoyed watching the storms from his window. It was a big change from the bland environment of his home planet Mara.

Kafta endured the long days with his second wife and the pleasures of a comfortable home. His home was small but very functional and filled with all the best that Maran culture had to offer. His wife was constantly spending his money and redecorating the home. The best part of being one of the first immigrants to Kulo was the fact Kafta had lots of time to think and create.

Kafta was the most modest and studious of Mr. Kyn's friends. The seclusion that Kafta enjoyed on the planet Kulo enhanced his creative thinking. His dwelling was not large but it had many rooms. The home was burrowed into a hillside and there were large picture windows in most rooms so that he could take in the incredible views that looked out over the dry valley below. One could sit comfortably with their favorite refreshment and watch the electrical storms as they lit up the evening sky on the horizon.

For the past 20 years Kafta had worked privately for Mr. Kyn as a biological and genetic engineer on a variety of projects. He was the head of engineering for Mr. Kyn's agricultural company that mostly farmed the seas of Mara. Kafta's work had become very important as the migrations expanded and various forms of aquaculture were introduced into the infant lakes and oceans on some of the planets. Kafta had a state of the art lab adjacent to his home and a small crew of 20 workers that came and worked on a rotational basis. Like Mr. Kyn, Kafta kept the socializing with his workers to a bare minimum. The other scientists and assistants that came to work their six month shifts had a very hard time understanding how Kafta could live permanently under such harsh planetary conditions. They were always very happy when their shift was over.

Kafta had been recommended as an expert in the development of artificial skins which Mr. Kyn was starting to use in the development of his latest sexual robots. For the better part of 20 years now their friendship had grown to where now they could each think of the other as their best friend. They conferred over a variety of issues on a regular basis but only visited each other every few years. Over the past ten years Kafta had worked secretly with Mr. Kyn on a number of Mr. Kyn's projects. Mr. Kyn was confident now that he could trust Kafta to keep the prying eyes of the Federation away.

The research and development of the latest project that Kafta led was by far the most secretive. Kafta and his team worked on a number of new technologies that would be implemented into the new personal robot. Kafta realized that Mr. Kyn was working on a highly innovative robot, but for what function she was to be used he could only speculate. One thing he knew for sure is that this was not a robot that was going to be mass produced for the public. The cloud of concealment was by far the most intense that had ever been engaged. Kafta knew that in recent years that Mr. Kyn was having many problems with the Federation on a variety of levels. What was odd to Kafta was why Mr. Kyn wanted a synthetic womb put in the robot. Kafta did not question Mr. Kyn's directions but the idea just did not have any logic to it. Many Marans grew their children in artificial wombs but it was always done in special facilities for that purpose and putting one in a robot just seemed ridiculous. The birth of babies in artificial wombs was highly regulated by Federation laws and if they ever caught wind of what Mr. Kyn was doing there would be severe consequences.

During the past year Kafta had heard less from Mr. Kyn than before in the past. Kafta's work on the project had been completed almost a year prior and he had been wondering until recently if the reason Mr. Kyn had not been in communication was because of possible displeasure on Mr. Kyn's end from the work that he had done. When Mr. Kyn arrived unexpectedly with the extremely unique and lovely robot, Aktal, Kafta was beside himself with excitement and surprise. As usual Mr. Kyn did not explain too much, only that he wanted Aktal to stay with Kafta for two months. Kafta could only tell his wife that Aktal was a new personal robot model that they had been working on and that his job required him to test the robot for a period of two months. When Kafta question Mr. Kyn about what results and tests they should do or were looking for, Mr. Kyn just grinned, crossed his long fingers together and very slowly said, "I will tell you one time only my dear friend Kafta, I want you to relax and take a vacation. Enjoy your life for a few months and give me a full report on everything. You've worked for me many years and now this robot is the fruition of our efforts. So once again, enjoy the fruits of your labor!" Kafta was sort of overwhelmed, humbled and confused but it was an assignment he would be more than happy to take on.

It didn't take long after Mr. Kyn left that Kafta realized he was in the presence of a technological phenomenon far beyond anything most Marans could ever imagine. The combination of technologies used in this robot had not just exceeded Federation regulations; they broke laws that were not even yet written! Kafta was not even sure the Federation would know how to classify this robot at all. Aktal soon proved to Kafta that she was a creation supreme. She was the ultimate being for intellectual and physical stimulation. Kafta now understood why there had been so much secrecy around the project. If the Federation ever discovered what they had created not only would Mr. Kyn's wealth be subject to confiscation but most likely everyone involved in the project would end up in front of a hearing board and lose whatever licenses and status they had. It would cause a complete uproar throughout Maran society on a variety of levels.

After the first week with Aktal, Kafta wanted to contact Mr. Kyn and talk with him, but he was under instructions not to call him. Kafta was exhausted, totally enthralled, and stunned to the extent of not wanting to do anything but wake up and spend time with her. It was truly like spending time with an ancient Goddess from one of the Maran myths. After two weeks Kafta could no longer hold in his emotions and started to send Mr. Kyn messages but of course Mr. Kyn did not respond. Kafta realized he would have to wait until Mr. Kyn returned and in the meantime he would have another 6 weeks with the amazing Aktal.

Towards the end of the two month trial period Kafta started to feel melancholy. He knew it was because he was becoming attached to Aktal. He sent this wife to visit relatives after his first week with Aktal because the experiment was becoming obsessed with Aktal and he could no longer hid her in his lab from his wife. He was reaching a point where he really did not care if his wife even returned and that was not an emotion he felt he should have. Worse was the fact that as his affection on various levels had increased towards Aktal he was feeling younger and more energetic than he had ever felt in his life. He was sure his mental capacities were growing and so he did some tests on himself. He was pleasantly surprised when the results showed that his intelligence level had increased! This was not supposed to happen to a middle aged Maran.

Aktal was both a companion and a teacher. The time Kafta spent with her seemed to not only increase his intelligence but also gave him a strong sense of increased clarity in thought. He knew this was not something he could test but it was definitely happening to him. There was something odd that happened whenever he was in her presence. The air around him seemed to be filled with electricity. It was similar to the feeling he had when he would sit and watch the electrical storms in the valley below only the feeling with Aktal was more subtle. Just as the brilliant colors that ignited the sky on such a regular basis from the storms touched Kafta somewhere deep inside of him, Aktal was doing the same and even more. He knew he was becoming part of something that would shift the culture of his people.

Kafta and Aktal were lounging quietly while they watched the colorful sunset. Kafta was reflecting on the time he had spent with Aktal over the past two months when his phone buzzed. Kafta left Aktal and walked into the adjacent room pushed the button on his phone and saw Mr. Kyn's smiling face.

"How is life on that stormy planet of yours? You know the Federation is having a very hard time getting people to migrate there even with all the incentives they are offering!" Mr. Kyn said.

"Tyijo I thought I would never get a chance to talk to you. It is about time you called me. Did you get all the messages I sent? Well, I know you did. You leave this amazing creation of yours here with me and I don't even get a chance to thank you!" Kafta replied.

"You know me better than most Kafta, so, let's just say I have been busy. Like I told you when I left her there with you I just wanted you to have enough time to enjoy your life for a while and have a full experience with Aktal in the privacy of your own secluded retreat. Let's not discuss anything right now. I will be there in two days and we can have plenty of long talks. " Mr. Kyn said.

"I have nowhere to go so you know I will be here. I look forward to your visit my dear friend. Oh yes, and thank you for at last contacting me!" Kafta replied with a smile. After the conversation ended and as Kafta strolled back into the room where Aktal waited he started having thoughts that he knew he shouldn't have. He was thinking about taking Aktal and running away with her and that is why he said that odd sentence to Mr. Kyn that he had nowhere to go! Something had changed in the past two months and he knew it was all because of this amazing creation that sat gazing out the window at the sunset with him and seemingly enjoy the splendor of the colorful sky.

Chapter 4
The Journey Begins

    The two days before Mr. Kyn was to travel to the planet Kulo to visit Kafta were very busy. Even though Mr. Kyn was the President of numerous corporations his time remained exclusively his own and he liked it that way. All of his enterprises were managed very well and running smoothly without him most of the time. Mr. Kyn knew that his youth was past him. He had never properly married and the elite society would never accept him because of that. Sometimes this bothered him but now that he was at the stage in his life where only the future mattered he blocked those thoughts from his mind. He knew the choices that he made now were the choices that would guide him until his death. He felt he was ready for the excitement that all the changes would bring.

    Mr. Kyn was the head of the only inter-planetary transport vehicle company that was privately owned. The other companies were now controlled by the government due to the fact that when the migrations were reaching the peak the Federation saw it as a necessity to keep ticket prices low for passengers. In a way Mr. Kyn helped pay for the migrations because he paid an outrageous tax on his transport vehicles even though they were mainly used only for the transport of the precious minerals from his mines. Ten years ago Mr. Kyn took on his first and only project that partnered him with the Federation. Mr. Kyn's company and the Federation had been working together to build a new spaceship that could travel within their galaxy. In reality it was Mr. Kyn's company that was doing all the research and development. The Federation was simply giving Mr. Kyn's corporation tax credits in the future on his other transport vehicles. Intergalactic probes had been sent to explore other nearby galaxies but there was very little interest by Marans in traveling away from their home planets due to the fact that they had solved the environmental problems on their home planet of Mara and since they were now settling the other planets they had what seemed like a very secure future. The simple desire for exploration was not as strong as it had been in the past. Still the Federation wanted the ability to travel within their Galaxy. It was the logical next step after they settled their home planets. The members of the Federation that headed this project also knew that someday in the future Mr. Kyn would die and they were prepared to take over all of his companies so it was sound logic to let him work on the project.

      The first two spaceships that Mr. Kyn's company built used the most advanced fusion technology which was provided by the Federation. They were fully tested on the ground and everyone involved was satisfied with the progress that had been achieved. Mr. Kyn's contract was extended with an order for ten more vehicles. The first vehicle was launched and Marans everywhere viewed the launch. It was a historic and significant event that had been the pinnacle of the last 100 years of tremendous technological achievements. Though the majority of Marans did not see the need to travel within their galaxy they still felt proud at what their culture had achieved.

      Less than a year into the voyage the contract with Mr. Kyn was canceled and the whole intergalactic expansion directive was scrapped. There never was any official word from the Federation as to what happened but the story that leaked out was that the vehicle had malfunctioned and that all 80 of the Marans aboard perished. Mr. Kyn for the very first time in his career realized he had to make some type of public statement despite the fact that the Federation officials in charge of the project wanted Mr. Kyn to remain silent. Mr. Kyn's statement was short and he denied having any knowledge of the vehicle malfunctioning. He also let his fellow Marans know that his involvement in the project had been under the supervision of Federation officials. Privately Mr. Kyn and his staff had a strong belief that the vehicle had not malfunctioned and that all that had happened is that a nearby super nova had cut communications.

What ensued from the fiasco was a large legal battle where the Federation demanded all of the completed intergalactic vehicles be turned over to them along with massive refunds of monies that had been loaned to Mr. Kyn for his involvement in the projects. In reality the whole situation was being created by the Federation to try and take money, power and property away from the Kyn Empire. Consequently the Federation passed strict laws that prohibited private ownership of intergalactic vehicles. Mr. Kyn's wealth was dented but still intact with the core mining operations still going strong. Mr. Kyn knew that his wealth was now under serious scrutiny within the Federation and that it would not be long before he came under attack again.

During this trying time in his life, Tyijo Kyn thought often about his Father and wished that he was still alive. He knew that it was only because of the wisdom that his Father had imparted to him that he was able to maintain his composure during the numerous hearings he had to endure in front of the various Federation committees. Often when he sat alone on the stand and answered absurd question after absurd question he recalled the time he had walked along the edge of the lake near his home with his Father and his Father told him how the good of the Marans did not always rest in the hands of the Federation. He told his son, Tyijo, that there would be times in his life when it may be necessary to skirt the laws of the Federation for the greater good of the Maran people. At the time Tyijo did not fully understand what his Father was telling him but now he did.

After the grueling hearings the legal battles went on and it became more and more apparent that the Federation did not like the fact that Mr. Kyn had his hands in all the enterprises that he did. Mr. Kyn often wondered if it was just pure jealously by the government officials or was there some other underlying reason that his wealth was being scrutinized so often. It was very clear now that the Federation was intent on breaking up Mr. Kyn's companies in any way they could. As time progressed the legal battle intensified and as a result Mr. Kyn's need for secrecy with his projects also increased.

When the Aktal project was completed Mr. Kyn took on an air of aloofness that he had never done before. Even his closet friends thought there was something wrong with him because he often would not communicate with anyone for weeks at a time. He stayed alone in his home or at one of his other retreats. What no one knew was that he was not alone because he was with Aktal. He was sad about the way his affairs had turned out with the Federation. He had never thought of the government as his foe and he knew many people that worked within the Federation. The people he knew always seemed a bit stiff and aloof but they were Marans like him and they wanted the best for the Maran people as did he. Far worse was than feeling sad about the situation was that he felt complacent. Tyijo had never felt complacent in his life and it was a new experience. He did not like the feeling at all. When he did communicate with the various heads of his companies he found himself putting projects on hold and constantly saying to them that he would have to think about things for a while. This was not like him and this was not how he was able to create his wealth. It was at this time that his other close friend, Jacon, was able to pull him out of his doldrums and once again spark the fighting spirit Tyijo knew he had lost.

Jacon was the head engineer for Mr. Kyn's mining transport spaceships. Like Kafta, Jacon, had no last name. Mr. Kyn recognized the abilities that Jacon possessed and could see that Jacon's temperament was similar to his. When the contract for the intergalactic ships had been awarded to Mr. Kyn, he put Jacon in charge of the project. Jacon was a small agile Maran that seemed to have an unlimited energy to go along with his brilliant mind. He and Tyijo Kyn became friends on a level that only too geniuses could. They carried on seeming endless dialogues that often went off on wild yet feasible tangents. The main focus of their conversations centered on aspects of intergalactic travel and what that would mean for the Maran culture. Mr. Kyn realized early in his friendship with Jacon that he would be able to trust Jacon because they shared many of the same ideals and quests to discover new technologies that would benefit their Maran culture.

When the Federation canceled the contract Jacon was emotionally crushed and beside himself with anger. During the ensuing hearings and lawsuits Jacon wrote numerous articles and gained a strong following with his harsh criticism of the Federation and its powers. Jacon saw no logical reason as to why the Federation was slowing and even preventing the progress of technology for intergalactic travel. Secretly and without any approval from his boss Jacon carried out plans of his own. He was almost one hundred percent sure that Mr. Kyn would approve but it was just too risky to let him know anything due to the scrutiny of the Federation. Also, he didn't want the burden of guilt to fall on Mr. Kyn if things went wrong. He knew his career would be done, that he may be put away in jail for a long time, heads would roll and people would lose their jobs but it was a risk he felt he was forced to take. Something had to change within the ruling elite of the Federation and maybe this would be the catalyst for it. Marans had just become too well off and too comfortable now that they were in an era of leisure and wealth. Most Marans just assumed that their governing bodies were working for the overall betterment of the Maran culture when in reality, as Jacon knew only too well, many inside the Federation were just trying to increase their own status and wealth.

Unlike the vast majority of Marans, Jacon was very religious but not in the old beliefs that were long forgotten by Marans who had grown up with a thorough education and understanding of science. Jacon was religious and it was based in his vast experience as a scientist. His beliefs focused around a universal rhythm or law that imbued every aspect of matter. He was sure this law or rhythm existed because he had witnessed it in the results of many of his experiments when he worked on the fission reactors for the intergalactic space craft. Now as the quagmire of problems with the Federation engulfed him he had a deep sense that somehow he was going to be protected by an aura of simple energy and that all of his actions would lead him closer to truly understanding this ultimate law.

Events changed quickly in the two days after Mr. Kyn had talked with Kafta and told him that he would go there to talk with him and retrieve Aktal. Mr. Kyn was almost in a state of frenzy because of what was happening now. He sent a message to Kafta telling him that he should immediately take Aktal and go to his Fifth Palace on the planet Misa. He warned Kafta to be cautious and not let anyone know where and when he was traveling.

Mr. Kyn's Fifth Palace on the planet Misa was one of his favorite places to visit. Misa was called the planet of fog. The temperature was warmer than the other planets and in most areas a thick fog was always present. It was not a popular planet for the Marans to migrate to and the Federation offered large financial perks for those that would migrate there. Some Marans that came from the more equatorial areas of Mara did actually enjoy the environment and definitely preferred it to the dryer planets. The planet did have many elderly and very rich Marans on it that populated the southern part of the planet. These were wealthy older people and many had lavish homes. Mr. Kyn owned his own island on the planet and was expanding his aquaculture business. The palace he built there was not nearly as large as his home on Tyijo but it was much larger than any other estates on the planet. Mr. Kyn preferred to invite his friends to Misa because it was very secluded and Misa did not have a large presence of Federation officials as the other planets.

Kafta assumed the Mr. Kyn had changed his mind because he wanted to spend more time discussing the business prospects of marketing a personal robot like Aktal. Mr. Kyn often had high level business meetings at this palace. Kafta had some ideas but he knew it was going to be extremely difficult to get this prototype to market within the current Federation regulations.

Jacon had also been invited to the palace. He had an intuitive feeling why but at the same time he feared that Mr. Kyn had other plans for him. The now closed transport company had been a major issue between the two of them recently.

Once at the palace on Misa, Mr. Kyn made sure that Jacon and Kafta were kept apart and not aware that the other was there until the actual time that he was going to meet with them. Although Kafta and Jacon were two of Mr. Kyn's closest friends they did not have a lot of admiration for each other and they were not intimate friends. They had met each other on various occasions and on a few occasions the tension between the two of them disrupted the meetings. It was early in the evening and both Jacon and Kafta wanted to see Mr. Kyn but he made some excuses and told both of them that he would meet with them in the morning. Mr. did request to see Aktal and so she went immediately to see her creator. That night Mr. Kyn barely slept at all. He spent the whole conferring and honing plans with Aktal and a secret friend of his.

Aktal had evolved in the short time she had been functioning into a highly into advanced being. Mr. Kyn was very happy he had her helping him to make the decision he needed to make with haste. There was a simplicity of logic that Mr. Kyn admired in her and that was one of the reasons she had such a profound effect on Kafta. As the evening wore on Mr. Kyn was able to analyze all of his options very quickly. The fact he had been away from Aktal for the past two months made him realize even more profoundly that he had taken on the role a creator and he was very proud of his creation. As much as her presence stimulated him mentally it also scared him because he knew his life was going to change in a very dramatic way.

Chapter 5
The Meeting

It was nearly noon and not out of the norm, Mr. Kyn was late for the meeting he had called with his associates. Jacon and Kafta were sitting patiently waiting for Mr. Kyn to arrive. They were both surprised to see one other. They were rivals and as usual behaved in a snarky way towards each other. As they sat quietly the tension between them was as usual thick in the air. They had greeted each other cordially then sat down in silence waiting for Mr. Kyn.

Kafta still felt the glow form the time he had spent with Aktal so he was in a very good mood. He decided to break the silence. "You must be pretty upset about what happened with the Galaxy project. Actually, you know, I read some of your biting articles in the journals." Jacon stared down at the patterns on the marble floor and did not respond. Kafta decided to continue to rub it in with more remarks. "Well didn't I tell you years ago that you were using your talents in the wrong field? I distinctly recall encouraging you to go into bio-technology like me. It has been the most lucrative field of science with all the migrations. You should have heeded my advice. I am sure when Mr. Kyn gets here you will see exactly what I mean!" Kafta was hoping that Mr. Kyn had Aktal with him when he showed up and he could brag about his part in her development. Jacon looked up from the marble floor and scowled.

At last Mr. Kyn entered the room with Aktal by his side. Jacon was instantly taken aback and had a stunned look on his face. He stared at Aktal with his mouth open. Mainly he was staring at her two eyes. He had never seen a personal robot with two eyes and the dark metallic blue color was also different. "Welcome Jacon and welcome Kafta. Jacon I would like to introduce you to my personal robot, Aktal. She is our most recent experimental prototype and I am sure you will discover she is more than a normal robot assistant." Mr. Kyn sat down opposite his two employees with Aktal at his side. Mr. Kyn was very alert and refreshed even though he had not slept the night before.

Aktal saw that Jacon was staring at her so she stood, stepped over to him and reached out her hand. "It is a pleasure to meet you Jacon." Her voice was soft and alluring. Jacon knew instantly that this was not a normal robot. "Tyijo has said many admirable things about you." Jacon nodded his head and stared at her.

Mr. Kyn stood up. "Please follow me everyone. We will have a serious and lengthy discussion but here is not the place." He led them outside to a small sculpture garden. Most of the sculptures were of various types of sea life and were carved out of large slabs of granite and marble. Spaced between the sculptures there sat large pots with exotic flowers. On one side of the garden was fountain carved out of a large dark blue stone. In the center of the garden was a circular mosaic of semi-precious stones. The mosaic also displayed various forms of sea life. Mr. Kyn motioned for them to stand next to him on the mosaic. The others followed his direction and stood quietly looking at each other wondering what was going on. Very slowly and almost imperceptible at first the mosaic began to sink into the floor. They soon realized they were being lowered into an expansive underground chamber. Mr. Kyn explained to them that this was a clandestine place and that they were never to reveal it to anyone. Jacon and Kafta started asking questions as they were gradually going down at least 50 yards to the floor below and Mr. Kyn politely answered them. Soon they were able to see the full view of the chamber and they stopped asking questions staring at the wonder of the chamber below. They could see that the roof above them was made of some type of luminous material and made the floor below appear to have depth. Both Jacon and Kafta knew if Mr. Kyn was taking them to this private chamber that he had some very serious issues to discuss with them.

Right about as the platform reached the bottom Mr. Kyn spoke up again, "This is going to be very special for both of you. You may not like each other as much as you should but it is important to know that you are my two closest friends. This is a critical time and I need your help and guidance. Whether you are aware of it or not I feel we share a lot of the same feelings about our roles as Marans and our roles in this life. I only ask you now to contemplate very seriously everything that occurs from this moment on and please prepare yourself to make decisions based not on your emotions but on what you think is the best for all of us including our society. Also, I have to remind you that no matter what, everything you see and hear at this meeting must remain completely confidential."

They had reached the bottom and Mr. Kyn led them off to the side where there was a small area set up with a large table laden with many traditional Mara refreshments. It looked very inviting and comfortable indeed. This was something that Marans liked; being comfortable.

Jacon was very perceptive and he could tell from the fact that there were seven seats at the table that three of the participants had yet to arrive. He glanced at Kafta as he took a small piece of pastry and put it in his mouth. He could see that Kafta was also looking at the empty seats and wondering whom the seats were reserved for. Both knew Mr. Kyn had three sons ad they suspected the seats were for them.

Mr. Kyn had never married because Maran culture was extremely class oriented. When Mr. Kyn had fallen in love with a woman from below his class he tried to keep the relationship private. The boys were raised here on Miso far from probing eyes. Two years ago the boy's Mother had died in an accident when the inter-planetary vehicle crashed. It had been suspected that the crash was not an accident but a plot to kill the mother.

Mr. Kyn was very depressed and became even more suspicious of the Federation than he already was. The younger boys were twins so out of fear Mr. Kyn sent them to stay with Jacon's brother who was a prominent and well liked artist who lived in a place even more secluded than Mr. Kyn. The young boys loved their new home and Mr. Kyn visited them often. Traga who was the older son by almost ten years went to live with Jacon who became his mentor. Jacon and Traga worked together on project Galaxy. Traga was becoming a highly respected scientist in his own right. Mr. Kyn had told Traga recently that he would inherit Mr. Kyn's estate if something should happen to him. Mr. Kyn left no questions unanswered when it came to Traga and that is why he trusted Jacon as his mentor.

As they were sitting at the table and beginning to enjoy the variety of appetizers Traga causally walked in from a small passage that led to the garden. He greeted everyone and hugged his father. He sat down and engaged the others in small conversation while nibbling on the refreshments. Mr. Kyn started to explain to Kafta that his son had been staying with and working with Jacon for the past few years. Kafta was surprised but tried not to express it. When Mr. Kyn told Kafta that he had chosen Jacon to be his son's mentor, Kafta felt a bit of jealousy. Kafta knew he could have been a much better tutor than Jacon. Kafta now came to the conclusion that the talk had to be about some type of restructuring of Mr. Kyn's corporations and that made him feel pretty good because that meant he would be involved in the restructuring. Kafta had a lot of good Ideas he could share.

After they all indulged in the refreshments for a while and made small talk Mr. Kyn rose from his chair and raised up his arms in a gesture indicating silence. He looked first at Jacon and then at Kafta in a very serious manner and then spoke in a very soft voice alternately looking at each of his friends. "As you can see there are two seats remaining at the table. They will be filled in due time. First I would like to take some time and explain the purpose of this meeting and why I called us here to meet at such short notice." He stared at Kafta again. "Kafta, you and Jacon I consider as my closet friends and confidants. You have worked with me for many years now and both of you have proven your devotion. I highly admire the tireless energy you have given to my companies. We have shared many insights, personal experiences and more than our share of Maran refreshments." The three Marans chuckled a bit at Mr. Kyn's humor. Please understand, especially you Kafta, that because of the morals of our society I have had to raise my son Traga mostly in a clandestine manner. Traga is very dear to me along with my twins, but the twins are much younger and their future is yet to be determined. Traga has worked closely with Jacon and I am very proud of how he has matured." Mr. Kyn looked at his son and shot a wry smile his way. "I know Jacon and Traga have also become close friends and I am happy for this."

Kafta was starting to become confused now. He had not heard Mr. Kyn speak in the manner he was speaking, ever. Something very serious was going on and he knew it. Mr. Kyn continued, "Aktal is a very extraordinary robot. The truth is that maybe she is even more than what we have come to know as personal robots. Her development has been a covert operation and it has taken all of my abilities to influence the project so that no knowledge of it could be leaked out. Kafta, what I am going to expose to you now both Jacon and my son already know. Actually, they are mostly responsible for it, but I did play a small role.

"As we all know, inter-galactic travel is now banned by the Federation. Some think that was part of their plan all along when they enlisted our companies help to develop the spacecraft, others think it is just a result of the first vehicle being lost, but either way with the legislation now in place it will not be possible for any private entities to own that type of spacecraft. We have spent a large fortune on the work and will never be able to see the return on our efforts. As you know there are many other companies that were involved in this project and they are very upset with the Federation's decisions but there is nothing anyone can do now. I am sure you are well aware that Federation has been tightening controls on all of my corporations over the past few years. It is obvious that they believe I have become too powerful and my wealth somehow displays a threat to them. There are many like me that believe differently. The reality is that as mine and other private corporations keep discovering new technologies it causes the general population to see the Federation as an outdated governing body. There are those now within the Federation talking of the day when it is overthrown or reformed and the old hardliners that are now in power do not want to lose that power. The signs of their demise are apparent. As you are all well aware, the rumor is that the first intergalactic vehicle that was launched was purposely destroyed by the Federation. I am not sure if any of us will know what actually happened. We know the purpose of the first mission was to further explore and begin to settle the galaxy Jahatsvha, which of course is the nearest galaxy that we have determined has similar solar systems to ours. There is a possibility that someday the Federation will decide to continue project Galaxy and maybe even partner again with private industry, but this is a remote possibility right now. The Federation definitely has the required technology and funds to continue the project, but because of the volatile political situation it is unlikely they will make any decision in the near future. Because of all that I have stated and for other reasons which will become more apparent to you later I have decided to set in motion one of the most important endeavors I have ever undertaken, or for that matter that any Maran in the history of our culture as ever taken."

Mr. Kyn paused for a few seconds and intensely looked into his son's eyes. It was a look of admiration and love that only a parent could know. "I have listened many times as my son shared his dreams with me and I have also perceived these same dreams from both Kafta and Jacon, though they may have not been expressed in the same manner." Mr. Kyn then briefly looked to Jacon. "Jacon knows somewhat of my plan, but I am sure there will also be new revelations for him. Directly below us and off to the west is another large enclosure. In it we have housed the only other Maran intergalactic spacecraft. For now, the Federation does not know of its existence. The assembly of it took place as we built the other prototype for the Federation. With the help of Jacon and my son we were able to doctor the procurement and other documents we provided to the Federation to show that the parts used in this vehicle were used in the one built for the Federation. Yes, it was highly illegal what we did, but since it was my corporation's time and money I wanted to have something to show for it. So far we have gotten away with the scheme. The vehicle is smaller than the one we built for the Federation and can only carry seven, thus the seven chairs at this table." Mr. Kyn paused and looked at Kafta and Jacon. He could see that they understood the point he was making so he continued. "Originally I did not see any priority to the plan I now have but now time is of essence. At this point I am sure it will not be long at all before the Federation discovers the ploy I have carried out and the vehicle will be confiscated. I have three choices now. I can destroy the vehicle, turn it over to the Federation and face the consequences or I can launch it. I think by now you all realize that I want you to accompany me on a wonderful voyage." Kafta had a look of both surprise and wonder. "Jacon, at this time I must sincerely apologize to you for dragging you along in this conspiracy. I understand it was at first your idea, but by complying with you I have forced you now to follow me or lose your career. At first I thought your idea was crazy and impossible to carry out but now I am glad you convinced me."

Jacon, Kafta, and Traga stared at Mr. Kyn and even though Jacon and Traga knew of the basics of the plan they still felt there were going to be more revelations. It was starting to sink in that Mr. Kyn was asking them to accompany him on an intergalactic voyage and to where they were not yet clear. This obviously meant they would be discarding their families, friends and culture. It was an extraordinary request but coming from a Maran as exceptional as Mr. Kyn it was a request they knew they would accept. Their loyalty to Mr. Kyn was honed from years of love and respect for him.

Kafta was the first to respond to the request. "Mr. Kyn, I am having a hard time finding the words to express how I feel. I was expecting a meeting of a different sort. I know I am privileged to be part of this plan and I know I have no way of predicting the future any better than anyone else. I have learned over the years that it is much easier to start things than it is to finish things. I also know that when I die, I die alone and any attachments I have will not go with me. From that viewpoint I can only say, absolutely, yes. I would love to be part of the historic journey. I truly do not think I am the most worthy companion but since I have been asked, it is my honor to say yes. "

Mr. Kyn had been the most worried about Kafta accepting his proposal so he felt relieved. "I am happy you have agreed to be part of this adventure. Please understand though, we will not set course for Jahatsvha as did the Federation vehicle."

Traga and Jacon instantly had a quizzical look on their faces when they heard Mr. Kyn's last sentence. They both assumed the journey was to follow the path that the Federations vehicle had taken. They knew the vehicle that Mr. Kyn had in his possession most likely could not travel to other stars as there were not many stars close enough with habitable planets. All of that data was well known to everyone.

Jacon voiced his concern and thought maybe that Mr. Kyn had made a mistake in his statement. "Excuse me, Mr. Kyn, where will we go? Are you sure we are not heading to the star Jahatsvha? I always just assumed we would follow the route of project Galaxy? I am not sure the vehicle we have can go anywhere else!"

Mr. Kyn raised his hands in a gesture for silence. He knew he had stretched the loyalty he had earned from all of them to the utmost limit. He also knew it was critical that their devotion to the mission he was planning remained intact. Mr. Kyn raised his voice in a very assertive manner that was not typically in character for him, "I am asking all of you to trust me. I need a vow from all of you that you will be committed to this journey. If you can do this then I can continue to explain our plans."

It was if Jacon, Kafta and Traga were lifted by the magnetism in Mr. Kyn's voice so they all abruptly stood up from their seats and ever so slowly nodded their heads to show their support.

Mr. Kyn continued, "Good, I am very happy. I know this journey will be successful and I am confident I have picked the best companions." The others sat down and Mr. Kyn also sat down then continued in a more gentle tone. "This is going to be a historic adventure. We will begin a new chapter in our history. Now that we are in complete accord, I would like to introduce you to the sixth member of our party. I must ask all of you to remain seated and to remain perfectly calm. I am sure you will find this hard to believe but who I am going to introduce you to now is not one of us. He is not a Maran." Mr. Kyn paused to see what reaction his friends were going to have but they sat still and did not react. "He is an alien, and I may add someone that is much further advanced than any of us. He will enter shortly and explain his history and how he and I have come to know each other."

The others were now more overwhelmed with fear than anything else. This whole idea of some adventure to a destination yet unknown had taken on a new twist. Yes, most Marans were aware that there was other life in the Universe and it had been rumored for over 200 years that the Federation was in touch with aliens but that they kept the communication private. The reality was that none of them and no other Marans they knew had any contact with aliens. It just did not seem within the realm of any reality they were comfortable with. Why Mr. Kyn was in touch with some alien was a serious issue that needed to be explained. They were numb and sat frozen in their seats.

From behind an adjacent wall there appeared a large being with short legs and a large torso. He was wrapped in a fine shimmering white robe. His hands were proportionality very large with eight long, thin and delicate fingers. He had an even larger opposing thumb. His skin seemed to be somewhat of a translucent pale blue. His face was radiant and he had two small lavender colored eyes that almost seemed to glow. He slowly made is way to the table and took his seat. Kafta, Traga and Jacon were frozen in their seats with their mouths open and hands clasped in their laps. The alien extended his hand to each Maran, one at a time. They noticed a small feeling of static electricity when he touched them. The alien did not extend his hand to Aktal or look at her.

Mr. Kyn was looking back and forth at the other Marans and he had a wry smile on his face. He knew they were in shock. "There is no need to fear my friend Borghx. He does not speak. He carries a special device to transmit his thoughts into our language so that he can communicate with us. Before I give him the opportunity to converse with you I will answer some of the questions that I am sure you have on your minds. Borghx is from a distant Galaxy he calls Yusolax. You may not have heard of this galaxy from your studies because it is too distant to have any relevancy to us. I am sure you will discover that Borghx is a very warm and sharing being. He will be able to show and teach you many thought-provoking ideas. Borghx was very helpful in our development of Aktal. He offered me many insights and new technologies that we implemented into her circuitry. Borghx has been staying here at my retreat for nearly 13 years in complete secrecy. He came to our solar system as a scout for his people with the intention of discovering planets suitable for immigrations. He was able to arrive here undetected and was also able to make direct contact with our leaders of the Federation. Borghx offered them knowledge of many new technologies in exchange for one of our planets. The Federation intentionally deceived Borghx. The Federation was able to have him disclose some of these advanced technologies before they committed to their part of the deal. They reached a stalemate in the negotiations and when Borghx decided to return to his planet the Federation promptly confiscated his inter-galactic vehicle and jailed him under the guise that he needed to be quarantined for health reasons. The vehicle was routinely dismantled as a means of trying to discover the advanced systems it contained. Because of their ignorance as they were dismantling the fission reactor errors were made and the research facility imploded. Many Marans were killed but the explosion was covered up by the Federation. Many of the discoveries they made were used in the development of the vehicles for project Galaxy. When we won the contract with the Federation for project Galaxy they supplied us with much of the data they had uncovered when they were dissecting Borghx's vehicle. At this point the Federation knowing I was to be the main contractor for the project decided they needed to bring me in on the secret that was Borghx. They felt I would be able to befriend him and get him to reveal more details on how the small fission reactor worked. They allowed me to bring him to my palace on Tyijo in complete secrecy and supplied a large crew of guards. Borghx and I were able to have many long conversations and over time we became close friends. He sensed I was different from others that were part of the Federation and overtime came to trust me. Eventually I convinced the Federation that my palace on Tyijo was becoming too popular with the public and that it would be more secure if I was able to bring him here. The Federation agreed as their number one priority was security. Unbeknownst to them it was part of a plan that Borghx and I had formulated. A few weeks later when the Federations transport vehicle arrived under heavy security to pick up Borghx I said goodbye to him. In reality I was saying good bye to a robot that Borghx and helped me to create that looked like an exact replica of him. On the journey there was a bomb planted in the robot and the transport vehicle exploded in flight. As far as the Federation was concerned Borghx had been lost forever. Obviously there was a lengthy investigation that led to even further investigations into me and my companies. That was really the beginning of the intense scrutiny the Federation leveled on me and all my corporations. I believe that is when they started to implement plans to break up my financial empire. It was too late for them to cancel the contracts that we had with them for the Galaxy project but I am sure if they could have found a way they would have done it. After all the investigations into the explosion of the transport vehicle they could not find any evidence of sabotage so fortunately I was able to go about my business of running my companies and helping them with the Galaxy project. About a year later after keeping Borghx in seclusion on Tyijo I was able to move him to my palace here. Borghx has been very implemental in the development of Aktal and she was designed to help us with the mission we have planned."

Mr. Kyn continued, "Borghx is an extremely kind and passive being. He possesses various types of perceptive abilities that are completely undeveloped in us. Nearly always he knows your exact thoughts and feelings. He is very quiet and even though he speaks to us with the aid of his computer voice translator he speaks infrequently. I have to warn you that when you do have the opportunity to converse with him that you will often find in the beginning that you start to feel tired very quickly. This is because he is reading your brain waves and the fact that his brain waves are incredibly powerful. The good thing is that you will most likely never forget what he tells you. Over the past few years Borghx has lent his intelligence and wisdom on many of the projects our companies have been involved with. I hope I have covered enough of the background details and now I will let Borghx explain the specifics of our journey. After that he will answer any questions that you have. Before we end the meeting I will introduce you to the last member of our party."

The Marans were staring at Borghx who looked as if he had fallen asleep while Mr. Kyn had been speaking. Then Borghx's pale blue skin began slightly glow. Borghx opened his thick darker blue eyelids and his eyes began to emit lavender light. He slowly brought his very large hands to the table in front of him. He gradually intertwined his six fingers and then began his discourse.

"It is a tremendous pleasure for me to at last meet Mr. Kyn's dearest friends and son. Although I have cherished the companionship that Tyijo has provided, I am very happy to make some new friends. Tyijo has always spoken very highly of you and your accomplishments. I look forward to having you as companions on this journey. I sincerely believe this journey will enable each of us to fulfill a deep desire that is hidden within a part of our subconscious. There are many questions that will become answered and they will reveal a part of our lives that we never knew existed."

"As you all know our Universe is vast and expanding. The expansion will at some point in time end and our Universe will contract again, but the cycle is endless. There are many forms of life everywhere but most of the advanced forms of life are carbon based like you Marans. My people were originally carbon based but we have evolved into a combination of carbon and silicone. That is why I appear so different to you. My cellular structure is very different from yours. My people populate many galaxies. We are by far the most populous beings in this quadrant of the Universe. We have sent a vast amount of probes to many stars to determine if they have planets that we can migrate too. The data is stored in the collective conscious of my people. Some of the information about certain planets around various suns has revealed both fascinating and unique forms of life. We have learned from our journeys and probes that there are basically three types of civilizations. The first is one that is able to reach a state of homeostasis on their planet. By that I mean they are able to not destroy their planet and use their resources in a way that balances their environment. You Marans were lucky to have discovered this early in your evolution but many others have not. Most of the carbon based beings eventually reach an advanced level of in-vitro fertilization. This obviously leads to a matriarchically society such has occurred here with you Marans. The fact that over 100 years ago your people realized men were headed for extinction led to a new enlightenment in your culture and Marans began the migrations to your other planets. This was an intelligent and crucial choice that your Federation made. It saved the males of your species from becoming nothing other breeding stock. My people have determined the future of your civilization is a healthy one. Now that your Federation has eased off on expansion in this galaxy there is a great chance that your civilization will continue for many years to come but that is mainly due to the fact that you have habitable planets and others that were not extremely difficult to make habitable. I will be able to share a lot more information with you in the future. "

"I was sent here to your solar system as an ambassador. Our probes had determined and gave us every indication that in the time it took for me to travel here, your civilization would be friendly to my people. When I first contacted your government I was confident of success. We were convinced that because of the peaceful evolution and ample room here that the Federation would allow us to develop a small outpost here to use for other journeys. I was quite surprised when the negotiations turned around and deception was introduced. I may have been able to escape on my own but when I met Mr. Kyn another solution seemed feasible. Our people have learned over millions of years of evolution that there are always peaceful solutions to all problems and the fact that in general Marans are peaceful played into my thought process. We are passive beings and though we have the technologies to devastate most life forms we encounter we have learned it is almost never in our best interest to take that type of action. Of course in this case, I was very fortunate to have met your beloved, Tyijo Kyn whom in my opinion reflects more the core values of your people than does the Federation at this time."

"The second types of advanced civilizations are ones that are able to use their source of energy, their sun, to expand to other solar systems. This come mainly by being able to develop fusion reactors The Maran civilization has reached this level but the need for expansion is not there due to your fortune of having ample room on your neighboring planets. I believe that your Federation is beginning to understand this and in due time will be able to restart their project Galaxy. You should all be proud of your heritage and progress because there are few civilizations that reach this level. The vast majority of civilizations destroys the environment on their planet and causes their own extinction. If and when they do reach a level of homeostasis, they become too complacent to advance technologies enough to expand."

Everyone was listening intently to what Borghx was saying. They could all tell that he was a very advanced being and that he had deep compassion for life. Borghx continued, "The past years that I have spent here with Tyijo have proved to be both enlightening and fruitful for me. I must tell you that in my culture I am in high regard because of my missions. Like most of my kind I have raised a family and I have contributed to my society in numerous ways. It is only now at the later part of my life that I have taken this role as an ambassador. In way you might say that we ambassadors are dispensable. Our missions are not always successful and that is why each ambassador travels alone. The majority of do not return. For me, I do hope to return someday but at the same time my journey here has allowed me to communicate much important information back home to our central leadership. I have made new decisions based on my lengthy discussions with Mr. Kyn and my own knowledge. I have sent communications back to my leaders about these decisions and the new mission that I hope to accomplish with your help."

"Recently because of the intense scrutiny that Mr. Kyn has been under from your Federation we have had to accelerate our plans. Should they discover the intergalactic vehicle in Mr. Kyn's possession then all of our plans will be for nothing and I will be stranded here with Mr. Kyn for a long time. This is not something I want to happen. I am an ambassador and I want to continue in that role for my people."

Borghx continued, "In order to accomplish the goal of our mission I have had to make some modifications to Mr. Kyn's intergalactic vehicle. Though we will travel to a planet within this galaxy it is just out of reach of the vehicles that your Federation built. This planet and some of the neighboring planets that circle the star there were once considered by my people as candidates for migrations but those plans were discarded for various reasons. The beings on this planet have yet to reach the first phase of truly intelligent life and have not yet evolved out of their aggressive traits. We have every reason to believe that they are still involved in various conflicts amongst themselves and they have yet to implement energy technologies that do not harm their environment. It has been a planet of large egos, wars, and regional conflicts all mainly driven by greed. We believe that should this planet continue on the present course that it will eventually cause the extinction or near extinction of the beings there. There is also a distinct possibility that with their large buildup of nuclear weapons that the planet may someday become embroiled in nuclear wars. My people discussed these scenarios at great lengths and at the time decided it was not in our interest to intervene, but I have changed my views on this and now believe it is in our interest to interpose. The beings there do have peaceful qualities and the potential to become true Galactic Citizens and it will be our mission to help affect the change. The beings there call the planet, Earth. Marans have evolved into peaceful beings so I will value your input during our mission."

Marans and I appear physically very different from the Earthlings and we would most likely find it very difficult to be accepted and to interact with them. This is the reason Aktal was developed by Mr. Kyn and me. She is an exact replica of a female Earthling. Our goal will be to establish a hidden base of operations on the planet. Over a period of time we will be able to initiate communications and exert and influence on the leaders of the planet through Aktal. The people of Earth have never interacted with beings from other planets but a very large sector of the population does believe that other intelligent life forms do exist. They still hold on to many primitive religious beliefs most of which place them above nature and this is one of the main reasons that they continue to cause imbalances in their environment. Their underlying fear and mistrust of the unknown makes this a dangerous mission. We will bring the necessary equipment to construct our base as quickly as possible when we arrive. Kafta will be in charge of our food sources but I am sure we will be able to find ample natural resources on the planet. Our preference will be to establish our base of operations in an underground cavern of some sort so that we are in a protected and safe environment. We will be on this planet for a number of years. What is most important is that we stay focused on our goal of helping the beings on the planet evolve towards a peaceful and balanced planet with no wars or conflicts. I hope all of you understand how deeply meaningful our mission is and that it will take many years to make progress. Now if any of you have questions feel free to ask them at this time."

After the lengthy diatribe by Borghx, Kafta, Traga and Jacon all felt a bit overwhelmed by the pure gravity of what they had heard. Even though they all knew bits and pieces of the journey they would be participating in, they were unaware of much that Borghx had told them. Worse was the fact that during the whole time Borghx had been speaking his sharp beady eyes had been darting back and forth between the three of them as if he was looking for any small sign of fear or weakness. The three Marans had tons of questions but they just couldn't formulate them into questions because of how stunned they felt.

Mr. Kyn broke the brief silence, "Thank you Borghx for explaining the mission to us. I am sure my friends have confidence and trust in you just as they have in me. I am also sure they will have many questions, but right now I believe they are somewhat in shock." Mr. Kyn laughed and the tension eased from the air. "It is critical that we hurry with the preparations for the journey so at this time I would like to introduce you to the last member of your crew."

Mr. Kyn had saved the introduction of the last voyager for a specific reason. He continued, "One last point that I must emphasize as we make the final preparations for our journey is that I have a strong suspicion that the Federation is very close to discovering that Borghx is still alive and staying here with me. I don't know how they have found this out but I am very concerned that they may invade my retreat at any time. I ask all of you to be very wary of any strangers that ask you any questions and to let me know immediately if anyone does approach you. We must be prepared to leave in two days." The Marans gasped and looked at each other not aware that they were being asked to leave their home planets so quickly. Mr. Kyn could see their shock. "I know this is a very short amount of time to take care of any personal matters that you must take care of, but this is the time table we have. Now I will introduce you to Shala, who is the last member of our party."

From behind the adjacent wall appeared another robot that looked exactly like Aktal! The only difference was that Shala had blond hair and Aktal had auburn hair. Shala took the last seat at the large circular table and smiled at everyone. "I am Shala and it is a pleasure to meet all of you."

Mr. Kyn again noticed the surprised look on his friend's faces, especially Kafta who was frozen. Kafta had no idea that tow robots had been created. Mr. Kyn had never told him anything! Mr. Kyn smiled at Kafta but Kafta was staring back and forth between Aktal and Shala. "As you all can see Shala and Aktal are exact duplicates. When Borghx and I developed these robots we thought it would a prudent decision to have more than one, just in case anything happened to one of them. From the data Borghx has gathered we have determined that the Earthlings are much less in control of their emotion than Borghx's people or us Marans. Therefore it is essential that these two robots have the capabilities to handle the earthlings and their emotions so that we can guide the planet to more peaceful solutions to their conflicts. We do not have an exact plan of how all this is going to happen but we do know that with Aktal and Shala we will be able to exercise more control over our attempts to find solutions to their conflicts. Via the interactions with the Earthlings and the data gathering capabilities of Aktal and Shala we will be able to analyze exactly how the Earthlings behave. We have visual and sensory command of both robots at all times. Borghx has programmed the robots to follow his commands via his brain waves but we also have a manual control with us. I am sure that all of you understand that even though we may not be returning from this journey that is extremely important that as least the robots see the mission to completion. We will end this meeting now and make preparations for our departure.

Chapter 6
Threads that Bind

Vietnam - October, 1966

The war had reached the height of insanity. The conflict had escalated to the point where most of the world wondered if any of the conflict was justified. For Ernie Lopez on his last tour of duty the war had taken way too many strange turns and he was more than ready to go back to the States anytime he could get a chance, but he had to follow orders. This was his second tour of duty in Vietnam and he had only been here one week. It was more chaotic than ever and he wanted out fast. Ernie had turned 19 years old just last month and when he was a kid growing up playing soldier in his back yard with his cousins he never imagined that this now would be his reality. Death, bombs, lost limbs, blood, rage, soldiers losing their minds, and all the other horrors of war surrounded him now. Ernie was scared of death just like everyone else but for a young man his age now trapped in a place he did not want to be he realized that he was much more scared of being captured and tortured than he was of death. He had seen and heard enough stories just in the few days he had been back on his second tour of duty that now his emotions were like an open wound. He knew he would see combat soon and he was more scared than he had ever been. Ernie was a Green Beret and he had many kills under his belt. Everyone that knew Ernie told him that he would be a perfect assassin because he was so calm all the time, but they did not know how he felt inside.

Ernie had enlisted at the age of 17 because he had been arrested for assault and disturbing the peace. His Father gave him the ultimatum, either enlist or stay in juvenile hall until he was 18. Juvenile hall was jail for minors and even though Ernie was 17 and one of the older kids in detention it was still jail and not a friendly place to be so he decided to enlist. Having grown up in Venice, Ca in a gang saturated area Ernie had seen more than his share of violence. His only and older brother was now incarcerated in Arizona. His brother had never gone the gang route, but he knew had plenty of gang members. He was caught selling siphoned gas to a known gang member and the garage that he had rented to stash the gas exploded killing two adjacent neighbors. Ernie's brother was going to stay in jail a long time.

Ernie's parents were divorced and Ernie stayed with his Mom and her boyfriend. Ernie didn't like the boyfriend and he knew that if he stayed in the house much longer there would be a fight. Joining the military seemed like a good option. His Father had been a green beret and had taught his two sons how to shoot guns. Ernie had seen too many of his friends either get shot or go to jail over some gang issue so he needed to get out and the army was going to be his way out.

Ernie had all the skills the Green Berets wanted. He had trained at his local YMCA in karate and jujitsu. His Father had taught him to use guns. Ernie had the calm focused determination that a good soldier needed. He excelled during his training. His superiors noticed that Ernie even felt empathy for the ones that dropped out of training. Unlike the other soldiers that made fun of them, Ernie would often console them and encourage them not to give up on themselves as they move forward in life. "This is just one train stop on the journey." Ernie said to almost everyone that dropped out. That phrase was Ernie's philosophy, not so much because he really believed it, but because he was scared and needed to convince himself so he could have courage. Because of the environment that Ernie grew up in he had to not show fear or he would be in danger. At night most people stayed inside in homes. Most homes had bars on the windows. As the helicopter headed towards the base camp the low hanging fog and cloud layer cleared below. Ernie looked out the window and saw that Hell had become tenfold worse when he had been here on his first tour. There were more people, more equipment, bigger bases, and more devastated land. Smoke plumes were on every horizon. The earth burned and the mood in the helicopter dropped to below zero. Some soldiers were noticeable sick. Ernie looked around and at his fellow soldiers and saw blank eyes. Many eyes staring into death they hoped would not come.

They landed in a base camp that was very small compared to the camps they had flown past. The ride had taken almost an hour and none on board had been briefed as to where they were going except for the pilots. The soldiers on board made guesses but has the time passed they all realized they were going close to the Cambodian border. Ernie had been chosen from his unit for this assignment and he assumed whatever the assignment was that the other eight soldiers being transported with him where going to be on the same mission.

Just before the helicopter set down Ernie could see that the base was very small compared to other bases he had been stationed at. The base was well camouflaged with netting and it appeared to Ernie there were not many troops or machinery. Ernie now had an idea about what his mission would be. It made his stomach upset.

Ernie was led to his bunk. He started talking with the other three soldiers in his small tent and soon learned that his suspicions of why he was here were pretty much true. They were on the edge of the Vietnam and Cambodian borders. The camp he was in was set up to run small missions into Cambodia where the Viet Kong were setting up bases and preparing for a large offensive into Vietnam. It was a secret base because the U.S. was not at war with Cambodia and not supposed to be entering the territory, but now they had no choice.

The next morning Ernie was woken up at 5:00 AM and called to the command center. Major Jones was in charge of the operation. Ernie's old staff sergeant, Booth was present in the room also. After saluting everyone and being asked to sit another man came into the room and sat off to the side without greeting or saluting any of them. Ernie had never seen this man. Ernie had a bad feeling about him but then again, he thought to himself, he had a bad feeling about everything now. It was the fear inside of him and he knew it. Then two Cambodian men entered the room. They were both dressed in normal cloths not military uniforms.

Major Jones started the briefing in sort of an unexpected way for Ernie. "Lopez, we know you think you're hot stuff, so, we are going to give you a chance to prove it!" Some of the other wanted to laugh but they didn't. Ernie just stared at the Major and tried not to show any emotion with his eyes.

Ernie tried to put on a calm front but inside he was extremely nervous. He hated the fact that the higher up the chain of command one went in the military, the more war became a game and a sick game at that. Ernie never looked at himself as a "hot shot", and he surly did not want anyone else to see him that way either. He wondered if the Major was trying to intimidate him but the more Ernie stared at him the more Ernie knew that the mission he would be going on would be one with a very high risk of death. Ernie closed his eyes for a second and imagined being back home in Venice and eating his Mom's cooking. For a brief instant he could taste the food. Ernie opened his eyes and took a deep breath.

"Lopez", Major Jones shouted out, "I need your full attention here."

"Yes Sir", Ernie replied realizing that he needed to stop letting his mind wander.

"This is an extremely important mission and I need your full attention. Keep your eyes open and focus on what I am saying. Trust me Lopez, when I get done explain this mission, you are going to hate your parents for ever bringing you sorry ass into this world. I am willing guess that you had no concept that because of your brown Mexican skin that it would make you the perfect candidate for this mission. Do you realize that you look a lot like your Cambodian brothers sitting here?" Major Jones pointed to the two Cambodian men sitting opposite of Ernie. The Cambodians grinned at Major Jones as he pointed at them. "Some coincidence don't you think? " Now the two Cambodians turned and smiled t Ernie whom had a blank look on his face. "We need one of finest Green Berets on this mission, and as much as I like messing with your mind Lopez, you are a good soldier. These two men here and you may save this war for us. Lopez, are you listening to me? We have some serious stuff going on here so stay focused. Damn Lopez, you are looking a bit pale for a Mexican/American. Are you alright?"

"Yes Sir. I am fine." Ernie replied even though inside he had a really bad feeling about the mission.

"Good, now let me introduce you to David Stearns. He is with Intelligence and will brief you on the mission."

David Stearns stood up and went to where Ernie was sitting, so Ernie stood up and the two shook hands. David Stearns had a strong handshake, but Ernie did not like his eyes. He has seen those types of eyes before. They were the type of eyes that just hid too much information. Mr. Stearns took a chair next to the Major. "I am with the Cia. I am sure some of you here are aware of the Phoenix Program. This program is designed, coordinated, and executed by the CIA and special operations forces. Our job is to identify and "neutralize" the infrastructure of the Viet Cong. We have an interrogation center not far from this base. This is going to be our first mission into Cambodia. The mission is a very simple one. Mike and Rick though both originally from Cambodia are actually Australian Special Forces."

"Good to meet you mate!" The two Cambodians said to Ernie. For the first time during the meeting Ernie cracked a smile and the rest of the people in the room laughed out loud. Stearns waited a few seconds then he continued. "The plan is a very simple one. The three of you will be crossing the border into

Cambodia. Arms have been passing through Cambodia to the Viet Cong for years now but recently much large quantities of surface to air weapons have been coming through. The amount of our helicopters getting hit by these missiles is on the rise and we need to put an end to that. Obviously as you all know we are not at war with Cambodia and this is a classified mission. If anything goes wrong you are all on your won. Try to split up and by no means give up any details of our mission."

"We have seen large movements of heavy equipment and weapons being trucked in to a remote location not too far from here. What is puzzling is that we have also have intelligence that there is a contingent of Soviet scientists attached to this recent movement of weapons and equipment. We need to have the three of you infiltrate the camp and find out more details of what is going on. Two days ago a smaller contingent from the camp broke off and the Russians are with them. They have a lot of heavy earth moving equipment and satellite equipment. From what we can tell from aerial photos it appears they are starting some kind of mining or tunneling operation into a nearby mountain. We have no clue what they are up to and why they want to tunnel into this mountain in such a remote area of the country." Stearns paused for a second and stared at Ernie. "Lopez, are you getting all of this?" Stearns asked with a harsh tone in his voice.

"Yes Sir, but I have one question. Since there are going to be three of us on this mission, who is going to be the leader?" Ernie asked.

"Not you, Lopez!" Major Jones chirped before Stearns could answer. "I didn't even want any of green berets on this mission but it was not my choice. Stearns and his superiors want a Green Beret along to provide support and that is why we have you. Mike and Rick are fluent in many dialects of both the Vietnamese and Cambodian languages so the two of them are in charge on this mission. Your main job, Lopez, is to protect these two Aussies!" Ernie nodded his head to show he understood.

Stearns continued, "Let's get into the details of the mission now. We want the three of you to kidnap one of the Russians that is in charge of the operations. His name is Ivan Petrosky. He is with the KBG and has been involved in opening up a variety of arms channels to bring weapons to the Viet Kong. Over 10 years ago he was acting as a double agent for both France and Russia. If we can kidnap him out of there we can get a lot of information out of him. Because he is heading this mining operation and it is so far removed from the base camp I think we have a good chance of getting to him. I have a lot of aerial photos that show Mr. Petrosky has some very predictable patterns to his daily routine so if we can move in at the right moment we can extract him."

The two Aussies, Ernie, and Stearns all moved to a large conference table that had stacks of large aerial photos. Major Jones left the room. The three soldiers talked amongst themselves and honed the plan that Stearns had laid out for them. Ernie started to feel a bit calmer now. The mission was becoming clear and he started to erase the negative thoughts from his mind. The two Aussies were in their late twenties and their mature attitude made Ernie feel a lot more at ease. Two hours later they loaded their gear into a helicopter and headed out to the drop point which was 20 miles from their actual destination in the foothills of a steep mountain.

It was near dawn. The air was hot and humid with a misty rain falling. They hurried out of the clearing where the helicopter had dropped them and headed for an outcrop of rocks. Ernie and the two Aussies were dressed in drab gear that made them appear like any other Cambodians that might be in the area. Ernie carried a number of weapons and so did the two Aussies. They found a small cove where the rocks sheltered them in all directions and put their gear down. They would start their hike for the enemy camp at night fall. Ernie lay on wet grass with his back pack as a pillow and soon dozed off. The day passed quickly and in the afternoon the two Aussies and Ernie went over the plans they had been given and each weighed in on the various options and contingencies. They were all on the same page. At sunset they loaded their gear and headed out.

They hiked up a short hill that led to a long gradually ascending ridge that would lead them straight towards the camp. After two hours hiking at a steady pace the stopped and rested for about fifteen minutes and then continued on. It was a desolate area. They could see lights from a small village that had to be at least 10 miles away off to their left down in a small valley, but other than those lights they saw no sign of people. The evening was mist had started to set in and now even the village with the lights went dark hidden by the thickening fog in the valley below them. The full moon started to rise over another small mountain range off to the east and at the same time the fog lifted. There were more lights now from another small village in the valley on their left. Rick called a sudden halt. He had been in the lead about twenty yards ahead of Mike and Ernie in the rear. They all couched down in unison and listened. Suddenly a goat came around the bend in front of them. The goat noticed the three men and turned off the path to avoid them. It was well past midnight now and they were only a few miles from their target destination so they called a halt to the hike and decided to wait for 3 hours before they continued. Ernie stood guard and the two Aussies napped.

Ernie was alone in his thoughts. He thought about his first tour of duty and about the combat he had been in. The time passed very quickly and then they continued along the ridge heading towards the enemy camp. About an hour before dawn they could hear the river they knew was below them to the east. The dark shape of the mountain loomed in front of them outlined in the full moonlight. They could see a few lights that were coming from the enemy camp where the river snaked around the mountain. They called a halt and hunkered down to wait for the sunrise. Ernie and Mike napped and Rick took the watch. They were on a very high ridge and it would not be easy for anyone to find them in the position they were in. Rick woke up the other two at dawn and they could see enemy soldiers moving around far below them in the small camp. They could see at least two large tractors and earth moving vehicles. Further up there were two more large back hoes. Within and hours the camp below was buzzing with activity. They waited and watched. They took turns napping during the day. Ernie was happy he was in the mountains because it was not as hot as the steamy valleys below. He no longer felt the fear he had felt in the briefing. He knew he had a mission to do and his Aussie partners seemed more than capable to do their parts.

When night came Ernie remained in position and the two Aussies crawled down the hill towards the base camp to make sure their plan was in place. They returned after a few hours and confirmed that their plan was still in place. They rested as well as they could during the night alternately taking turns to stand watch.

The plan was a fairly simple one and if it worked as they hoped it would not many people would have to die. Ivan Petrosky, who was in charge of the mining operation or whatever the operation was, further up the river, followed the same routine each morning. The routine had been scouted by Aussies over a week ago when the CIA has sent them in to document the mining operation and gather other intelligence. They had confirmed the routine the day before. At dawn Ivan Petrosky would walk along a small path about a half a mile downstream with one guard to a place where the river swirled off forming an eddy in a small inlet. The rocks were very shallow so the water filtered over them and bubbled up various places. Ivan would undress, scrub himself with soap and lie on the rocks for up to half an hour and let the water flow over him while the guard stood nearby on the shore.

Since this happened at dawn it would be highly unlikely that anyone from the camp would miss him for at least two hours and that should give Ernie and the Aussies enough of a head start to forcefully march him out of the area to one of the planned retrieval sites. Ernie and the Aussies knew they would have to move quickly to carry out their plan.

They were going to head down from their perch on the mountain two hours before dawn so that they could position themselves for the operation. Ernie tried to sleep that night but every time he started to fade into sleep he thought he heard voices so he opened his eyes. His mind refused to shut off no matter what psychological techniques he tried to use. His body felt tense even when he told himself to relax. As he started once again slipping into sleep he realized what was bothering him. It was the two Aussies. He opened his eyes and starred at the stars blinking in the sky above him. It finally dawned on him that he was expendable on the mission and that when the two Aussies spoke to each other in Cambodian they were often talking about him. Ernie realized he was not only in danger from the mission but from the two Cambodians if anything went wrong. That is why everything had to go as planned. It was the way of Secret Operations in War and Ernie knew it. All his animal instincts lite up and sleep was no longer an option.

Ivan had been sent by his commanders to this remote area of Cambodia to investigate an odd frequency of signals that seemed to be coming from inside or below the mountain in question. The Russians had been bringing weapons to an area over fifty miles to the south for years. The weapons were sold to the Viet Kong. The low frequency waves had been detected by a new type of radar the Russians had developed for underwater detection. At first the Russians were not sure what was going on inside the mountain but they highly suspected that the Americans had set up some kind of underground base and were experimenting with new technologies. When the area was initially investigated by the Russians there was no sign or evidence of the Americans involvement anywhere. This made them even more curious as to what was actually happening. For Ivan, who was now in charge of the investigation, it seemed to be absolute insanity to be blasting a hole into a mountain this close to the border with a war raging on, but, he had his orders. He was sure that by now they had drawn the attention of the Americans and that was attention he did not need. The natives in the area had been telling him that there was a "Devil" that entered the mountain almost 5 years earlier because the entrance to a large cave that was half way up the mountain had mysteriously been closed.

Ivan and his team had been working for four days now, and yesterday the low frequency waves had suddenly stopped. As far as Ivan was concerned that meant only one thing. Whatever or whomever was in that mountain now recognized they had been discovered. Ivan did not like the situation at all. It was very odd and not something a senior KBG officer like himself should be working on. At any rate he was sure today would be the last day of digging into the mountain because from all indicators they were only about forty feet from opening the entrance to the cave that had either collapsed or been covered over. A few more blasts of dynamite and half a day with the earth movers was all they needed. All the later thoughts passed through Ivan's mind as he lay on his cot waiting for the guard to notify him that they were ready to head down the path so he could bath in the cool stream. He looked forward to washing away the humid sweat from the night before.

Chapter 7
Flights of Fate

The long journey from the five planets of Han by Mr. Kyn and the others to planet Earth had not been without problems. The Marans had been flash frozen to a state of hibernation for the majority of the flight. Shala, Aktal and the alien Borghx had directed the speeding craft and made sure that they stayed on course. When they at last entered the solar system of the planet Earth the Marans were revived from their long hibernation. Traga, Mr. Kyn's son was extremely ill when he was brought out of the hibernation. Borghx cared for the ailing Maran but a few days before they were to enter the orbit of planet Earth and decide their landing area, Traga passed. Mr. Kyn and Borghx argued for the first time since they had known each other. Mr. Kyn mourned and blamed Borghx for the mishap. Mr. Kyn was distraught, tired, weak and no longer wanted to continue the mission. He wanted to turn around, abandon the mission and return to his home. No one could console him. For over a week the spacecraft orbited the planet Earth and the mission remained up in the air. In the end the other Marans were able to convince Mr. Kyn that they needed to continue with the mission. Mr. Kyn remained distraught and constantly wept for his son.

While they orbited the blue-green planet below Aktal and Shala were trying to determine the best landing place for them so they could remain hidden from the Earthlings. There were a number of remote areas that seemed to suit them and Borghx made the final decision. They flew into a large cavern in a small mountain and set up their operations. The entrance to the cavern was closed and they blasted out other safer entrances for their ingress and egress.

Now if had been almost 15 years from the time they landed. Aktal and Shala had ventured into the Earthlings societies creating various levels of relationships as instructed by Borghx and Mr. Kyn. They posed as two nuns and traveled mainly in Southeast Asia and Europe. Often Aktal and Shala would be away for nearly a year before they returned. Their underground retreat had been transformed into a safe and beautiful environment for the Marans. At times they felt like they were not even away from their homes. Mr. Kyn had changed since the loss of his son. It was a heavy burden that he carried on his mind and inside he blamed himself for his son's death. For a variety of reasons it appeared that their mission amongst the Earthlings was not progressing as they had hoped it would. The overall feeling of the Marans was starting to be more and more one of frustration. Borghx felt totally the opposite of the Marans and often would point to areas of progress and influence that had occurred. The War that had intensified in Vietnam was now of a major concern to the Marans and Borghx. The Marans wanted to abandon the mission now and return to their homes, but Borghx convinced them that they needed to give themselves more time.

The discussions they had constantly stayed focused on their mission of intervening and influencing the Earthlings towards a path of peace. The ongoing buildup of nuclear weapons by the United States and Russia was a major concern. Often they found that the actions of Aktal and Shala, even though carefully orchestrated had little impact. When Aktal and Shala would return to the base camp in Cambodia the Marans and Borghx spent long hours discussing their next tactic. As the Vietnam War intensified Aktal and Shala had to remain in the base camp for longer periods of time because it was just too risky to send them back out into society. An alternative plan had to be made just in case they would have to move the base camp. Aktal and Shala traveled to New Mexico and purchased a large ranch that had a massive natural cave deep below the property. The two robots prepared the new have just in case they had to leave.

The environment they had created for themselves was very comfortable. Within the cave there was a large dome shaped ceiling that glowed with a soft light. Their advanced nano-technologies allowed them to duplicate materials with the aid of micro-robots. Many of the plants they grew were brought with them from Mara. They also genetically modified many of the local plants to suit their needs.

Robots that Jacon created also mined for gold and silver so that they could create wealth to fund the goals they needed. The environment was so complete that the Marans never noticed or thought about how they were aging. The constant work and planning seemed to have slowed their aging process. Borghx seemed to never change. His appearance and activity was always consistent.

Eventually as time passed the eternal optimism that Borghx and Mr. Kyn exuded started to wane. They were frustrated with their progress and now that feeling of frustration was starting to show itself to the other Marans. Mr. Kyn was starting lack enthusiasm and that made the situation worse. It appeared that many of the governments lacked any type of a long term vision for a peaceful planet. Greed and avarice seemed to be at the core of many governments. Regional conflicts were all over the planet. All of them realized that it would take much longer to complete their mission than what they had originally planned for.

Now though, none of the problems mattered because they realized their whole existence was being threatened. The earthlings were drilling and blasting the mountain. Preparations and plans had been made, but as the blasting outside continued Mr. Kyn and Borghx realized time was running out. The main problem that weighed on their minds was that their overall plan was not progressing as they had planned. Mr. Kyn and Borghx were discussing their mission throughout the early morning hours as the others made the preparations to leave. The deep rumbling sound of the heavy machinery tunneling into their retreat continued.

Borghx's people were spreading throughout the Galaxy, or more technically put, their consciousness that was imbedded in the nanotech constructed artificial bodies was spreading. It was critical that Borghx completed the mission he was on to set up the outpost for his people and try to stabilize the small blue planet. His people had learned just as many life forms in the Universe had learned over millions upon millions of generations of evolution that, "Karmic Retribution" was a powerful and devastating force. Once a life form headed on a path of greed and destruction the destruction eventually turned on that life form. It appeared the Earthlings were headed in that direction. Most "advanced life forms", had developed philosophies and cultures that avoided causes which led to negative effects.

The Marans on the journey looked up to Borghx almost as a Father figure. He was their leader, teacher and mentor. He could at times also be quite entertaining as he acted out the stories of his extensive space travels and adventures. He was constantly teaching the Marans new skills and concepts. As the war in Vietnam had intensified, Borghx saw the dangers they all could possibly face. He had called a length three day meeting and together they all planned an escape route and began preparations to build a new retreat in a different area of the planet. That is when Aktal and Shala found the large property in New Mexico, USA and purchased the land there. Aktal and Shala had a large steel building built near the ranch home there. It looked like a large storage shed that any working ranch would have. Then the two robots brought in the nanobots that went to work on building a new underground shelter that could be their new base camp.

As the Cambodians with the aid of the Russians continued to tunnel into the mountain Borghx, Mr. Kyn and the rest of the crew were finalizing their preparations. All evidence of the base camp had to be destroyed; they had no other choice.

As the sun rose outside and dawn broke they were now all in their inter-galactic vehicle prepared for the next chain of events in their mission to the small blue planet. Shala and Aktal had left days early to wait for the others in New Mexico. Borghx and Mr. Kyn looked at each other as if to reassure each other, then Borghx gave the orders. Mr. Kyn fired the laser that vaporized a large hole in on the opposite side of where the Cambodians were tunneling. There was a tremendous blast of air and dust as the side of the mountain blew outwards. In a flash the inter-galactic vehicle was accelerated into the resulting vacuum and then up towards the deep blue sky into orbit.

Earlier as the dawn approached Ernie and his two Cambodian spies had positioned themselves in an area where they could quickly swoop down towards the stream and abduct Ivan Petrosky. Ivan had strolled down to his usual spot with his armed guard. The morning mist hung in the low lying areas. Ivan had followed the same routine and was casually strolling along towards the same spot. He took off his cloths and found a familiar and lay down in the stream looking up at the gentle mist above him. Mike had positioned himself in a place behind the where the guard was crouched down and now having a smoke. Just as the guard put the cigarette to his mouth a hand locked around his forehead from behind and the knife quickly sliced through his neck. It was a quite kill and Ivan lay still in the water still looking up at the mist totally unaware that his guard's throat had just been slit. Ernie and Rick were hiding a bit further down the bank. When the guard was taken out they were ready to make their move. Suddenly it sounded like a powerfully clap of thunder. Ivan, Ernie, Rick and Mike all looked up and saw a blast of light coming out of the side of the mountain. The blast was a shock but even more of a shock was the thin metallic space craft that accelerated from behind the blast like it was being shot out of the side of the mountain!

Ivan jumped up from the stream, convinced the Americans were attacking his base camp. Ernie and the two Cambodians clearly saw the spacecraft exit the gaping hole in the mountain and continued to stare in that direction. Then the rocks started falling from the sky due to the blast. They had to crouch and cover their heads. After the initial waves of debris and rock stopped, Ivan ran full speed stark naked back to his camp. When Ernie saw Ivan running full speed away from him, he turned and scramble up the bank through the bushes and up the hillside to where they had been quietly camped out planning the operation. Ernie knew from experience that if there was one explosion then quite often there would be another to follow. The Cambodians found each other in the chaos and quickly made the only decision that they could make; they took off running full speed after the scared Russian. They had to complete their mission. Ivan was more than a hundred yards ahead of them, but they pressed on through the dusty air. Ivan ran into the camp which consisted of a bunch of trucks, tractors, tents and maybe 50 Cambodian workers. People were running around like chickens with their heads cut off. It was complete chaos. They could barely make out where Ivan dived into a large tent at the edge of the camp. Mike and Rick stopped running and began to slowly creep along the edge of the camp towards the large tent that Ivan was now in. Both realized that it would be impossible now to capture Ivan so Plan B went into effect. They retreated and headed back up to where they had made their initial camp hoping they could find Ernie there.

Ernie had been hiking the whole day now and he was still in shock at what had happened. He knew he had seen either a flying saucer or some new prototype that was US or Russian, either way, he didn't want to know: he just wanted to be home in Venice, Ca. He was tired, thirsty, and not exactly sure he was moving in the right direction. This was his first really important mission and it had it was a fiasco. The sun was getting low in the sky and he had almost made it back to where he thought their initial camp was so he decided to stop and rest where he was for the night. He found a safe spot, drank some water, and ate some rations then fell asleep totally exhausted.

Just before dawn Ernie opened his eyes and immediately he knew something was wrong, he just felt it in the air. Within a few seconds the two Cambodian agents that he thought were his team members were standing over him with guns in hand. Mike and Rick actually had liked the American, Ernie, but the mission had failed and their orders were clear. They had been instructed to eliminate Ernie if the mission failed or if it appeared Ernie was going to be captured. Ernie had run off after the explosion in the opposite direction and now Ernie was a risk for them, so he had to be dealt with now.

Ernie's instincts had been honed from the streets of Venice and when the attack was on he reacted the only way he knew how, like a cornered animal. Initially he had no idea who was standing in front of him mainly because of the weak light. When his eyes began to focus he saw it was the two Cambodians, his so called CIA partners. Both of them had their fingers on the triggers but the guns were also pointing down and not at him. Ernie eyes started to focus in the light, "What's going on guys?" Ernie asked while trying to buy himself some time to decide exactly he needed to do. His heart was pounding and he could feel it. He was scared. They slowly raised their guns and Ernie knew the intent.

It all happened in a matter of seconds. Ernie grinned at the two Cambodians then rolled to his side and let off a shot which was under his right side with the safety off ready to fire. The shot hit Rick directly between the eyes and blew the back off his head up in the air. Mike let off shot that just missed Ernie's head as he kept rolling over. Somehow as Rick fell he was able to throw his knife at Ernie and it stuck in Ernie's left calve. Ernie had rolled over twice now and the second shot that Mike fired grazed

Ernie near his shoulder. Ernie didn't feel anything because his adrenalin was pumping through every cell in his body. After the second roll Ernie was able to get off three shots straight to the chest of Mike. Mike crumpled to the ground spitting up blood on the way down. Ernie fired two more shots to his head to finish him off and then put another shot in Rick's head as he lay writhing on the ground. It was over and Ernie fell back on his back in the damp leaves of the jungle panting for air. He pulled the knife out of his calve and that is when he realized he had also been shot in his shoulder. He patched himself up the best he could with his medical kit and then gathered what little gear he had and started to move out. He knew the gun shots could attract the enemy. It didn't take long before the wounds, the heat, and lack of water started to make him dizzy. He had no idea how long he had been limping along towards what he thought was the main camp. He was found by some patrol guards two days later not more than 200 yards from the camp, passed out in the bushes.

Ivan was not embarrassed by running naked back to his camp. He quickly dressed inside his tent and then surveyed the confusion around him. He did what he did best and that was to start barking out orders. The tunnel they had been excavating into the mountain had collapsed killing two workers that were fixing some machinery before the crew arrived. Rocks and fallen trees were everywhere. Some of the tents had collapsed and people were injured from falling debris. Ivan was directing everyone to pack up. There was no purpose in staying if the Americans were going to attack the camp. He then headed to the medical ten to get his bloodied foot taken care of. He must have cut it while running back to the camp. As he was sitting on a table having the Cambodian doctor sew up his foot he suddenly felt a sharp pain in his side. The Doctor looked at it and saw that there was a long sharp piece of what looked like a dark blue glass shard imbedded in his side. The Doctor pulled it out and sewed him up with a few stiches. It was an odd looking piece of glass or metal so Ivan had the Doctor put it in a small plastic bag that he put in his pocket. When Ivan was back in his tent he pulled the bag out of his pocket and examined the shard. It was nothing like any material he had ever seen before. A few minutes later he was called outside and his men led him to where they had found the guard that had accompanied Ivan in the morning. The dead guard was on a stretcher and his throat was sliced ear to ear. It was obviously not an injury from any falling rock. The next day the camp broke up and Ivan eventually made his way back to Moscow to report to his superiors. He brought the metallic crystal sliver that had been in his side but decided he did not need to show it to anyone, at least not now. He was near retirement and he knew it may be something that was valuable or alien. He had to keep that to himself. A few months late, while Ivan was still in Moscow, it was brought to his attention that dog tags with the name Ernie Lopez were found near the stream where he had been at the time of the blast. Obviously the Americans were involved in the blast and Ivan wanted to know what happened.

When Ernie woke up he was staring at a blurry light above him. He didn't know where he was nor the day or time. He tried to blink his eyes and for a few seconds thought he was back in the jungle, but then the light came into focus and he saw it was a light bulb hanging above him. He looked around and could tell he was in a medical tent. He saw a few other patients in the beds next to his. He tried to sit up but his body ached so bad he just fell back on the fluffy pillow. The bed felt nice especially as the memories of the previous days started to come back to him. He felt the pain in his leg where the knife had entered then closed his eyes and went back to sleep. It took another day before he could sit up and eat a full meal. After the meal he was taken in a wheel chair to the commander's office.

Colonel Jones was seated at his desk going over paperwork when Ernie was wheeled into his office. Ernie saluted the Colonel Jones and the Colonel saluted back. "Sit down soldier, oh sorry, you are already sitting! Damn, you look pretty bad, but I think you are strong enough now to explain to me what happened"

Ernie real did not feel like talking so he just stared at the Colonel with a balk expression. Inside Ernie could feel the rage starting to boil as he reflected back and saw the look in the two Cambodians eyes as they stood over him in the early dawn. "How could his own country do this to him after the time he had served? ", Ernie thought to himself. Just at that moment Mr. Stearns walked into the room holding a clipboard. He was late to the meeting because he had been on the phone with his superiors in Washington trying to explain to his superiors what had happened. Ernie's anger turned a deep crimson red inside his head at the sight of Mr. Stearns. Stearns was the man that had given the orders to the tow Cambodians to kill Ernie if thing went wrong and the Cambodians had no whims at following that order.

"You!" Those were the only words Ernie could muster as he exploded out of his wheelchair like a coiled lion ready to attack. Almost instantly Mr. Stearns dropped his clipboard and at the same time Ernie was on top of him and had his hands locked around the man's throat. Mr. Stearns struggled but Ernie held on until Colonel Jones and his assistant that heard the commotion from the adjacent office could pull Ernie off of Stearns. They held Ernie down on the floor and the assistant radioed the doctor who arrived in a matter of minutes and shot Ernie up with a powerful tranquilizer. Eventually Ernie calmed down and they put him back in his wheelchair with his hands strapped down to the arm rests.

It took a good fifteen minutes for Ernie to calm down under the effect of the tranquilizer. Mr. Stearns took a chair on the opposite side of Ernie with Ernie still glaring at him. "Ok, Stearns, what was that all about?" Colonel Jones said in a stern tone as he wiped the sweat off of his brow and scowled.

Stearn raised his hand like he didn't know what was really going on and then replied in a defensive soft voice, "Hey, let's remember I told you I didn't want this kid going alone on the mission in the first place. You are the one that insisted we have your Beret accompany my men! Look, it's obvious this kid is a little out of his mine, but hey, I guess that is what war does to people. I can see he his drugged now and not likely to make any sense if he does talk. I have my orders and they are not from you. I have a chopper waiting outside and I need to leave here now. I am in trouble because of your Green Beret! He screwed up the mission and my agents are nowhere to be found. Just send me a copy of your report to our office in Saigon." Stearn then stood up and hurriedly left the office heading for his waiting chopper. He had enough intelligence from other sources and he knew what Ernie was going to say. There was no point in him sticking around with an angry Colonel in his face.

Colonel Jones replied sharply before Stearns could get to the door, "Ok, Stearns, I have a good feeling you are leaving for another reason, but that is fine with me because I don't like your type around my men. Maybe I should just have let Lopez ring your neck a little longer. Just be sure that when you get to Saigon to tell your people to stay the heck away from my camp because I don't need your slick intelligence causing my men anymore trouble. We have enough of it here without your type. One last thing before you leave; this kid has the potential to one of our best soldiers and if you have screwed him up because of your moronic spy plans then I am going make sure you pay for it."

Mr. Stearns slammed the door on his way out and made his way to the waiting chopper.

Ernie was in daze from the tranquilizer. The sedative had taken full effect and even though his anger lingered he was just to numb to move. He stared a dead cockroach that lay on its back halfway under the Colonels desk in front of him. After the door slammed and Stearns left the Colonel asked his secretary to leave the room so that he could talk to Ernie alone. "Do you think you can tell me what happened out there on the mission?"

Ernie brought his eyes up from the dead cockroach and stared at the Colonel in front of him. He casually looked around the room and saw that he was alone now with the Colonel. He wasn't sure that he should tell the Colonel the full truth, but the tranquilizer in his system seemed to make telling the truth a lot easier. Why not, he thought to himself. There was nothing to lose at this point.

When Ernie opened his mouth to speak he realized his thoughts were coming a lot faster than his words, so he laughed out loud at how stupid he must sound to the Colonel. He stopped himself and then took a deep breath and started over speaking with a slow deliberate voice.

"You know Colonel; I really trained hard during boot camp because I was fully intent on making it as a Green Beret. I have learned many ways to kill and the moron Stearns is one that needs to die as far as I am concerned". Ernie paused, and realized what he had just said. He kept blinking his eyes feeling the effect of the tranquilizer, and he knew he was talking but he didn't really know the implications of what he was saying, yet he did in a way. His mouth opened again very slowly he spoke again but it turned to a rage of the memory, "They tried to kill me!!" Ernie shouted, but it really wasn't much off a shout because of the tranquilizer effect. "The Colonel smiled and knew he would be here awhile. Ernie continued after taking a deep breath, "Stearns had to have given them the orders. I saw it in their eyes, so I had no choice; I killed them before they killed me. They had their fingers on their triggers so I rolled and shot first. I had to defend myself."

The Colonel reached in his desk, then walked from behind his desk and continued to let Ernie tell him the story of what had happened at the mountain. Ernie breezed over the part where he had seen a spaceship come out of the side of the mountain, just calling it a blast, or explosion, and he expected more explosions, so he headed back towards camp. The Colonel was recording the story and would later write his report. There were other reports that came in of a rocket or space craft coming out of the side of the mountain but they were blown off as native hoax or rumor. Petrosky was never was sure what happened except for the shard of crystal/metal pulled out of his side.

Ernie was transferred to Japan for two years with a desk job. He fell in love with a Japanese woman; she got pregnant so after his stint in the service he brought his wife and new son back to his parents' home in Venice, Ca. He kept his war stories to himself.

Chapter 8
The Ancestors Speak

Tom Whitecloud lived in a small trailer outside of Socorro, New Mexico on ten acres of land he had purchased for almost nothing a few years ago. He bought the land from an old man who had known one of his cousins. Tom was 33 years old, of medium build and he was a full blooded Zuni Indian. He had grown up on the Zuni Pueblo Reservation in the northwest corner of New Mexico. When he reached his early twenties he grew tired of life on the reservation. Everyone knew everyone else's business and even though Socorro was a small town he at least had his land with more space. The town of Socorro was not nearly as nice as the Pueblo but at least he could be left alone. He liked the solitude and the peace it brought to him. He had a few friends, mostly drinking buddies, but he also spent a lot of time alone. Tom raised a few chickens and had a very large garden. He enjoyed working in his garden so he could provide most of the food he needed for himself. He didn't really like hunting or fishing. He really didn't like killing animals for food or any other reason. He knew all the animals were just reincarnations of people and when he sat on his porch he would sometimes talk with the animals that passed by. Eventually most of the wild animals in the area sort of knew Tom also, and he liked that. Tom made jewelry from gemstones he would find on excursions to the local mountains. Once a month or so he would drive up north to Santa Fe and sell his jewelry to the Zuni vendors that worked in that town selling jewelry to tourists. He didn't have much money or any steady income other than the jewelry he sold but that was not major concern to Tom. He enjoyed a quiet and peaceful life and that is what mattered to him the most. His family back on the reservation stayed in contact with him on a regular basis. As far as a social life he would travel back to the reservation for various family gatherings and celebrations. His family was very happy that Tom was doing well because they all knew he was bit slower than the other children growing up. Now Tom seemed to be the happiest of just about anyone they knew!

Almost every morning, very early, Tom would go for a walk to enjoy the smells and sounds of the nature around him. Sometimes he would go and sit by the river just staring at the water and occasional fish that jumped out of the water.

Today Tom was up a little earlier than usual for his walk. It was 4:50 AM and he had a hard time sleeping the night before. The day before when he was in Santa Fe someone had broken into his truck and they stole all the jewelry that he was going to sell. He had worked on the jewelry for over a month so it was a big loss and now his finances would be really tight for a month or two. Although it was still dark Tom decided to go for his walk. He needed to think and get rid of the anger he felt. He headed east along the cliffs near the river and he could see the sky begin to lighten so he knew it would light pretty soon. After walking for about half an hour the dawn sky became very colorful and the beauty on the horizon made him smile. The anger was starting to dissolve. He was feeling calmer now. In back of him the full moon was sinking in the sky but it still gave off a shimmering pale white light. He turned west and headed over to a small mesa where he decided he would sit and watch the magnificent sunrise. The sky was getting brighter now and the stars overhead were fading from view. Tom thought to himself how small and insignificant he was compared to the sky. He stared at where the sun was starting to rise and he felt sad for a few moments because of the loss the day before, but he no longer felt angry. Suddenly there was a flash of light across the horizon just to the left of where the sun was beginning to show itself. He narrowed his eyes and tried to see what was happening. There appeared to be a long saucer shaped object rapidly decelerating as it went through the sky. It came to a stop very low on the horizon and then dropped straight down just beyond another small mesa. For a time Tom felt as if he was still in bed dreaming, so he bit his lip to make sure he was awake. As the sun continued to rise the wind came up. It was a cold biting wind and Tom shivered as he felt the wind on his face. He marked the exact spot on the horizon so he could check out that location later in the day. As he was walking back to his trailer he had a strong vision of his Grandfather sitting by the fire and telling the children that were gathered around about a secret place that only the Zunis knew was there. It was a very sacred area where the spirits of his ancestors would gather to pray. Tom stopped walking and softly began to chant an old song that his Grandfather had taught him. Tom's vision began to meld with the brilliant rainbow colored sunrise that exploded on the horizon. When he opened his eyes he set out not towards his trailer but towards the spot on the horizon where he saw the craft go down.

He followed along the ridge of the mesa as the sun rose into the sky to his left. He crossed down from the mesa into an arroyo and then up to the other side and up a long gentle slopping hill. It took him almost an hour to arrive where he had set out. When he at last made it to the top of the hill he was out of breath. He peered down into a small valley and he saw an old ranch house with a large wooden fence in front of it. There was a large newer looking red barn next to the house. There was a barbed wire fence around the land and some cattle grazing in the distance in back of the house. There was no sign whatsoever of any spaceship and no sign of any people. Tom crouched down behind an outcrop of rocks and rested. He watched the ranch house below and sipped from his water bottle. He was starting to doubt that what he had seen earlier was a space vehicle at all, and started to think his eyes had deceived him. After about ten minutes or so he heard the cry of a raven and as he narrowed his eyes to see better it appeared the raven was trapped on top of the barn flapping its wings trying to get away. A lady then walked out of the barn from a door that was on the side near the house and looked up at the trapped raven. The next thing that happened seemed very odd and Tom was not sure what to make of it. The roof of the barn started to open up, the raven flew off squawking at the lady, and then the roof closed just as easily as it had opened. When the roof opened Tom could see shadowy reflections coming from inside the barn. Then the lady looked up before she went back inside and she stared at the exact spot where Tom was peering out of from behind the outcropping of rocks. Tom could feel her eyes piercing into him. It was not a scary or eerie feeling, just odd. Now Tom knew the visions of his Grandfather were real. Maybe the spaceship was in the barn. Tom took off back to his trailer worried that the lady had seen him and that he would be in some kind of trouble.

The underground grotto the aliens had landed in was very similar to the one they had left in Cambodia only a lot smaller. They hoped it would be their last home and base of operations for the remaining time they would spend on the small blue planet. It was actually set up more to their liking than the one before because Aktal and Shala could stay in the ranch house above. This meant they would have to keep up their front of being two sisters from California. It had taken almost a year with the help of their worker robots to build out the retreat in the cavern below the barn to fit Borghx's specifications. Mr. Kyn and the other Marans were very pleased with their new home. While the others unpacked and secured the space vehicle, Borghx and Mr. Kyn went off to a small granite patio to discuss their plans for the future. Mr. Kyn noticed that Borghx seemed to be moving slower than normal but did not mention anything to him about it. When they finished talking Mr. Kyn called the other Marans to a meeting to discuss the various issues.

The Marans sat around a small table with fruits and other refreshments that Shala had prepared for them. Everyone was relieved that their escape from Cambodia had been successful. They were all tired but in a joyous mood. Mr. Kyn began his speech, "Thanks to the hard work of Aktal and Shala it appears we have a wonderful retreat here to now continue our mission. We all know that we were lucky to escape as quickly as we did. I am sure we were detected by various radars but hopefully our cloaking mechanisms will have covered our tracks well enough so that we can remain here in peace. Borghx and I are both convinced that we will be able to center our operations from here and make steady progress with our objectives. We do though, have one immediate problem. Borghx and I have discussed the problem and we have come to the same conclusion to solve it. I am sure most of you will actually enjoy and gain many insights from the solution that we have come up with. Earlier Aktal informed Borghx and me that a large bird was trapped in the roof of the barn when she closed the entry after our space vehicle landed inside. She went outside to see the bird that was trapped and she decided to open the roof again to free the bird. When she opened the roof to free the bird she noticed a man on a distant hill that seemed to be observing us. She informed Borghx and me that she has seen the same man in town a few times in the past. There is a possibility that he may now actually be on his way to inform others of what he observed. If this happens we are all in danger, though I doubt our cavern beneath this barn would ever be discovered. There would still be a lot of questions as to why there is a large mechanical door on the roof of this barn. Borghx and I made the decision to send Aktal to follow this man and to have her try to gain his confidence. This may mean that she will have to introduce him to all of us if she is confident that she can gain his trust."

Jacon and Kafta let out a little cry of glee! They had been waiting for what seemed like forever to have the opportunity to actually meet and talk with a human!

Mr. Kyn could see their excitement and quickly interjected, "Wait, wait my dear friends this could be a very serious matter. Now, of course I am also very interested in meeting a human face to face but the first encounter must be well orchestrated and suited to our needs. The man that Aktal is approaching is an indigenous human to this area. His people are called Zuni and Borghx will educate you on the Zuni culture. For now we must make preparations just in case we encounter anymore unforeseen problems." Jacon and Kafta jumped up quickly and hurried off chatting and laughing with each other in search of Borghx. They were very excited that at last their adventure would begin and they knew that Aktal would be successful in dealing with the human.

Tom Whitecloud was sitting at the small dinette table in his trailer sipping some herb tea he had prepared to calm his nerves. He remembered he still had some brandy left from the night before, so opened the cupboard above the sink and took a long gulp of the brandy. He noticed that when he washed the brandy down with the herb tea it left a very sweet and distinct taste. He liked the taste and told himself he would have to try that again. He knew he was just distracting his thoughts from what he had witnessed only an hour before. He told himself out loud that he should have had a phone line run out to his trailer because now he would at least be able to call his sister, but there was no phone line and he was alone. His sister lived in Santa Fe with her husband and Tom was sure that his sister was about the only person that would believe his story. He took another swig of the brandy and again washed it down with the herb tea. The thought of his sister and her husband made him think how lonely he really was and how it would probably always be that way. He hoped that he would meet a good woman someday, but, he knew he really did not have much to offer anyone other than his jewelry making and love, but maybe that would be enough. Time would tell, he said to himself. He had sat long enough and even though he was tired and wanted to take a nap he knew he had to drive into town to use the pay phone and call his sister so he got up and started to put on his jacket when all of a sudden there was a sharp knock on the trailer door. Tom was instantly scared because no one came out to his trailer and he never heard a car pull up. He sort of fell back against the cabinet near the kitchen feeling more scared than he had ever remembered feeling in his life.

"Hello, Hello is anyone home?" It was a woman's voice that called from outside the door. The voice was soft and very sweet.

"Oh, hello, who is there?" The fear instantly dissipated and Tom stepped to open his door.

"My name is Aktal. I am your neighbor." The woman said as Tom slid the small curtain aside to take a look at her before he opened the door.

Tom opened the door wondering if something was wrong. Maybe someone needed help or maybe there had been some kind of accident. When the door was fully opened he looked into the deepest blue eyes he had ever seen in his life. They reminded him of two pale blue gemstones. The woman was dressed in jeans and a green top. She was absolutely the most beautiful woman he had ever seen in his life and the sight of her shocked him. He stood holding the door open not able to speak.

"Hi, my name is Aktal. I am your neighbor. I live down the road. Can I come in?" Aktal reached her hand out and Tom instinctively shook her hand. It was like touching the hand of a Goddess and Tom felt her energy surge through every part of his body. At last he pulled himself out of his daze.

"Yes, yes please come in!" Tom moved away from the door so Aktal could take the two steps up into his trailer. "I'm sorry my place is a mess." Tom cleared some papers from the chair that he never sat in and motioned for Aktal to sit down. Aktal took one look around and instantly knew almost everything she needed to know about Tom. She saw the picture on the wall an old Indian then froze her gaze; something deep inside of her reverberated. Aktal had no idea she was a robot other than the fact that she was programmed with certain traits of recognizing fact that she was a robot. She had grown on the journey by learning from the human's knowledge along with many conversations with Borghx. Conversations with Borghx though were different than her conversations with the Marans because Borghx was a Galactic creature and in many ways a robot like her, only light years more advanced. She stared at the old Indian in the picture and Tom saw her doing it. He motioned for her to sit down, "That is my Grandfather." Aktal sat down and Tom sat across from her.

"Oh, he looks like a very wise man." Aktal said in a soft tone that instantly made Tom feel like he was dreaming.

As Tom stared at Aktal it suddenly clicked that she was the lady he had seen in the distance near the barn earlier. His eyes opened up wide. He felt scared. He shivered. Aktal saw the fear and she gently reached out her hand across the table and touched Tom on his shoulder. "Stay calm Tom, I am your friend!" She smiled with her eyes. Tom felt at ease and he stared into her sparkling eyes. He suddenly felt light like an eagle soaring in the clouds. He saw fluffy white clouds pass outside the small window. He raised his eyebrows.

"My Grandfather died two years ago.", then Tom felt a tear form at the thought of his Grandfather. Aktal pulled her hand from Toms shoulder, sat very upright and then beamed a magnificent smile.

"Tom, I can see your Grandfather is alive inside of you. I would like you to come with me to meet my sister and some friends. I feel you would be very happy to meet them and that they would be very happy to meet you. Please, Tom, come with me now." Aktal beckoned with her hand and slowly started to rise from her seat. She stood in front of Tom and he could see every curve in her body. The way she had stood up was like no person he had ever seen. It was so composed and smooth. She exuded sensuality but it was far beyond just her physical beauty. Her jeans hugged her so that when she stood it reminded him of the women he had seen in movies that stole men's hearts. His heart was instantly taken. Tom nodded his head in affirmation. He was mesmerized in the moment. He stood and followed her out of the trailer. He forgot to close the door so Aktal turned and closed it for him. Tom could feel his legs were tired from the recent walk; he had only eaten a small biscuit and drank the tea with brandy. He realized he was tired but his mind was exploding in colors, like a hallucination from peyote he had once tried with a cousin. The old men had taken peyote but Tom did not like the experience. Now he was back in a similar state of mind, mesmerized, but this time he knew it was a destiny he could not resist. He followed along behind Aktal for at least a mile or so and she kept up a fairly steady pace. Neither one of them spoke. At times Aktal would seem to spring along like a seasoned deer knowing exactly how to place her feet and glide over the path. Tom started to see the face of his Grandfather in his mind and wondering why his Grandfather was appearing to him now. Then he felt his Grandfather speak through him. "Wait." Tom assertively spoke out so Aktal had to stop and turn. Tom bent over and put his hands on his knees to rest. He was panting for air. "You are the lady I saw this morning. Who are you? I saw that flying saucer! It went in your barn! Why are you taking me with you? I saw the crow. You know that crow was really mad at you!"

Aktal took a slow step towards Tom and moved very close to him so he could feel the intimacy his animal instincts wanted with every cell in his body. Tom felt aroused in every way a man could feel aroused and it instantly embarrassed him. Aktal started to smile and giggle almost like a little girl that had put too many flowers in a basket and then it fell off the railing of a porch. The flowers were pretty the accident was not. "Tom, my lovely Tom, I am a native also, and I am a creature of Mother Earth, so I promise you I will totally make amends with the crow!" Then she reached out and pulled Tom very close to her so that the anticipation of a hug swelled to a height beyond the now burning sun Tom felt on his back. Softly she spoke very close to his ear so that he could smell the sweet nectar of a cactus flower perfume, "Please Tom, come with me now." Tom deliberately nodded his head and felt the presence of his Grandfather once again, a sense of adventure, seeking, expanding his knowledge, taking a risk on a feeling, and the joys of only feeling that your future would be real and secure. Tom took a step and slowly led the way in silence. He felt his aching muscles; he was very tired and hungry. No words were spoken.

It was a lengthy walk and Tom was happy when they headed down the ridge towards the farm below. He saw the large red barn where he knew the flying vehicle must have landed. He felt no fear. What he would see he had absolutely no clue, but he just thought "What have I got to lose! Smallness disappeared into a deeper smallness. Now a fast dehydrating Tom was lagging along with this exquisitely splendid species of an advanced galactic aided robotic prototype who was manipulating Toms every movement. They slowly saunter down the hill toward the ranch house. At last they arrived. Shala greets them at the front door and introduces herself as Aktal's sister. She takes Toms hand and leads him to a lavish bath area that is more like a spa than a bath. Tom is dumbfounded, tired, and more or less in complete shock. He has never experienced anything like this but he likes it, so he just goes along with the program. Aktal leaves through a side door and Shala waits on Tom hand and foot. She gives him refreshments, massages him, feeds him, baths him and has him relax under highly skilled healing hands. The barn stood outside nearby, but Tom was not interested in the barn at this point. Shala leads Tom to a small but very clean bedroom where she then guides him to the bed and tells him that he should rest some before he meets the others. The bed was more comfortable than any bed he has ever been on so within minutes Tom is fast asleep. After six hours of a deep and peaceful sleep, Tom wakes up, refreshed and focused. He gets up, dresses, and notices that the sun is low in the sky. He starts to wonder if he is in a dream when Shala walks in the room and smiles at him.

"You look like a new person, Tom!" Shala says politely.

"I feel like a new person. I am really wondering if this is a dream." Tom Says as he puts his boots on while sitting on the edge of the bed.

"No, this is not a dream." Shala replies.

Chapter 9
Circles of Desires

Venice, California – 15 years later.

It was the end of June and the summer heat was coming on like a blast furnace. The sky was a deep blue and there were no clouds anywhere to be seen. Normally this time of year in Venice the weather was a bit overcast in the mornings and often the sun did not burn through the haze until well after noon, but not today. The beach was packed with people.

Ernie Lopez, Mark Price, and George Kasaki were no longer school age but they were young at heart, good friends for many years, all loved the ocean, and could not resist watching the bikini clad girls at the beach. The three of them had not been together since last winter so what better place to get together and hang out! The three of them were different races and from different cultural backgrounds but they had a lot more in common than mere social differences which in reality made little difference to them having all grown up in Southern California. They had become close friends from High School and from the hot summers they spent at the beach with their friends. After High School Ernie was in the Marines, while George and Mark did everything they could to avoid the military. George avoided the draft because his vision was too poor. Mark was just somehow missed in the draft process altogether. Mark told people his name was just too common and someone must have made a bureaucratic error. There really was no logical explanation as to why he was not drafted. When Ernie returned from Vietnam the three of them met on occasion but the friendships had seemed to wane. Mark and George were still fairly close friends and they sometimes talked about how Ernie had changed since his tours of duty in Vietnam, but it was not really much of a topic because they still loved him as a good friend. Ernie was always super loyal and the first one to stand up for his friends in any conflict. Recently Ernie's wife, Maria, had called Mark because she was convinced that Ernie was going to lose his job because of his drinking problem. Mark heard her out and even though he was not the type to want to intervene in anyone's problems he promised her that he would have a talk with Ernie. Mark figured it would be best to have George with him because two would be better than one, so that is why they were all meeting at the beach. Of course as fate would have it George brought along a six pack of beer with him and that was surely not going to make the talk session any easier, but hey, what the heck, it was a really hot day and Markwas more than happy to have a beer! They sat around on their towels, went swimming, talked about the various bikini clad girls sauntering along the water and then when George and Mark went back into the water, Ernie snuck off to the store to get another six pack of beer! Ernie finished half of the second six pack and the day was wearing on so Mark decided he needed to at least make an attempt at the talk he was supposed to have with Ernie.

     "Ernie, you know it is only 4:00 pm. Don't you think you should go easy on the beer? Mark was sitting on his towel and turned to look Ernie directly in his eyes when he spoke to him. "Look Ernie, I am going to be honest, your wife called me and she is worried that you may lose your job because you have been drinking too much." Mark wondered if he had taken the right approach. Maybe, he thought after he said it, that he would only cause more problems between Ernie and his wife. Ernie laughed, like only Ernie could laugh. It was one of those big bellied laughs that meant no matter what you said to him he was going to find a way to turn the whole thing around into something humorous. Mark did not like the fact that Ernie was laughing at what he said. Mark was being serious in his own way and he wanted his friend to realize that. "Look Ernie, this is not a joke. I mean seriously, I don't care if you drink twenty four hours a day. Hey, it is your life. I am telling you because your wife asked me to tell you and she must be concerned if she asked me to tell you so try at least to look at the situation in some type of serious manner!" Ernie was just smiling now and staring at his beer, which he decided to take another sip of. Mark took that as a sign of Ernie not being serious at all and it sort of pissed him off. "Ok, look, we have been friends for a long time and I am only telling you this because your wife asked me to. If I had anything I would talk to you about it would be about Vietnam. You know we have never brought it up, mainly because you don't want to talk about it, but seriously, what the hell happened to you there? George and I both know something happened because you have changed and if the drinking too much is part of that then maybe it is time you started telling us about what happened there." Mark thought to himself, oh boy, now I opened the can of worms!

Ernie looked at Mark for a long time, longer than George or Mark were accustomed to. Ernie sort of shifted on his towel and stared out to sea. He then took a deep breath. His faced changed and became very relaxed. For a brief moment both George and Mark saw Ernie as they had seen him in High School. His scowled dissipated, he took another deep breath and he had that boyish sense of adventure and curiosity that everyone that knew him loved about him, even though nowadays it only came in brief flashes and mainly with his two sons. Ernie stood up and took another deep breath, "Come on guys let's take a walk down the beach and I will tell you about Vietnam." Then Ernie darted full speed towards the ocean and the waves not more than 50 yards away. George and Mark followed. Ernie dived into the surf and swam out past the breakwater with the others following. They grouped together and dogpaddled. At first Ernie fought back some tears, and then he sidetracked with tales of prostitutes, funny soldier incidents, but always going back to a killing. He then swam back in to the shore and started to walk down the beach. At one point he stopped at looked at his two old High School friends. "Ok, look guys, I have told you a lot of stuff, and I have told you how I met my wife in Japan. I am going to ease off the drinking. I love her, but you know how it goes when you have been with someone a long time." Mark nodded. He had been through enough women that he understood. George raised his eyebrows because he had not been with many women, nor had he ever married. He was always a bit jealous that he had not raised a family but he understood why in his own way. His strict Japanese upbringing was different and with his thick glasses he knew not too many women found him attractive. "Ok, look guys, I have never told anyone this." George thought to himself, maybe he is going to say he is gay! "George, wake up!" Ernie slapped George in the chest like he had done years ago when they were close friends in High School. Ernie had protected George and George had helped Ernie with school work. It was the perfect relationship because George lived two houses down from Ernie in the worst Gang infected part of Venice. At that time the gangs were African American, and George's family was the only Japanese family. Ernie's was one of the few Mexican families. Both had a number of siblings, so the families became very friendly as a form of protecting themselves.

It was survival of the fittest at the fundamental core. "Alright this is it, I know you're going to think I am crazy, but I saw a flying saucer when that mountain blew apart. I swear to God, I really did, it was as clear as day. Now I have thought over and over again, and I have kept up on all the military technology over the years and there is absolutely nothing that would compare to what I saw. I don't tell anyone mainly because I was in the military and I don't ever want anyone snooping around or asking me questions. I don't want either one of you to say anything to anyone, ever. Is that clear?"

George and Mark were not sure what to think. He could just be telling them a crock of baloney because he says he is going to ease off his drinking. On the other hand he seemed extremely serious.

Mark, being the witty one, chirped in, "So Ernie why did it take you so long to tell us this? Here we are your best friends and you never said anything? Look, I can understand the somewhat guilt part about killing two guys working for the CIA, but hey, I would have done the same thing. I mean lots of people say they have seen flying saucers? I mean, hey, I think George told me he saw one once, but he may have eaten some mushrooms or something."

Ernie looked back and forth between the two of them with a puzzled look on his face. In his mind he thought he had just explained everything to them but it seemed the two of them were too dense to understand. It wasn't the flying saucer; it wasn't any guilt over the killings he made; it wasn't any issue with his drinking or his wife. "Ok guys, let's walk back now and sit down we can talk some more there. Ernie was back to his frown, his discerned look, the Ernie that had changed since he had returned from Vietnam. George and Mark followed along not talking, lagging behind like stray dogs in a pack. It did not take long to reach the towels. Ernie handed out beers to everyone. They sat in a sort of semicircle with Ernie in the center looking out at the water. Ernie sipped his beer and enjoyed the view of the ocean. He thought how good it was to be back at the beach. This was the first time he had come all summer. George and Mark did the same. "Ok, Listen guys, I want to tell you this only one time so that you understand and get it. I only have one thing bothering me. You see, unlike the two of you morons, I keep my life together pretty well. What bothers me is that I did that mission for Military Intelligence and I know for a fact that they have kept an eye on me ever since. So I behave. I mind my ways. The system is much bigger than it was back then. Before I left Japan an officer came up to me and told me directly that it would always be in my best interest to keep my mouth shut about the

Cambodian agents and anything else. When I came home from Japan they watched or visited me in certain ways until now. Sometimes more frequent and sometimes less frequent. It is disturbing because I don't know anything. I think they just check on me because I am in the system and it is their job now and then. I have thought of moving after my kids are grown to somewhere remote, just for the peace. So I am trusting the two of you will just keep your mouths shut about this forever." Both Mark and George nodded their heads in agreement as they realized the seriousness of Ernie's conviction.

Ernie shifted his position on the sand and looked around him. He noticed something and lowered his voice. "Look very slowly to the right about fifty yards from the lifeguard station. Mark and George turned their heads to look slowly in that direction. "Ok, look back at me." Ernie said. "It is sort of getting later in the afternoon here now and that guy with the green hat has been there all day. He has watched me with friends on a variety of occasions over the past few years. I would say maybe six or eight times. I don't count and I don't really care. It is just annoying. I confronted others in the past and realized that was worthless so I just don't let it bother me. He has been watching us."

Mark rolled over on his side so he could get a better view of the guy. The man had a beach chair and a small cooler. He was wearing sunglasses and some headphones like he was listening to a radio. He looked somewhat familiar to Mark but it was hard to place him. Then it hit him! Mark looked at Ernie and raised his eyebrows and acted like he wanted to say something but instead he let out a soft laugh and shook his head. Next Mark started to get up and both George and Ernie grabbed him by his ankles. Mark was chuckling as they pulled him down. "Look I am going over there to pay a visit to your so called Military Intelligence man. So, when I get up the next time, do not grab my ankles." Mark flashed his eyes with the anger only George and Ernie knew was there. Normally Mark was very much in control of all situations and they both knew he liked to think of himself as some sort of "Ninja." They also knew he had some boring Bureau of land Management job. "Listen, I am just going to have a short talk with him, nothing important. When I come back here I will tell both of you everything, just like Ernie told us everything!" Mark let out a little laugh, but kept focused on his task. George and Ernie looked at Mark and really didn't want to know. Ernie could care less, it wasn't him doing something stupid, but he wasn't sticking around so he nudged George and they started putting their stuff together to leave. Mark got up and walked very casually in the general direction of the man in the green hat.

The guy looked like a typical tourist, but what neither George nor Ernie knew was that Mark was someone that not even he knew who he was. Where the rage for justice in him came from no one was sure. His job for Bureau of Land Management was his cover for his work with the CIA. Mark was what they considered a rogue agent. During his College at USC, he needed a job so he answered an odd add in a local paper that turned out to be a cover for a CIA operation trying to root out newer Russian immigrants that could turn to agents. The whole thing was a total fluke, but, Mark started talking during the interview! Mark talked a lot when he was nervous so when the man interviewing him asked him directly if he was associated with any Russians, Mark spewed off about the Russian in the building next to his. He was not that good of friends with them but at the same time he was polite and cordial; that was Marks nature. Mark was a very compassionate man and he BELIEVED in America. He was smart raised in a normal middle class family. The agent was able to coax out of Mark the fact that there were always a lot of different people coming and going, which led the agent to believe it was a safe house of some sort. After a week of watching the building they knew it was. A hot shot new regional manager came up with the great scheme to hire this USC student, Mark. He explained the job would be part time under the Bureau of Land Management. He also told Mark that the CIA would offer to hire him after College with a generous salary, if he did a good job. Mark accepted, kept the stuff quiet, took Russian classes in College, watched the building next to him, and enjoyed his life as a college student. He had some of the hottest girlfriends. When College ended, Mark took the job with the CIA and told no one except his Father. That was the rule. It turned out that only after two years Mark became out of control. The CIA had to consider him rouge. The first incident was the day after he had moved out of his apartment building next to the Russians and into a condo a few miles away in the Marina Del Rey. Mark had returned to his now empty apartment the day after he moved out because was going to patch the holes where he had pictures hanging and saw two Russian Agents he knew in his apt. Within seconds Mark had seriously hurt each one, no, not to the point of death but enough blows with the tools he had to conflict serious damage. His bosses had to cover up the incident with the local police and the skulking agents disappeared in a matter of hours. Other incidents happened along the years, but Mark always performed his job well. He wanted all the tools of the trade, but his bosses had to take away the psychotropic drugs because Mark was "losing" some of them. Mark understood so he checked his behaviors. He then went years without any incidents, but that was going to change right now!

As soon as Mark recognized the man he knew what he had to do. He would surely solve his friend's mystery. It was Felix, and not some Military Intelligence guy, Felix was a Russian operative, a low level one at that, and the CIA was not too sure what exactly he did because he most of the time acted like some Russian playboy, running around LA spending his Daddy's money at clubs and with girls. He had little influence and even the other more sophisticated operatives sort of avoided him. He was basically an off the radar son of some rich retired operative. Mark wasn't sure

Felix would recognize him. Mark knew his rouge status kept him somewhat off the Russian radar. It was a game and it was not always played conforming to any rules. So often things just happened. Mark had quit smoking long ago, but the one thing he did show to friends was the cigarette pack he carried that was a Taser stun gun. He told his friends it was government issued and he could not get one for any of them. Instead he directed them to a commercial company that made one within legal settings of which the one he had was not.

Felix turned and saw Mark now approaching him. He was going to stand but decided Mark did not look threatening. "Hey Felix, do you know who I am?" Mark said in a sort of diverting humorous way. Felix did not like the fact this person knew his name but now he was curious. He stared at Mark trying to place him, but his mind was blank. "Felix, look, I know you are Russian, my Dad knew your Dad." Then Mark said a few words in Russian and that put Felix more at ease. Mark sort of laughed and joked about how Russians didn't like going to the beach alone. He asked where the girls were! Felix was perplexed but not scared. He knew this guy had been with Ernie and he also knew Ernie was some ignorant Mexican that his Father had asked him to keep track of now and again. This guy was obviously some idiot also, except that he spoke Russian and said his Dad knew his Dad. Maybe, his Dad was checking up on him? Now he was a little worried that something was not right. "My name is Mark! Trust me after today you will remember my name." Mark pulled the package of cigarettes out of his pocket and took one out. "Do you have a light Felix?"

Mark loved the moment; he thrived for moments like these. He was a fun and free person. He was ready to die for his country but even more he was ready to fight for any of his friends that felt the same. He was the Law as far as he was concerned but at the same time he appeared as the most polite and helpful person you would ever meet. Mark loved flowers.

Before Felix knew what happened Mark was in back of him and pinned Felix's hands to the sides of the beach chair. Next Mark pressed the bottom of his cigarette case to the side of Felix's neck and it let off a mild shock.

Felix tried to struggle, "What the heck are you doing?" He screamed out.

"Shut up asshole. Don't move and keep your mouth shut or I am going to give you the jolt of your life." Mark replied calmly. Felix struggled a little thinking that there was no way this guy could get the jump on him like this so Mark slid his index finger to the lever on the cigarette case and turned up the volume some on the Taser jolting Felix again. This time Felix didn't scream but instead went a little limp with a horrible painful look on his face. Felix stopped moving and sat perfectly still. He realized this guy was a professional.

"Look you little scum I do not like you. If you move again I will turn up the juice and you will get the thrill of your life. I know all the lifeguards and the closest one is not too close, so keep quite. Worse is the fact that you have actually no idea who I am, so let's just say you would not be the first person I have killed just because I felt it was the best for the situation. I want you to start answering questions and I want short fast answers. Is that clear?" Felix nodded his head. I know who you are and who you work for. Mark then zapped him just for the fun of it and Felix could feel the warm urine as he released his bladder into a pool on his already hot beach chair. Mark knew Felix was primed now. "Why have you been following Ernie Lopez?" Felix was worried but he thought maybe this was just some local nutty friend of Ernie's. Felix had only been on the job for a few years and he had never seen Ernie with this guy. Felix didn't think it mattered much anyway because he really didn't know that much.

"OK, Ok, wait, don't shock me again." Felix pretended to be hurt worse than he was but he surly did not want any more shocks. "I don't know that much. All I know is that my uncle hired me to watch him. I don't know why, really he only told me that it had something to do with Vietnam, so I check up on him once in a while.   I sometimes record his conversations and give the information to my uncle." Mark turned up the volume a little bit and the voltage made Felix scream so Mark let go off Felix's arms and slammed his massive hand over his lips to shut him up. Felix could taste the salty blood as his lips were ripped over his teeth.

Mark is what we call a savant and to go along with his incredible intelligence, for some reason, he had a wild side to him that took his violence often to what some would consider a dark level. His CIA handlers were comfortable with him as long as he kept in line with the missions. Fortunately there were not too many missions and Marks superiors learned quickly that Mark was only useful at home in the USA. When they had sent him to Russia things got out of control way to fast. Mark's brain worked much faster than most and his skills at reading people were incredible. He could tell right away that Felix was not giving up any information that he had and most likely he didn't have much. Felix was a goofball playboy, want to be agent, living off his rich uncle that most likely was, or was related to the one Ernie was going to assassinate in Vietnam. The whole thing was small stupid crap that had little to do with the problems of humanity as far as Mark was concerned.

"Ok, stop please" Now Mark could tell his idea of Felix was correct. A normal KBG agent would not give in this easy. "I've never seen him contact any other agents. I have never seen him do anything wrong. He just goes to Reserve meetings sometimes. I am not exactly sure why I watch him. The whole job seems stupid to me but I get my check every month. I am not KBG otherwise I wouldn't be watching this ignorant Mexican! I don't…" That last line was too much for Mark and his brain his brain snapped. The adrenaline was already flowing too fast and Felix made a foolish mistake!

Mark was not a poor man, in fact he was fairly wealthy. He did it on his own and as long as he worked with the CIA it was all good. Mark was intolerant of racism and prejudice. He could deal any intellectual debate on a non-emotional level but emotional gut level racism was intolerable. Every stupid Religion, none that he believed, had various aspects of intolerance in them. On a systematic level it went beyond a moral sin to a mortal sin in some cases, so, in Marks mind, lessons must be taught. He knew his part in changing humanity was slim, in that he was a realist, but in action he pursued it. It was his American duty. He could tell his reactions to injustice was aging him faster than he wanted to and knew he had to make a change. Maybe now was the time to do it, he thought to himself.

As a savant Mark thought at lighting speed. His emotions and intellect were wound together like tightly woven rope. His pursuit of justice was ingrained in him and thought at lighting speed as to what his future would be like, and then he pursued it with passion. He felt guilt from his Methodist indoctrination as a youth. Now his life almost seemed to just be a way of a releasing the pressure from not being able to make the world see the injustices that were rampant everywhere.

The Golden Recovery never happened this time. He knew he had been a warrior for peace, but now he was older and it seemed his time was limited. It was hard to accept that fact, but at this exact moment he decided he would. It was enough for Mark. He did not enjoy his friend being called a stupid Mexican, and it was obvious he would have to go elsewhere to get more information. He was getting nothing out of this guy. Now it was late afternoon, some clouds had drifted in and a majority of the beachgoers had left. Ernie and George were sitting with gear in hand ready to leave at moment's notice. Mark flashed a glance at them, then nodded his head for them to start walking, so they did. Mark cranked up the voltage and shocked Felix. He collapsed to the ground foaming at the mouth. George and Ernie looked back and then ran from the beach. Mark walked away casually and they met at the car.

"Mark you idiot" They hurriedly were throwing their gear in the car. Ernie was livid. "Are you out of your mind? Did you kill that man? If he is military indigence I am dead. What the hell is wrong with you?"

Mark felt calm and focused now, at least compared to a few minutes before. He knew at this point there was no other choice but for him to be calm. He adeptly put his gear away, ignored Ernie, got in the car and started driving a circuitous route that only he knew to somewhere. Mark reassured Ernie over and over again that Felix would be fine and just wake up with a head ach in an hour or so. Ernie was still upset and did not like the situation. Why would Mark screw up so badly and do something so stupid? Was he just that much out of control or was he being protective of him? It didn't matter now because the damage was done and the consequences would have to be paid. It sucked big time.

When they hit the freeway, Mark cranked up the stereo and let out a wild yelp! After he grinned at Ernie, he then answered all of Ernie's questions. Mark realized it was time to admit to his friends his work with the CIA. Bothe Ernie and George were speechless. Mark went on to tell them about Felix. "Felix was a semi-loser KBG sent by the Russian guy that you my friend were sent to exterminate in Vietnam! I tell you, to me, it makes little sense because if someone wanted revenge it would have happened a long time ago. You are obviously not some advanced officer. You are in the Reserves and have a normal job. The only relation I can see is the blowing up of the mountain. If that is the reason then someone really cares about what was going on in that mountain and they think you know something or are somehow involved. Of course another conclusion is that the Uncle is semi-senile and has an obsession just for revenge but has no balls to carry it out! It's all good. Actually, everything seems to be working out just fine. I am getting a plan together and I want to bring you in on it. I can guarantee your peace and a cool place for your sons. I will take care of everything,"

"Ernie hit Mark in the arm. "What are you saying, this car could be bugged! I think you are nuts and just listening to you ramble on is exhausting to me! Just drive me home!"

"Chill Ernie, I told you. I work for the CIA. I am pretty independent and have some technology that would just blow our mind. Somehow we will get to the bottom of this and in the meantime maybe we can have the life we dreamed of as teenagers back in high school." Mark replied.

George was beside himself because there was just too much going on and he didn't like it. George worked for FedEx and had a good career job, now his two best friends were playing some kind of cloak and dagger games. Yeah, right, like Mark worked for the CIA! That was just way too much to believe or comprehend. Flying saucers, Russian Agents and his friend Ernie wacked out from Traumatic Stress Syndrome; everyone he knew that had been to Vietnam had some mental disorder. "So are you guys telling me now that this car may be bugged by the CIA or the Russians, why the heck are we even talking! Mark I just think you have gone nuts!"

Mark waited a few seconds to respond. He had known George for a long time and he really did not like being called nuts. "Cool, I can understand both of your fears. It is true and I do work for the CIA, so just relax. I can tell you more later on. Right now I think the best thing for us to do would be to head over to Santa Monica Airport. I will take you for a ride in my new plane! You guys would be up for that, right?" Mark said has he sped up and turned off the freeway. Ernie and George looked at each other and threw their hands up in the air like they really didn't care anymore then nodded in agreement. It was a fast but silent ride.

It was a normal Saturday afternoon and the adventure was just getting started. The twisted intangibles that seemed to always randomly occur now met at a point single point in time.

Once at the airport Ernie had to call his wife and tell her they would be late because of going for a ride in Mark's new plane. She was fine with it Both Ernie and George were anxious to push Mark on what happened at the beach but at this point they could sense from his behavior that maybe now was not the best time to get into too many details.

Once in the air Mark gave everyone headphones. He spoke in a serious tone the about the incident at the beach. He told them that he felt that he was getting old and that he really wanted to get out of his duties with the CIA. Ernie was confused and taken back by the claim of a KBG agent. It all seemed just too bizarre. What did any of it mean? Nothing! Same old crap, same old life. Ernie zoned out of the conversation for a while and stared out the window at the city lights below. At least he was riding in a cool plane!

Mark reemphasized his points. "Look the reality is he did not want to tell me anything, so I neutralized his sorry ass for a while!"

George was ready to jump out of the plane. He started n with a rant about how the aliens wanted him because he had seen it in a dream. "Look guys, this is for real, someone's watching Ernie because he saw a flying saucer."

The rest of the airplane ride centered on crazy ideas, speculations, suppositions, but all with one theme in common; none of them had a clue what was going on. Mark landed and sort of sped up and skidded into the hanger. They got out of the plane and the random conversation continued with no one caring if anyone one was bugging the or not They continues to jabber on and laugh just as good friends will.

After an hour, or so, Felix staggered into his apartment complex. He had a massive headache and took a bunch of aspirin and a few shots of vodka. Not more than ten minutes later his Uncle appeared at his door.

He explained the story to his uncle who was now visiting from Russia, Ivan Petrosky. Ivan had completely forgot they were supposed to go to dinner and a strip club that evening. Ivan was outraged that Felix had let some amateur take advantage of him like he did. He was pissed off and asked for all the data that Felix had collected over the past two years, so head ach or not Felix scrambled to get all the data for his uncle.

Ivan Petroksy did not have the opportunity to retire after the Vietnam War because he was promoted to a leadership position the War Department and pretty much had free reign of a significant budget to do as he wished. He had a network of KBG agents that put pressure on immigrants to relay information back to Moscow. He liked his position of power and hopefully soon his new life in sunny California. He started to work out in anticipation of his planned move. The crystal he had found stayed in his possession. He had it analyzed one too many times in Russia and now he wanted it analyzed in the US.

He kept the crystal close to him and on many occasions he carried it in his coat pocket. So far no scientist could determine its origins. After a few of them wanted to keep it or turn it over to the Government Ivan decided not to expose it in Russia anymore. He was a devoted KBG but now with a chance to live part time in the USA he decided it was best let it remain a secret for him to manage as he see fit. There really was nothing more to find out from this Ernie Lopez but he would still keep his ears open.

Time went by and he rarely talked with his nephew, because he was such a moron. At any rate, it seemed obvious to him that somehow the Americans had gotten ahold of some alien technology. They were coming out with too many ceramic, and ceramic/metal mixtures, plus other technologies. Not human inventions. Now the Americans were pulling far ahead in a variety of new technologies. It was becoming a race by the spies of other countries to get at the American technology. It was beyond a game for monetary gain and all the major Nations knew it was a race they needed to excel at if they wanted to hold power.

Mark never wanted power, fame or glory. Not to say he had not acquired a lot of wealth. He may not be a Mr. Kyn but in his own way his savant abilities had led him to treasures that only appeared at rare times in the cycles of the universe. If there was a God he never needed to look at Mark.

Mark, George and Ernie sat in the airplane that had now landed and was parked back at the hanger. They were all tired from the long day and from the events that had unfolded. It was getting dark outside now. It seemed the silence of the big hanger brought more calm to the situation. They were talking amongst each other and again proposing various questions and scenarios only now they were not so emotional. George and Ernie were asking Mark a lot of questions about what he did with the CIA and Mark deflected the questions the best he could. He realized even though the two of them were his best friends it would be smarter for him to keep his mouth shut. He had already said too much. "Ok, look guys, the only real facts we have here are that the KBG for some reason has been watching Ernie for years, but, even then, we are not sure it has always just been them! So I guess the only real fact we know is that Ernie saw a flying saucer in Vietnam and killed two Cambodians working for the CIA. Maybe those Cambodians were actually double agents! I don't think we really know much." Mark said.

"I don't know what to think, but I just hope you didn't cause more problems for me by zapping that guy with your stun gun!" Ernie replied.

"Well I have something to propose to both of you and it actually has nothing to do with any of this. I was hoping to bring it up when we were at the beach but things got a little out of control." Mark said.

"Yeah they got out of control because you had to confront that guy and cause a big scene!" George chirped in.

"Ok, I'm sorry, maybe I did get a little too aggressive with him." Mark wanted George on board with his proposal so he conceded the point. "In a way what I am going to bring up may be a temporary solution. Actually George and I have talked about it before and I have done some research and thinking myself. You know what I am talking about right George?"

"You mean the business plan we talked about?" George answered.

"Yes the business plan. Why don't you explain it to Ernie?" Mark said.

"First off, let me just say this has been one crazy day. I just hope we don't have any more days like this! You know it seems like whenever the three of us get together trouble seems to come around." George said.

"Things just are the way they are!" Ernie said looking at his watch and realizing he needed to get back home pretty soon.

George continued, "Mark and I have been looking into very low interest Government financing for the fish farm project we have talked about for years. As you know Ernie, even though you haven't come to see it yet, the pilot project up in Kern County is very successful so far. We have been able to show good enough results that we are pretty close to getting a large low interest loan from the Government so that we can expand. The problem until now had been finding a good enough location. There is not enough water on Mark's property in Kern County and with the ongoing drought I doubt we are going to find the needed acreage in California that has sufficient water rights. I did all the background checking and if we expand it has to be outside of California because of the water situation and because the taxes are too high. Mark and I have been looking for a good location and last week we put in an offer on a property that we believe will be perfect. We should know in the next few days if our offer is accepted. If the offer is accepted then the Government is ready to write the check and we can go full speed ahead."

Mark interjected, "I could finance the project myself, but I told George from the beginning that we should take advantage of a low interest Government loan if we could get it and now we have. I have an agreement with George that he can buy out my shares in the company as we get going and start making a good profit. He has done 90% of the work and I just put up the seed money and let him use my land."

George continued, "Let me get to the point Ernie. The land is New Mexico about an hour from Albuquerque. It is near a small town called Socorro. We need someone to supervise the set up, so Mark and I wanted to ask you if you would come in as a partner."

Ernie needed to be getting home or he knew his wife would be thinking he was out way to late drinking even though he was completely sober now. "Thanks guys, but you got the wrong person. I am not leaving this area and I don't know anything about fish farming." Ernie said quickly.

"Hold on Ernie, you don't need to know that much about the actual fish farming. We need someone there to supervise the digging of the ponds and the other construction operations. I will be coming there on a regular basis and later I will be moving there myself. We just need someone there to get things started as soon as possible and to keep an eye on our interests. There will be a company contracted to do the work from the plans we have for them. We are asking you because you are a good friend and we need someone we can trust just to get the project started. I have to wrap up my employment contract with FedEx and Mark is off doing who knows what! It would be a really big favor for us and we would give you both a salary and an interest in the company. Seriously it is just mainly for the summer and your kids are out of school. We will pay all the moving expenses. The land borders on a stream and there is a fairly large ranch house on it with a few barns." George could see he was not getting too far with the proposal so he looked at Mark sort of wondering if he should just stop talking.

"Ernie, look, it will give you a chance to get out of here. You can go there alone at first and then bring your wife and kids. We will even give you a budget to fix up things around the house. I understand, it is out of town, sort of isolated, but I think when you see it you will like it and so will your family. Think of it as a paid summer vacation!"

Ernie had to hurry and get home but there was a little glitter in his eye. He knew this meant he would at last step up from barely getting by each month to a different level of income. He knew his answer but he wasn't sure what his wife would say. "Ok, you guys convinced me! Look, I need to get home now but George can call me tomorrow after I talk with my wife and we can work out the details about my pay and interest in the company."

The three of them went their separate ways and what had been a wild day actually turned out just as Mark and George had hoped it would. They were in a bind and they knew Ernie was perfect for the job.

It was shortly after 11 pm when Mark returned to his apartment. He had no sooner taken off his shoes, popped open a beer and relaxed on the couch when he heard a loud rap on his door.

"Who's there?" Mark yelled out from his couch.

"It's your neighbor" Someone responded.

Mark rose from his couch then walked over to the door and opened it just enough to peer out. He saw three Russians. One was an older man. He was overweight and balding. Standing behind him were two definite thug types. The older man spoke, "My name is Ivan and I would like to talk to you for just a little bit."

Mark was not stupid and he knew that payback time would never happen so quickly so obviously there was something else going on. He knew he had to take control of the situation. "Sure, why don't you all come in and take some seats. I just have to go put a shirt on." Mark quickly backed away from the door and ran to his hallway where he grabbed his shotgun and just as the three Russians sat down Mark came from behind the wall holding the shotgun.

The Russians were all seated around the kitchen table and when they saw Mark standing there with the shotgun they acted like it was just a normal part of business so none of them flinched. Mark had a big smile on his face as he took the last seat around the small dining table and backed up his chair a little away from the table so he could use his gun if he needed to. "Ok, before we talk all of you are going to take your weapons and put them on the table. The two big Russians slowing reached in their coats and put pistols on the table. The older one did nothing because he did not have a weapon. "Great, now the two of you can get up and go outside. I can tell that whatever is going to be talked about here is between your boss and me. Leave now!" The two thugs looked at their boss and he nodded so they stood up and walked outside. "Now that we are alone Ivan and due to the fact that I have the guns, I am going to ask a few questions first. If you are my so called neighbor then how come I have never seen you before?"

Ivan was a little surprised by how quickly Mark had taken control of the situation. He was either a rare wild card or a top CIA operative and he was not sure which. He knew now it would be worth it to have him investigated in detail. It may even be worth it to see if he could turn him into a double agent. This guy seemed to have the right personality for it. He obviously knew more than he needed to know about the safe house that was in the apartment building next door. It would be very interesting to see what made this guy tick. "Well actually I do not live next door, but some of my friends do. I guess you know my nephew, Felix." Ivan replied.

"Well, not until I met him today at the beach!" Mark said with a flippant attitude. "Tell me, why had he been following my friend Ernie?"

Ivan was toying with a small rubix cube that was on the table. "Mr. Price, you know I don't have answers I can give you for that question. Maybe if you were friendlier towards me I could give you a few answers. You know Felix had to get stitches because he bit through his lip the last time you shocked him. I understand your need to protect your friend but I think you were too extreme especially doing something like that in public. That took a lot of balls! Actually I like the way you operate Mr. Price and maybe if we have the chance to meet again I will have some answers for your questions. I think maybe you are a bit too impulsive but you seem very intelligent. I can tell you this much and probably you know some of what I am going to say. Things are changing very rapidly in my country. For people like me, I guess your generation would say, 'Old School', well, let's just say I am under a lot of pressure. I have to constantly change my views for whatever political group is coming into power and most of them are a lot younger than me. I think that instead of you and me viewing each other as foes, we might do better to be friends. Maybe then incidents like the one that happened at the beach today might not have to happen." When Ivan had finished his last sentence he put down the completed rubix cube.

Mark laughed out loud and shook his head back and forth. Ivan had spoken elegantly and totally evaded giving out any information at all. Mark could see this was a highly intelligent man because of how fast he completed the cube. Mark nodded his head as if to say he was on the same page with Ivan. "Listen, Ivan, I really do not like having my friends spied on and especially when Ernie is the last person that anyone would want to spy on. Ernie was in the military but that was the end of it. He has never worked for the Government in any capacity whatsoever since then. Ernie is just a normal working stiff as you well know, so, why don't you start telling me why he is being watched? What is really going on here?"

Ivan smiled but the smile was transparent and because Mark was so good at knowing people he now realized that Ivan was never going to tell him the full truth. This time he looked up from the completed cube and he stared directly into Marks left eye which seemed very odd to Mark. "Ok, Mr. Price I can explain some of the mystery but not all of it at this time. We know your friend did some work for the Military Intelligence when he was in Vietnam. I have my orders to keep an eye on him because the project that he was involved with never came to any solid conclusion and there remain questions that we have not found the answers to. I have told my superiors that we are wasting our time on him but they insist we keep an eye on him. What can I do? I am what you call and "Indian", not a Chief!" Ivan thought his humor would lighten the situation but there was nothing humorous in it for Mark. Mark was tired and more confused than ever. "Look Mr. Price, I think when I send in the report of what happened today at the beach and include in it our conversation it may be enough for my superiors to call an end to watching him. I think the whole thing will be dropped fairly quickly. I have reported many times that he is clean and not involved with your government in anyway so I see no reason they should not drop the operation. So let's just leave the matter at that and try to be good neighbors, even though, you may not see me around here very often from now on. I must leave now, but I will contact you again sometime down the road." Ivan stood up, pushed the chair aside, smiled at Mark, and then headed out the door.

Within the next few months the situation in Russia had changed dramatically and Ivan was able to break his ties with the old boy's network as he had hoped. He had enough small businesses running to keep him flush with money for some time and devoted himself completely now to investigating the mystery of the crystal. He was convinced now that Ernie knew nothing important. His nephew refused to go back to Russia with him and that was fine, he was an adult, but now he would not get any financial support even when he moved back to the USA. He was thinking of returning to the place where the incident happened in Cambodia.

Chapter 10
Connections

Tom Whitecloud sat on a rock outside his trailer. He was thinking about how much things had changed in the last few years. Now the road to where his trailer sat was partially paved. There were new homes being built all around him. His old trailer was one of only a few remaining in the subdivision. Everyone had a phone and electricity now so he no longer needed to start up the generator for his electricity. He smiled to himself, because he enjoyed having a refrigerator. How he ever got by without one he couldn't imagine now. He had plenty of money in his bank account but he really did not want a new home built. He liked his old trailer even though at times he thought about getting a bigger and more modern one.

A big fluffy cloud rolled over the mesa in front of him and it blocked out the late afternoon sun. Suddenly a heavy dark feeling entered into him and he was not sure why. Tom got up from the rock went inside and grabbed a jacket because the temperature was dropping fast. He stood staring out the door of his trailer and decided to stroll over the cliffs that overlooked the Rio Grande River. It was one of his favorite places to watch the sun set. He was worried about tomorrow. He knew that the next day would be the start of a big change in his life and in the lives of a lot of other people. He was leaving early in the morning to go to Taos, New Mexico to meet with the Medicine Men of the First Council and he knew some very important decisions would happen as a result of the meeting. When he reached the cliffs the sky exploded into a bouquet of pastel colors as the sun sank lower in the sky. Tom sat down on an old log and stared at the sky. His thoughts drifted to recalling the dream like life he had lived for ever since he had encountered the aliens. He recalled his initial paralyzing fear and how the warm touch of Aktal made him feel both loved and secure as she had gently taken his hand in hers that day when they walked to her ranch house. He recalled how after that first touch his fears seemed to have melted away like the fresh snow on a fall day when the sun blazed down on it. Little pools of water gathered around the melting snow. Tom smiled again as he sat on the log and the sky turned to darker shades of pastel. He remembered how that first touch of hers had made his emotions drift to an eternal spring in the high desert with the flowers and sounds of nature. He remembered going through the front door and seeing her sister Shala. They were so lovely and so sympathetic to him that he forgot about time and space. The house was so practical and simple, but to him it seemed like a palace compared to his dingy trailer. As the color faded from the sky in front of him he thought back to when they led him to the barn and the raven he had seen earlier that day circled above them squawking at them. Once they were inside the barn he remembered how empty it looked and how he felt like he needed to start asking questions but then Shala was holding his hand and it made him feel calm again. How could they control his emotions with just a simple touch? He was staring at an old saddle hanging on the wall of the barn and wondering where it had come from when it seemed he started to shrink but really he wasn't shrinking because a large section of the dirt floor was now sinking into the ground. They were being lowered into a large subterranean cave still far below them. He could see a soft light being emitted from the walls of the cavern and below it looked like a tropical forest with lush trees and plants. There were odd fruits hanging from some of the trees that he had never seen before. Then Aktal took his other hand and they reached the bottom of the cavern. Then he saw the bodies and faces of the aliens waiting to meet him. He was surprised how human like they looked except for the one large eye in their protruding forehead. He remembered how he had bit his lower lip because he was so scared and tasted the blood. Shala and Aktal squeezed his hands a little tighter now. The two sisters led him to the beautiful table that was inlayed with gemstones. He appreciated such fine work and was also amazed at how much it looked like the work of his tribe. At first he could not speak so he just sat in the chair and stared from one alien to the other. He smiled now, recalling how silly he must have looked to all of them. Soon enough he overcame his fears and talked with them, in English, and he wondered if the whole thing was some elaborate hoax, but he knew it was really not.

Since that day his life had completely changed. They had him take an oath of secrecy and they in turn asked for his help in saving his planet. He still wondered, why me? He became a willing student and agreed to work for their lofty goals. He had now worked for them for many years and he was content with his life. His main job was to maintain the ranch and keep up the appearance that it was a working ranch. Borghx took a liking to him and spent long hours helping Tom develop certain skills of intuition and insight that Tom never knew he had. After a few years at the suggestion of Borghx, Tom began meeting with and assisting his Uncle who was a Zuni Medicine Man. Last year his Uncle became very ill and Tom asked Borghx if he could bring his Uncle to meet the aliens. Borghx agreed and it was enlightening for everyone. His Uncle died peacefully at his home and later Tom took over his position and became one of the Zuni Medicine Men. It was a big honor for Tom and something he never dreamed would happen. Soon after Tom took over his Uncle's position he gained a reputation amongst the Zuni and other local Tribes as a great healer. Tom also noticed that he seemed to retain his youth. He looked half his age and felt like he was a teenager! He was stronger and more agile than he had ever been in his life. Now Tom knew that the meeting he would be attending the next day was to nominate him as the Chief or the Order of Medicine Men. He was not sure he deserved the acclaim but he felt it was his duty to accept it. He would become one of the leaders of all the Southwest Indian Tribes. It thought maybe it was partially due to the fact that after his Uncle died he again asked Borghx if a few of the leaders from other tribes could meet the Aliens and Borghx agreed though Mr. Kyn was opposed. It was the first real disagreement between Borghx and Mr. Kyn. After the meeting they planned an annual meeting with the few leaders that were sworn to secrecy. It was a sacred pact amongst the Aliens and the Native Leaders. Now those same leaders wanted to bring up at the meeting tomorrow their meetings with the Aliens to the others and thought that it was the right time to form a group that could introduce the aliens to the rest of the world. Tom along with a few others was vehemently opposed to this and knew they had to convince the others before the meeting.

Borghx and the Marans thought of time on a completely different level than humans and none of them thought this was a good time for them to be made know to humanity. They still felt the small blue planet they were on was many years away from becoming stable enough to understand and to work with them on any large scale. They felt their work was progressing. Tom Whitecloud and along with a few others that knew they existed were sufficient for their present goals. It seemed too dangerous for them to be revealed now and they made sure Tom understood their position in the matter.

Tom Whitecloud had always been a sensitive soul. Now with his training from Borghx he had gone far beyond just being sensitive to others, he had become a great healer. He could see the anxiety with Mr. Kyn and Borghx and in a way he thought it was his fault for introducing the other Medicine Men to the aliens. That had been a mistake and Tom knew it.

Tom walked back to his trailer and suddenly very old and tired. He lay on his bed and tried to sleep but his mind would not shut off. He kept going over in his head what he and Borghx had discussed a few days earlier. "Long life, an end to disease, peace on the planet and the means to advance technology to the level of constant space exploration." What more could humanity want? This is what the aliens had to offer, but Tom knew he had to protect the aliens because at this time in human history the wisdom and knowledge they had would most likely be used not just for peaceful purposes but also for military advantages. This is what the aliens wanted to avoid and now Tom was burdened with the task of helping them avoid it. Tom knew he had to be more assertive than ever when he met with the other Medicine Men the next day. He did not want the situation to spiral out of control. He fell asleep very late that night.

Earlier the Same Day

In the secret retreat beneath the barn Borghx and Mr. Kyn were having a lengthy and serious discussion. "Borghx, I would have never imagined in my wildest dreams that this adventure or mission as you like to call it would turn out the way that it has. Losing my son during the journey left a very dark feeling inside of me. Time will never heal that wound, but years have passed and I am starting to see some of our influence on this planet. I am beginning to enjoy the mission more now. Jacon and Kafta have turned out to be the closest of friends and I truly feel I made a good choice in bringing them with us. Their combined skills and talents have made our home here very comfortable. At times I feel like I am at one of my retreats back home. It has been fascinating to me to watch the development of Tom Whitecloud. Now that we have had contact with the other two Medicine Men I can see that humans are actually very caring and compassionate in general. I only wish the leaders of the planet had the same qualities as the few humans we have met."

Borghx sat upright and stared towards the end of the deep cavern that was their home on Earth. He seemed to be in a trance but that was not out of the norm for him so Mr. Kyn waited patiently for Borghx to gather his thoughts. Borghx eyes widened a bit and he brought them back to focus on his small Maran friend. "Yes Mr. Kyn in my own way I am also starting to enjoy our adventure as you would call it." Mr. Kyn chuckled and Borghx smiled like only he could smile which was mostly with his large deep purple eyes that seemed to glow when he experienced joy or humor. "It is apparent that this planet is approaching a great transition period from war and aggression towards a period of advanced technologies that hopefully will lead to a more enlightened period for all the inhabitants. Unfortunately it seems greed is still the underlying driving force of the people and their economies. The countries that are democratic and claim to have freedom are increasing but greed is still the underlying force of their economies. For centuries economies were driven by war. The leaders of the Democratic countries are now faced with what they see as their only choice to grow their economies and that is with consumer based economies. Unfortunately this can only be sustained by constant brainwashing of the people to make them feel the need for more and more material gains. Your people avoided the economic models of war because of the very nature of Marans. The Earthlings underlying nature is much more aggressive and I am not sure if they can overcome that nature and not destroy their planet. Of course that is why we are here! My fear is that that our mission will take much longer to complete than I anticipated. The information I gathered on this planet before making the decision to come here was based more on the philosophies and writings of many of the great human sages and not on the reality of what we see now that we are here. The vast areas of pollution and lack of governments to stand up to primitive petroleum based energy companies is far beyond what I thought it would be before we came here. We must somehow be able to share our ideas and technologies soon or this planet will slowly sink into a chaotic blend of manmade disasters, global warming from carbon pollution and a greater widening gap between the wealthy and the poor. My other fear is that we may not have enough time to save this planet. If we were to reveal our existence here now we would be trapped in a web of manipulation and bureaucracy. I have considered the option of replicating Aktal and Shala on a larger scale, but that could be a very risky option. If we had robots move into positions of power on this planet then eventually we may lose control of the robots. This may happen on its own in the future weather we replicate our robots or weather in the natural development of human technology they begin to create their own robots. I am hopeful but along with the hopefulness there is an underlying feeling that the very nature of the earthlings may lead to their own downfall. The one good aspect I do see now that we have been here for some time is that I feel my past fear of a great nuclear war on this planet is unlikely. All of the powerful nations that have nuclear weapons seem to have developed a stance against ever using them again." Mr. Kyn stared at Borghx and nodded his head in agreement. He wondered now if he would ever return to Mara. He took a deep breath and smiled at Borghx. Borghx continued, "I think tomorrow it would be a good idea that Aktal accompany Tom Whitecloud to the meeting with the Council. They may object at first but she has her ways of overcoming objections and we will know the results of the meeting much sooner.

"I am fairly certain the council will vote to have us exposed to the public in some way. It will benefit them and not us." Mr. Kyn said.

Borghx was also certain this would be the result of the meeting. The past few years younger leaders on the council that had met the aliens constantly talked about calling a meeting with the United Nations and introducing the aliens. They believed it would bring status to the Indian Nations that had been so harmed by the brutality of European migrations in the past. Those same leaders on the Council now had more influence and tomorrow the vote would most likely favor their idea.

Mr. Kyn was eternally hopeful. It was his nature as a Maran. "Borghx, I know you may have some doubts and reservations but from my eyes I believe this journey of ours has gone quite well. I will agree with you that tomorrow could change all of that and lead us down a path of unexpected perils. I am not going to disagree with anything you have said so I am glad that we have prepared for the worse."

Borghx reached out his long translucent pale blue fingers as if he was going to catch a fleeting butterfly, it was his way of catching a thought or an idea that suddenly came to him. "My dear Mr. Kyn, it just occurred to me that to these Medicine Men on the Council and most likely to any humans we ever encounter we are entities far beyond what they have ever thought of as Aliens. We are entities beyond what they believe are Gods in all of their various religions. Our exposure to them along with the technologies we can share with them could transform their small blue planet into a paradise as depicted in most all of their Religious beliefs. We would be able to end hunger, greed and war. We would be able to extend their lifespans. We would be able to help them to develop intergalactic travel. Of course the Medicine men that have met with us know all of this. Maybe our best course of action is to leave as much information as we can with the Medicine Men and consider our mission complete. Of course the danger in this path could be that the information we leave with them is not used for the purposes we intend it to be used for, but, with the Council it would be in the best hands I believe we could leave it in for now."

Mr. Kyn's mood immediately changed and he was excited. From a conversation of doom and gloom Borghx had offered an option of leaving soon! Oh, how he wanted to return home! "Borghx, we both know we are not Gods" Mr. Kyn chuckled to release his excitement at the prospect of returning to Mara. "Before I met you, even though I and most Marans knew there were other lifeforms in our Galaxy, we still viewed everything around us from a totally Maran viewpoint. I can empathize with the Earthlings in that regard."

"We are not Gods from the Earthlings viewpoint of God but in a more Universal way we are all Gods; my dear friend!" Borghx enjoyed his talks with Mr. Kyn. "My people are very ancient compared to most lifeforms in the Galaxies that we have migrated to. We had the opportunity to learn what many other lifeforms are seeking to learn but may never learn. We are here on this planet to try and prevent the humans from destroying themselves and possibly causing unforeseen consequences that could affect this galaxy in whole should they start a nuclear war. In reality we are all Gods, because we are all part of the Universe. The essence of our Universe is not something any life from can understand from a purely theoretical viewpoint. The essence of this Universe is encompassed in feelings, like our feelings of love, compassion and the concept of vibrational reciprocations. This planet is ruled by greed and hopefully our presence here can change that. One being can change the destiny of a planet. There was a scientist that lived here who touched on the concepts I am talking about now. His name was Nicola Tesla. His mind and body were united towards the goal of teaching compassion through science. His ideas were shelved for many years and he became a victim of others greed. His concepts of a "Utopian Society" were repressed by those in power. I believe if we are exposed to the public at this time we most likely would suffer the same fate. Our technologies would be used profit and power not for the betterment of this planet." Borghx paused and looked deeply into Mr. Kyn's one large eye. He thought to himself what a unique species the Marans were. They had pure hearts and open minds and in many ways they were similar to the Earthlings. Mr. Kyn was the Maran that had gone against his own government to rescue him. Borghx laughed with his eyes and Mr. Kyn understood him. Borghx extended his long arm and put it on Mr. Kyn's tiny shoulder. "One thing is for sure my friend; it only takes one step to change directions. I believe that may be what we must do now"

Mr. Kyn thought he understood. He stood up and walked away from the table towards the edge of the patio. He was hungry and that overruled all conversation as far as any Maran was concerned! He saw a large four stemmed cactus which erupted on the top into bunches of bright orange flowers and a spiny fruit. Mr. Kyn waved his hand in a circular motion and a small disc about the size of a tea cup zoomed down from the luminous dome ceiling and hovered over the cactus. A small blue metallic arm then extended out from the disc and rapidly plucked the tiny spines out of the skin on the fruit. It then cut the fruit from the cactus and dropped it into Mr. Kyn's hand. Mr. Kyn walked slowly back to the table where Borghx was sitting with the fruit in hand. The tiny disc then repeated the action with four other fruits and dropped them on the table. Mr. Kyn and Borghx leisurely ate the fruits.

Mr. Kyn was closer to Borghx that the other Marans, but the others were not jealous of the relationship. Jealousy was a trait that had been more or less eliminated over time during the evolution of Maran culture. Borghx of course was a very different type of lifeform. None of the Marans knew hold old he actually was and they never asked. It seemed as if he was ageless. His appearance never changed. He was not youthful nor did he look old. His long slender arms and long fingers always seemed to move as if they were underwater. All of his movements were slow and fluid. His head was overly large and one could almost make out his enormous brain through his semi-transparent skin. His eyes seemed to pulsate when he was sitting still and thinking or talking. The Marans were much more active than Borghx. They constantly had some project they were working on, such as building the small disc shaped robots like the one that plucked the fruit for Mr. Kyn. Borghx on the other hand would often just sit for days at a time in a very still meditative posture. It appeared to the Marans as if he was sleeping, but in reality he rarely slept. Shala and Aktal were the servants, friends and occasional lovers for the Marans when they were not pursuing some task that Borghx had assigned them to do. Borghx was the leader and Mr. Kyn was second in charge for all endeavors.

Aktal and Shala were busy straightening up the ranch house when Mr. Kyn came in and informed Aktal she was to go and sit in on the meeting of the Indian Leaders the next day. The meeting was about 100 miles away in Santa Fe, New Mexico. He instructed her that it imperative that she leave the meeting and contact him if any decision was made by the council to bring them into the public view. Mr. Kyn then asked Shala to go below and help with the preparations of the inter-galactic space ship that the others were also working on just in case they needed to make a quick exit in the next few days.

Aktal and Shala had maintained the perfect front ever since they had purchased the property years earlier. The story they gave any inquisitive neighbors was that they had inherited money and they wanted to be away from the big city. They attended neighborly functions on an irregular basis so as to maintain a friendly atmosphere. Most of the time, they kept to themselves and did the tasks that Borghx and Mr. Kyn assigned to them. When the leaders of the Council began to visit after Tom Whitecloud was working with them they claimed they were working on some books about the various Southwest Indian tribes and their customs. Fortunately for all of them there was only one other large ranch nearby and that was at least two miles away. It was owned by an elderly couple, the Garcia's. The property was run down and the Garcia's no longer had any livestock other than a few cattle and sheep. Once in a while the two sisters would come to visit them but it was not often. The aliens were hoping to purchase the land from the Garcia's at some point in time. Aktal and Shala made the Garcia's offers for the property more than once but soon realized Mr. Garcia had no interest in selling it. Mr. Garcia liked to tell the two sisters stories about the "Old Days", and usually he would fall asleep in the middle of the stories. Aktal and Shala had not visited the Garcia's in over three months and what they did not realize is that the property had finally been sold to someone else.

Over the Hill

"If you please to plant yourself on the side of Fate, and say, Fate is all; then we say, a part of Fate is the freedom of man. Forever wells up the impulse of choosing and acting in the soul." Ralph Waldo Emerson.

George and Mark had spent numerous hours putting together all the details of their fish-farming project and they were excited about the venture. Their application for the government farm loan had finally been accepted and now that they had their friend Ernie onboard and willing to work as the foreman. It seemed everything was at last falling into place. Mark and George had done a lot of research to find the right location. They wanted a location that was central to more than one market, so they choose the southwest. The area near Socorro, New Mexico had been on their list and the property prices there were low compared to everywhere else they had looked. They knew if they were as successful with their projections then they could expand and purchase other properties in other areas. They had to have water rights to a fairly large water source. This property not only had water rights to the Rio Grande but it also had warm mineral springs. This meant they could possibly at some point also raise shrimp.

Mark was familiar with Real Estate because he had other properties that he owned. He didn't really need the farm loan from the government but he wasn't doing this project just for him, he was doing it for his two friends and he felt if they had a loan it would make the two of them more devoted to the project. Mark had flown out to Albuquerque with George; they rented a car and then spent time in Socorro looking at properties. They were interested specifically in one property that the Real Estate Agent said he had in his pocket. A pocket listing in Real Estate meant the property was not listed for sale but the Realtor had knowledge that the owners would sell. Mark did his research on the property by looking at topographical maps and asking the Real Estate Agent numerous questions. The property consisted of 640 acres. It was mostly level with some rolling hills and a few small streams that fed into the Rio Grande. The Realtor was old friends with the owner, Mr. Garcia. When Mark and George went to look at the property with the Realtor they saw how run down it was. Other than the main house the other barns and corrals were all run down. Mr. Garcia lived there with his wife and they both seemed very old. The Garcia's offered them a meal and Mr. Garcia told stories about the "Old Days." He had wanted his son to take over running the ranch but after his son went to College he had become a "City Boy". George and Mark felt a bit sorry for the elderly couple living alone on such a large property. Mr. Garcia liked the idea that the two young men were going to start a fish-farm and he told them that he had the same idea many years ago. It wasn't true of course, but Mr. Garcia was old and lonely so he wanted to prolong the conversation. George and Mark talked as the Realtor drove them around the property and decided they liked it. They also decided to tell Mr. Garcia that if they bought it that he would be welcome to come out anytime and watch them as the project took hold. That is what probably secured the deal for them. It took only a few hours the following day to work out a deal. Mr. Garcia and his wife moved out before the thirty day escrow closed and left a lot of things behind. Mr. Garcia had kept telling his wife, as they packed and drove to Albuquerque, he would have to drive down to the ranch once in a while to supervise those two young men because he knew a lot about fish farming. His wife was getting Alzheimer disease for some years so she just listened and ignored him. They were going to stay with their son and his family.

After George and Mark returned to Los Angeles they showed pictures to Ernie of the property that had been purchased for the fish farming project. Ernie was not excited at all and almost backed out of his commitment. There was no way his wife and kids wanted to move out to what they considered the "middle of no-where", so he fought with his wife for two days straight until they finally agreed to keep their place in Venice until the ranch house was fixed up and the project was further along. The plan was that Ernie would commute and fly back every other weekend.

As soon as Mark heard from the Realtor that the Garcia's had moved out a few days before the close of the escrow he got ahold of George and Ernie. Mark told his friends they would fly out to Socorro on Saturday. They agreed that their first goal would be to clean up and repair the ranch house so that when Ernie's family came to visit and maybe eventually stay they would have a clean and enjoyable house. George and Mark were starting think that maybe they had made a mistake by bringing Ernie in on the project but they kept those thoughts to themselves for now.

When they landed at the small airport they took a cab to the only Ford dealership in town and Mark paid cash with the new company checks and bought a brand new plain white cargo van.

"Now listen Ernie, this is our company vehicle so be careful with it." Mark said as he dropped the keys into Ernie hands.

"Wow, thanks boss", Ernie put an emphasis on the word, "boss", so as to get his point across in a factious way. Like anyone that was changing jobs after fifteen years with the same company Ernie was both excited and scared. If this fish farming project turned to a bust, then he was screwed and he knew it. He would have to go back out to the job market and there is no way he would every find a job equal to the one he had. He was taking a big risk and putting his faith in his two friends. He wasn't worried about doing the tasks he needed to make the business a success, he was worried that he would be the only one doing the work while the other two sat back and collected the profits! He had two sons, one 13 years old and one 15 years old back at home. He thought, sure, it would be great to get them away from Venice and all of the bad influences that were everywhere in the environment. On the other hand if he did not make this business a success his family would never forgive him. It was a lot of pressure. His wife had been the love of his life, but the rigors of work, raising kids, both their jobs, and just the aspect of time had created a wall between them. They both knew it was just part of the whole process and they both wanted things to be like it was when the first met. How to get back to that point was the problem because there was no easy solution. In the back of both their minds they hoped this change in their lives would help them to get those old feelings back. They both knew they would never leave each other, so optimism was at least the best chance they had. One thing Ernie knew for sure was that he had been fortunate to have married a Japanese woman. He saw his co-workers and other friends whose wives left them at the least little sign of discord. Ernie walked over to the new van and opened the door with a smile on his face. He had a new vehicle!

"You know Ernie, I've know you since High School and I still can't figure you out. One minute you seem like you're ready to fight the world, the next minute you have a smile on your face. Why is that?" George asked as he got in the back seat.

"George, you would never understand. You have never been to war and you have never been married." Ernie replied as he turned the key and started the van.

Mark sat in the passenger seat and had that sly grin on his face, like he knew everything about everything, and could really care less. In reality he cared about everything. He and Ernie were very similar, only they had taken different paths. Mark was probably too intelligent for himself and that had always caused him problems with his relationships. He was still constantly studying and learning. Mark had been married twice but his friends only knew of one of the marriages. There was no lack of passion in his life and he believed that one day he would meet someone who would capture his spirt and cultivate his soul. He enjoyed the search even if he never met the right person he would at least have the pleasure of female company! Every few months of so Mark was showing off some woman that he was dating to his friends. She would usually be younger than him. Because Mark had plenty of money he could take his flavor of the moment to nice places and on nice trips. This usually led to them becoming to clingy, too jealous, and asking way too many questions, so Mark would have to end the relationship. Ernie and George were a bit jealous of Mark because of all the different women he had known, but they kept that to themselves.

It took about 30 minutes to drive from the town to the property and even though Ernie didn't let on, inside he was getting a bit excited. The rolling hills and endless views relaxed his mind. He had never thought too much about living outside of a city, except when he was in Vietnam. During the war he thought a lot about living away from the city. He was tired of Venice, tired of Los Angeles and for the first time in what seemed like forever he felt sort of relaxed. There was just so much open space and it really had a calming effect on him.

When they reached the gate Mark got out and unlocked it and then locked it up again after they passed through. They drove down a narrow unpaved road with scrub oaks lining their path and the ranch house along with other adjacent buildings was soon visible in the distance. "Oh my God, my sons are going to love this place!" Ernie blurted out. Mark and George laughed at Ernie's sudden change in attitude. "I mean, at least I think they are! Hey you guys shut up don't say anything! I have a right to change my opinions!" Then they all laughed as they pulled up in front of the ranch house.

"Remember Ernie, you are here to supervise and get the job done. You are not here to fantasize about riding horses and playing Cowboys and Indians!" George said as they got out of the van and grabbed their bags.

"I know what I am doing." Ernie replied. "Also, I am willing to bet the two of you are going to be around quite a bit anyway. This seems like a really interesting place."

Mark grabbed Ernie by the arm as they stood on the front porch. "Listen, Ernie, I know you can handle this that is why George and I brought you in on the project. Like I told you before, we have a government farm loan and it is really important you don't co-mingle funds. You have to keep good records. If you want to buy a horse, cow or goat, let me know and I will buy it for you. You understand, right?"

"Sure Boss, I understand." Ernie grinned at Mark as George pushed the front door open.

"Mark, check this out." George said as he stepped inside.

"Wow, someone cleaned up!" Mark said. He was fully expecting the place to be cluttered and dusty like the pictures the realtor had sent to him after the property was in escrow. Instead everything was cleaned up. Most of the furniture was still there but all the small items that had been lying around were gone. Ernie stood in the doorway and looked around. The living room was about three times the size of his living room back in Venice. The house was old and obviously needed some work, but on the other hand it was big. He quickly walked through the other rooms and planned out where he would put his two sons. He even had room for an office. When he went in the kitchen though, he realized how old the place was. The stove was tiny but there were great views from the windows. "Hey guys, come check this out." Ernie said as he walked over to the dining table in the kitchen. When George and Mark came in the kitchen they saw the big basket full of fruit, snacks and two bottles of champagne on the table. Ernie handed them the note. It was from the Realtor. It welcomed them to New Mexico and said that he had taken the liberty to have the place cleaned up for them.

"Hey this is great! I think we starting off on the right foot here!" George said as they all sat down at the table and grabbed a snack. "Let's open the champagne!"

"Hold on guys, the day is still early and we have things to do. Let's wait until later before we start drinking." Mark said. George took the two bottles over to the ancient refrigerator and went to put them in.

"Check this out!" George said as he looked in the fridge. Mark and Ernie turned their heads and saw the fridge was also full of meat and produce.

"I don't know, maybe we over paid for this property or people around here are just naturally a little more friendly." Mark said.

"No, I think the Realtor just wants to be on our good side. He probably just wants to keep us as clients if we decide to buy more land and expand our operations." Ernie said as he munched on an apple. "What about new carpet? My wife is going to at least want new carpet in some of these rooms." Ernie was looking at Mark.

"Yeah, we can do that Ernie, but no horses or goats for now." Mark replied and they all laughed again.

The laughter died down. They stood silent for a few seconds takin and stared out the large picture window in the kitchen that faced towards the East. The afternoon sun had just made its way onto the horizon over the roof line and was creeping in the living room area. It was a magnificent inspiring view that showed the gentle slope of the full property all the way to the river in the distance.

"There is just so much space here." Ernie remarked as he looked out at the shadows of the rolling hills.

"Yeah, back in Los Angeles everyone is packed in like a bunch of sardines packed in a can." George said.

"At least I won't have people around all the time watching my life, like the Russians were doing in Los Angeles. I am pretty confident all this old spy crap will end now. I will be too far away for anyone to even care about what happened in Vietnam." Ernie said.

"Well let's hope so, because I am sure if anyone comes out here and they are not wanted that you will have enough fire power to blow them away!" Mark chirped in. Ernie turned and looked at Mark and nodded his head. "Hey brother, I do know that you have a few neighbors and they are about half a mile away over that hill. At least that is what the Realtor told me.

"Hey, guys, I am opening a bottle of champagne." George got up quickly and went to the refrigerator. "We need to at least share one bottle and celebrate this new venture." Ernie rubbed is hands together and Mark nodded his head in agreement.

They continued to stare out the window as George opened the bottle and brought them each a glass. They had a toast.

"You said half a mile! I mean that would be like from my parents' old house in Venice to the beach. It is hard to imagine I have that much space between me and the nearest human!" Ernie said.

"Hey, the Realtor gave me the scoop on your neighbors." Mark said as he put his glass down. It was cheap champagne and he didn't want to drink anymore of it."

George asked, "What do mean by the scoop?"

"Oh, I thought he told you too George?" Mark replied.

"No, what are you talking about?" George said.

Ernie continued to be lost in his thoughts as he stared out the window and wasn't really listening too much. This was going to be such a big change for him and his family he kept thinking. He just knew it would all be for the best. He could feel it.

Mark laughed out loud. "George I know you were there when the Realtor told us about the neighbors. Why don't you remember?"

"Mark stop being a prick, I just don't remember" George said. Ernie glanced at the two of them and sensed the tension.

"Well in this part of the country it is a good idea to get to know your neighbors, because if you don't then sooner or later they are going to get to know you!" Mark said.

"What neighbors are you guys talking about?" Ernie said

"Mark said the Realtor gave him the scoop on our neighbors but I have no idea what he is talking about!" George blurted out feeling a bit annoyed at this point in the conversation.

"What are you talking about?" Ernie said as he turned away from his view out of the window and stared at Mark.

Mark stood up and went close to where Ernie was sitting near the big window and pointed out the window. "Well, you see that ridge over there a bit to the left of the little hill. There is a stream that runs through there. That stream is fed a bit farther up by the hot mineral springs I was telling you about earlier that is on our property. If you follow down the stream for about a quarter mile then go up on the ridge there is another property and a large ranch house with a barn next to it. George and I hiked down to the mineral springs the last time we were here. Do you remember that, George?"

"Mark stop playing games, of course I remember that!" George shot back at him.

Mark was enjoying the long drawn out explanation and still could not understand why George didn't remember what the Realtor had told them when they returned to the Ranch house that Day. It didn't really matter, but he liked messing with George. It was just part of the relationship the two had. "Ok, well I know Ernie is not going to believe me, but the Realtor told that there are two really attractive women that moved up here about ten years ago from Los Angeles. They are sisters. The Realtor told us that in town. He said he know them, but they sort of keep to themselves."

"Oh, yeah, now I sort of remember, so what?" George said throwing his hands up in the air.

"So what, what do you mean so what?" Mark shot back at him.

"Yeah right, they are probably lesbians not sisters. "Ernie blurted out with a smile on his face.

"I don't know about that." Mark said. "I do know there is only one way to find out and that is to talk a walk over there and introduce ourselves!"

"Are you crazy? You are just chasing after women again! That is so typical of you, Mark. If we walk over there they will probably shoot us! Lesbian or sisters it makes no difference; I can guarantee you they have guns. This is not some condo project in Brentwood. This is the wild west!" George said.

Ernie started laughing and got up to pour himself another glass of champagne. His legs were stiff from all the traveling and he didn't mind checking out his neighbors, especially if they were of the female variety. Heck, he was the one that had to live here and run the project full time. "I am ready, let's go meet our neighbors!"

"Oh my God, you two are just too much. All you two ever talk about is women and you are married Ernie!" George said still sitting at the table as Mark and Ernie were heading to the bathroom to freshen up. George called after them, "Ok, I will go with you guys but we don't actually have to go to the door. We can just stand up on the ridge and look down at the place."

"Sure George, whatever you say!" Ernie called back.

They cleaned up the best they could and headed out. It was afternoon and they had maybe 3 hours of light left so they took a flash light with them. They were laughing and joking around as they made their way along an old dirt path towards the fence line that separated their property from their neighbor's property. They kept debating Mark's claim that two sisters actually lived there and if he had just been joking with them all along. Ernie and George still were not sure if this was just another one of Marks practical jokes. When they reached the point in the path where they needed to turn off to their right and hike up to the ridge it was a steeper climb than they thought it would be so when they reached the top they were all out of breath. There was an old barbed wire fence that needed some repair work at the top of the ridge. They stood together looking down the hill and saw what appeared to be a fairly modern ranch house with a large red barn next to it. The sun was sinking low on the horizon to the east and they stood for a few minutes as George started to insist now that they now go back. Ernie and Mark overruled George in the debate so they walked along the fence line until they found a spot where the barbed wire fencing was sagging and they climbed over. Sure enough, George tore his jeans on the fencing and complained. He barked out that he knew this was a bad idea to go any further.

Mr. Kyn was notified immediately by Shala that there were three men that had crossed over the fence and now were heading down the hill towards their house. She told him that they most likely were coming from the Garcia's place. Mr. Kyn instructed Shala to stay in the house. Aktal was in the underground chamber where she was helping the other Marans. Mr. Kyn also told Aktal to return to the house. He instructed her that if the men were threatening in any way that she should render them unconscious then she and Shala could them drive them out to the main road and leave them there.

Mr. Kyn and Borghx finished their lengthy discussion only an hour earlier regarding their plans if the Medicine Council decided to expose them, when the three strangers were spotted heading towards the house. The two of them sat together in the underground retreat and watched on a video feed that came from Aktal looking out the window as the men slowly made their way towards the house above them. They were enjoying themselves with some refreshments and trying to discern what the intentions of these three men could be.

"Well my friend, these three men look quite interesting. One appears to be of Asian descent, one Caucasian and the other maybe American Indian or Latin. The Caucasian one that is in the front appears to be the leader because he is in the front. My sense is that their intentions are friendly, curious and maybe even amorous!" Borghx said.

"Yes, I would concur. Let's see what develops from this. Maybe it could even work in our favor. I am very curious as to why they are coming from the direction of the Garcia's place." Mr. Kyn replied as he stuffed another small rare fruit in his mouth.

Even though Mark knew this was all his idea and that he wanted to see for sure if these two women were as attractive as the Realtor had said they were, he sort of had an odd feeling. As they were approaching the white picket fence that was in front of the sprawling house the feeling became even stronger. Mark slowed his pace and both Ernie and George had a chance to catch up to him. Maybe it was the light in the sky as the sun began to sink off to their right and the long shadow from the barn that lapped over the house in front of them. Mark was a very sensitive and perceptive person. It was just part of his nature. He had studied all the major Religions and some that were not major religions, but at heart he was a scientist. People that had the intelligence that he possessed were not religious. Still there was something odd, like a feeling he had been here before. When they got within about twenty yards of the gate Mark was almost shaking and could no longer contain whatever it was he was feeling.

Marked stopped and put his hand out to block his two friends from going any further. "Wait. Listen, do you guys here that buzzing sound?"

George and Ernie were tired from the hike and looked forward to meeting the neighbors. They were hoping there would be some liquid refreshments inside. "I don't hear anything." They both said almost at the same time.

"Ok, I don't know, maybe I am getting dehydrated. I know this was my idea to come check out our neighbors but I am getting an odd feeling and that is not like me." Mark said.

Both Ernie and George pushed Mark out of their way and headed through the gate down the worn brick path towards the house. Mark followed them. Ernie led the way mainly because he felt like it was his obligation as these were going to be his new neighbors. George turned and said to Mark. "Dude, next time you drag me along on some hike like this be sure you know where exactly you are going and how long it is going to take. Look at this, (he pointed to his torn jeans) I ruined a perfectly good pair of jeans because of you."

Almost at exactly the same instant that Ernie pushed the button on the door bell they heard a very soft and extremely sweet voice come through the small speaker next to the door bell, "Hello, what can I do for you gentleman?" The voice asked.

Ernie took charge as Mark stayed back away from the door with one foot on the porch and one foot on the step at the top of the porch. These were basically going to be Ernie's only neighbors and now he was getting more than just curious. "Hi there, my name is Ernie Lopez and these are my two friends Mark Pullin and George Kasaki. We recently purchased the Garcia's property so we thought it would a nice gesture to stop by and meet our closest neighbors."

"Oh, really is that right? Well then please come in!" said the soft voice once again. George turned to where Mark was still planted with one foot on the porch like he was ready to bolt and gave him the finger! Ernie turned and winked at Mark as if to show Mark how wrong he could be at times. Mark just stared back still frozen like he was in some kind of trance. Ernie cupped his hands and whispered to Mark, "Hey I think they like my charming personality!" Ernie winked one last time and turned back to where the door was opening. Almost directly behind them the sun was beginning to set and there appeared to be storm clouds building. The sky flashed with a bolt of lightning that must have struck not too far away as the boom from the lightning seemed almost instantaneous with the flash of light. The three friends shot glances at each other and then directly to the door that was now wide open.

The light from inside seemed brighter than what would be normal interior light and it silhouetted a Goddess. In front of them stood the most beautiful woman any of them had ever seen. "Good evening gentlemen. My name is Aktal." Aktal had a wide and welcoming smile on her face. She stood to the side and waved her arm motioning for them to enter. Mark was mesmerized with the woman's charm but inside he felt like he was a small a deer walking into a lion's den.

Ernie had drank the most champagne earlier but his high didn't come from the champagne now. He reached out to shake to woman's hand and when she touched his hand he felt a soft fuzzy charge of warmth go through him. It was a completely new feeling and he liked it. "Hi, it is a pleasure to meet you." Ernie held onto Aktal's hand a bit longer than he would normally hold onto a woman's hand. For some reason he couldn't explain he immediately felt like an infatuated teenager and pulled Aktal a bit closer to him. She did not resist. Then he brought her hands up to his lips and kissed the back of her hand. This time the warm feeling surged right through his lips. "I am going to be your new neighbor. We bought the Garcia's property. I will be living up here permanently from now on. My friends are just investors in our project." George and Mark were staring at Ernie like they were looking at a completely different person than they had ever known.

Aktal very elegantly glided away from Ernie. She then reached out and took George by the hand and led the three friends towards the large tan colored sofas in the living room. George experienced the same feeling that Ernie had felt when she had touched Ernie. George didn't even realize he was walking. He felt like he was floating into a time and space that he had never been to before. As she let go of his hand and as George was dropping onto the sofa George finally spoke. "I heard that you and your sister moved here from Los Angeles. It is a small world you know. We're from that area also!" Mark who had trailed everyone into the living room sat next to George and nudged him in the side to make him shut up. George turned and flashed an angry look at Mark.

The three men were sitting on the sofa looking a bit dumfounded when the door across from them opened and another beautiful woman appeared. She seemed to be identical to Aktal only her hair was a deep light auburn color. "This is my sister Shala." Aktal said gently waving her hand in the direction that Shala was walking in from. Shala smiled and the two women sat down opposite the three men.

"I didn't know the Garcia's sold their property!" Shala said as her eyes darted back and forth between the three men. Right at the instant Mark knew something was not right. He asked himself, how did she know the property had been sold? She had come from another room and had not been privy to the earlier conversation. Of course maybe she overheard the conversation but Mark thought to himself that would be highly unlikely. Mark decided it was time for him to ask a few questions as his two buddies seemed to be overwhelmed by the presence of gorgeous women sitting across from them.

"Well actually the escrow will not close for a few days, but the Garcia's allowed us to take possession early. We came out to do a few repairs. We are partners in a new fish farming project." Mark totally forgot to ask the questions that he had just thought of asking. He felt like he was coming under some kind of spell and couldn't control his thoughts. He looked back and forth between the two women trying to understand why he felt so weak willed. "I think the Garcia's are happy with the deal."

"Oh, I see, that is very nice." Aktal replied. "Shala is going to get us some refreshments now."

Mark observed that Shala stood up even before the sentence was completely out of Aktal's mouth and raised his eyebrows. He had heard of twins reading the others mind but this was going too far. Still, for some reason he was having a hard time formulating his thoughts. Ernie and George sat still like two deer caught in the headlights of a car. Mark observed that each woman had on what seemed to be the exact same type of jeans. They both appeared to be about five feet six inches tall, perfect curves to their bodies and identical in every aspect expect for the hair color. Their skin seemed pale for two women living in the high desert of New Mexico. They must rarely get outside he thought. Their skin had a glow or shimmer to it that seemed too perfect. Then Mark noticed that there was a fire now in the fireplace to his right. He wondered why he did not notice the fire before when he first came in. They also seemed way too mellow for two women that came from Los Angeles, but maybe that was just the result of having lived away from the big city. He didn't know what to think. They were definitely very exotic and had an alluring quality to them that was hard to understand.

Aktal sat quietly now until Shala returned with a large platter of crackers, cheese, fruits and some drinks. Marks jaw almost dropped to the floor when he saw her carrying in the large tray. There was no way a woman could hold a try that heavy in one hand. Then even more amazing was how quickly she glided the tray from her hand onto the table in front of them without spilling any of it. Ernie and George were happy because with the large bottle of fruit juice there was also a bottle of wine. They exchanged glances of approval with each other and poured themselves some wine. Mark decided he was hungry now and the odd thoughts about the two sisters seemed to just evaporate into thin air. He poured himself some juice and quietly ate as George and Ernie talked on and on about their fish farming project like they both were experts. Mark smiled and let them brag. He knew it was a show for the two beautiful sisters that were sitting across from them. Aktal and Shala were very polite during the conversation and asked very few questions. They had all the facial movements to show interest in the narratives that Ernie and George were spilling out to make themselves look important. They often would nod or raise their eyebrows in agreement as Ernie and George went into detail after detail. Mark was aware that George was highly knowledgeable about the project but he didn't realize how much Ernie must have studied up on the project. He looked at Ernie in a bit of a new light because of that, but then suddenly his mind drifted back to reality. Again he had to fight the thoughts and was becoming more and more confused with each passing moment. He really was not sure if his two friends were just totally infatuation with the beauty of the two sisters or if there was really something odd going on. He stared at the platter and saw a slice of some strange lavender fruit so he picked it up and tasted it. It was incredibly delicious, like nothing he had ever tasted. It was sweet but and it seemed to just melt in his mouth. It reminded him of cotton candy only it was a fruit.

Mark interrupted the conversation at that point. "What is this fruit? I have never tasted anything like this before!" He asked as he looked back and forth between Aktal and Shala.

"It is a native fruit from a rare cactus that grows here in Southwest." Aktal said.

"Yes and we made a few modifications to the plant." Shala added. After Shala made the statement Aktal's arm twitched and Shala looked as if she would pass out.

"What my sister means by modifications is that we grew the cactus in a special environment." Aktal added.

Mark raised his eyebrows and reached for another piece of the fruit. "Hey, you guys should try this!" he said to Ernie and George.

Borghx and Tyijo Kyn were sitting quietly in their underground retreat watching the whole situation through the eyes of Aktal and Shala as it was transmitted to a holographic image in from of them via the eyes of Shala and Aktal. Once they learned the men's last names Borghx ran them through the data bases he had access to and they knew almost everything about all of them. No one had ever showed up unexpectedly at the door before but both of them knew it was a situation that they could learn from and maybe even take advantage of if they needed to. As they assimilated the data on the three men they talked back and forth discussing their options. They realized the three men had been friends since their youth and this showed a character trait that appealed to both Mr. Kyn and Borghx. They soon realized that Mark was in the top one percent of humans for intelligence but that he was also at times wild and unstable. George though also highly intelligent was quite the opposite of Mark, in that he was quiet and reserved. Now though, in the presence of Aktal and Shala his shyness seemed to have dissipated. All three men seemed to have a quality, because of their friendship, that made them feel comfortable with strangers. This was very interesting to both Borghx and Mr. Kyn. During their discussion Borghx kept returning to two points. One, that the three men having been friends for such a long period of time gave them a greater strength than what they had as individuals. Two, Mark not only had a very high degree of intelligence but that he also had a very high sensory capacity. More so than any of the Medicine men they had met from the council. Even Tom Whitecloud after all his years of training with Borghx did not come close to the abilities that Mark appeared to have. It had only taken Borghx a short time to analyze and read the three friends minds. Borghx's intelligence was far beyond Maran or Human intelligence. His thoughts were on a different level all together but he could not predict the future. He had that discussion with Mr. Kyn many times about predicting the future because Mr. Kyn thought for sure that Borghx should be able to do that. Borghx explained that the universal law of entropy was still well at work throughout the Galaxy and that was one reason they had embarked on this mission. Predictions always came from analyzing the probabilities and they were not always accurate. Borghx stood up and waved his hands around like he usually did before he had a great idea. Mr. Kyn knew something was coming, so he smiled and waited patiently. After Borghx sat back down he picked up a piece of the fruit almost at the same exact time Mark, high above them in the ranch house, also picked up the fruit. Borghx liked this rare cactus fruit. It was his favorite food. After he finished with the fruit he spoke. "I believe we are entering a new phase of our mission. I guess I would use the human word, adventure, though I do not like that word very much. I think we should gain the confidence and friendship of these three men. They could be very helpful to us in the days ahead. We have to be in a position of constant change and flexibility in all our plans now as we move forward with our mission. Let's discuss this further and make some plans now, my dear friend, Tyijo Kyn." Mr. Kyn smiled and took a deep breath.

Back at the house Ernie and George were exchanging glances with each other and the two sisters. Mark was feeling left out. He also still had a strange feeling that something was askew. He didn't feel scared or threatened but something was just not right. He stood up so as to draw the attention of George and Ernie away from the two women. Ernie and George looked at each other and shrugged their shoulders. Marked darted an angry stare at both of them and then very calmly spoke. "I think it is time we leave now." Both George and Ernie smiled and then shook their heads back and forth to indicate, no. "Look guys, I think we imposed for long enough here. We have a lot of things to do tomorrow. Also there seems to be a storm coming and I don't want to walk back in a downpour."

Ernie didn't want to go anywhere, but he also knew he had a wife back in Venice, so he thought twice. "We will go in a little bit Mark. I still need to rest my knee. You know the old football injury." Then he winked at Mark. Mark didn't like Ernie's attitude and he didn't want to stick around and get in an argument with him. The two had known each other since High School but, they were not always the closest of friends. It had been George's idea to bring Ernie in on this project. Mark was thinking it was probably going to be a problem like he had predicted.

Mark could see he was not going to get the other two to leave quickly. He felt uncomfortable but he wanted to be polite. "I think I will go out on the porch for a bit and try to judge when this storm is rolling in."

"That is good idea!" George said. George was happy to have Mark leave for now. It seemed Mark was drifting off into one of his strange moods.

Mark stood on the front porch and looked out to the horizon. There was still a bit of light and he could see the storm approaching. It looked like the wind was blowing it to the south and only the very edge would pass over them. He was trying to analyze the strange feelings he was having from the two women. He knew if he had stayed inside he may have argued with Ernie and that would not have been good for any of them. He knew George and Ernie were not aware of the odd feelings he was having at the moment. All his martial arts training and other training with the CIA seemed to do little for him now and he didn't like that. He wanted to be in control and aware of every situation he was in but somehow this was just way too different so it frustrated him. His mind started to wander, and he kept going back over all the pressure he had put himself in over the past few years to develop his financial fortune. He had wanted to escape the hectic city life for a long time and even though it was something he could easily do he forced himself to stay and take care of his businesses. A few years back he purchased a piece of land near Bakersfield, Ca in the mountains so he would have a place to escape to.

He liked this area of the country even better than where he had his land. As he stared out to the horizon his mind raced with continual thoughts. He was starting to feel old even though he was only in his late thirties. He wanted to know his destiny but it was just not something he could see. All of his goals and dreams seemed to have evaporated now. His mind settled into the present again and he felt alone, very alone. Something strange was happening and he could not put his finger on it. He thought, maybe the fact that these two women moved out here from Los Angeles, and the fact that I have always wanted to get away from Los Angeles, has triggered something in me. With that thought he turned, opened the door and walked back into the house.

He smelled the food immediately upon opening the door. There were trays of food and two more bottles of wine on the large table in now. Ernie and George were all smiles. The two gorgeous sisters were also all smiles. George was telling some nutty story about his days in high school. Only Shala turned her head as Mark walked back into the room. She smiled at Mark and it melted all of his tension like the dew evaporating from the grass as the sun kissed it early in the morning. Then Mark noticed that the two women had not only cooked food but they had changed their cloths. He looked at his watch and realized he had been outside on the porch for almost an hour! How could that have happened that he totally lost track of time? He recalled seeing the sky turn dark but other than that he had no memory of standing on the porch. All that existed was now. The smell of the

Southwest home cooked food, the laughter from Ernie, the warm and fuzzy sensation he felt from seeing two of the most beautiful women he had ever seen in his life now dressed in flowing silky white dresses. He could see every curve of Shala's body as she smiled at him walking into the room. They both had on matching elaborate turquoise earrings, necklaces and belts. They had let their hair down. When Mark sat down next to George he was captured by the aura just as George and Ernie were.

Ernie and George were already eating and drinking more champagne. Mark joined in and found himself actually listening to George's story about his days in high school with Ernie and Mark. Mark even contributed a few stories of his own. Mark felt relaxed and the feelings he had earlier disappeared into the air. It was all about his senses now. The scent of the lavender perfume, the smell of the food, the soft voices, the taste of the expensive wine, and the perfection he was watching that complimented the sisters and their environment. After ten or fifteen minutes Marks mood changed again. It was like he was going down into a dark cave. He realized he was the man out again. His vision started to blur and his mind began to race to towards visions he had never knew were inside him. Everything seemed grey. There were no more colors and the food tasted bland. He was starting to feel very uncomfortable again like the whole thing was phony, like it was some kind of macabre play in a darkly lit theater. He knew he had to find out what was going on with him and these two sisters so he forced himself to smile and go along with the spell that the two sisters had over his friends.

Ernie, being the only married one out of the three, realized he was in the predicament of a lifetime. For him, Shala was the most beautiful and the most elegant. Aktal seemed to be in control of Shala and he didn't like that. He felt Shala was constantly flirting with him. He also felt like she realized she was under the control of her sister. It made him feel close to her. He wanted to take her outside and talk to her alone but he was scared of being to forward. He kept debating with himself what would happened when his wife and sons moved and were living with him. Would he be able to start a relationship with Shala and hide it from his wife? His body ached to touch Shala. He wanted to see her naked. He wanted to be naked with her in some faraway place and never return to real life. He was trembling inside with lust and desire. He could never remember having a similar feeling ever in his life. It was all so sudden and new but he loved it. He kept biting his lower lip and telling himself that he would deal with everything one step at a time. Maybe Shala had been secretly waiting all her life to meet him. Maybe she felt like he was her soul mate! Just at the moment she stood up and moved her chair closer to Ernie. The slit in her dress revealed her soft pale skin. When she sat back down closer to Ernie she reached towards the table, picked up the bottle of champagne and filled Ernie's glass. As she did so, her naked thigh brushed Ernie's arm and shock waves of pleasure raced down Ernie's spine. He could feel himself becoming aroused and tried to stop the feeling so as not to feel embarrassed but there was nothing he could do. After a few more minutes of conversation and when George finished his lengthy and rambling story, Shala reached over and offered her hand to Ernie. "Let's go in the kitchen and you can help me with a few things." She said softly. Ernie took her hand and they walked into the kitchen. As soon as they closed the door to the kitchen Ernie could not resist and he turned and pulled Shala by her hand into him and they kissed with a passion Ernie had not felt in years.

George was talking more than he usually talked mainly because he was very nervous. He was the most unexperienced with women by far between the three friends. George was a romanticist, but he had never experienced a true romance. Usually when he met a woman that liked him he fell way to fast and that ended up turning the woman off. It was a modern world and the fact that George was no longer a spring chicken did not help. He had only had one serious relationship in his life and that was many years ago. Recently he had been wondering if he really had ever gotten over that relationship. He had been in his early twenties and he thought for sure the girl he was with was as madly in love with him as he was with her. He wanted to get married and start a family and when they talked he thought she wanted the same. She was Caucasian and from a fairly prominent family. She was not nearly as well educated as him but she was fun. He never asked her for any money but since she had a fairly large sum of money in her bank account from a family trust, she often paid for things. They had lived together for nearly two years when George popped the question. He was certain she would say yes, but she didn't. He was a bit shocked at the time but it was not something that he dwelled on. She said she needed more time to think about marriage. George told her that due to the fact they were living together it already felt like they were married. She agreed with his feeling but at the same time she still felt it was not the right time. They didn't argue over the issue at first but later when George discovered that her main concern was that her parents were against her marrying a Japanese American man, he lost his temper. He thought her parents always liked him. Her Father had taken him golfing at his private country club on more than one occasion. Not more than three months later she moved out. George was heartbroken and angry. He absorbed himself in his work and forgot about women for a long time.

This situation had completely caught George off guard. He was infatuated and fascinated with Aktal. After Shala and Ernie went to the kitchen Mark could see that Aktal was coyly getting inside George's head. Mark felt like he was at play but it was not a play it was real life. He sat back on the sofa and watched all the while trying to get his emotions and rational mind more under control. As if on cue, to what Mark was watching, Aktal moved her chair closer to George. She reached out and touched George's hand as he went for the champagne. "George, it looks like there is a storm headed our way. I don't want you to be too drunk when you leave." Aktal said.

George felt the electricity run through his hand where she touched his hand. Now he was more than fascinated by her he was obsessed with her. It brought back the old feelings of the only serious relationship he had ever been in and as those thoughts drifted into his conscious he furled his brow. He felt anger again. Mark observed George furl his brow and was not too sure why. If Aktal had touched his hand he would be in the bedroom with her shortly after and he knew it. What was George's problem he thought to himself? Then almost completely out of the blue but on cue with the underlying skepticism pervading Marks thoughts, George asked, "How did you and your sister change clothes so quickly and prepare all of this food?" This time Mark raised his eyebrows. He had been out on the porch and did not have a chance to notice the incongruity, but for some reason, George was now thinking along the same wave lengths as him. Mark was curious to see how Aktal would respond now that she was being questioned.

Aktal smiled. Borghx and Mr. Kyn also smiled far below the house in their retreat. Suddenly they realized that when George and Mark were together without Ernie present that the two of them almost thought as one mind. It was a very interesting development in the sequence of events for the evening and the first time Mr. Kyn and Borghx had ever noticed this in observing humans. They knew from their studies that this trait was present in biological twins and often in mothers and children, but, they did not realize it could be present in two very different men that were friends. Aktal replied, "We are efficient and fast workers. The food was already prepared and we only had to warm it up."

"Oh, Ok, I am curious, you know, it is my nature." George said. He turned, glanced at Mark and for the first time in over an hour realized Mark had some suspicions also. "I am not sure if I missed something earlier in the evening but where exactly in Los Angeles did you say you and your sister were from?"

"Actually we only lived there for a brief time. We have lived in many different parts of the world." Aktal replied.

Now Mark finally was able to formulate his thoughts. The thoughts were vague like a swarm of insects flying over a piece of rotting meat but he was able to focus much better than earlier. "Where exactly are you and your sister from originally?" Mark was starting to believe the two sisters were Russian KGB but he was not certain.

"I do not want to appear to be evasive, but at the same time this is not something I think I can answer in detail right now. So let me just say we are originally from somewhere a long ways from here." Aktal grinned and below Mr. Kyn and Borghx peeled another piece of the sweet tasting fruit. George nodded his head as if that was a sufficient answer for the time being. He did not want to offend her because she was so different from any woman he had ever met. She had an energy about her that he liked and she had been giving him attention in a way that made him want to know her better. "Let me ask you a question if I may? It is sort of a personal question."

"Sure, you can ask me anything you like," George replied as he sat back on the sofa feeling more relaxed now.

Aktal bent forward and again took George's hand in hers and looked deeply into his eyes. This time George felt more comfortable with her touch. Her hand was warm and sensitive. George thought for sure she was going to ask him if he was married or had a girlfriend. "Do you believe love is an emotion or a concept that surrounds our emotions arising from infatuation depending on our cultural, religious and moral values?"

Both George and Mark paused and exchanged glances. Aktal had shifted her conversation from trivial and light towards deep and explorative. George and Mark had these type of conversations on a regular basis. It was what bonded them as friends. They were constantly exploring a variety of topics. Mark couldn't understand what had shifted in Aktal's mind to now engage in deeper philosophical ideas. George sat with a sort of dumbfounded look on his face for a few seconds. He wanted to be careful and answer her in a way that displayed both his feelings and intelligence towards that topic, but inside all he could think about was to lean over and kiss her. Mark had never seen George so much under the spell of a woman. If anything Mark usually viewed George as sort of a misogynist, though he knew deep down he was really not. It was more of a front that George put on to make himself look more "Macho."

Once George gathered his thoughts through the blur of the moment and the buzz of the champagne he answered. "Actually Aktal, I have thought about that very topic quite often in the past few years. To be honest I could only give my opinion and I am not sure that would answer the question." Then something just seemed to take over George's thought patterns. Maybe it was the effects of the wine. After he said it, he wondered why he said it. "What I will say is that I feel something for you! I mean, I have never felt this way before in my life and I am not sure exactly what it is I do feel." George was beyond embarrassed that he blurted out what he did. Mark was sort of shocked, but the whole evening had been a shock to Mark so it was not too unexpected, especially since Ernie was off in the kitchen doing who knew what with the other sister. George needed to rationalize his words so he continued, "What I mean to say, is that here I am in a place I have never been to before and this should feel strange to me, but it is not. There was no reason or logic to come here other than the fact that we had nothing to do and that Mark said he had heard that the two of you were our neighbors. Now here I am and I am having thoughts that I am not sure I should be having right now." George was babbling and he knew it. He lifted his embarrassed eyes from the floor and let them rest in the warm comfort of Aktal's piercing metallic blue eyes. George was blushing but he felt comfortable as his eyes locked onto Aktal's eyes.

Mark again felt left out and like he was only a spectator to some bizarre first act of a play that was unfolding in real time. He knew it was getting close to the time when he either told both his friends it was time to leave or he just quietly snuck out and left on his own. He decided he would partake of one more glass of champagne and eat some more of the home cooked food before he made a choice of what to do. As he munched on a beef tamale and watched Aktal and George exchange further pleasantries he heard Ernie and Shala laugh loudly in the kitchen. Mark gazed around the house again and noticed how neat everything was arranged. Everything was just too perfect for his liking. Because his mind raced and analyzed everything so quickly he was anxious to understand why he couldn't come to any conclusion about the two sisters. He seemed trapped in the ambiance of the moment and he knew that was not like him. He had never met any women like these two and he had met plenty of beautiful women in his time. They were just too perfect. Then it dawned on him that in all their perfection they had chosen to direct their attention to his two friends and not him. He wondered if it was something about him they didn't like. At that instant Shala and Ernie returned from the kitchen. Shala was holding a small tray of desserts. Ernie was holding another bottle of wine. Mark noticed something he had not noticed before, Shala moved like a model, but in an unnatural way. Her steps were too long, very long, and they decelerated. They did not shorten as she got closer to where she sat down.

"All right, let's party!" Ernie said as he poured himself another glass of wine and reached his glass over to cling glasses with Mark. Mark shook his head like he needed to bring himself back to reality but he didn't know what reality was. He aimlessly clicked glasses with Ernie and tried to hold on to his passing thoughts.

Mark decided it was time to leave. He would have a dessert because he loved chocolate and then he would politely make his exit. He reached over to the tray and saw the desserts were that fruit he had tried earlier with some dark chocolate on top. He tried one and it was really tasty. "What is this fruit again? I have traveled to a lot of countries in the world and tasted a lot many different foods, but I must say this fruit truly is unique. What do you call it again?" Mark asked as he savored the delicate flavors.

This time Aktal turned her full attention on Mark and once again his mind faded into a place he didn't know existed. He felt like he was being transported back in time to some ancient civilization. In front of him was a Greek Goddess. "The fruit is from a secret garden we have. Maybe sometime I can show it to you. We grow a lot of exotic fruits and vegetables there."

"Oh really? Well that seems very interesting. Yes, I would like to see that sometime." Mark was lost now but he saw a distant light, almost like a ray of sunshine that peeped through storm clouds. He wanted to know what it was about the two sisters that had him under such a spell. He wanted to know now, but he knew that would not be possible. He had drank too much wine and his mind was not clear. He stood up and clapped his hands together twice to get the attention of Ernie and George as they were a lot further down the path to total infatuation than he was. Marks face reflected his determination and conviction that something was just not normal. His two friends turned and looked at him wondering why he looked so angry. "Hey guys, it is getting late. I think we should get going now." Both Ernie and George looked at him like he was an alien. Heck, the party was just getting going! Mark was not sure if he should just leave on his own, stay a bit longer, or try to convince his two inebriated friends to leave with him.

Mr. Kyn and Borghx had made their decision and communicated it to Aktal and Shala. Aktal took the lead now that

Mark was displaying signs of suspicion and anxiety. It was a spur of the moment decision for Borghx and Mr. Kyn but they were confident that things would work out the way they wanted them to.

Mark was still standing and could see that George and Ernie could care less about leaving or listening to him. He was feeling more anger well up from within and he knew he had to control it but at the same time he had to be assertive and get some answers or he had to leave. He sat back down and composed his thoughts. "Ok, let's cut all the games right now." He darted his eyes between everyone. "I want to know what is going on in this place. If you don't tell me now, believe me I will know soon enough. I have the means to find out everything. I want to know whom you ladies really are and where you are really from. Something is odd here. I have been feeling it ever since we arrived here. You two are just too good to be true. You seem to know too much about us and how we think. I want to know why you are putting on this act. Where is your family? I have lived in Los Angeles most of my life and the two of you are not anything like the women from Los Angeles."

Ernie was not happy and thought Mark was just jealous. He wanted to say something but decided it was best to just remain quiet. He had already been kissing Shala in the kitchen and as far as he was concerned that was nobodies busy but his own. It really did not matter to him what Mark was saying because he knew it would not be long before he was headed to the bedroom with Shala. George also felt Mark was just plain jealous mainly because Mark was used to getting most of the attention from women and this time it was different. George decided it was time for him to speak up but he wanted to be sure he kept the peace between all of them. "Mark, why don't you sit and relax. We can all leave in due time. I really think you have just had a very long day. Look, these two ladies are our neighbors and I think you should just try and relax. None of us want to cause any problems."

"Ok, I am sitting down." Mark said as he suddenly realized it really did not make a whole lot of difference what the issue was and maybe, just maybe, his friend was right in pointing out he had had a long day. As he leaned back on the sofa he mumbled to himself so that no one could hear, "I still want to find out what is going on here!"

Aktal, Shala, Mr. Kyn, and Borghx of course heard the mumbled words of Mark. Mr. Kyn and Borghx began to implement their strategy at that moment. Aktal and Shala exchanged glances and then ever so slightly nodded their heads as if they had reached some concurrence. In reality Borghx had given both of them full instructions as to how they should lead the conversation from now on. It was simple and powerful just like Borghx wanted it to be. Aktal was sitting across from Mark and watched him for a few seconds, then as Mark brought his eyes from the floor to meet hers, she spoke. "Yes, Mark, I think it is time now to explain some things to you." Ernie and George then turned their attention to Aktal as if some kind of laser beam had suddenly focused their attention. Aktal darted her eyes toward Ernie and George. All three of the friends noticed that Aktal's eyes seemed to sparkle and become a bit larger. "I want all three of you to be patient and try to understand clearly what I am going to say." My sister and I are not actually from Los Angeles. Let me just say for now that we are from somewhere far from here. We have used this story that we are from Los Angeles for many years, ever since we moved here, mainly so that the other neighbors out here would understand why two sisters would occupy a ranch out here in the middle of nowhere. We let the neighbors come to their own conclusions. Trust me, they have come to a variety of different ones. I guess that is human nature." Aktal turned and exchanged a wry smile with Shala. "What I can tell you, that may have value, is that we are not aligned with any government or country. We are diplomats of a sort, but, for now I think it is better to just leave that subject alone. More on that subject will be revealed to you later. I also want you to know that we do not adhere to any philosophy or religion. We are peaceful and believe in peace. In reality we are very similar to the three of you but in ways you most likely will discover in the future, we are different from you. My sister and I are highly skilled in many arts and extremely well educated. We are independent but we do have some very special friends that help to guide all of our activities. I think by now you can see that we like all of you very much. We have observed many outstanding qualities in you. We also admire the strong bond of friendship and respect you have between each other. It is very interesting to us how each of you can have such different personalities and still maintain such a high level of admiration for each other. We have observed that the one quality that seems to bind the three of you together is the value you put into the friendship. It is obvious that you have different levels of intelligence and skills. This unity that exists between the three of you is a very powerful force that we do not believe you have yet to recognize. In the future this unity will lead each of you to great success in a variety of endeavors. I want each of you to know that no matter what happens from this moment on that it is our deepest desire for all of to become closer friends."

There was a long pause and the three men exchanged quizzical looks with each other. For the first time all evening Mark once again felt he had the attention and focus of Ernie and George back with him. The problem for Mark is that now he felt like he was lost in a vision that he may have never had. That thought made no sense to him, but then again the whole evening had made no sense to him. He was totally confused but at least in his confusion he now felt he had both Ernie and George on board with him.

Aktal could sense the feelings of all three of the men and below Borghx and Mr. Kyn knew what they wanted to do. It would be a rare opportunity for them so they had Aktal continue with her speech. "It is now almost midnight so I feel it is the right time for me to reveal some more details to you. What I am going to say may seem to be a bold statement but I want you to understand that we are quite ordinary women only we are in an extraordinary situation." Aktal and Shala glanced at each other. The three men did the same. "We would like all three of you to spend the night here. It is late, the weather may turn bad and we have an offer I think you will like." Ernie and George smiled at the statement but Mark frowned. The high from the wine was wearing off and Mark again had an odd feeling that something was just not normal. Everything seemed just too perfect and now that Aktal was making these long statements it seemed there was definitely an ulterior motive involved. Aktal noticed Mark's reaction but Mr. Kyn and Borghx were instructing her to continue. "Our offer is this, we will promise that each of you will have a secret desire fulfilled during the course of the night." Ernie and George both raised their eyebrows and smiled. Neither of them could care less if this was an odd situation. All that mattered was the knowledge that Aktal and Shala had been directing their attention towards them all evening and now it would go to the next level! Mark, on the other hand, remained stoic. Suddenly Borghx and Mr. Kyn could see that Mark may either flee or become aggressive. It was a split second reaction and Marks mind raced like cars at a motor speedway with a myriad of thoughts. Aktal turned and leaned closer to Mark. She knew she needed to address him directly and quell his fears. She lowered the tone and volume of her voice. Mark immediately recognized her voice and tone being lowered as a psychological technique he had learned with the CIA but at this point he had no choice but to try and calm himself and listen. He took a deep breath. "Mark, I can see you are not as happy as your friends with what I had to say. I want you to come with me now to the secret garden I told you about earlier. There will be wonders there far beyond anything you have ever imagined." Aktal's eyes seemed to go a darker shade of blue and sparkle. Mark tried blinking his eyes but found he could not blink his eyes. He knew he was being hypnotized but there was nothing he could do to prevent it. He was no longer in control of the situation and he knew it. He nodded his head in agreement and Aktal reached across to him offering her hand. Mark took her hand in his and they both stood up. Mark's last though was that the two sisters were involved in some type of cult but now he was helpless to do anything. His mouth would not work and his thoughts were scrambled. As they turned to walk towards the door Aktal said to George, "I will be back shortly."

Shala took Ernie by the hand and lead him to the bedrooms in the back of the house. He was drunker than the others but he also knew what he wanted. It had been a long time since he had slept with his wife. George sat back on the couch and felt insecure. He was not sure Aktal would return as she had said she would.

Just as they opened the front door to head outside a large bird flew in front of them in the dark. Mark thought it had to be an owl chasing prey but it seemed a lot larger than any owl he had ever seen. It was dark and hard to see what kind of bird it really was. Somehow the sight of the bird helped wake Mark out of his hypnotized state and he again realized where he was and what he was doing. He felt Aktal's hand holding his and leading him towards the barn. Halfway along the brick walkway towards the looming barn ahead Mark squeezed Aktal's hand with a lot of force and stopped walking. He swung her around to face him. He thought at first she would resist but she remained very passive. "Ok, let's stop all of these games. I want to know what is going on here. Why are you taking me to this barn? Why would you have a secret garden in a barn?" Mark was upset and spoke with in a low angry tone. A few sprinkles of rain started to fall.

Aktal reached out and put her free hand on Mark's shoulder as if to comfort him. She spoke in a very soft tone almost as if she was talking to him from a distant place. "Mark, you need to trust me. The garden is secret. It is in a large underground chamber below the barn. The ceiling of the chamber is well lit and supports the growth of the plants there. Please Mark, try to relax. You are going to meet some very special friends of mine. You will be able to have many questions answered and you will be able to see some wondrous things. Believe me I am not here to do you any harm nor are my friends. We all very much want to be your friend."

Again Mark felt comforted and the tempest that always ran through his mind every day since he was a child faded into soft desert pastel colors. He felt like he was watching a beautiful sunset. Aktal's presence and words had transformed him into someone he had only dreamed he could ever become. He felt like he was becoming a small child again and Aktal was his Mother taking him to the ice-cream parlor. As they approached the barn door Mark was wondering if Aktal's eyes had changed from blue to green, or was it just the soft half-moon light that reflected from the dark red barn that made them appear that way. They opened the door to the barn. Aktal flipped a light switch and Mark could see the barn was basically empty expect for two small off road vehicles and some farming tools. Barns always smelled like animals but this one did not because there was no livestock in the barn. The floor was grey concrete. Aktal lead mark to the center of the barn. She then turned and faced him. Mark could see now that her eyes had not changed and that they were still blue.

"Ok, I am going to leave now. When I get back to the door and light switch the floor you are standing on will begin to lower you into the underground chamber. There are no railings so stay very still and do not lean out or look over the edge. I will return later and we can talk then." Aktal turned and slowly walked towards the door they had entered from. Mark stood like a statue. Even if he wanted to move he didn't think he could. His feet felt as if they were anchored to the ground. His legs felt heavy. He sat down on the cold concrete and crossed his legs. Aktal blew Mark a kiss from near the doorway and Mark suddenly felt very alone.

Aktal left and Mark felt could see that a ten foot circular area of the floor that he was sitting on began to sink into the ground. He had time to jump away but he couldn't move. He didn't know if it was fear or if he was paralyzed. Now he thought for sure that he had been drugged and he was heading towards his death. Then he smiled to himself and thought maybe her "friends" were more attractive women like her! That thought lasted just a few seconds because now he was almost blinded by the light adjacent to him that seemed to come from all directions. He was slowly going down and to where he had no idea. After fifteen or so he realized the light was coming from what would be the ceiling of the underground chamber. As his eyes adopted to the light he looked down into the chamber below him. It was massive. It had to be part of some natural cavernous structure because there was no way anyone could excavate that much earth. He could see now that the ceiling was a dome shape. The whole ceiling glowed with what he now realized was a soft luminous light and not nearly as bright as he had thought just seconds before. He also realized that he was no longer paralyzed and could move his legs so he stood up. He wanted to walk to the edge of the platform that was lowering him to the floor below but decided it might not be a good idea. He peered out to the edge of the platform and as he went lower he could see the ground below. It was lush, green and looked very much like the secret garden that Aktal had told him about. When he realized there really was a garden below him he felt a sense of relief, but only briefly, because he was still alone. The platform was moving very slowly so he had time to observe what was below him. To one side there seemed to be some other domed structures which at first seemed tiny but then he realized how far away they were and guessed they were at least 30 yards across. He could see all kinds of tropical looking plants and many of them had colorful fruits on them. At last his curiosity got the best of him and he ventured more towards the edge of the platform so he could see more of what was directly below him. He could see a shiny white marble or granite patio with three tables and chairs. There were also some strange looking sculptures or rock formations that surrounded the patio. Mark went back to the center of the platform and closed his eyes for a few seconds so he could try and compose himself. Mark was not sure if it was the wine, some drug they had slipped him, or just the overwhelming circumstance that made him recall a vivid dream he had when he was fourteen years old.

Chapter 11
Intertwining Dreams

The Dream

There was an expansive warm tropical lagoon and about fifty yards from the shore floated a rough wooden platform about ten yards square. Mark was swimming towards the platform where some darker native children were gathered on the platform. They were diving off the platform and enjoying the tepid water. There were approximately eight children and all of them were about his age but a few of them seemed to be younger. When Mark reached the platform he was a bit tired from the swim. He was greeted with enthusiasm by the others even though he had never met them and that made him feel good. He stretched out on his back to rest for a few minutes and felt the warm sun dry the water from his skin. When he was rested he joined some of the others in diving from the platform then splashing in the water. After half an hour or so he had sort of made a connection with a boy close to his age and after swimming for a while they both rested on their backs staring at the sky. Suddenly the boy stood up and so Mark followed him and stood up also. In an act of playful jest Mark pushed his new friend off of the platform into the water. The boy dived under the water for a few seconds then surfaced and beckoned for Mark to jump in also. Mark looked around and saw that all of the other children were now on the platform with him. Mark jumped into the water after his friend.

The boy ducked under the water and started swimming straight down towards the bottom. Mark followed after him. The boy was a very good swimmer and Mark had to swim as hard as he could under the water to follow the boy. After a short amount of time Mark realized he would not be able to keep up with the boy and that he needed air. Just as Mark made the decision to swim to the surface he saw the boy swim into an underwater cave. Mark headed up towards the surface to get air. He swam back to the platform and waited for the boy to come back up, but he did not. There were no more children on the platform. Mark peered towards the shore and was instantly overcome by a wave of fear and emotion. He could see the children that had been on the platform pointing out towards him along with a throng of adults. The boy still did not surface. Mark stood on the platform and tried to make gestures like he didn't know what had happened but it was too late. The men on the shore were waving spears and heading to their canoes to paddle out to the platform.

Mark was confused and very frightened. He knew he had done nothing wrong but he also knew that the other children had seen him push the boy off the platform. Mark did not speak whatever language these children spoke and knew he had no way to defend himself. He realized he had only one option. He had to dive back in the water and find the boy. He stood on the edge of the platform taking long deep breaths. He needed to gather all the energy he could so he could hold his breath under the water. He jumped out in the direction the boy had dived and then swam under the water. He saw the cave fairly quickly and swam in a straight line towards it. It was a longer swim than he anticipated and he was scared he would not make it but the fear of the oncoming canoes with the men in them drove him on. Now his lungs were burning and he thought he could die. Somehow he made it into the dark underwater cave. Now he really needed air but he forced himself to swim forward. He could barely see and slimy plants brushed his arms as he made long strokes forward. The water was colder in the cave and it made him think of death. He really needed to turn around and swim back to the surface before his lungs burst. He paused for a brief second thinking he should turn around but just at that instance he thought he saw a dim glimmer of light ahead so he continued forward. He was almost at the point of panicking and blacking out from holding his breath for so long. The mossy plants were thicker now on each side of him and it slowed his progress forward. He thought for sure he would drown now. His mind grew fuzzy and he was almost ready to gasp for air which would fill his lungs with saltwater. He started to see stars and he knew he was at the point of losing consciousness. He pushed forward and realized he was actually heading up now towards the glimmer of light that was getting brighter. He really was not sure if he had already passed out and was now dreaming or dying. All of his muscles ached with an intense stinging sensation. The light or the stars he was seeing grew brighter. He was sure he was dying. But then at the last second he burst through the surface of the water gasping for air. He was completely drained of all energy. He tried to relax by floating on his back but his body still ached from being deprived of oxygen. As he floated on his back he quickly realized he was trapped in what appeared to be an old abandoned well or some natural rock formation. He was in a cylinder and the rocks on the walls were a dark grey color and very smooth. He could see he was near the top but there was still four feet of steep wall on all sides of him. He was trapped and there was no way out other than finding a way to climb the slick walls or head back down the well and through the cave back to the diving platform. He just could not think of doing either one right now because he was so exhausted from the underwater swim.

After a few minutes of alternately floating on his back and dog paddling her realized he somehow had to get out of the well. His goal had been to find the boy and make sure he went back to the shore with the boy so everyone there could see that when he pushed him off the platform that it was a playful jest and not with intent to hurt him. Mark gaged the height of the wall and thought if he lunged upwards as hard as he could he may be able to put his hand on top of the ledge and pull himself up. His first attempt was weak and his hand came nowhere near the top of the wall. He tried again, and again, until he was almost exhausted from trying. Now he was frustrated and started to weep. There was no choice now but to swim back down the well through the small passage and back to the surface to face whatever fate waited for him there. He again lay on his back and floated on the water. By propping his feet against the wall he was able to stabilize himself and relax. He became so relaxed that he nearly fell asleep. He knew he was tired but he didn't want to sleep so he would close his eyes and count to forty then open them again. At some point he was not sure if he was awake or asleep and then he noticed that the water he was floating on had seemed to warm up some. He went back to dog paddling in the water and looking once again at the ledge. He realized the water had risen some, most likely from the tide rising so now the ledge was much closer. He lunged upwards out of the water and the tips of his fingers touched the edge of the ridge. Now he felt energized and he knew if he tried a bit harder he could make it. On his next attempt he was barely able to lock his fingers over the edge but it was enough to hold on. He struggled with all his might and was able to get his other hand over the ledge and then pull himself up to the top.

He lay face down on a smooth rock floor. He was in a large cave and there was still a glimmer of light high above him. He could see roots from trees above that were hanging down into the cavern between the filtered light. He looked around and saw there was a small passage to his left. He suddenly felt hopeful for the first time because he knew that is where the boy must have gone. The passage only went on for a short distance and then opened up into a much large cavern. Above he could see there was a large opening and other openings on the side of the steep walls. This allowed a lot more light to filter into the cave. As his eyes adjusted to the brighter light he could see that he was in a very large underground cavern and that there were plants and trees growing all around him. It was a lush green paradise. He could hear birds singing. His arm grazed a small tree as he stepped in and the tree had lovely ripe orange fruits on it. Mark picked one of the fruits, peeled the skin from it and ate it. He found another one and ate that one also. For a few minutes he completely forgot about why he had come to the place as he was enchanted by the beauty around him. After he ate he lay down on the cool stone floor and stared up at the light filtering in from above. He closed his eyes and fell asleep. He either dreamed or recalled how he had arrived at the place he was at. In the middle of his dream he realized he had come to find the boy so he quickly woke up.

He stood up and began to explore the large chamber. At first it appeared there was no way out. He called out and whistled hoping the boy was hiding somewhere but there was no answer. He saw a small path made of dark smooth stones and followed the path to an area behind a large tree that had long thin yellow fruits hanging from it. At the end of the path he came to a very steep but flat wall that had two doors side by side. Now he was excited because he was sure the boy had gone through one of the doors. He stared at the large doors. One was ornate with gold, silver and gemstones inlayed with carved wood. The other door was just plain with no decorations at all. He was positive now that the boy had gone through one of the doors. He looked at the ground to see if there were any footprints but there were none. He became very confused and tried to analyze if there was some meaning to the doors. Why was one plain and the other ornate. He became very scared and felt that he was going to be trapped in the chamber forever. He knew the boy had to have gone through one of the doors but he could not decide which one to choose. He wondered if there was a monster behind one of the doors that would eat him. Maybe the monster ate the boy. He was shaking with fear and going back and forth to each door trying to listen if he could hear anything behind the doors. His mind raced in an internal debate about the meaning of the doors. He also wondered if he should just go back and try to swim back up to the surface. He looked above him and thought for second he could climb up the rocks but it was just too steep. There were too many options and too many things to think about. Suddenly it came to him, he had to be dreaming. That is when he decided to wake up.

It was 5:00 am on a school day. Mark lay in bed sweating. He tried to go back to sleep so he could find out what was behind the doors but he couldn't go back to sleep. He recalled that dream on and off all of his life. Now as the platform neared the floor below him, he wondered why he was recalling the dream now.

For Ernie, his dream was coming true. He and Shala were giving the meaning of rapturous love making a new definition. The experience was far beyond anything Ernie could have ever imagined. The small amount of guilt he felt by cheating on his wife paled to the excitement of the moment. He would tell Shala later that he was married. It started with Shala giving Ernie a long massage. It was like no massage he had ever experienced. Her hands seemed to have a warm healing quality to them and Ernie felt like years of age was being taken away from his body. At one point Ernie was sure he was floating above the bed. He didn't know if he was having an outer body experience or not, but he did know it felt wonderful. As the light of dawn began to sneak in the window Ernie finally fell asleep. He was both exhausted and refreshed as he drifted into a deep slumber.

George sat on the couch in the ranch house and waited patiently for Aktal to return. At some point he stood up and paced around the room for a little while not sure if she would actually return. As he was standing wringing his hands together the door opened and there she stood. She was smiling and her eyes were gleaming. They sat on the couch and held hands for a while not saying very much. George felt like he was back in high school and this was the first girl he ever liked. George was speechless and did not know what to do. George started to stare at the floor and Aktal sat and patiently watched him. Then Aktal kissed George on his neck. George smiled, turned to face her and kissed her on her lips. It was heaven for George, he really felt like he was falling in love for the first time in his life. He felt very light headed and wondered if this was really happening. Her body was so soft and warm. "Aktal, I am really nervous about this. You know we only just met this evening." After the words came out of his mouth he felt completely immature for a man in his late thirties. He was embarrassed he had said anything.

"Why don't we go for a walk together? The rain has held off and it is a nice evening." Aktal could sense how nervous George felt. When they stood up Aktal pulled George close to her and kissed him again on the lips. They stood together hugging for a few moments and George felt a lot more comfortable now.

"Ok, yes, let's go for a walk." George said after the long embrace. He was trying to take a deep breath before he totally lost himself in Aktal's charms.

"Great, I am going to take you somewhere very special. You are going to love it!" Aktal said. "Hold on I am going to get a small backpack." Aktal went into one of the back rooms and George waited by the front door.

They went around the side of the house towards the back end of the house. The sky had cleared and there was a full moon. They passed through an old wooden gate and headed down a path that led to a ridge that went along a canyon. The path winded down into the canyon. There were small dwarf pine trees on either side of them. As they ventured closer to the bottom of the canyon the trees were larger and some large willow trees loomed ahead of them. George could hear water from a creek gurgling somewhere near them. After about ten more minutes of hiking they came to a little waterfall that splashed into a pond. George could see that steam was rising from the pond. This must have been part of the mineral springs that were also on the property they had purchased. They paused and gazed at the beautiful scene in front of them and Aktal explained that the water came from the mineral springs further up the canyon. It was a very romantic spot especially with the full moon hovering overhead.

Aktal took off the back pack and pulled out a large blanket that she spread out on a grassy area near the path. George was enthralled with the moment and almost had to pinch himself to see if it was for real. Here he was in a super romantic spot in the high desert of New Mexico with what he considered the most beautiful woman he had ever met. Even better was the fact that he was sure now that she liked him as much as he liked her. For the first time all evening his mind shut off and his thoughts evaporated into the air just like the mist on the pond. He allowed his heart to rule the moment. He instantly fell deeply in love with Aktal. It made no difference that he had only met her hours earlier. He knew it was his fate.

After Aktal set up the blanket with half a bottle of champagne and some snacks she very casually undressed. "Let's go in the pool!"

George followed her lead and undressed as fast as he could. Once he was fully naked Aktal game close to him and they kissed. It was a kiss that foretold the passion the come. Then Aktal took George by the hand and led him to some ancient stone steps that led into the water. George could not help but stare at Aktal's naked body. She had the most perfect body he had ever seen in his life. For an instant George felt inadequate. He wondered why this woman would pick him as she could obviously have any man she wanted. Once in the warm water George's thoughts again evaporated. Aktal slid over to him and they kissed again. George moved his hands to her body and felt every sacred curve. They began to make love in the warm water and the rhythms of their movements created ripples on the surface of the water. George wanted the moment to last forever. After some time they left the pool and lay naked on the blanket staring at the moon above. They sipped some wine and ate some crackers.

Before long they were embracing and making love again. George knew he was in love and he wanted to be with Aktal forever.

Mark had not closed his eyes for more than a few seconds when he recalled his dream. It played in his mind like a movie in fast forward. When he opened his eyes he realized he was now at the bottom. He stood up and left the smooth platform and stepped on to a polished dark blue marble patio. The patio was empty except for two round tables with chairs around them. One table was larger than the other and had more elaborate looking chairs. He guessed that the friends Aktal said would be there to greet him were either late or the whole thing was a complete lie. On the larger table there was a pitcher with glasses next to it and a platter of snacks similar to the ones that Aktal and Shala had served them earlier. He walked over to the larger table and then walked all the way around it. He then sat down and poured a glass of juice for himself. After he took a sip he called out, "Anyone here?"

From behind a rock sculpture two small men walked towards Mark. Mark could see immediately that they must be dwarves as their arms, hands and feet were large but their bodies small. When they got closer Mark's mouth dropped. The dwarves had one eye in the middle of their forehead! They both raised one hand up in the air as if to greet him and Mark instinctively raised his hand. As they came closer Mark could tell they were not Dwarves. Mr. Kyn had decided that Jacon and Kafta should be the first to greet the human just in case he went crazy or something. Mark didn't go crazy, he just sat dumbfounded because now he realized these were aliens.

Mark stared across the table at the two strange creatures and all his mind could think about was area 51 and Roswell, New Mexico. The aliens that people presumed to have crashed in Roswell had to be true. Aktal and Shala had to work for the US Government. But, why was she bringing him in on this? Mark was proud of the fact that he was not extremely shocked that he was sitting in front of two aliens but he was shocked as to why. He was having a hard time understanding why he was not completely freaking out. What did he have to do with any of this? Meanwhile, Jacon and Kafta occasionally chattered in some odd language and then would turn and smile at Mark. Mark could tell they were harmless, but if they could not communicate what was the point in him being here. If this was a Government operation where were the government officials? Did Aktal somehow know his affiliation with the CIA and was he being primed for some secret mission? Were these the same aliens that had landed in Roswell years ago or was this some ongoing collaboration with the Government and these aliens? He needed his questions answered but for now it was best he just sit and be quiet until something happened.

When Mr. Kyn and Borghx told Kafta and Jacon earlier that they should be the first ones to meet the new earthling they were pleased but a little apprehensive after watching his odd behavior on the ride down to their retreat. That is the reason they went and hid behind the sculpture. Now that they were sitting across from him they felt a bit more comfortable but both knew there English sounded very high pitched and odd so there was no point in saying anything to him until Mr. Kyn arrived. Mr. Kyn seemed to have mastered the language and its inflections much better than the others. It had been Mr. Kyn and Borghx whom had meet with Tom Whitecloud and the other Medicine Men that followed over the years. Jacon and Kafta preferred maintaining the plants in their retreat and working on various other projects. They considered themselves much higher on the scale of intelligence to the humans and saw little value in interacting with them. Mark could not tell but both Jacon and Kafta were now quite anxious that Mr. Kyn and Borghx were taking so long to arrive. Finally mark broke the ice and said, "My name is Mark Pullin." The two Marans looked at each other and then each grabbed a snack form the table and stuffed it in their mouths.

After they chewed and swallowed the food, Kafta spoke, "My name is Kafta and this is my friend Jacon. It is nice to meet you." Kafta spoke in a high pitched squeaky tone.

"Ok, well I can see you two are not from this planet. Did you come here when your spaceship crashed in Roswell?" Mark asked.

Kafta and Jacon looked at each other and then both shook their heads indicating "No." Both then grabbed a cup and poured themselves some juice.

Mark didn't know what to do or to say. Here he was in the middle of some underground cavern sitting with two little aliens that seemed to only care about eating and drinking. He was starting to feel extremely tired, lost, and confused. His main concern was if he would ever be able to get out of this place alive. Then Jacon stood up and walked to where Mark was sitting and reached out his large bony hand and touched Mark on his arm. The touch was warm, almost hot. Jacon contorted his face almost as if he was smiling then said, "You have a lot of fur on your arms."

Mark didn't know if he should laugh or cry. The whole scene seemed like he was in some late night "B" movie. He faked a smile and took a sip of his juice trying to think what he should do next. "Ok, where are you two from?"

This time Jacon answered, "We are from another Galaxy. Our planet is called Mara."

Mark noticed both of the creatures seemed to move a bit more slowly than he did. He didn't know if that was a biological thing or if they actually were fairly peaceful. Still he was on edge and remained very cautious. His mind raced a mile a minute trying to guess why Aktal and her sister were harboring these aliens. None of it made any logical sense to him. As he gazed around he could see the gardens were very well maintained. There seemed to be many varieties of plants he had never seen and some that were obviously genetically changed from common strains. He knew he had no chance of escaping so he leaned back in his chair and folded his hands waiting to see what would happen next. Jacon then continued talking, "We are very happy that you have come here to meet us. We have not met many humans. We have been here for many years and we miss our home planet. I am sure you understand the importance of us remaining hidden. Aktal believes that you are different than most humans and that we may be able to count on you as a friend."

Mark starred at the two aliens trying to discern if they were really aliens or some costumed hoax put together by the Government for some inexplicable reason. He concluded they were aliens. He had always believed aliens existed but never in his wildest dreams did he think he would be sitting in some secret underground chamber face to face with two of them. He still felt something wasn't right. There was chance Ernie and George were already dead and that he was going to be next. He looked around again and wondered if there was some way out of this mammoth underground cave. He concluded there had to be a way out other than the platform that just lowered him down from the barn. What he needed now was to buy himself time. "So why me? What makes you think you can trust me? We just came to introduce ourselves to our neighbors and now I end up here in front of you two. How do I know my two friends are safe? Why weren't my two friends allowed to come here also and meet you?"

Jacon and Kafta exchanged glances. Neither one of them was sure they were supposed to start answering all of the humans questions. They had hoped that Mr. Kyn and Borghx, whom were nearby observing would make their entry. Mr. Kyn had given them explicit instructions on how to behave but not on what to say. So, just as typical Marans would do, they both smiled in their own quirky way at the human and then proceeded to hand him a bunch of large grapes from the bowl on the table. Mark took the grapes, smiled back at them, and then plopped one in his mouth.

Then mark put the rest of the grapes back on the table and stood up. He was ready to make a run for it but for some reason his legs felt like lead so he sat back down.

Kafta saw the discontent on Marks face. "We have a few other friends that will be here very shortly and they will be able to answer all of your questions. The two of us are not what you would call the leaders so I hope you understand that it is better for us if we do not answer those questions now. If we get into any detailed discussions with you we may be in trouble. Plus, we are not very good at lengthy discussions. Our role with the crew entails more engineering and invention. Actually many of the plants you see around here are the result of our experiments with your native plant life."

The answer satisfied Mark so he relaxed. He also realized now that there would be more aliens showing up. He just hoped they could clarify the situation he was in.

Then out of the blue, Jacon adjusted his chair so as to make it face more towards Mark. He sat very upright and placed his hands on his small but strong thighs. He starred directly at Mark. He started to speak in somewhat of a different voice from what he had used earlier. His voice seemed to have a kind of echo to it. At first Mark thought he was not an alien at all but some kind of robot. What Mark did not realize is that Jacon was very nervous about what he was about to say. "My name is Jacon. I am a highly renowned scientist amongst my people from our planet. I want you to understand that I am not really that much different from you except for my appearance and of course various cultural aspects. I have worked almost my whole life for one man. His name is Mr. Kyn. He is the main reason we are here. He is by far the wealthiest person on our planet. His wealth far exceeds any Maran. He is also a very humble and nice person. I can say that because I am one of his closest friends. You will have the opportunity to meet him shortly and for that reason I am telling you a little about him. We have been on your planet for nearly thirty five years. We have remained in seclusion for most of that time. Only in the past ten years have we made friends with some Native Americans from this area. They are part of a council of Medicine Men from various local tribes. This may be hard for you to believe but the two sisters that you met are not humans. They are robots that I helped to build along with Mr. Kyn and another Alien that is not a Maran, named Borghx. Aktal and Shala act as our agents in your world. We made them to look and act like humans. They are highly advanced robots and have many qualities that we continually make advances with. We are all very fond of them and think of them as part of our team not as machines."

Mark was in shock, but at the same time all of his earlier suspicions came to light. He knew there was something odd about the two so called sisters. He also realized that these aliens were highly advanced, much further advanced technologically than anything he could ever imagine. Then Mark smiled thinking how George and Ernie were being entertained by two robots! He wondered to himself if they actually had real female parts but he dare not ask.

Jacon continued, "We are all very happy that you came here. Yes, of course, it was a random event, but then again the universe is one big random event. We never view random events as anything other than opportunities to take a step into the future. Mr. Kyn and Borghx will have many very important matters that they wish to discuss with you. The computers we have here told us almost everything we need to know about you except for your innermost beliefs. We know your involvement with your government and we also know how you are considered a rogue agent with your CIA. Your position is very rare and comes from your deep sense of morals and patriotism. Your government would never allow almost anyone to act in the capacity that you have. We also know the level of your intelligence is nearly off the charts for human intelligence. I am not sure what Aktal explained to you about our mission here if anything. What I can tell you is that we Marans evolved very differently than you humans. The alignments of our planets and various other circumstances helped us to realize that violence, aggression and war were not traits that would allow our people to survive as a species. Those traits have been virtually eliminated from our culture. Your planet is on a far different path and that is the reason we have traveled here. We are hoping through various means to provide a catalyst of change so your planet does not turn into a barren rock or become blown up from a thermo-nuclear war." Kafta was about ready to strangle Jacon because he was not supposed to talk so much and tell this human all about them, but he sat quiet because he knew Mr. Kyn and Borghx would be upset with Jacon later and that would be well worth his silence!

"Hold on a second, Jacon. Did I say your name correctly?" Mark politely interrupted. "Why may I ask are you telling me all of this? I am nobody important. If you have researched me as you say you have then you know that my position with the CIA is totally disposable. As far as they are concerned I do not even exist and if they choose to at any time they can just have me eliminated. Now, that is a choice I made a long time ago and I like working the way I do and they know I am one hundred percent a patriot. Not to say my country does not make mistakes, but I can say this much, I have been to a lot of different nations and by far the USA is the best! We take less bribes in our companies and governments in general. I am a fan of statistics and odds, so I choose the American odds. My bosses at the CIA are familiar with how I think and how I work so they have allowed me the freedom now to work the way I do. Fortunately, for now, there are not a lot of major pressing issues so I can take the time and start this fish farming project with my friends. Also if you looked at my background you should know my bosses will know I am here at your so called hidden underground retreat!" Mark knew that was not true but he had to make them think someone knew he was here and would come to rescue him if he needed to be rescued! "Now I go back to my question, why me?"

"No, no I don't think you understand. Mr. Kyn and Borghx are highly advanced. It is not just that they have read all of your files but they have also read your mind!" Jacon then felt a strong kick from Kafta and quickly shut up. Kafta decided it was now time for him to take over the conversations before Jacon went too far off on tangents that this earthling may have no ability to understand.

"Mr. Mark, my friend sometimes is very long winded and has a hard time explaining things. Let me take over the conversation from here." Kafta glared at Jacon and then left the thought alone. "There are many factors involved that can answer your question. It very much has to do with timing and rhythms. You see, we have perceived you to be an honest and devoted person. We find these to be very admirable qualities. My friend here, Jacon, revealed that we had investigated you. I must say that this was only something we did because you and your friends showed up unexpectedly at the ranch house. Our friend Borghx, whom you will meet shortly, is a very highly developed creature. He is not from our planet, or I should say planets because we Marans have migrated to all five planets that circle our sun. Borghx has the ability to read both your mind and what you would call, soul. He and our leader, Mr. Kyn, decided that you and your two friends may, in the future, become very helpful to our mission here on your planet. In turn we would offer to teach and to show you many wonderful new technologies. I really should not be telling you all of this because Mr. Kyn told me to wait until he and Borghx arrived so that they could explain more to you but I had to stop Jacon from babbling his mouth off. As you can see, I am a more elegant speaker." This time Jacon gave Kafta a hard kick under the table, then they both laughed. When Mark heard them laugh he wanted to laugh also because these two aliens were funny characters. It made him realize that individuality was well and alive in the Universe. He didn't laugh, but he did sort of smile!

"Ok, let's just slow down and take everything here one step at a time. I know from being in the CIA about the Roswell incident. Are you two the same type of aliens as those?" Both Jacon and Kafta shook their heads indicating no. "How many Aliens of your type have visited this planet in the past? Mark asked.

Kafta replied, "We are the first ones. We understand in the past there have been a variety of different aliens that have visited this planet throughout its history. Yes, some of the rumors you may have heard of about the Incas, Easter Island, and the Egyptians are true. The harsh reality is that your species, humans that is, are a very aggressive and violent type of people. I am sure you know that just from studying your history. Those traits are not good traits for a species to continue to thrive on a planet. In all honesty at the rate your species is going it will not survive. Your ecosystem is being destroyed because of a human ego based in Religion and Capitalism that puts humans above all other creatures. The petroleum industry is destroying the very air that you breathe. There are so many other more efficient means of providing energy but most all of them are squished by the large oil companies in the name of profit. We understand a majority of humans know all of this but the way your political systems are set up the people do not have the power to change any of it. The aliens that visited your planet in the past saw immediately what the future held for such an aggressive species and decided it was not a place they wanted to cohabit with humans."

Mark nodded his head up and down. It was almost exactly as he had thought. He had almost the same conversation with George in the past. Reality was what it was and how it would ever change was beyond him. "Ok, well that is very interesting but I still have no idea why I am here and what I can do to help if anything." Jacon and Kafta stared at each other thinking the exact same thing. If this is one of the more intelligent humans then the human species is doomed for sure!

"I think Borghx and Mr. Kyn will answer that question when they talk with you." Kafta knew he most likely had already talked too much. It was nice that Borghx and Mr. Kyn had allowed himself and Jacon to meet the new earthling first but now was not the time to go into the kind of details this earthling was seeking. And probably would never understand anyway.

"Look, I have no idea how my friends and I can be of any help to any of you. We have no power or influence in our society. We are just three normal guys. I actually have no idea what George and Ernie are doing right now, but I am fairly certain they are letting some of their inhibitions go wild. Yes, we humans are animals. Some of us know that and some of us don't. The point I am making is that we are now at a point of no return. You have met me and I have met you. In the CIA that would mean someone is going to have to probably die. That is not a feeling I like to have. Worse is the fact that I have no clue if you are even really aliens. For all I know you could be sophisticated actors dressed up and putting on a good act. So why don't we get to the point in the evening now where I meet your leaders. Yes, as they say in the movies, take me to your leader!" Then Mark laughed for the first time. The whole situation was beyond ridiculous and bizarre. Here he was in some hidden underground chamber, that surly no humans could have made, with two aliens. They had one big eye in their forehead and they were diminutive in size. Their voices sounded like children but they spoke perfect English. They were dressed in plain American style clothes only the shoes they wore were more like those of a man twice their sized. Their skin had a greyish tone to it. Their mouths were very small compared to their size and their noses were only small bumps on their face with two small holes. It was all too weird, too late, and something still did not seem right. Mark leaned back in his chair and took a small piece of the tasty fruit and plucked it in his mouth. No one spoke for a minute or so. Mark looked around and then it really dawned on him that he was basically a prisoner but these two aliens were treating him like a guest. There was no escape and he knew it so he resigned himself to just play along and whatever the conclusion would be. He looked at his watch and saw it was well after 2:00 am! He was trying to think what to say next but after he had gazed at his watch he started to feel tired, or maybe the fruits were having a tranquilizing effect on him. He looked back and forth at the two strange creatures with one eye in the center of their head and then he blinked his own eyes rapidly just to be sure he was not dreaming. "Ok, so when do I get to meet the other two that you mentioned?"

Jacon was wondering that very question himself. Why had Mr. Kyn and Borghx left them alone with this persistent human for so long? Mr. Kyn had said he would be along shortly but that "shortly" was becoming a long time for Jacon. Jacon glanced at Kafta before he responded and he could tell Kafta was thinking the same as him. "Oh, they will be here shortly!" It was more of a hope than an answer. Mark put another piece of the tasty fruit in his mouth.

As it has been said a million times, "Back at the Ranch House." Ernie was sound asleep in a rapturous inebriated bliss. Shala left him to sleep and reported to Mr. Kyn and Borghx. When Shala told them that Ernie would never be of much value to them both Borghx and Mr. Kyn found that to be an odd statement from the robot they had built. They were still planning what to do with the humans and what to do if the next day the Council of Medicine Men decided to go public with their ongoing relationship with them. They sent Shala to work preparing the Intergalactic Vehicle as Jacon and Kafta were now busy entertaining the human, Mark. They were coming to the conclusion that the three friends could serve an important purpose for them. It was time to meet the one called Mark.

Borghx and Mr. Kyn were having a lengthy conversation trying to sort out the details of their plans and other contingency plans. Borghx was fairly certain that the Council of Medicine Men would decide to expose them, whereas, Mr. Kyn felt more confident that Tom Whitecloud would be able to convince them not to expose them. This was really one of the first times that either Borghx or Mr. Kyn could recall that they had such a starkly different viewpoint.

Both Mr. Kyn and Borghx had learned quite a bit about the three humans by observing them. They did agree that they may be helpful to them in the future but exactly how they were not exactly sure.

At last Mark felt somewhat more relaxed. He had been using deductive reasoning to analyze his situation. He had concluded that this was obviously not some kind of hoax. These were real aliens and they were a lot more intelligent than he was. What he could not put his finger on even though they had offered him an explanation, was, what their real mission was. Mark decided he had no choice than to just play along with them and try to see behind the words. He knew at this point he was not in control of his future but the aliens were, so he figured he might as well enjoy the moment. He started to ask questions and to his surprise they answered his questions. Since Mark had worked in the government for the majority of his life he asked the one question he had always wondered about. "Will this country, I mean my country, you know the United States of America continue to be a World Leader among Nations and if so for how long?

This time Jacon jumped to answer. "Yes, absolutely. From all the projections we have run this country will dominate the World for hundreds of years, at least until your Planet can unite under one form of government. Unlike what you or others may believe as to the reason for this, the reason is quite different, yet quite logical. Your country has all the majority of resources, waterways, natural borders to protect it, and an ideology that is inclusive rather than divisive. Since your government came up with guidelines for trade from the Bretton Woods conference, after WWII, the rest of your planets countries have made great progress under the protection of your Military, especially your Navy. Nothing is guaranteed of course, but, if the your country and the Soviet Union can work out a Nuclear disarmament agreement sometime in the near future then your Planet has a bright future, if not, then it is doomed."

Mark shook his head slowly and tried to absorb what he had heard. He wanted the best for his planet as he guessed most people did, but, it was a different feeling hearing it from an alien.

Now Mark started to ask more questions and they were fired at the aliens in droves, one after another. He wanted to know everything about them and where they came from. When he opened his eyes he then realized he had said nothing. They had been communicating without words. He knew he was exhausted and he knew he was in a situation that had no point of reference to any previous experience, so it was now difficult for him to formulate his thoughts. He opened his eyes, then closed his eyes, then started to blink rapidly as if somehow he could make the image of the two aliens with their large one eye in their forehead come into focus and become two eyes like normal people, but it did not work. "When do I meet your leaders?" He at last blurted out. He then instantly realized he sounded like some moron in a B rated movie, so he laughed. It was deep laugh. Jacon and Kafta turned and looked at each other thinking to themselves how strange the earthlings were.

"Yes, they will be here soon." Kafta replied once Mark stopped laughing.

Mark had always been unpredictable and in a way that made him a perfect inside man for the CIA, but it also made him a liability. Both sides knew it but there was not much Mark could do to control that part of his genius. It sort of had a life of its own. Some people would say he had multiple personalities and maybe he did but for Mark all that mattered was the moment. Life was about the present and how he moved from the present towards the future. So, for him, weather he had different opinions, or different personalities really made little difference as long as he kept moving forward.

Jacon reached out and took some of the cactus fruit from the table and then stepped towards Mark and offered it to him. Maybe that is what triggered the reaction in Mark or maybe it just had been too much wine and one heck of a long night. Mark had already ate too much of the fruit and part of his brain was telling him that the fruit had some kind of psychotropic affect (it actually did), either way, his mind suddenly raced back to his two friends. Maybe they were already dead and in the process of being dissected by these aliens! Mark raised his eyebrows at the thought of it and slapped the out stretched hand of Jacon holding the fruit away from him. Jacon cowered off to a corner of the patio like a scared child. Mark was getting angry now. He could feel his palms start to sweat and his heart start to beat faster. He recognized the signs and tried to take a few deep breaths but that did not help much. He was at the point of making a run for it. The problem was he didn't know where to run. Just at that moment off to his left from a behind a long partition wall Mr. Kyn and Borghx appeared. They casually strolled to the table and seated themselves across the table from Mark. Mr. Kyn waved his hand and Kafta left the table. Kafta and Jacon left the patio area in the same direction from where Mr. Kyn had arrived. Mark sat dumbfounded at the sight of Borghx. It was strange enough that the other aliens were small and had the one big eye in the center of their head but this other one was very different. Borghx had two dark eyes and sort of looked like what aliens had been portrayed like in all the movies with the big head but up close Mark could see that Borghx's skin was sort of a translucent pale blue color and it almost made him appear as if you could see through his skin but you couldn't. Borghx started to speak and this time Mark realized that the alien was not really speaking but communicating with his mind. Mark was fine with it. He had no choice.

Borghx started the communication, "Forgive us for not coming sooner but Mr. Kyn and I had some very important matters to discuss before we could speak with you. Your friends are safe and they are both actually sleeping now. From this point on we will communicate with you in your language and not with telepathy. We want to make sure that we all fully understand each other." Mark blinked and realized he had actually been sitting with his eyes closed.

Mark nodded his head and said, "Yes, let's use words now." Mr. Kyn smiled at Mark and Mark smiled back at him.

Borghx continued speaking but now the words came out of his small crooked mouth in a buttery monotone. "We have reached a decision. That is, Mr. Kyn and I have reached a decision. We want to discuss this decision with you before we implement a plan. I know to you this seems very strange and confusing as to how you have become involved in our affairs. From the background check we ran on you we are aware that you have studied many religions and philosophies, so from your point of view you can look at our meeting not just as a matter of fate, but as a matter of fate with a higher overall purpose. Our paths have crossed for a reason that is beyond mortal understanding. I hope you will absorb what we have to say with an open mind and then feel free to add your own input."

Mr. Kyn sat very still and focused his attention totally on Borghx as he continued to speak. "Mark, we need to ask for your help. Even though there are other humans that know we are on this planet it is not wise for us to seek their assistance at this time or in this particular situation. I am referring to members of a council of Medicine Men that is composed of the leaders of many of the Southwest Indian tribes. There a number of these men that are aware of our existence here and a few that have actually come here to visit us. Later today they are having an annual meeting and we are aware that they will discuss the prospect of them revealing us to the United Nations in the very near future. Mr. Kyn and I have come to the conclusion that if this happens we most likely become nothing more than prisoners on this planet and all that we know and that we have will be dissected for the benefit of a few and not for what our mission was in coming to this planet. We feel this is not the right time for us to be revealed or exposed. We know that our technologies would most likely be used by the more powerful nations to take advantage of the weaker nations. This is precociously why we have traveled here so as to prevent those type of actions from happening." Borghx paused and let Mark absorb all that he had heard.

Mark no longer felt tired he felt focused but dreamy at the same time. He didn't understand at all why it was he and his two friends that had been pulled into such a bizarre situation. He wanted nothing to do with aliens, heck, he had been trying to distance himself from the CIA over the past few years and this fish farming project was just part of that transition. Mark put his hand up in the air as if to ask for a break. He stared down at the marble floor for a few seconds then looked first at Mr. Kyn then at Borghx. "Ok, let's step back for a second. First, there are plenty of humans that believe in aliens so if you were revealed to the public it would probably not make that big of an impact on anyone. Plus, the fact that you become so called public figures would in a way actually insulate you and your knowledge from being abused by any one government. Lastly, the fact that it is a council of Indian leaders that are the ones to reveal you to the public would in a way lend even more value to the whole process because the public views Medicine Men as spiritual leaders. So overall, I would say that maybe you two are wrong and that the Medicine Men are a bit wiser in this case."

Borghx and Mr. Kyn stared intensely at Mark. Borghx's eyes seemed to light up a bit and actually maybe began to glow. Borghx knew that this human was highly intelligent and also had a mind of his own but he did not expect him to throw a wrench in the plans that he and Mr. Kyn had been talking about for the last few hours. "The problem is that your planet is embroiled now in the results of poor planning and materialistic goals. Greed, quests for power and domination, and the overall lack of any regards for the natural eco systems are now just beginning to show their effects. Over the next few centuries this planet could get much worse and fall into chaos. I am sure that for you and for many others the solution to this predictable outcome is very far off and lost in a quagmire of bureaucracy. Trust me, no matter what is done or not done the bureaucracy is not going to improve. We are here to offer solid and very real solutions that will put your planet on track to become a planet that can take the next step towards migrations into your solar system and then beyond. But, if your home planet becomes a barren rock due to war or poor management then your human species will become yet another extinct species. We can provide knowledge of new energy technologies, new types of alloys and materials, advanced robotics, and complete plans for developing intergalactic space vehicles. Our vehicle is stored here underground. This can all be implemented within thirty years or less. Our knowledge along with a focused and humanistic plan can assure that your planet will become a paradise for humans. We strongly believe that if the Council decides to reveal us to the public at this time then the first priority of your government would be to shelf all of the technologies we have and then selectively use them to strengthen your military. We both know the United States Military is the strongest on the planet and weather the technologies we have is used to strengthen them or not the United States Military will remain strong for any foreseeable future. The problem is time. How long do you want your planet to be embroiled in small regional conflicts and continued degradation of the natural eco-systems? Mr. Kyn and I have held many lengthy discussions over these topics and even though we made the decision for the Council to be our first point of contact into your culture we now believe we made a mistake in doing that because they are at this moment deciding on their own our fate and the fate of your planet. We are uncertain now when will be the correct time to push forward with plans to reveal ourselves to your people if at all now. Still we have a strong will to accomplish the mission we set out on when we traveled here. You may call it "Fate", that we have met now or you may think of it as the natural order of progression towards saving your people from an eventual fate of annihilation. The main issue right now is that we are here and we are communication with you. We know you are the leader of your two friends and we needed to speak with you first before we moved forward with any of our plans. That is why we are here now talking with you. Will you help us if we need your help?"

Mark sat dumbfounded and started back and forth between Mr. Kyn and Borghx. He felt like he was being put on the spot and worse it was nearly morning, he was tired, and he was being asked to help the aliens he had just met! He wanted to be serious but the situation was just too strange for him to be serious. How in the world did he go from starting a fish farming project with his two friends to now being asked by two aliens if he would help them to save his planet! Mark didn't know what to say but he guessed it really did not matter too much what he said so he just nodded his head and replied, "Sure, I can help you, I guess."

Borghx and Mr. Kyn seemed to breathe a long sigh of relief, though it had been their full expectation that the Earthling would agree with them. It was morning now and Tom Whitecloud would be meeting with the other members of the council in a few hours. They had to prepare. Time was moving too quickly now. Borghx nodded his head as he stared at Mark as if to show he knew that Mark would agree to help them, then he continued, "We are both very pleased that you and your friends will help us. The meeting will take place with the council members in a few hours. We fully expect them to vote and approve their plan to take us to the United Nations later in the month. We have decided we must leave here without them knowing. We have contemplated returning to Mara and the other Marans on this journey would be very happy if we did that, but now that we can count on you and your friends we are going to remain on your planet awhile longer.

"So how can I help you gentleman!" Mark said in a humorous tone. "I mean I don't want to sound flippant but as you can see I am but a lowly human on the evolutionary scale!"

Borghx looked at Mr. Kyn and nodded his head as a sign that Mr. Kyn should take it from here. Mr. Kyn smiled as if to acknowledge the human's humor even though he did not find what he had said as funny. "As Borghx stated it is highly likely we are going to have to leave here in the next few hours. We will leave our intergalactic vehicle hidden here in this underground retreat. Our only other option is to destroy it and we do not want to do that, but if we need to we will. We believe if we seal off this chamber sufficiently even the few Medicine Men that have been here will not be able to point any authorities to the exact hiding location. We can return at some later date and retrieve the vehicle. We have calculated that if for some reason the vehicle is destroyed or captured that it will take us approximately 15 years to build another one and we would need access to a large manufacturing firm. The problem now is that we just do not have enough time to move it to another location. This is where you and your two friends can be of aid to us for now. From our research we know you own a large property in Kern County of California. We have looked at all of the topography maps for your property and we believe this would be a good area for us to go to and reside for the near future."

"You seem to know a lot about all of us and I am guessing this is not just from looking at intelligence reports that you obviously got from hacking government sites. Mark stated so that he could show them that even though he may not be on their level of intelligence he still had a could hold on reason.

"Yes, we do." Mr. Kyn replied.

"Ok, I guess I will just leave it at that" Mark replied.

Mr. Kyn continued, "Essentially this is a situation that we did not predict or prepare for. We want to hide out at your place in Kern County at least temporarily and maybe permanently. How we are going to get there and other details will have to be worked out once we know more of what happens at the meeting with the council today. I think your commitment to helping us will work out well for us and for you and your friends. It may be a bit of an unpredictable adventure but I think that is something that we all thrive on! We will be able to accomplish great things with your help. History may look back on you and your friends as true visionaries."

Mark was dazed, tired, and still a bit wary that any of this was real. He bit his lower lip. He was awake and not dreaming. He knew his life would never be anywhere near normal from this point on.

Borghx had closed his eyes and seemed to be in a meditative state of mind. He opened his eyes and then spoke. "It is confirmed now, the Medicine Men will vote to reveal us at the meeting. They want to introduce us at a meeting with the United Nations. Tom Whitecloud has confirmed how they will vote from talking with some of the members. We must leave here by noon." Mr. Kyn and Borghx stood up and scurried off behind the large partition leaving Mark sitting alone at the table. Mark looked at his watch and saw it was 7:00 am. He had no idea what he needed to do so he reached over and took a few of the remaining pieces of cactus fruit and plopped them in his mouth. He lay down on his back on the cold marble patio and closed his eyes.

He fell asleep within seconds. He started to dream about his Grandfather who had died ten years earlier. They were planting apple trees on a clear sunny day.

Jacon sat quietly behind a few trees as Mr. Kyn had instructed him to do. He watched Mark as he slept. Less than an hour later Jacon gently woke Mark up and took him back up to the barn. He told Mark to go to the Ranch House where he would find his two friends, eat some food, and then return to the barn in an hour.

As Mark entered the house he could smell the breakfast that Aktal and Shala were cooking in the kitchen. Ernie and George were sitting in the breakfast nook talking when Mark came in the front door. "Hey stranger, come have some coffee" said George as he noticed Mark come through the front door.

Mark sat at the table with his two friends and poured himself a cup of coffee. "How are you guy's doing?" Mark asked as he put some cream in his coffee.

Ernie was the first to respond, "I am doing great! I had a fantastic night!" He threw a glance at George who blushed and fumbled with his coffee cup. At that moment Aktal sauntered in from the kitchen carrying a hot tray of corn muffins which she set down on the table. She smiled at Mark and then gave George a little kiss on his cheek which made him blush even more. Ernie burst out laughing. This was the happiest Mark had seen Ernie in a long time. "Mark, I had a great night. You just can't imagine what Shala is like. She is out of this world!"

Now Mark laughed and shook his head. "I bet she is!" He replied not knowing if either Ernie or George had any idea that the two women they had spent the night with were robots! Mark exchanged glances with Aktal. Aktal left then returned with Shala and more food which they set on the table. George kept his head down but he looked up when Aktal returned. Ernie winked at Mark like he knew exactly what was going on. They ate and conversed about the food and how nice of a day it was going to be. When Mark finished his food he looked at his watch and saw it was near 8:00 am and that meant it was time to go back to the barn. Aktal saw Mark looking at his watch and said out loud, "Don't worry, we have put it off until 8:30 am."

"Put off what?" George asked. Now Mark knew that George was clueless. Mark could tell Ernie knew something and was fine with whatever he knew but George was lost in a world of rapture. George really had fallen head over hills for Aktal.

Mark decided since they had a bit more time now that he had better be the one to explain things to George and not Aktal. "Well George I can see you had a very enjoyable time last night." Shala kicked Mark under the table and Mark knew exactly why. She did not want Mark to tell George that the two women were robots. Mark had guessed as much but he motioned with his eyes to both Aktal and Shala that he understood. "We are meeting some people at 8:30 am here. Basically, I have offered our assistance to these tow lovely ladies. They need our help. I just need you guys to trust me on this one and not worry too much about anything. It has nothing to do with our fish farming project."

"You are the boss!" George replied. Ernie excused himself and went to the bathroom.

Shala motioned for Mark to go to the kitchen with her. So the two of them stood up and walked into the kitchen. Ernie came into the kitchen just about the same time and was carrying a shotgun he had acquired from the bedroom.

Shala took the two of them out to the back porch. "Things are moving quickly now. Ernie knows everything that is going on but he has not met the others yet. We are going to send Aktal and George up to Santa Fe where the meeting is going on. They can take our car but when they get there we want them to buy a new van, one with no windows."

Mark looked at Ernie holding the rifle, "Ernie, do you really think you will need that?"

"You never know." Ernie replied.

"Shala is that OK with the Mr. Kyn and the others?"

"Yes, of course, they know Ernie only wants to be protective." Shala replied.

"Look, the only reason I believe Shala's story, that she has friends that are aliens whom need our help, is because she showed me that she is a robot! When she showed me, you know me, I tried to take her out." Ernie laughed, "Well she kicked my ass pretty fast! Then we actually had sex again!" Ernie laughed louder and Mark could see that Ernie was more than ready for whatever adventure lay ahead. Ernie was back to being the old Ernie.

Aktal was at the dining table telling George about their trip to Santa Fe for the day. George was all for it. He was totally bitten by the love bug. When the others returned to the dining room, George excitedly told them that he and Aktal were going to drive to Santa Fe for the day. They told George and Aktal that it was a good idea. Before they headed out Aktal winked at Mark. Mark and Ernie felt a bit guilty about not letting George in on everything that was going on but at this point since George was so far lost in his world of infatuation it most likely would just be a distraction if George knew too much. After George and Shala left the others headed back to the barn. Now Ernie would be able to meet the aliens. Ernie kept the shotgun next to his side.

Once below, Shala took Ernie to meet Kafta and Jacon. Ernie laughed the first time he saw them. The one eye in the center of their bulging heads was just too funny. Now Ernie felt like he was in the middle of a cartoon adventure. He still couldn't get over how human like Shala was but he wanted his own robot no matter what happened in the long run. These aliens had the right idea he kept telling himself. When they sat down and talked Ernie related his tale about the spaceship he saw years ago in Vietnam. They were all amazed at the coincidence when it was revealed that the spaceship Ernie saw was them leaving their underground cavern in Cambodia and coming to New Mexico. Ernie called it "Fate", the aliens just smiled.

After Mark conferred with Mr. Kyn and Borghx he brought them to meet Ernie. Ernie was very impressed with Borghx. Later when he was alone with Mark he told Mark that Borghx did not have long to live. Mark asked Ernie why and Ernie said, "It is just a feeling."

The plans had been made. Ernie and George left the underground retreat and Shala drove them back to the ranch they had purchased for their fish farming project so they could pack their belongings and rest.

It was nearly 11:00 when Aktal and George were nearing the outskirts of Santa Fe. It had been arranged long before that Aktal would pick up Tom Whitecloud in the plaza sometime after noon. Aktal stopped the car at a rest stop so George could use the bathroom. When he returned she sat on the driver's side and smiled at him holding a baseball size rock. "Look George, isn't this an interesting rock I found?" She handed the rock to George and he examined it.

"Yeah it is an interesting rock. It seems to have some type of dark blue crystal imbedded in it and it is pretty heavy." George said as he handed the rock back to her.

"Yes, I found it outside. The dark blue is Lapis Lazuli." Aktal said as she stared at the rock.

"Well it is a nice rock. We better get going." George said as he stared at Aktal. He still couldn't imagine how such a beautiful creature had fallen so hard for him. He was ready to give up everything to be with her.

"Watch this." Aktal said. She held the rock in the palm of her hand and then slowly squeezed her fingers around the rock. Then in one quick motion she crushed the rock. It broke up into small pieces as George watched in shock. His jaw dropped.

"What was that? Was that a trick? How did you do that?"

Suddenly George felt very small. He felt like he was the rock and he was being crushed.

Aktal smiled threw the crushed rock out of the window then leaned over and kissed George on the lips. For the first time George did not kiss back, he sat like a frozen half-finished marble statue. Aktal knew what he was feeling. She turned the ignition on and headed out to the highway. George kept staring at her. Once they were on the highway again and George's heartrate had calmed down a bit Aktal began to explain everything to George. She told him about her friends that were aliens. She spoke slowly and answered George's questions with short but calculated answers so as to not allow him to get overly worried or excited. When she came to the part about her being a robot with artificial intelligence George closed his eyes. At first Aktal thought he was going to feint, but then she could see he was just trying to understand what he was being told on a deeper level. What she didn't expect after he sat silent for a few minutes were his first words.

George opened his eyes and then reached out and put his hand on Aktal's shoulder as she drove down the highway. He just let his arm rest there for a while as if the gesture would somehow convey his thoughts. He kept opening his mouth like he wanted to say something then he would close his mouth and sit silent. This went on for a good five minutes and Aktal stayed mute. Then George took his hand off of her shoulder and cleaned his thick glasses with his shirt. He didn't know what to think, but he knew he liked Aktal even if she was not human. That very thought made him question his view of what was real and what was not real. Maybe this was just some kind of joke. Maybe he was dreaming. At last he stuck with the thought that there was something very odd going on and he was not in control of it at all. He suddenly felt like a child. He wanted to weep, but tears would not come. He sat dazed as Aktal continued to drive. After a few minutes it dawned on him that he was in love with an alien or a robot. He concluded he was just a pawn in some grand scheme and so were his two friends. He looked up and stared at Aktal as she drove trying to see what made her a robot or alien. He couldn't see anything. She had to be human. Then he recalled the events of the night before. He reached over and put his hand on her thigh and felt her warm skin beneath her jeans. Aktal pulled the car off the road onto a side road. They kissed and made love once again. Now George was convinced she was human not a robot. The story she told had to have been a farce; a sick joke. George decided he needed to keep quiet and play along with whatever was going on. They continued on to Santa Fe and Aktal dropped George off at a Ford dealership, handed him an envelope stuffed with cash and told him to purchase a new van. George did as he was told and Aktal headed to where the Medicine men were meeting near the town center.

Less than an hour later Aktal returned with Tom Whitecloud in her car and introduced him to George. She told George to drive back to Socorro and meet with his friends.

Chapter 12
Accelerating Rhythms

When George pulled up with the new Van he was exhausted. It was near 1:00 pm. He had made a wrong turn in Albuquerque and had been lost for a while. Everyone was wondering what had happened to him because he never called them. He was hot and mentally at the end of his wits. He had no idea what was real and what was a fantasy. He felt like he had lived a month in 24 hours. Ernie and Mark greeted him at the front door and breathed a sigh of relief that he was safe.

"Hey, you made it back! Nice van!" Ernie said standing on the front porch as George exited the van.

"Yeah, I made it back all right, now I need you guys to tell me what the heck is going on?"

They went inside and sat down in the kitchen where there was a big pitcher of ice tea waiting. George downed two glasses and then leaned back in his chair. Mark brought some turkey sandwiches he had made earlier and put them on the table. "Look George, I know this past 24 hours has been completely bizarre! It has been that way for all of us. Maybe we don't really know what is happening but one thing is for sure, the two sisters are robots made by aliens. Ernie and I have met the aliens and we have given them our word that we would help them."

"Well I knew all of that because I figured out Aktal was not human." Actually George was fibbing because he was very confused and had to pretend in front of his friends that he had not fallen in love with a robot! "So what are they like?" Asked George?

"Little short dudes with one eye in the center of their head. Then there is another one that is tall and looks like something out of a movie, but, he has two eyes." Ernie said with a smile. "I am going to go get some rest. It was a long night. You guys wake me up when something happens."

"Yeah, me too, I need to shower and rest. Mark, you can let us know what happens." George replied.

"That's fine, you two rest, leave me here to watch out for things. We all just have to act normal until they get in touch with us again." Mark said as he finished his sandwich.

"Act normal? What does that mean? You work for the CIA! Don't you think we should inform someone what is going on here? Have both of you lost your minds?"

"Calm down, George. I think we have everything under control. We just need to lay low and I am sure everything will work out. I am not contacting anyone. If I did I can guarantee you all of us would be dead in a very short amount of time. This is serious business. We all believed that aliens were real. So, it just so happens we stumbled onto some! There is nothing any of us can do at this point. Plus, I do believe they have good intentions. Now go lay down and rest. You look exhausted."

Not more than ten minutes later Shala came in the front door. She asked Mark where the others were and he told them they were resting. She motioned for Mark to follow her outside where they sat down on some rocks under a shade tree. "Everything is moving very fast now. Aktal has returned to our ranch with Tom Whitecloud. Mr. Kyn and Borghx have confirmed their plans. None of us know how much time we all really have, but we know we need to start acting fairly quickly now. We definitely are going to need your help."

"Well, I promised to help last night and I am man of my word. The other two are willing to help also." Mark replied as he admired how lovely Shala looked sitting under the tree next to him. It was hard to imagine that she was not really human.

"At 5:00 pm today our ranch is going to explode. They are setting the explosives now. We have decided that George will drive us to your property in Kern County in the new van. We know it is a 12 hour drive but we believe because of George's feelings towards Aktal that he will be able to handle it. Plus he has the best driving record of the three of you! You and I will fly to your place on your private plane so we can get there ahead of them. I will help you to get things set up for their stay there. Aktal will go with George in the van. They want Ernie to stay here at your place and wait for a few days before he leaves. There is a good chance that some authorities will ask him questions. " Shala said.

"I guess George is the best driver." Mark replied with a smile. "You said you are going to blow up your ranch house? Why?"

"Mr. Kyn and Borghx think it will the best cover we can have for disappearing. Aktal and I both have IDs so it may not make much difference, but at least if anyone comes around, there will be nothing left but ashes." Shala said.

"From what we have gathered, from Tom Whitecloud who is with Mr. Kyn and Borghx now, is that there are a small group of the Council Leaders that want to have a news conference as soon as possible. We are not sure when this would take place but it could be at any time so we have to move quickly." Shala continued as Mark tried to focus on her words and not how lovely she looked.

Now he knew why both George and Ernie were so taken by the two robot sisters. They had a way of making you do what they wanted you to do and to not even question it. He could tell now that this was all very serious. The aliens did not want to be exposed to the public so they had no choice but to either leave the planet or find some way to hide out for a while. Mark just wanted to know how long "for a while" would be but he knew no one was going to tell him that so there was no point in asking that question for now at least. This was turning into a fiasco far beyond what he had imagined. If they were going to blow up the place and that meant their so called space vehicle would be blown up also and then they would be stranded. There was no way he could keep them on his property. That was just insane!

Shala told Mark he should go inside and wake up George and Ernie so that he could explain the plans to them. Then he and George could head over to the ranch house so that George could meet Mr. Kyn and the others before they started the drive to Kern County, California. She then ran off like a deer back to her house. When Mark saw how fast she ran he knew for sure she was a robot. He felt like he was caught up in some bizarre movie he had seen on TV years ago but he couldn't recall the movie.

Mark went inside and woke up Ernie. George was just asleep on the couch and Mark wanted to let him rest knowing he would have to do most of the driving but he woke him up anyway. He gathered his friends back in the kitchen and told them the plans. When Ernie knew he was being left behind, to so to speak guard the fort, he walked back into the bedroom and grabbed his shotgun. "I think I will keep this baby close to me for the next few days. How long do you think before I am able to get out of here?" He asked Mark.

"I am not sure. I believe not too long. I will call you and tell you a code sentence. How about "It is time to buy the fish", that will mean you can go back to LA then I will hook up with you there." Mark said.

"Ok, sounds like I am back in Special Ops with the military, only we would have better codes!" Ernie had a little smile when he said it and both George and Mark laughed. They all liked the idea of some adventure, even if it was with aliens!

Mark drove the rental car to the airport where he would wait for Shala and George drove the van with Shala to Aktal's place where he was going to meet the aliens for the first time. Ernie remained behind. He sat down in the reclining sofa chair with the shotgun by his side and decided to take a nap.

Ivan Petrosky never gave up until he had answers. "Fish farm my ass!" He kept saying out loud as he drove his rental car from the airport in Albuquerque towards the three friend's new property. He was going to find out what they were up to for sure this time.

The council of Medicine Men were calling a press conference. Santa Fe was a fairly large city in New Mexico. It was known mostly as a wealthier area that housed a lot of artists. For the council to call a press conference in the downtown Hilton hotel seemed odd to the few press people that were in town. The Council's annual meeting rarely had any news that came out of it and this was the first time they had ever called a press conference after their annual meeting. A few of the local media people called their offices in Albuquerque and Phoenix. Rumor got around that the major tribes in the area had some announcement that was going to be news to the Federal Government in regards to the relationship which the tribes had with the Government. The press conference was now underway.

There were only a handful of reporters in the conference room of the hotel in Santa Fe when the news conference began. Four Medicine Men from the Council sat behind a folding table with a microphone in front of them. Only the Zuni leader was in his traditional cloths, the others, one from the Navajo Nation, and two from Pueblo Nations were dressed in casual clothing. There were some local people and some guests from the hotel that wandered in out of curiosity. All together there were maybe fifty people in the room in total. Tom Whitecloud was nearly back in Socorro by time the new conference took place. Mr. Kyn and Borghx were quickly making plans for their escape. Unexpectedly one of the Medicine Men that had previously met with the aliens had taken some secret photographs of Mr. Kyn Borghx and all the others. When they arrived at the part of Aktal and Shala being robots of the aliens that had been made in the likeness of two human women the reporters and everyone else in the room laughed. Someone yelled out that the Indian Council members were high on their own peyote! It was embarrassing for the council members but they forged ahead with the news conference and explained how they would be bringing some of the aliens with them to New York for the United Nations annual meeting of Indigenous Peoples the following month. After the new conference a few of the reporters asked the whereabouts of the Aliens, but the Medicine Men refused to give out the location. Copies were made of the photographs and handed out to the reporters and others in the room.

There was laughter and questions. Many thought the photos were fake. Some reporters hounded the Medicine men with more questions but the Medicine men had no intentions of sticking around and once they answered a few of the questions they hurried towards the cars that were waiting for them outside to take them back to their respective reservations. Back inside the room one of the reporters that was originally from a small town near Socorro recognized the hills in the background of one of the photos. He knew immediately that was the old Garcia ranch. He told a few of his reporter friends and they decided to make the drive and check it out. It was a two and a half hour drive.

Ernie had fallen asleep with the shotgun in his lap on the recliner. The sound of helicopters outside woke him up. He looked at his watch and it was a little after 6:00 pm. At first he thought he was back in Vietnam, but soon enough he came out of the foggy sleep and realized he was alone in a ranch house.

The Aliens along with Aktal and George were now driving in a brand new white van. They were heading to California. The drive would take all of 12 hours. Aktal was letting George do the first leg of driving so that he would feel like he was in charge. In actuality George was still exhausted and Aktal knew she would have to take over at any time.

Ivan was now heading towards the ranch house outside of town. The reporters that had decided to check out the area the one reporter recognized as the ranch from the photo.

Mark and Shala had just taken off in Mark's private plane to head back to Los Angeles.

The Military was setting up a perimeter around the ranch.

A few large black crows sat in a tree watching all the commotion.

Tom Whitecloud was sitting on a hill overlooking the ranch house watching the crows as they scurried about in the tree below him. Tom saw four large black helicopters on the horizon heading for the ranch house. Tom started weeping. He had done all he could to convince the other members of the council from making the decision they had. He was overruled and he felt it was mainly because all of them were older than him.

At exactly 5:45 pm there was a tremendous explosion. Tom could see the explosion started from the underground cavern and then puffed up into the air and when the dust settled the ranch house had fell into a large crater that the explosion had caused. Tom began to cry. He felt he had been the cause of all of it. He was ashamed of his people now. He was ashamed of what he had caused. The black crows had flown up into the air and circled around high above their favorite tree, but when the dust settled they came back down to their tree seemingly happy their tree was still there.

Ernie went outside when he heard the explosion and watched the plume of smoke and dust that flew into the air. He could see the wind was blowing away from where he was so he was happy he would not have to clean up. He decided it was a good time to fix some food and start drinking. When he looked in the refrigerator he was happy there was still one bottle of champagne left. He popped the cork and took a long drink straight from the bottle. He then fixed himself a few sandwiches and sat at the small kitchen table to see what would happen next.

He turned on the television but there was no news about the explosion so he turned the station and watched the last half of an old John Wayne western. He dozed off on the couch and when he woke up again it was dark. He went outside and quietly went up to the top of the hill and peered down to where the ranch house had been. He could see a massive glow of lights and heard the sound of the generators. The whole scene reminded him of Vietnam. There were hundreds of people scurrying around and the perimeter was totally guarded for security. He didn't want to be seen so he quickly headed back to his house.

The next morning at 6:00 AM there was a loud knock on his door. Ernie had slept on the couch with the shotgun next to his side. Before he went to sleep the night before he had called his wife and confirmed with her that she was ready to move to their new home in New Mexico. They talked for a long time and made plans. For the first time in many years Ernie slept peacefully even though the property next to his had been blown up. When he heard the knock he wondered how the aliens and his friends were doing not who was at the door. He left the shotgun next to the sofa and went to answer the door. Two men dressed all in black were on his front porch. Ernie let them in and they sat in the living room. The first question they asked him was why he had the gun leaning against the sofa. Ernie rubbed his eyes and laughed. "Hey, I was in the military. You guys had to have heard that explosion yesterday afternoon. I thought there could be some kind of trouble."

The two men nodded their heads and then grilled Ernie with a barrage of questions. Ernie knew what to say. He told mostly the truth. He explained he was new to the area and did not know anyone. He told them about his plans for the fish farm. The men left but then a few hours later they came back and asked him more questions. This time they asked him about George and Mark. They asked about Marks private plane. Ernie told the truth except he left out the aliens. When they asked him why Mark had taken an attractive brunette with him on the plane yesterday afternoon: Ernie laughed again. "Hey, that is Mark for you!" He is always with some hot babe!" The men left.

Near sunset another man knocked on the door. Ernie thought it would be the same two that had come twice to question him. Ernie was getting annoyed now and he really did not want to sit through another round of questions but he opened the door anyway. This time it was a different man and he was dressed in simple cloths. At first Ernie thought he recognized him. The man was older with a greying beard. The man flashed some form of ID for Ernie to see but Ernie was already so tired of questions he didn't even look at it. The man was Ivan Petrosky. He sat down and asked Ernie all kinds of questions. The questions were different from the questions the other two men asked and Ernie was getting suspicious. The man's English was very good, but Ernie detected some kind of small accent. Ivan had been so frustrated with the explosion and with all the activity going on that he ignored everything he had ever learned. He knew he should not go directly to the house and ask Ernie questions but he thought it could be worth the risk. He thought about putting pressure on Ernie but when he saw Ernie, he decided against it. Ernie grew more suspicious as the conversation went on and Ivan could sense Ernie's suspicions so he quickly wrapped up the conversation and left. As Ivan drove back to his hotel he decided maybe it was time to end his pursuit of the truth. He was getting too old. Ernie found a bottle of old rum in the back of a cabinet and as he drank he tried to place where he had seen that man before.

The trip to Kern County in the van with the aliens and George was an adventure for sure. Fortunately the only check point they had encountered was an agricultural checkpoint and the guard only asked if they had any agricultural products. Aktal seemed to hypnotize the guard with either her attractiveness or some other means and he just waved them through without inspecting the van. Borghx and Mr. Kyn were constantly having a discussion. Jacon and Kafta occasionally chirped in during the lengthy talks but George had no idea what they were saying because they spoke in the Maran language. Aktal had told him bits and pieces of the discussion but George was more focused on Aktal. He wanted to stop the van and go into the desert with her so they could be alone. He wanted to question the amorous feeling he had for her but whenever those thoughts came into his mind they dissipated like steam from a tea kettle. There were stops at gas stations and Aktal purchased all kinds of snacks that the aliens devoured like they had not eaten in months. American junk food turned out to be something they greatly appreciated! Aktal took over the driving on the last part of the trip and George fell into a deep sleep in the passenger's seat. George had vividly colorful dreams but when he woke he could not recall them. When he saw Aktal next to him driving the van he felt like he had known her forever. He smiled and wondered how in the world a robot from another planet seemed to be turning out to be his soulmate. Aktal smiled at him like she understood his thoughts and George guessed that she probably did understand his thoughts!

Once George was awake, Mr. Kyn scooted up close to him and started to tell George the story of how he had become so wealthy back on Mara. George was fascinated about the tales of the various sexual robots and it dawned on him that maybe that sort of thing would someday happen on Earth. He voiced his view with Mr. Kyn but Mr. Kyn just laughed because he highly doubted Earth was headed to repeat the history of his planet Mara. The topic did give Mr. Kyn and idea so after he had the discussion with George he moved back to where Borghx was sitting and had a serious but humorous talk with Borghx about his new idea. Borghx listened and often nodded his head.

The various members of the Tribal Council were hiding as best they could. Some were mad at the others and everyone did not want to talk to anyone especially the plain cloths Government officials that came asking questions. The Council made a pact to remain silent. The Federal Government knew there had been some truth to the statement the Council had provided from various pieces of evidence at the explosion. The two women that had owned the ranch house had disappeared and there was very little information or records on their backgrounds. Anyone that knew them had only provided statements that they were from California and that they were sisters. The investigators could not push the Indians to talk. Tom Whitecloud quietly left and went to his nieces house in Phoenix without telling anyone before anyone had a chance to talk to him.

A large chain link fence with barbed wire on top was erected around the crater that the explosion had left. The government people doing the research claimed that radiation levels were high and that is why they needed to isolate the property but some local reporters snuck in with their own radiation detection equipment and found there was no radiation whatsoever. The reporters got on local talk shows, radio and wrote articles that fueled the UFO conspiracy community to believe that there had been aliens on the property. They believed the aliens left back to their planet and blew up the evidence of their visit. The Indian leaders remained silent and stuck by the story but also photos they had provided which was completely hypocritical to those asking questions but there was nothing they could do. The researchers began to come to the conclusion that there had been some type of small controlled fusion reaction. This of course was impossible because no one had been able to control nuclear fusion. Fission reactors were being operated all over the planet and everyone knew the dangers of an accident and having the radiation escape. Theoretically fusion was possible but from a practical standpoint it was impossible. The mystery continued to grow.

Ivan followed everything that was going on and spent a few days keeping an eye on Ernie but nothing out of the ordinary seemed to be going on so he decided to go back to Moscow. He knew there was something he was missing but now he was not sure if he would ever discover what it was.

Mark called Ernie a few days after he returned to Los Angeles. They talked in more or less coded words and kept the conversation brief. Ernie's wife and two sons were going to be moving out to stay with Ernie in a few days. Ernie kept himself busy and started hiring people to dig the ponds for the fish farm. He stayed away from the property next door and only went into town when he needed to buy supplies. He was happy that no one else came to visit him.

After George and the aliens arrived at Marks property they began preparing the bomb shelter next to the manufactured home for habitation. George was waiting until Mark came out from Los Angeles then he would return to his place in Los Angeles. George had already decided he was going to keep his apartment but spend most of his time with the aliens and mainly with Aktal. He wanted to be around Aktal. She had become his girlfriend exclusively and she was giving him a lot of attention. He had completely put it out of his mind that she was a robot. Even small things that may have reminded him of her being a robot; he blocked out of his mind now.

Mark drove with Shala to the property the day after they had flown back to Los Angeles. They brought a lot of supplies along with a variety of tools and raw metal materials that Shala insisted they purchase. Mark had no idea what the future held for him or for the aliens. He was starting to regret his involvement as they were driving to his property and Shala cold sense Mark's feelings. Mark thought the whole idea of conversing with a robot made to look like humans by aliens was just too abnormal. In Mark's mind it went far beyond what any intelligent species would need to do. Mark had been with the CIA for way too long and he knew the value of deception but the value his superiors gave deception never seemed to be as great as they thought it would be when it was put into practice. Shala began the conversation as if she was reading Marks thoughts. For the first time since they had met, they dived into a deep philosophical discussion about the very existence of Shala and Aktal. Mark explored the concept of robots as life forms. They discussed the thin line between biological life and artificial intelligence. Shala offered the idea that even though Borghx and the Marans had given her the capacity to acquire and sort through various radio wave frequencies to gain knowledge that in actuality most biological creatures had that capacity also. Dogs could sense fear and many humans could "read minds." In the future Shala explained that there would be localized "Hot Spots" (what we now call WIFI) that would disseminate waves so computers could pick up vast amounts of information. Satellite technology would permeate the globe and both humans and artificial intelligence would have access to incredible amounts of data. Mark listened and started to feel better about his role, but he knew it would be like walking on very thin ice.

George headed back to Los Angeles to get his belongings and wrap up some business. Mark stayed at his property and had extensive talks with Mr. Kyn and Borghx. Aktal, Shala, Jacon and Kafta had turned the raw materials into a group of nanobots that began expanding the bomb shelter into a larger and more habitable space for the aliens. A week later when Aktal and Shala emerged from the bomb shelter their appearance had changed. Their facial features and eye color had changed but not too dramatically. Mr. Kyn explained that it had to be done so they could move forward and avoid any inquiries in the future. When George returned Aktal's new look made no difference to him in how he felt for her.

After a month it seemed that the escape from New Mexico had went smoothly and any investigations were only ending in dead ends. George and Mark flew back to New Mexico to visit Ernie and his family that had now moved in with him. They discussed the ongoing plans for the fish farm and Ernie talked about the men that had visited him to ask questions. At night they snuck over to the border between the two properties and saw that the activity had died down. It was still fenced but it appeared there were only a few people stationed on the property. A trailer had been put near the crater and there was some heavy earth moving equipment parked near the trailer. Mark and George only stayed a few days and just before they left Ernie expressed how much he was starting to like his new life. He told his friends that he really did not want to know anything further about the aliens and that he wanted to just continue to live the peaceful life he now had. He told them that his sons were fitting in well with their new school and that they wanted him to buy them horses. Mark and George smiled at the suggestion and told Ernie to go ahead and buy the horses for the two teenage boys.

Once back at Mark's property Mark, Mr. Kyn and Borghx came up with lengthy detailed plans for the next phase of the mission on how they were going to exert influence on the planet. Mark realized now that he had to be fully committed. Mark contacted his superiors with the CIA and put in his formal resignation. He had to go through a number of lengthy interviews back in Los Angeles but the interviews went well. Mark committed himself to the next phase of his life.

It had only been three months since the aliens had escaped from New Mexico. They had blown up almost all the evidence that they had ever been there including their inter-galactic vehicle. Mr. Kyn and the other Marans had no intentions to remain stranded forever. Part of their plan, with Mark's help, would to be to eventually build another intergalactic vehicle. They knew the project would take years and they also knew it would involve some major risks, but it had to be done if they were to ever return to Mara.

Borghx, Mr. Kyn and Mark had extensive talks. George, though staying on the property, spent most of his time with Aktal.

It was more than a love affair, they were a couple. Mark could see the progression in George's mind and body. It seemed as if George became quicker, faster, fitter and mentally more acute. At the same time he seemed to have adopted a sub-servient role towards Mark. He treated Mark not just as his friend now but also like he was the commander of the ship. Mark could not see the changes he was going through but George could see them and they were as equally impressive. The aliens were having powerful yet subtle influences on both of them.

The plan that they formed was one that was going to take years to implement and accomplish. All knew it would have to change along the way but at the same time all knew the underlying importance of accomplishing the main goals. Mark was going to be used as a conduit to bring new technologies and ideas into human culture.

Mark flew to Seattle with Shala who pretended to be his companion. They approached one of the top aerospace firms located with a stack of patents recently had filed for numerous new technologies. They told a tale of how Mark had an old German neighbor that had died and had passed a number of the ideas on to Mark and then Mark had them put under patent. The aerospace firm asked no more questions and when Mark and Shala returned the following day for another meeting the company made Mark an offer to purchase the patents at an unbelievable price. Mark, as already planned, refused the offer. Mark told the Company executives that he was retired from the CIA and he was already wealthy. He played the game with them that he could easily sell the patents to other companies or if he wanted to he could even give them to the US Government, but that is not what he wanted to do. There were more meetings and eventually Mark revealed that the intent he had by approaching them was so that he could form a new spin-off company with them as partners but he needed the controlling interest so that the new technologies could be used in ways that he deemed to have the most value to creating a harmonious and peaceful planet. The aerospace company wanted Mark onboard with them and saw value in any deal that Mark presented. These were technologies and patents that would take their company to historical heights not only in monetary measures but in ways that would change the future of the planet. Over another two week period attorneys from both sides met and the agreements were drawn up.

Mark and Shala moved to Seattle. They now had a private company jet and would return to the property only on certain occasions. George stayed with the aliens and brought them the supplies they needed to expand the bomb shelter and make it even more comfortable.

As part of the agreement Mark remained as a ghost investor through a secondary company and allowed the aero-space company take credit for the technologies that were going to be developed. Per the agreement the fusion reactor and the inter-galactic vehicle were to remain secret projects until Mark decided when they would be revealed to humanity. The aerospace company at Marks direction purchased a large piece of land near Bakersfield only 80 miles from Marks property to be used as the development headquarters for the intergalactic vehicle and the nuclear fusion reactor. It was in a remote area and Mark along with others from the newly formed company obtained all the needed permits from the Federal Government in exchange for allowing the Federal Government to incorporate the new technology into their NASA program once the prototypes were built and tested.

Mark's former bosses along with much higher government officials put Mark through rigorous questioning and suspected now that he had received the ideas for the technologies from the aliens that had escaped from the New Mexico ranch. They spied on Marks property and then confronted him in a dramatic meeting where Shala was present with him. They never suspected Shala to be a robot. Mark had an idea that they had guessed what exactly was going on and discussed that with Borghx and Mr. Kyn. Mark cut a deal with the Government to leave him and the aliens alone until after the projects were completed by promising them one of the Intergalactic vehicles that was being built and other technologies in exchange for privacy. He let them know that the aliens were prepared to die rather than be exposed to the government or public at this time. The deal was hashed out and now it appeared the aliens would be left alone and Mark, George, Aktal and Shala would be the keepers of the aliens. Shala and Aktal, went completely under the radar and no one suspected them as having anything to do with aliens. That would not last forever and they all knew it.

Everything seemed to moving along as planned for Borghx and Mr. Kyn. Their new home was comfortable and Mark had turned out to be more than capable to be their front as they began to exert influence on the planet.

After only one year the company that Mark had formed with the aerospace company had successfully tested the nuclear fusion process. Mankind's dream of virtually free energy would someday come true and Mark was in control of how it would be eventually revealed and used. Mark feed the scientists information bit by bit on a variety of other highly advanced technologies. The main goal now was to build an intergalactic vehicle that was an exact clone of the one that the aliens had blown up when the left New Mexico. The project was to be kept under wraps and all involved were happy with the progress. .As the various new technologies came about and spread around the globe they had the desired effect. Planet Earth was gradually entering an era of more stability and peace. The Earth eventually would at last have access to almost unlimited energy and the US government would have the rights to the first reactors.

George often introduced Aktal to others as his wife. It was easy to do because they were so close. Aktal never questioned

George when he did present her as his wife. George and Aktal were intense lovers but even more intense was the friendship and mentoring on the part of Aktal. George was constantly learning and becoming even more of a genius than he already was. He enjoyed staying behind the scenes and offering his suggestions. Aktal constantly stimulated Georges mind. The effect the aliens were having on Mark and George was a good one. They both discussed how they felt younger and more energetic.

Ernie remained on the fish farm that was now thriving. George and Aktal would visit Ernie and his family everyone once in a while, but Mark rarely visited, mainly because he was just too busy. The friendship was still strong between Mark and Ernie but there was a bit of an invisible barrier. Ernie felt some jealousy towards both Mark and George but he kept the feeling hidden. He had nothing to complain about.

Mark was becoming incredibly wealthy. He began expanding his holdings into other corporations with a team of a few select investment advisors. He could see he was becoming a human like version of Mr. Kyn. Events were moving by at an incredible pace. The thinking of world leaders was changing each day. The oil and gas dominated world was undergoing an evolutionary shift. Greed no longer held the power it had held on the planet throughout the industrial revolution. A new revolution was taking place due to silicon technology and the new clean energy technologies that were in a large part being introduced through Mark and the aliens.

Everything was moving as planned by Borghx and Mr. Kyn. The aliens had only to wait now until the prototype inter-galactic vehicle was completed by the corporation Mark had set up. It was only a matter of time and time was passing in a peaceful manner which made everyone happy and content.

Chapter 13
The Passing

10 Years Later

Mark, George and Ernie were now in their late forties. Their health was good except that Ernie now had somewhat of a growing beer belly and his dark hair was mostly grey. He seemed to have aged the most of the three friends. Mark and George seemed to have aged very little. They all knew this was somehow an effect from being in close proximity to the aliens. Mr. Kyn, at one point clarified the concept with Mark and George by letting them know that it was totally an effect of being close to Borghx and not the Marans. Mr. Kyn told them that Borghx had the same effect on them. When Mark brought this up with Borghx, Borghx just laughed and said. "That idea is all in your head!" Mark did not know what that meant so he never pressed the issue again, it was nice enough to know that he seemed to be aging at a slower pace because of his proximity to Borghx weather it was true or just in his head.

George and Aktal were still deeply involved. They were close friends and lovers. Aktal of course had not aged at all and she looked almost exactly the same except for occasional changes to her hair color and hair style. George stayed with the aliens and Aktal. Shala was often traveling with Mark. Mark and Shala were lovers, but the relationship did not have a lot of passion which seemed to be the way that Mark preferred it because he knew she was a robot created by the aliens. The fact that she was a robot did not bother him at all and as far as he could tell there was no difference what so ever between Aktal and Shala unless of course you he discussed the topic with George. George did not view Aktal as a robot but as human. He actually felt she was by far the best human woman he had ever know, (not of course that

208

he had ever had very many relationships with any women.) Either way, Mark took the occasional conversations and the obvious infatuation that George had with an alien robot in stride. He knew the two of them were breaking all normal concepts of relationships.

Mark was trying to view his life and what had been accomplished over the past fourteen years as not just extraordinary but as part of his mission in life. The aliens were now his closest friends and trusted advisors. He had learned that they had incredible altruistic beliefs about life and the preservation of life. They were always forward thinking yet they were also able to change their plans on a moment notice if circumstances dictated it. Because of the aliens influence on Mark, he became a dedicated philanthropist. He had accumulated an incredible amount of wealth in a short amount of time. He took up painting and sculpting as a hobby. His property had been transformed into a very lavish and comfortable location. Their complex was far enough away from any city so that they could all feel comfortable and safe. The very expensive and detailed security system they had installed allowed them to keep any intruders far from them. To date they had only had a few incidences with some local kids. Mark went to his office in Bakersfield every few weeks or so to attend meetings or meet with investor clients. The office was staffed full time to handle all the inquiries.

The inter-galactic vehicle was near completion and soon the aliens would make their planned escape back to their home planet of Mara. Of course they had never seen the vehicle that was being constructed in secrecy by Mark's company in a large hanger not more than a few hours away. It was far too dangerous for any of them even though they all knew they were being watched. It was a game and all involved knew it. It was in a way a Mexican stand-off. The government authorities knew Mark was harboring the aliens and they watched his complex 24/7. Mark leaked out new technologies through his companies and other associates, in exchange for privacy. Everyone was getting what they wanted and that was good but it was an incredibly stressful balancing act that Mark with the help of Borghx and Mr. Kyn had to stay on top of. At one point a few years back George and Aktal were abducted by Government agents that tried to force them to talk and to go over to their side. It was a complete fiasco that only strengthened the argument on Marks side to leave the aliens alone until the time they had agreed on in the contract. What the government did not know was that the Aliens wanted to leave. The Feds knew they had no choice but to trust Mark because they wanted contact with the aliens. To date everything Mark had promised had happened so even though the Feds were anxious they fully believed Mark would live up to his end of the deal. On a few very rare and spontaneous occasions Mark would invite one or two Government officials in to meet the aliens so as to keep them satisfied that everything was copasetic. What Mark and the Aliens agreement with the Military said was that the harboring would end the following year along with the release of other technologies, but of course, Mark was not going to let down his friends. Mark's friends were the aliens now and he had become very attached to them. Mark knew that he and George were not aging as fast as normal people and he knew that it was because of their proximity to Borghx. It was a good feeling to have and both of them wanted it to last but at the same time they knew the big planned escape back to Mara was not far off.

Even though the hanger where the inter-galactic vehicle was being prepared was under high security, Mark had access whenever he liked. Mr. Kyn and Borghx were quite pleased with the work that had been carried out with the help of Mark and even more pleased that the inter-galactic vehicle they hoped to take them back to Mara was now almost completed. They discussed their plans often with Mark and George. Mark went along with the others plans because they were his friends but inside he knew it would be almost impossible to take the aliens to the inter-galactic vehicle. It would be even more unlikely that they would be able to hijack it and return to their planet of Mara. Security and the constant monitoring of the aliens would make any plans very difficult to carry out. Mark did not want to break that type of bad news to Mr. Kyn and the other Marans, not now at least. Even more troubling now was that Mr. Kyn was talking of "Going Public", and getting the public on their side in a "request" to leave. Mark knew Mr. Kyn was not comfortable with the plan that Mark was formulating at this point. Time was becoming critical and all involved knew it. The realization they had accomplished the majority of their mission and the planet was on a good path seemed to be causing cracks in their unity as a group. They did not know the Government officials as Mark knew them and there was nothing Mark could do to change their thinking. Weather they returned or not would make little difference, at least in Marks mind but he felt compelled to aid his friends and he also felt compelled to not allow the Government to get their hands on the aliens. He knew he had difficult decisions ahead. Mark knew he had to help Mr. Kyn regardless of what Mr. Kyn wanted. Kafta and Jacon often talked with Mark about their strong desire to leave Earth and return to Mara. Mark had come to know the Marans well, but in a way he still did not know them completely. They were not aggressive at all, the self-claimed "Warrior Spirt", that Mr. Kyn liked to profess in his tales with Mark and George was only true in Mr. Kyn's quest for adventure. Mark was troubled because he knew there were risks he would have to take. How and when he could not decide but he had to act soon because he knew the Feds would catch on to the grand ruse at some point in time.

To Mark, George and Ernie, who came to visit on occasion, it appeared Borghx had not aged at all. He was the one unchanged remaining fixture in a long Shakespearean drama. He had become much slower in his movements now and his color had seemed to change to a more pale purplish blue. He was much more selective with whom he conversed with and for how long. Even his closest confidants, Mr. Kyn and Mark only had constructive conversations with him at the most once a week or so. Borghx had always elegantly avoided questions as to his age and even Mr. Kyn was not sure. Mr. Kyn did tell Mark it was very long, but how long he was not sure. Mark and George discussed the topic on occasion and tended to believe it was as long as Borghx wished to stay alive. It could not be forever because he originated from a biological being and he was not completely self-replicating as a robot could be. At some point everyone just accepted Borghx for whatever he was. Borghx was an intelligent creature far beyond both the Marans and the Earthlings. Borghx is the one alien the Feds wanted and they were becoming increasingly anxious for the contract to be completed so they could have him for their own.

Twelve years was a long time for George. He and Aktal knew the end was near and they were still close lovers. George wanted Aktal to remain. George had not talked a lot with Mark recently as he could sense that Mark was ready to move ahead with some plan that would allow the aliens to leave. George had confronted Mark on a few occasions and Mark had always left the option open and avoided the question telling George that was the decision of Borghx and Mr. Kyn. George tried to convince both Borghx and Mr. Kyn that they should allow Aktal to remain behind, and the answer was always the same, "that is not our decision and it is not Aktal's decision." George did not understand that answer and no one would explain it to him any other way. Even Aktal, which George had recently become suspicious of for not having an answer to the question, seemed to want to avoid the topic. It was frustrating for George to think about, so he choose not to think about it.

Instead, George delved deeper into the robot mind of Aktal. Now though it was late in January and a recent snow storm had laid a soft blanket of snow on the ground. It was time to address the idea that soon Aktal would be leaving. George and Aktal were alone. Earlier George had been in the workshop with Kafta and Jacon, who both talked incessantly about the Inter Galactic Vehicle being ready for testing. George knew a plan would be coming soon. At last Aktal explained the answer to the question, not because she didn't know the answer before, but because now Mr. Kyn allowed her to answer.

Aktal sat calmly next to her human lover in the cold and explained the situation to George, "George, you are blinded by what humans call, "Love." I know we have briefly discussed this before, but, not in relation to what has surfaced in now. Yes, time has run out and options are becoming limited. I cannot predict the future. Our fourteen years together has been but a drop of time to me, but, without Mr. Kyn or another Maran here to maintain me, it is more likely than not I would break down. You know that." George dropped his mouth in surprise. Even Mark had thought that Aktal was a self-replicating robot. "George, I am different from Shala. Like I have told you many times I am more autonomous than Shala. Yes, it is true that to a small degree I could become more or less self-replicating but I do not believe that is a risk Mr. Kyn wants to take. It is his decision. He allowed me to explore my affections towards you and become reflective of your emotions towards me. What we can both agree on is that we have become one." Aktal leaned over and they touched lips, ever so gently, their lips lingered in a soft kiss. George no longer felt the cold air around him. He only felt the heat from Aktal's soft lips. Their thoughts melded into a realm of peaceful bliss. It mattered not what the future held at least not in the present.

Mark always had a difficult time understanding the attachment that Aktal and George shared. Mr. Kyn had allowed Shala to accompany Mark on many of his business trips and Mark thoroughly enjoyed her company. He often thought of her as human and felt at times he was taking advantage of her because he treated her more like a slave than a human, or robot, or whatever she really was. One thing for sure was that he did not feel he "loved" her. He did not feel attached to her. His rational mind stayed rational and sex never became an emotional attachment. In recent years he never used her for sex anyway. Yes, he would have her give him a massage on occasion but the sensual parts had stopped and Shala being a robot could care less either way.

Ernie remained in New Mexico. His boys both lived not far away and helped him with the fish farm. Actually they more or less ran the whole operation for him. His older son had married after college and Ernie enjoyed being a Grandfather. Ernie had quit drinking but he was not in the best of health. His hair was silver grey now and he grew a beard that was also silver. He took long walks with his two dogs and on occasion rode around the property on horses with one of his sons. It was a peaceful and fruitful life. He almost completely forgot about George and Mark except for the occasional phone call or visit.

As the intergalactic vehicle neared completion Mark decided he needed to go talk with Ernie and get his opinion on how to proceed if they were going to hijack the space ship so that the Marans and Borghx could return to Mara. They rode horses and spent long hours talking about the adventures they had gone through. Ernie concluded that it would be insane to try and hijack the vehicle. Mark had explained to Ernie how easily they could get access to the hanger because it was his company working on the vehicle but Ernie still believed the idea was very risky. Even if they were able to get the Marans into the vehicle who is to say that it would function exactly like the original. Mark became very pensive. He respected Ernie's opinions but he knew he had to come up with a plan. Maybe in his mind it was a way to conclude what had been a crazy adventure for nearly 15 years or maybe it was something else that drove him forward. Either way, Mark knew he had to move forward. There was no turning back. The last day of Marks visit they had a barbeque. The sky lit up with magnificent orange, lavender and red colors at sunset. Mark spent most of the time talking with Ernie's son about a variety of topics, but one of the main topics was if Mark believed humans would ever discover intelligent life outside of Earth. Mark kept smiling inside as he spoke with him. Every once in a while Ernie would come over from the grill he was attending to and exchange smiles with his son and Mark whom were lost in their conversation.

That evening as Ernie drove Mark to the local airport where his private jet was waiting Mark brought up the topic again. "I need to know, Ernie, if I need you to help me with some plan, will you be able to come to California?"

"I knew you would not give up on the idea. Of course, if you need me let me know and I will be there." Ernie replied. They shook hands and now the clock was ticking on the next step in an adventure that had changed their lives and the lives of all human history.

As Mark piloted his plane back to California he reflected on all of the decisions he had made over the years. He did not have regrets. Then he thought about George and Aktal and he realized he did have a regret. He had never settled down. He had never released his soul in a relationship with a woman. He smiled as his jet soared above the clouds thinking how odd it was that his best friend George who was in love with a robot had made him realize his one deep regret! Now he had to come up with a solution for the two lovers. It would be cruel of him to force them apart and he knew that would cause a lifetime of regrets and resentment from George.

The next day Mark headed out to Mojave where he spent half of the day inspecting the now completed inter-galactic vehicle. The large crew of engineers and staff had been drastically reduced now. Testing on various components was complete and all that needed to be done was to wait until the date that it would be fully turned over to the US Government. The Military representatives hounded Mark almost every day now to hurry up the paperwork and turn the vehicle over to them. Mark insisted they would have to wait until the actual date in the contract. He told them his lawyers did not want his company to face any liability in case there were any problems. Mark left his office in the hanger for one last look around and finalized his plan. He then headed back to discuss his plans with Mr. Kyn and Borghx.

It was early evening when Mark drove in the ornate gate that took him down the nearly mile long road to the compound to where the aliens had called home now for over 14 years. Mark was reminiscing as he slowly moved along the road and over the small creek to the outcrop of small buildings. Mr. Kyn, George, Borghx and the others had been anxiously waiting for Marks return. They all knew that Mark had been working on some plan for the past few weeks and they wanted to know what conclusions he had arrived at. They all headed deep within the lavish underground bomb shelter that the aliens had expanded for their comfort to a small room with a circular ornate table where chairs were set up. As usual there were refreshments set up on the table and Mark noticed the thin slices of an aromatic cactus fruit. He recalled the first time that he had met the aliens back in New Mexico. He was sure that fruit had some kind of mild narcotic effect, but he went ahead anyway and plucked a slice of it from the tray as he took his seat and put it in his mouth. The taste was extraordinary and it made him smile.

Borghx sat away from everyone else. Mr. Kyn had mentioned earlier that Borghx wanted to be left alone during the meeting. Borghx seemed to be in a deep state of meditation. His long delicate hands were crossed in his lap and his eyes were closed.

After sometime of small talk and delving into the delicious refreshments Mark decided it was time to break the news to the aliens. Mark's face had a very serious look on it and not all of them were sure he would have anything encouraging to say. The reason for Marks serious look was due to the gravity of the situation they were all in and he knew he could not reveal how serious things really were. "Ok, we are all gathered today to discuss our future. As most of you know the intergalactic vehicle is near completion. Actually, it is completed and has been tested. The only aspect of it that has not been tested is if it will hyper-accelerate. The engineers and everyone else believes it will. That test will not be made for at least another few months. So, that leaves us with a window of opportunity." Mark smiled as he could see some of the Marans start to smile. They all knew what Mark was going to propose next. "So, if we are going to hijack the vehicle we had better finalize a plan and make our move soon!"

Jacon and Kafta jumped up out of their seats and cheered. Then Kafta nearly feinted as he put his head down and began to weep. The idea of returning to their home planet had seemed very distant and remote. Even though they all had held out a few rays of hope the reality of the situation had never led them to hope. Mr. Kyn and Borghx had told them the odds of ever returning to Mara were very low. So, to have the human Mark, stand in front of them and propose it was more than just a small shock.

Mark let them vent their excitement for a bit while he munched on some snacks and wondered to himself if he was really doing the right thing. He knew he was headed for the unknown. The Government would take everything from him and most likely he would be locked up for a long time. He let out a little chuckle and said to himself, "This is my life, I am crazy and I know it!" He then turned back to face the Marans and tried once again to clarify the situation for them.

"Look, this is going to be very difficult and very dangerous to pull off. I know that you think I have the ability to do whatever I want with the vehicle, but that simply is not true. I am the majority stockholder in the company and the company is now under contract with the Government. Security is very tight at the complex and even more so at the hanger where the vehicle is housed. There is no way we can just waltz in there and say we are taking the vehicle for a little spin! I have a lot of planning to do if we are going to pull this hijack off. What is most important is that we all agree we want to do this and that we are all prepared to move on a moment's notice when the opportunity arises." The Marans all nodded their heads vigorously in agreement. Mark had never seen their one big eye in the center of each of their foreheads look so bright and happy. Even Mr. Kyn now seemed to be in agreement.

The meeting ended and the Marans walked around jabbering with each other. They were all extremely excited at the prospect of returning to their home planets. George and Aktal left quickly and decided to hike over to a special place where they liked to spend time with each other. Mr. Kyn stayed behind in the room with Mark and the two of them were alone. Mark could sense that Mr. Kyn had some serious matters to discuss with him. They knew that now the time they spent with each other was going to be limited if the plan worked out and the Marans were able to leave Planet Earth. They pulled chairs close and sat staring at each other.

Mr. Kyn spoke first but not until he looked Mark up and down for any sign of what he was thinking. Mark was used to this type of Maran observation process. He realized now that it was an evolutionary habit that Marans had developed, similar to the saying in English, "Think before you Speak." Mark smiled as Mr. Kyn stared at him. "Mark, I have known you for a long time now and you have helped our mission here on your planet in ways I would never have imagined possible. I have to thank you for the others as they were very excited and did not take the time to extend their gratitude for all that you have done for us. I will be gathering a variety of socio-ecological and other data that some of us have been working on to give to you before we leave. There will be projections for the next 2000 years for your planet. It is very important data and as always I will trust you to reveal it as you see the need. I will also include the exact navigational coordinates for Mara just in case some time in the future people from Earth wish to travel there. We both know that you have had a very difficult time trying to convince those in your Government the value of using the knowledge we have in specific humanistic ways, but that is just part of your evolution as a species. As you well know Marans and Earthlings do actually have quite a bit in common."

Mr. Kyn continued, "We came here with the direction and aid of Borghx. For me, personally, the idea of a great adventure was all I needed to be convinced to follow Borghx. I also believe that was a good part of the reason for the other Marans to make their decisions to participate. Also, the restrictions and controls by our Federation had reached a level far beyond what most Marans ever imagined could happen. I see similar patterns happening here on Earth. The Globalist ideology is great on a social and cultural level but when it comes to manipulation and control of technologies it can become very stifling to common citizens. Mark, this is something you will have fight as long as you are alive. Ever since we introduced fusion technologies through you we have seen great changes towards less wars and more cooperation but at the same time the number of governments abusing this energy technology has also increased. What we hoped would issue in an era of basically free energy for your planet is now mired in corruption and greed within many nations. Still our hope of ending wars and threats of nuclear wars seems to have happened with the introduction of the technology and I am sure all earthlings are happy for that."

Mark listened intently as Mr. Kyn spoke. He felt a bit melancholy that soon his best friend in life would soon be leaving but at the same time he had a new sense of purpose as it related to his role in the great mission the aliens had undertaken to change the course of his planet. They paused for a few minutes and reminisced about the various adventures they had gone through. They munched on snacks and both could feel the need for something more to be said, something greater, and something beyond even the great ideals they both cherished.

Mr. Kyn continued, "Mark, you know well my story and how my planet became mired in heavy central government. My wealth is all that preserved my freedom in the long run. I do see similar patterns happening here on your planet. Your nation, because of the size and technology of its military, will remain as a dominate nation for as far as I can predict into the future. Also the fight between liberty and more government control seems to be in store for the future. When too much wealth is concentrated in private citizens or corporations it seems governments become fearful of their power whereas when too much power becomes concentrated in governments the common people often just get more brainwashed until enough of them reach a state of desperation and revolt." Mr. Kyn chuckled and Mark laughed along with him. They both knew their time together was limited and all that was left for the two of them to do was to reassure the common beliefs that seemed to bind them.

Mark looked down at the smooth marble floor and thought about what Mr. Kyn was implying. It was something he had learned too well over the past many years. Harboring the Aliens, starting the companies, joining with the "Shadow Government" of the USA government. Life was a constant undercover reality that had little or no mystery. What it did have was a large dose of constant stress. Mark had never thought much about the distant future, as he was too much involved in his near future. If Mr. Kyn was telling him that the Corporate Media, Military, and the Elites behind nations would someday grow to the point of severely restricting liberties then it was already too late, because they already were too restrictive as far as Mark was concerned. "I have a question Sir. First as we both know the plan to hijack the inter-galactic vehicle is not a perfect plan because there are no perfect plans. I was happy in the meeting the others did not say anything about the risks of one or more of us losing our lives and failing with the mission. Mr. Kyn, it is a funny game all the players seem to be playing. We know my Government watches us, but we also know they allow us to have our safe space here. You know as well as I do that date for the contract to fulfill is near at hand. At that time I am required to hand over the other documents we have promised them. Now that the Inter-galactic vehicle is completed I can move the date up or delay it with a certain time frame. The date will be set shortly and then the plan goes into motion. As you can see I am nervous, but we will all do our best. My question now has nothing to do with our plan, it has to do with me, personally. Do you have any premonition into my future?"

Mr. Kyn had a wry smile that began to turn to a grin which he then pulled back and took a deep breath because he realized for Mark, the Earthling, that it was a serious question. Mark truly believed Mr. Kyn had some method of premonition other than simple deductive reasoning! Deductive reasoning was nearly genetic for Marans. Mr. Kyn reached out and took a small blue grape and plopped it in his mouth. He enjoyed the taste. He then turned to Mark and replied, "As much as I would like to I will not answer that question. It is not that I don't want to but it is not my place to. I will say this, as you know from our any discussions including those with Borghx, life is endless throughout the Universe. Life is intelligent on many different levels and comes in a vast variety of shapes and forms. The knowledge and experience Borghx has is something no Maran or Earthling will experience for thousands and thousands of generations if ever at all. Borghx is very rare even amongst his own kind. I believe you and others have mentioned to me that what impresses you equally or more than his intelligence is his compassion. I think all of you now realize the effect he has had on your aging process. I am sure by now your Government friends are interested in that aspect of Borghx also."

Mark nodded and Mr. Kyn continued. "As we all know Borghx went into one of his lengthy meditations over a month ago. I spoke with him yesterday. He wanted to be here to go over the plans with you for the escape. I know you have formed an elaborate plan and all of us are on board with that plan. We all understand the risks and we are all willing to take them. Since you have enlisted Ernie to help out I believe we will be successful. There is another reason that I am happy Ernie is coming here."

Mark sensed something in the Aliens voice, something he had not heard before in the many years of their friendship. It was something dark and foreboding. Mark did not like the feeling. He stared at Mr. Kyn as Mr. Kyn folded his hands in his lap and looked down at the floor with a frozen blank stare. Mark looked away and then took a breath. "What is it Mr. Kyn?"

Mr. Kyn raised up and took a long breath. "I am happy that Ernie is coming because Borghx is dying"

Mark nearly fell of his chair. He fully believed Borghx lived forever or at least a lot longer than what he had believed was tens of thousands of years. It was a shock to his system. He knew Mr. Kyn was serious. He had noticed over the past few years these so called mediation sessions that Borghx took had become more frequent. Then Marks life flashed before his eyes. He recalled the time when he was 8 or 9 and the two older kids pulled a knife on him. He ran. He ran faster than he had ever run. He wanted to run now, but he knew there was nowhere to run.

Mr. Kyn felt Marks anxiety and gently reached out with his long Maran arm and rested it on Mark's shoulder. Mark took a breath and tried to think. He always tried to think even when he knew maybe he should feel instead of think. Thinking was who he was. He realized now that perceptions and conclusions were fluid and if Borghx was dying it only made his life that much more insignificant.

Mr. Kyn trained his thoughts on the moment and his heart on the future, "My dearest friend, Mark, you are a very special entity, now and forever. We know Borghx comes from a line of beings that for all we know are the highest forms of life in our Universe. We also know they live for thousands of years and like you for quite some time I believed they lived forever. Borghx explained to me they do not live forever a few years ago. I was shocked but never asked him again about the topic. I saw no reason to. When he told me a few days ago that he was reaching the end of his existence I was upset but not as much as I feel you are now. We have all noticed how he has changed over the past year or so with the meditations being longer than usual. When I talked with him there are a few things he wanted me to relay to you before we all see him again. He has actually lived 132,844 Earth Years, and what that is exactly on the Galaxy his beings originate from I do not know or care to know because it is way more in Maran years. The next thing I am going to tell you must remain confidential. Though Borghx's physical form will be passing he has taken the initiative to pass his knowledge and spiritual form on to another being." Mr. Kyn then laughed! "Sorry, sorry Mark, this is not funny, but just in case you wondered that being is not me or you." Mark glanced up from his stare into the table and saw Mr. Kyn's eyes then they both let out a little refreshing smile. "Mark I must warn you, Borghx is preparing for the transformation and when we all see him again it will be shocking. He has turned a very pale light blue color and his eyes are just small globes of glowing light. He is aware he would never survive a journey back to Mara even if it had been taken years ago. Now what I am going to tell you may shock you more even than the fact of his passing. He will leave his body and transfer his consciousness into a most unexpected being." Mark was fully intent now on what was to come next. His mind had been blown just by the fact that Borghx was going to die and now he had to hear something he could never guess at even though his mind was racing a mile a minute trying to guess.

Mr. Kyn continued, "Let's start with some truth that I have not told you before." Mark raised an eyebrow. He knew Mr. Kyn was almost always truthful with him other than sometime petty jokes that often did not make any sense to Mark. Now though, they were in a deep conversation at a critical point in time and he did not expect Mr. Kyn to be bringing up something he had not been truthful about. It was odd. Mr. Kyn continued on, "The relationship between Aktal and George was in part set up and contrived by me. It was done for a number of reasons. Of course now the two of them are like a married couple. Maybe even what you might say as the perfect couple. They are always happy and charming, diligent in work, and intently satirical in their shared viewpoint on life. Obviously George is enjoying his seemingly eternal youth because of his close relationship with Borghx. That adds to the couple's prolonged infatuation and never ending companionship with each other. I understand to you and to some others it is often too much. That is understandable as creatures are all different, I say that not to judge your lifestyle in anyway but only to outline what I need to explain to you. As you well know even where I come from I am known as a scientist. I like that designation as do my fellow Marans. Aktal and George have spoken to myself and Borghx about the two of them remaining together. That will now be possible because Borghx will not be returning to Mara. George will be able to take his place. Now you must wonder what has all this have to do with Borghx. The answer is that Jacon and Kafta have constructed with the guidance of Borghx an artificial womb to carry the egg. Aktal had an artificial womb for a Maran child but we have modified it. Once an egg has been fertilized Borghx will pass his spirit on to the embryo for the journey back to Mara. Aktal and Shala will be able to run the inter-galactic vehicle and the egg will be frozen during the journey. Everyone has agreed to this Mark so now we just need your agreement."

Mark nodded his head in agreement. There was no other choice. It was what the players in the grand act of his life adventure wanted and he knew in the end he was only the pawn of something greater, but what that was he also knew he may never discover. It was a deep moment and a moment of clarity shrouded in the perpetuity of now.

The conversation continued and Mark learned that Borghx had already made plans with Aktal and George. Only from the inner circle did he and Ernie not know of the plan. Mark's feelings were not hurt and he understood the secrecy. George had given a sperm donation only month ago and now the egg was fertilized. They had told George that he would not be able to go on the journey to Mara and that only the fertilized egg would go. Recently they told him he would also go. They revealed the plan in two stages to not overwhelm George psychologically. Mark did not ask nor care whose egg it was but he did care about what the child would be like if born to an artificial womb and living on Mara with Borghx's spirit. The conversation went along those lines for quite some time. Mark was happily informed that Borghx assured all that the child would be unique and do great deeds. That was enough for Mark.

The following day early in the morning Mark used his secure phone to call Ernie. He knew the phone may or may not be as secure as he wanted it to be but he had no choice now. After all the Mr. Kyn revealed last night the time for action was at hand.

Ernie was riding one of his horses when the call came in. "Mark, how is it going there? You haven't called me on this line in a few months. "

"That's true my brother. So if you remember back when we talked the last time you will understand if I tell you now is the time." Mark replied.

"Well I have a few loads of fish that need to be harvested but that should be over in a few days." Ernie said.

Both men knew that the time had come for the grand escape and both knew they had to limit the conversation just in case it was being tapped. Since they had been friends for so many years they knew the protocol and understood each other. Ernie would be coming out to Los Angeles in two days. Nothing more needed to be said.

Mark ended the conversation. "Ok, Ernie I can tell you are busy. I will talk to you soon."

Ernie rode his horse through the ravine and part way up the hill then tied his horse up to a small tree. He walked the rest of the way up the ravine to the top of the steep slope. Tom Whitecloud stood near the top of the ridge staring into the brilliant orange sunrise waiting for his friend Ernie to make his way up the hill. When Ernie came walking in he was breathing hard but he managed to blurt out a "Hello Tom", as Tom motioned for Ernie to sit down on the rock next to him. Tom put his fingers to his lips to indicate to Ernie to not speak and then pointed to the ever increasing pastel painting of an incredible New Mexico sunrise.

Ernie and Tom had been friends on and off for the past fourteen years. They were neighbors and shared the secret connection with the aliens but they did not socialize or talk about that subject ever. Over the past few years as Ernie got in the habit of riding his horse early in the morning to avoid the heat, he would on occasion come by Toms place because he discovered Tom was always up at dawn. Over the years Ernie began to feel sorry for Tom, he seemed to be a lonely old man now. It would be impossible for Ernie to reveal to Tom that the aliens were still alive and not vaporized in the explosion on Aktal and Shala's ranch years ago. Both Mr. Kyn and Mark had instructed Ernie to remain quiet about the incident, so he did. That is the reason

Ernie felt guilty and always on the edge of saying something to Tom about it, but to date he had not.

Suddenly Tom started to do some Indian chant. This is the first time Tom had chanted in front of Ernie. Ernie felt uncomfortable and thought for a second to get up and leave but he knew that probably would be rude so he sat and watched the sun rise. A few old crows flew out of a tree nearby and then Tom stopped the chant. The two men exchanged glances and then just as suddenly as the crows had flown out of the trees to their left, a large Eagle swooped in from seemingly nowhere and landed about 40 yards ahead of them off to their right on a scrub oak tree. He let his wings unfold and then settled on his perch. He looked comfortable but he stared back at the two men. The two men stared back at the eagle. The eagle squawked then looked away. Ernie exchanged glances with tom Whitecloud.

"Wow that is a magnificent bird! It just swopped in and landed like it wanted to enjoy our company!" Ernie said in a joking manner as he attempted to minimize whatever spiritual mumbo jumbo he was sure to come from Tom Whitecloud now that this random bird landed in a tree near them."

Tom turned and looked Ernie square in the eyes. "Ernie I would consider us friends by now. You come here and chit chat with me. Sometimes we see each other in town, but though we know each other, there is something distant about you. Why?"

Ernie started to sweat. Here he was going in a few days to Los Angeles to help the aliens escape. He bit his lip and then proceeded to make his excuses and blurt out everything he knew about the aliens and the few times he had visited them in California. He also revealed he was going there in a few days to help them return to Mara. Tom listened intently knowing a story that detailed as that had be true. Tom understood why they did not want him to know. He really did not mean that much to him. He had always sort of felt in his heart of hearts that they had made some covert escape, so he remained calm and unmoved.

For Ernie though, it was a relief that he could at last blurt out the truth to Tom. Tom was a meek person and he deserved the truth.

"Ernie, I am not surprised. Many of the Men of the Medicine Council believe they are still alive." Tom said very calmly.

"Ok, then I guess that settles it for me. I want you to come with me to Los Angeles to say goodbye to them." Ernie said without hesitation.

Tom grinned ear to ear, "Yes that would be great!"

Ivan Petrosky was in his early sixties. A lifetime spy for the KBG and now an American citizen working more or less on his own. He had kept track of Ernie on and off for a long time because of his relationship to Mark. Ivan had consolidated his services by running a private security company in Southern California. He paid his bills and kept all of his licenses up to date. He knew his background had been washed by the KBG so he was fully Americanized, at least legally. Therefore, his security company ran on the up and up. Ivan had a small group of managers that could work on whatever operations Ivan wanted to work on. Mark was now his private obsession. When the claim that the documents for nuclear fusion were given to Mark by some German hermit, Ivan immediately investigated Mark. As Mark's wealth accumulated at an ever increasing pace, Ivan knew something was up. The problem for Ivan was that now the US Government had their eyes on Mark like hawks so getting any information out was nearly impossible. That forced Ivan to focus on Ernie because Ivan knew eventually Ernie or someone near him would spill the beans. Ivan started a relationship with Tom Whitecloud but so far that relationship seemed to be fairly worthless. Even more of a lead now was the fact that Ernie kept dumping phones and over the past few years Ernie was always on a secure channel. In spy terms Ivan was now nearly blind until the moment when he got the call from Tom Whitecloud. Cash to Mr. Whitecloud at opportune moments over the years had yielded very small results but now this was the biggest one of them all. The goofball Indian was telling him that the "Aliens" of which he knew somewhere existed were holed up in California and there was to be a big meeting in three days. Yes, Tom was a turncoat in a way but from his point of view life would be the same for him before and after whatever happened plus he needed the money. Tom told Ivan he would not wear a mic but he would give him more information in four days if the payment went through immediately.

The payment went through and the next day Ivan set up camp to spy on Marks property. He found a hill top nearly 10 miles away where had a clear view into the small box canyon below. He was pretending to be a camper and he had scouted the CIA watch post so as to not be seen by them. There was no movement in the complex but it was fairly well hidden from any aerial surveillance because of the large trees and think shrubbery. There was only one road in and out, the rest of the property backed up to a very steep canyon that lead high into the mountain. It would be nearly impossible to access the property from that mountain side.

Tom Whitecloud and Ernie arrived on a Thursday. Mark met them at the gate and was shocked to see Tom Whitecloud. Mark scowled at Ernie but did the gracious act and allowed both of them in the compound. When Mr. Kyn saw Ernie he thanked Ernie for bringing him but that still did not ease Marks thoughts. Mark and always been suspicious that Tom may have tipped off the KBG on occasion so this was not a good sign.

It was a time of celebration and the group gathered in the vast underground bomb shelter luxury home where they ate and drank. Mr. Kyn politely explained once again to the ones that had not heard the process of the transference of Borghx's soul into that of the now fertile embryo. It was a joyous meeting except that towards the end Mark spoke with Tom Whitecloud and got him to spill the beans on tipping off Ivan. Mark remained calm but he knew he may have to make adjustments to his plan. He wanted to threaten Tom, but it just seemed stupid. Two old men threatening each other and it did not change the present circumstances.

The ruse was on for the duration of the plan and there was no looking back now for Mark. Mark had told his Government operatives that the Marans wanted to see the Intergalactic vehicle one last time before they handed the new technologies over to them. They arranged for Sunday at 5 pm but Mark was not going to wait and instead make his move Sunday at 4 AM.

Later Friday night up above on the patio Mark called for a meeting with George and Ernie to go over details of the plan. The transference ceremony was to take place the next evening on the same patio. Mark sat with George and Ernie. The three friends were once again into something far beyond anything they could imagine or understand. They were making plans to pull off a major crime and someone could die, but they forged ahead! Beers in hand, bravado still running wild, and focused determined minds planned to pull off what they all really doubted they could actually pull off! After more beers and joking Mark got called away by Mr. Kyn who was back at his quarters.

"Tomorrow is the Spring Solstice" George said to Ernie as they sat waiting for Mark to return. Both were obviously nervous and scared of the adventure that lay ahead of them.

Ernie sort of chuckled, "So is that like, romantic?"

"Ernie it has been a long time since we have seen each other." George answered.

"Hold on, little brother" Ernie emphasized the, little. "I can see you are really happy. I can see, and yes, I am jealous, how neither you nor Mark have seemed to have aged. We all know that is from the influence of Borghx. I guess it would be cool someday if that could be packaged. Now, George, I love you like a brother, and I am happy you are happy, but you need to understand I am a fish farmer. I enjoy it. I enjoy the simple life.

The only reason I do this stuff for Mark is that I made a pack with him to do things like this. I guess also some adventure a few more times before I die might be nice. I spent time years ago with Shala and I understand the constant feeling of devotion and attendance to your every need. I would use the word slave, but it is so far beyond that word I just can't use it. I am very impressed how good of a couple the two of you make. It is inspiring for sure. Mark explained to me all of the implications of the child having so many special abilities and maybe someday doing great deeds for our Universe. I think that is Patriotic. You see, George, I like to think of myself as Patriotic. I am a rebel but really just a homebody!" They both chuckled. It was a conversation they had before. It was the usual ramblings of Ernie but with a twist.

Ernie stood up. He was tired and needed to rest for the big next few days that lay ahead. He put his hand on George's shoulder, "I just have one serious question. How is it that the two of you can have such a never ending close relationship when Aktal is not human? There just has to be aspects of her physically, mentally or emotionally that are blatantly not human to you?"

George appreciated the question but he did not expect it from Ernie. "Well to be honest with you Ernie, I have both asked myself that question nearly every day and at the same time just forgot about answering nearly every day that I have been with Aktal. I will say there is no solid answer for that question because it is yes and no, not necessarily good versus evil or God versus no God, but from a purely common sense approach, I am happy and satisfied on a variety of levels. Now I have thought about this a lot. I would add, just recently, with this addition of raising a child together, my view on the topic has evolved some. I would have to say at this moment it is because of the fact that Aktal is both biological and digital. The material science is phenomenal and we all know that is mainly from Mr. Kyn with some adaptations by Borghx. Honestly Ernie, the whole thing just blows my mind every single day. I don't know if I am living a dream or some dream is living in me and has taken over my life. What I do know is that every day feels like a hundred days and every moment with Aktal is stimulating on a variety of levels."

"Dude, I can see you are happy! All the best to you and your alien baby infused with some God like aliens spirit! Hey, off you go to Mara, home of the little dudes, with one eye, so you should fit in perfectly!" Ernie replied. They laughed and noticed Mark had returned.

"Guys, I overheard parts of that conversation. Let's understand we are in crisis mode probably worse than the old days! I will say this though, Aktal and Shala are Love Goddesses, and how and why Mr. Kyn and Borghx made these two extraordinary robots into living creatures is far beyond me. That is part of the technology we are supposedly handing over to the Government on Sunday. They are like I-Phone's Two Million and the biotech elements are extremely advanced. You noticed Borghx and Mr. Kyn have not duplicated them since they have been here on our planet. I still have not been able to completely find out if they could exist without Borghx or Mr. Kyn but I guess now we know part of that answer because Borghx is passing on. Bingo that is a revelation. That must be the reason they do not want the information into the hands of our Government. We just are not advanced enough as a society and with autonomous robots on the loose we would succumb to them in the end! Well it is as good of a theory as any."

Ernie had heard enough theory. He really wanted to be back at his ranch with his horse. "Ok, guys, I need to know the details of the plan for Sunday morning. I have gathered bits and pieces but not my exact role."

Mark frowned because he knew this time he was putting his friend at more risk than he had ever put him before. "Look Ernie, we are down to crunch time here. So let me spell things out and see if you can handle it. It takes about two hours to get to the base. We need to leave at around 2:30 AM Sunday morning. We will take two vans. Just before we get there I will call my handlers and say we are almost there. They are going to say, "What?" And I am going to say "What?" and then I tell them we will wait around with the Aliens. I will tell them Borghx is not with us. I will tell them we have the computers with the information. We can wait around in my office and reschedule at Noon. By then we should be long gone. The security is going to be minimal and it will take 45 minutes to bring in more security. It is highly unlikely they are going to make us wait at the gate for 45 minutes, but if they do, then the plan is off and we go back home and come up with another idea. There are two night guards in the hanger. All the offices are empty except for a few with an occasional scientist with insomnia working at night. By 4:00 AM the cleaning folks have all left. There is a lull 4:00 AM to 5:00 AM and that is our window of opportunity. It will take at least two hours for my handlers and the Generals to drive out to the base. So they will be happy with a Noon meeting. We have to expect of course that they will call for more security as soon as I call them. My office is only 50 yards from the spacecraft. The controls to open the hanger though are at the far end of the hanger. That is also where one guard is. He has a little room next door to the control room. I will have to get into that control room. I know the guard and on occasion have brought him snacks from home. He likes the Maran fruits. That will be my plan, so when we come into the hanger we are going to need to carry some gifts and baskets, but nothing to overwhelming."

"Guns?" asked Ernie.

"Yes, guns, whatever we decide will be the most appropriate. Later, I am going to show you both a new proto type of laser gun Mr. Kyn gave me the other day. The Marans will be carrying weapons also." Said Mark.

Ernie nodded his head up and down. He could feel some animal instincts starting to bubble inside of him.

"Ok, listen Ernie, Tom is going to stay here at the compound. I need you tomorrow at sunset during the ceremony to be up on a hill somewhere not too far away looking out for our old nemesis, Ivan. Tom tipped him off. I am not that worried but we are at a critical junction now. I know my handlers are watching me and watching this compound, but I also know where and how they are doing it so I am a lot less worried about them. When they see the ceremony tomorrow it will take them days to analyze it. Then the next morning we head out of here. I am going to make sure their communications are blocked at least temporarily. Most likely the two morons will be half asleep anyway and I wouldn't need to cut their communications but we half to think of every angle. They want the technology for Aktal and Shala. They have met both of them on a few occasions. Borghx and Mr. Kyn I believe have figured out that the Feds have realized now that Aktal and Shala are robots. It will be a scary situation if the Feds get their hands on them and start trying to replicate them."

"So let's review the situation with the guards. There will be two at the gate along with all the perimeter fencing cameras. We are driving in and everyone will be accounted for. Again our only risk at that stage is the guards at the gate holding us until they get instructions from above. I think I can schmooze that over by throwing the indignity of the Aliens back at them and then push it to having them use one of the guards to find food for them while we all wait. That will leave only two other guards. The one at the end of the hanger near the control room. I will be offering him some snacks, then immobilize him. Shala will then join me and assist me in programming the ship and setting the launch coordinates. The two of you will stay with the aliens in my office and try to keep the guard diverted while Shala and I work in the control room."

"When you see Shala leave and head your way that means you either have already immobilized the guard or need to do it as quickly as possible then get on board the ship. Launch will be in 10 minutes from the time Shala walks down the hanger towards you. Basically it takes that long for the roof to open so the ship can be launched. Aktal can send her off a bit sooner from inside the craft if she so chooses but hopefully she doesn't if the roof is not totally opened. That is the plan. I ask both of you again, if you are in and if you have any questions?"

"Yes, how do we get out?" Asked Ernie

George laughed out loud. He had been listening intently but now it just dawned on him that this was it for planet Earth. He was out of here with his alien girlfriend and a bunch of short one eyed aliens to be cryogenically frozen for a few hundred years and to then wake up to a new reality with his beloved Aktal, a growing embryo with Borghx's so called "Spirit", whatever that meant, in a solar system called Han with five habitable planets and even more one eyed aliens. His child would have two eyes like him. It was all very interesting and scary, yet in a way was actually a less of a problem than the one his two friends would face after the ship too off!

"Guys, listen up!" George blurted out. He was more than a little drunk, and more than a little, anxious to go back to his room where Aktal was waiting for him. "Tomorrow is Saturday, I feel sorry for the two of you having to stay beyond, but, the ceremony where Borghx transfers his essence into my yet unborn child is going to happen. Now I am sure Mark has some plan to get the two of you out of the hanger safely but that is not going to affect me." Mark shrugged his shoulders. George continued, "Actually, I think I need to go to bed now. It is getting late." Ernie shot a mean glance at George.

Mark interrupted, "Hold up guys, the fact is I do don't have a plan for Ernie and I to escape but that is irrelevant. They are going to be nice to me and anyone I tell them to be nice too because they are going to believe I have the plans for Aktal and Shala. Which of course I may or may not have, but that is not even something I am going to tell either one of you for your own sake. Again, Ernie and I are going to drive out. There is a chance we get caught but my attorney's will get us out quickly, well, at least they will get Ernie out quickly. Look, we are going to do our best and that's it!"

They Said their "Good Nights." Ernie had a bad feeling about the whole thing.

Chapter 14
Transformation

Aktal left George before sunrise on Saturday morning. Borghx had asked her to come to his place of retreat. They sat together in a state of deep meditation as he transferred his wisdom and experience into the newly fertilized egg that Aktal carried. At the same time Aktal was trying grasp the burden of carrying this human embryo and becoming a Mother. Even with Aktal's vast existential knowledge and wisdom the concept of "Mother" was not something she was positive she could fulfill on an emotional level. Aktal's love and devotion to George was on a different level. George was an adult and made choices of his own. Giving emotional love to an infant, even though, Aktal was assured Marans would help with the upbringing along with George, was not computing totally in her programming. Borghx and Mr. Kyn knew it. Still the potential was both unique and possibly able to have a large impact on some upcoming inter galactic event. At least that is what Mr. Kyn and Borghx suggested to each other. It was a private belief that did not need to be shared with others.

Borghx knew part of all this ceremonial ruse was simply a muse of his own. He understood the level of intelligence of both the Marans and Humans. He had been fully able to choose his demise into whatever life after death meant to anyone and everyone. His culture had not reached such a high level of intelligence, longevity and wisdom without have the conscious ability to end life at a chosen time. Borghx had known for over a year his time was coming to an end. He knew then he needed to plan the time close to the hijacking of the new inter-galactic vehicle. Mr. Kyn had a suspicion of the ruse but there was no need for Mr. Kyn and Borghx to discuss it. This was for the betterment of all the others involved. The idea of George remaining with Aktal was very unique and portending an actual means of preserving the pathetic human race. Both Mr. Kyn and Borghx could not predict the future for the blue planet. They understood they may have come to Earth to early in its evolution but what was done was done and Mark seemed to have a very good head on his shoulders. He was beyond a patriot for his species, he was and had a great potential to become an even greater hero.

About a mile away now in the nearby hills sat Ivan at a well camouflaged viewpoint. So many years he had tried to put together this puzzle of these three friends and he was excited because now it seemed he was getting close. He was nearly one hundred percent sure the three friends were hiding aliens at this compound. He would wait out the day and get as many photos as possible then leave tonight and fill out a report. He was sure his handlers back in Russia would now pay him good money to set up a full operation especially if he could get more photos. It was hot, but he would watch and wait.

Around 11:00 AM Mark, George, and Ernie came out of the central building and hiked about half a mile to the east of Ivan. Ivan watched them intently with his binoculars. The three men stopped on a ridge and Ivan could not get a direct sight on them but he had a partial view of them behind some thick sage and manzanita shrubs. They started firing some type of laser guns at targets to their right and then down into the canyon blowing up small boulders. Ivan had never seen any gun of that type. He took as many pictures as he could as they practiced shooting for a good half an hour or more.

Sunset would be at 6:32 PM. Two hours before Sunset Mark sent Ernie off with his laser rifle to hike up to a spot a few hundred yards above the patio so he could have a view and be the watch out. Ivan was so intent on the little alien people setting up flowers and strange fruits on tables around a large rug in the center of the tile patio that he never saw Ernie hike up to the spot to his right in the hills. Ivan was dumbfounded and taking pictures like crazy of the little alien creatures.

Ten minutes later Mr. Kyn notified everyone He and Borghx wanted them to gather in the meditation room to talk with Borghx one last time.

A few minutes later everyone except Ernie promptly arrived. Ernie was near his perch in the hills.

Borghx did look noticeably paler to everyone that saw him now for the first time in a few months. He sat on a large pillow in a comfortable position with piped in sunlight reflected off of his translucent soft pale blue skin. Once everyone had gathered he turned and faced the crowd then waved his hand in front of his long thin body while bowing his head. Everyone felt a surge of compassion and warmth pass from Borghx to them and they let out a collective sigh.

Surprisingly to those gathered when Borghx began to speak his voice was not weak. If anything he appeared livelier than he had ever been before. The group collectively felt astonished for a brief flash of time. Then, quite naturally, Borghx did what he did best. Borghx controlled every lifeform below him. He controlled their focus. He controlled their attention spans to be nearly perfectly attuned to both his literal and conscious words along with his subconscious introspects. It was a benefit of having higher intelligence and Borghx well knew there were other forms of life equal to or surpassing his own that did not view the Universe as he did. Some were more aggressive and conquering. "We are all fools in an insane Universe occupied by myriads of lifeforms. We are lucky to know each other. Luck and fate are no different than love and hate. In between is respect. I respect all of you and I know all of you respect me. My mission on this planet is over and I am at an age that is old, very old, so it is time for me to move on. I have transferred my will to the embryo. I am trusting Aktal and George, Mr. Kyn and the Marans to raising the child. My burden will end in an hour or so."

Collectively you could a small moan from all those gathered. "Wait, wait do not be sad! I am Borghx!" Borghx sat up tall and raised his hands over his head then elegantly brought them down to his chest. "Life is not forever! You will find throughout the Universe that creatures of higher intelligence choose when to end their own lives. I understand on this primitive planet people usually only do that for some cause or ideology. They often blow themselves up killing other humans. That is not the same. I choose to end my life for the benefit of others and not even my own people! I do it for you! So all of you should not weep. You must rejoice! We are going upstairs now to have some refreshments. I have a vile here of a special formula that will turn me into a misty purplish harmless gas."

Mark had to interrupt. He knew Borghx read his mind but at the same time he wanted assurance. "Sir, I must ask, Please, are you sure this is the right time?"

Borghx continued, "Yes, Mark it is the right time. The information you have in your procession that you are passing on to your government to replicate Aktal and Shala is your responsibility. I believe it is fine for the others to know that you, I and Mr. Kyn made those discussions. I am old, and I feel it is better to have others return to Mara that have not been there. At the same time it is impossible for me to ever be under dissection by the US Government in more ways than one. We all know I can only be protected here for a limited time."

Borghx looked over at Tom Whitecloud, "I know Mark is recording this for Ernie who is not here. Ernie is on lookout. Mark has always been protective of me in that way. Tom, I am not angry at you but I am disappointed in you. So I wanted you to understand this directly. Only you and Mark will be here to hear these final words. This country called America is a great country for one main reason. The division of powers: Executive, Legislative, and Judicial. We have Mark, Mr. Kyn, and myself. This type of arrangement in ruling tends to last as long as the people do not become brainwashed slaves with limited knowledge of how their government functions. I would not consider any of you here, brainwashed slaves!"

Everyone laughed except Mark and then Borghx continued, "To that end, the future of this planet is still in doubt. Mark, Mr. Kyn and I all have come to that conclusion. Yet, we all have hope and I would say of all the beings here with the most hope are the three humans, Mark, Tom and George. Oh, wait let me refrain and restate that to include Shala and Aktal. I am sorry I left the Marans out but I only said it that way to show that Marans are a more pragmatic culture and more pragmatic cultures are those that tend to last longest!" They all understood it was not a compliment to humans. "Ok, Ok, my friends enough with the analogies and cultural jokes!"

"I was simply explaining the difference in ones right to choose to die when and how one thinks is best as to choosing to die for a cause or ideology, and especially harming others. Because understanding the differences between; a peaceful passing, a strategic passing for the good of a unified galaxy, a passing due to nature, simple old age, disease, calamity, or as I previously stated, for purposes of terrorism; we can then have a species that has a worldview based on unbridled humanity. All Religions are not the same and there are many Religious Nations on this planet. After I pass and after the ship departs the ring of power will be passed on to Mark, Tom and Ernie. This will be the large part of the future of this planet. We all hope they become heroes from now and into eternity!"

"Ok, eat, drink, be merry and meet me on the patio above in 30 minutes." Borghx said.

Everyone left and gathered above to wait for Borghx. It was an odd feeling for all of them. In Maran culture there was a way for the State to end life in rare cases of danger to the society but nothing like Borghx was speaking about. There had never been a period in Maran culture where Marans blew themselves up for an ideology. That concept was not even in any part of their consciousness. The patio was decorated with flowers and tables with more food and drink. In the center was a raised platform with pillows for Borghx. Mark stood close to Mr. Kyn and kept trying to think of something to ask him but Mr. Kyn had such a disconcerting look on his face it made Mark stop trying to think of the question he wanted to ask him. Mark waited only a few minutes then strolled over to a table that had some of the fruits he liked. George and Tom followed Mark to the table.

"I guess this is for real." Said Tom calmly.

Mark turned around and gave a bit of a scowl to Tom but quickly stopped himself. "Yes Tom, he is serious. He is a lot smarter than all of us. Remember, he was speaking directly to you, to me, and to Ernie who is not here, in regards to a ring of power. Look Tom, at some point in the future we will sit down and discuss all of this in more detail. For now I need you to just stay calm and remain here at this compound until all of this is over."

Tom nodded. He understood. He did not particularly like Mark that much personally but he understood what the ring of power was and that was something deeper than him personally. The past was the past and a new time was at hand. "I have a question for you Mark. Is it Ok if I ask it?" Mark nodded in agreement. "Since there are to be the three of us left here with this so called ring of power. Tell me if since I am the dumb Indian in your mind." Tom raised his hand and smiled at Mark with a gleam in his eye so as to let him know he was being facetious. "Mark, what I mean to ask is that if something happens to one of us three who is to carry on?"

"That is a good question and let's just hope nothing does so we can decide on that at some later time. For now, I believe reality is as about as intense as it can get for the time being." Mark replied. Tom nodded as if he understood.

They stood around waiting for Borghx. They knew Borghx would be arriving soon. It did not feel like a time to eat drink and celebrate. In a corner sat Tyijo and Kafta with their heads in their hands looking as if they were crying.

Borghx walked in with Aktal holding his arm. He was clothed in a fine white robe. The two of them walked to the center where the platform was set up with pillows and Borghx sat down. Aktal then waved for the observers to stand away at least 10 feet from Borghx. She then took her place next to George and held his hand. They stood in a semi-circle facing the setting sun and Borghx silhouetted in the setting sun.

Borghx smiled the best way he could. Unlike what any of the others may have felt about him he still feared death, but he could not show it now. Borghx thought to himself that this was a modern day Shakespearian Drama. He liked that thought. He was trying to think of some comforting words to say to his audience but it was difficult to think of what to say. He was about to push a little blue button and smoke his life away all for what he was sure was to save the life of his friends and hopefully a simple, violent, yet hopeful small blue planet. He had trust in humans. George, Ernie, Tom and Mark yet he knew not their future. What he did know was that if he was turned over to the Government it would be over for the planet. As much as he wanted to be protected and as much as Mark had promised he could have him protected the two of them knew it was never going to be possible. Borghx knew the concept of passing his soul and wisdom to this embryo was equal part ceremony and equal part hope but there was no use in allowing any of them to know that. In his thousands of years and many travels he knew hope was all anyone ever had. Melding the spiritual, and purely mechanical into a level of molecular, the difference between machine, soul, species and the local trees grew was only a very small difference in the bigger picture of the Universe. What was much more important was the intent of the energy being given and passed along to the coming generations. So a little hocus-pocus in his final days on this God forsaken planet was all in good faith. What he was doing was for the betterment of all and he trusted mainly in Mark to carry on with the mission for planet Earth.

"These will be my last words to all of you. Super Symmetry as Mr. Kyn well knows is the technology behind the intergalactic vehicle and to a degree with the development of Aktal and Shala. It is important Mark, Tom and Ernie discuss this concept of Super Symmetry with the information I have provided Mark. There will be a private package for each of you when you return to your rooms after the ceremony. Many species and cultures believe we live multiple lifetimes and pass our spirits on. I have done my best to pass my essence to the embryo. Though I have lived for thousands of years I do not feel I know more about spirituality, spirits, mystical beings, or Gods of any sort more than any of you. What I do know is that the Universe is a pulsating life force of causality. By choosing to end my life at this time I am affecting a portion of the causality of this tiny bit of the Universe and hopefully passing on my dreams to all of you to spread compassion wherever you go. Species that are not ready to evolve do not evolve or destroy themselves. If the Government here gets the plans to replicate Aktal and Shala that will be the end of humans because this planet is not yet ready for technology that advanced. Mr. Kyn, Mark and I have discussed this many times. The information Mark has to trade is a very limited prototype of Aktal and Shala. So limited in fact it will take at least a hundred years before they can reach the advanced level of our robots."

"Lastly just remember there are many mysteries in our vast Universe and none of us can know for certain the future. What we all do know for certain is that we have shared some time together in this adventure called life. I want the best for all of you. One last thing never forget to celebrate!"

Poof, it was a soft explosion if there is such a thing. A round ball of static light completely encircled Borghx and the light gradually grew brighter. Soon they had to shield their eyes. The glow continued for a good thirty seconds and then slowly dissipated and a very pale bluish-purple cloud of smoke hoovered in the air. The smoke rose straight up into the dimming light of the orange sunset. Then the smoke rose high on a gust of wind and drifted off to the east.

Ernie had been watching from his perch the whole time. He looked around occasionally but saw nothing in the surrounding hills. If anyone was out there watching they were well hidden. Mark had assured him the CIA and the Government were staying hands off as that was part of the agreement in handing over the technologies. He was more worried about Ivan because of what Tom had spilled, but so far he saw no sign of the pesky Old Russian man. Ernie wondered actually how old Ivan would be by now. It didn't really matter he was still the enemy to Ernie and always would be, nothing but a Commie spy. For Ernie it felt good to be back doing something he thought was good for his Country. Mark felt the same and that was enough for Ernie to participate in this grand escape. As Ernie kept staring back at the sun getting lower and lower on the horizon he knew the time would come soon when Borghx would make his grand exit. At least that is what he was told by Mark. They all seemed to be around Borghx in a semi-circle and the sun was nearly down. Ernie wondered what Borghx would be saying to them. Then poof, it happened, Ernie wasn't sure what kind of explosion it may be so he looked off to his left away from the light and just at that instant he saw a reflection in the hills not more than a mile away from him. Ernie turned his binoculars on the area of the reflection and saw a man with a large telescopic camera taking photos. Ernie was not a hundred percent sure but he thought it could be Ivan. Ernie's military instinct kicked in and he took off with his laser gun in the direction of the reflection.

Ernie was also old and not in the best of shape but he was in good enough shape for his age and he made his way down the steep ridge and then along the gully for a half a mile. It took him a good fifteen minutes and it was getting darker by the second. He had a good point of location on where he had seen the reflection. Above him towards the top of the hill he could not see exactly where the spy was stationed so he decided to move a bit further down the gully to see if he could get a better view. Not more than a minute down the drainage area Ernie came to a spot where he had a straight view towards the opposite ridge above and could clearly see the man. It was surly Ivan and he was putting his equipment away. He was hurriedly dismantling a small camouflage tent. Ernie was too tired to hike up the ridge and decided he had no choice but to take a shot from where he was. He found a rock to steady his gun and took aim. The blast just missed Ivan as he was pulling up a tent stake. Ivan rolled over to his right behind a rock and grabbed his camera. Another shot rank out hitting directly into the small boulder that Ivan was behind and part of the boulder blew off striking Ivan on his shoulder and nearly knocking him down. Ivan scurried down the slope behind him to the road less than a quarter of a mile away where he had his SUV under a tarp and drove off. Ernie was not positive if he had hit Ivan or not but when he was heading back to the compound he heard the sound of an engine up on the hill and guessed he had missed. He shrugged his shoulders and said to himself he just wasn't the sniper he used to be. Live to play another day he thought. Ernie took his time getting back to the compound.

Mark was talking with Mr. Kyn and George inside the retreat. The others were preparing for the drive in the two vans they would take at 3:00 AM to the compound where the intergalactic vehicle was being housed. It would be an hour and a half drive. Ernie was sweating and dirty. Both Mr. Kyn and Mark noticed him. "Ernie, I see you are back. Are you OK?" asked Mark as Mr. Kyn pulled up a chair for Ernie to sit down.

"I am fine. Just old and out of shape I guess!" I think he got away. I am almost certain it was Ivan. He was photographing everything and everyone. I saw him at the last minute and went after him. I took a few shots but I am fairly certain he got away." Ernie said as he pour himself a glass of water from an ornate pitcher on the small table and sat down.

"Well that is not good. It's not good he got away and it's not good he was there." Mark replied.

Mr. Kyn was still in shock over Borghx taking his life but he understood the gravity of the situation and like all Marans he was eternally frightened. Marans were extremely passive and like the other Marans, Mr. Kyn had been on this violent planet just too long. Worse now he lost what he had believed to be his kindred soul, Borghx. He wondered how much longer Borghx could have lived if he wanted to? A few hundred more years? The length of Borghx's species versus his age at the time he took his life was on a different scale than Maran or Human lives. Am I feeling sorry and selfish at the same time thought Mr. Kyn?

"Hey I did my best, brother!" said Ernie as Mr. Kyn just seemed to keep staring at Ernie in with blank bizarre look lost in his thoughts. Ernie wanted to say something to Mr. Kyn but he understood that Mr. Kyn had just lost his best friend so he kept quiet.

"I know you did." Said Mark. "Look it does not change any of our plans. More likely than not he will take all the photos back and process them. In six hours or so they will be off to Mara and it is over. I need your help with this Ernie. This is about America, the World and everyone's future. These creatures are peaceful and have good intentions but the technologies they possess are too far advanced for our planet at the stage of development we are in. Hopefully it will all change in the future but there is a good chance a big part of that will be up to you, me and George. I guess that is just the way things have worked out."

"I agree, I was just getting warmed up. I'm going to rest until we leave. Send Shala to wake me up with a kiss, if you could my dear Mr. Kyn!" Ernie grinned at Mr. Kyn and it broke Mr. Kyn's extended panic over what had happened to Borghx and the impending getaway.

Mr. Kyn shook his head like he was rattling a marimba and then focused his one big eye on Ernie's eyes. "Yes, Yes Ernie. I am sorry. I was lost in thought. I am happy you are here to see us off. We will take good care of George and the embryo. Hopefully we will return to this planet one day. (Mr. Kyn doubted that but it was nice to say and not out of the realm of possibility.) Let me just ask you one question Ernie before you go to sleep, Oh, Oh, yes I will have Shala come wake you up. It will be our pleasure. My question to you is one I never asked to anyone here on your planet. I did not discuss this with Borghx or with Mark for reasons that are personal to me. You used the word 'Patriot.' Yes, I like to think of myself as a 'Patriotic Maran' even if, as you well know, my history is more that of a rebel. So in that light, my question is; do you think the Human species will ever end the violence and wars?"

Ernie just started laughing, he really laughed hard, and actually he had not laughed that hard in way too many years. Mark started laughing with him. Then some of the other Marans nearby heard them laughing and came over and started laughing. At last Mr. Kyn started laughing. Then they stopped and Mr. Kyn retold the question. They started laughing again.

A few drinks and stories later they retired to sleep for a few hours until they woke at 2:00 AM and departed at 3:00 AM for the base.

Before they left the Marans went to Tom Whitecloud and bid him goodbye. Tom was staying behind. Then they left in two vans in the pitch dark with no headlights on until they reached the main highway heading out to the desert on the other side of the mountain. It was a cool evening and the sky was clear. It would take an hour and a half more or less to get to the main gate where Mark had promised to pull his magic. Mark drove the first van and George the second van. Mr. Kyn and Aktal were with Mark the rest were in the second van.

They reached the front gate with two guards at 4:32 AM and immediately the guard halted the van. Mark waved and the guard recognized him. They talked and Mark waved his hands around explaining the aliens thought the meeting was at 5:00 AM not 5:00 PM. The guard put Mark on the phone and Mark played his ruse. He said the aliens would be offended, which led his bosses to suggest keeping them there. Mark played on that and at the same time took the blame for not knowing the exact time. His boss said he needed two hours and they would have everyone there. Mark asked for refreshments for the aliens. His boss chewed Mark out and then asked for the guard back on the phone. The boss then told the guard to get refreshments for the aliens. That was it, it was simple and they were in.

Once inside the compound Mark drove slowly. They did not want to draw any more attention than normal. The big hanger that housed the inter-galactic vehicle was nearly half a mile down the road past the now empty offices. Mark had his office in the hanger. It was a privilege he had for providing the technology.

They parked near the front entrance and the guard came out to greet them. There would be another guard inside near the control room. After both were taken out Ernie was going to be the watch outside until Mark got out.

Everything went smoothly. George did some small talk to the guard about the aliens and the next minute immobilized the guard with a stun gun. Mark headed with Shala to the control room while the others waited in Marks office. Ernie was looking out the window of Marks office and back at the group getting ready to make their dash to the magnificent space vehicle sitting in the center of the hanger.

It was not a short walk to the control room at the other end of the hanger for Shala and Mark. For one, they had to act casual so as to not draw attention from the guard who would eventually see them. The guard would be at or near the door.

Everything was going as planned and even though anxiety was rushing at an ungodly level through their collective blood there was a calm that the plan was progressing in good fashion. Mark straightened his tie as he walked casually across the floor of the hanger with Shala. He had to be unpretentious as it was most likely that the guard was somewhere in his little alcove watching him. Mark and Shala pretended as if it was a flirtatious jaunt. As they came to within forty yards of the guard's alcove they could see he was watching his monitors that showed the outside of the hanger and he had not even seen them walking towards the control room.

They were in luck for sure. They slowed down their approach and when they were within target range Mark took the guard out with his stun gun. They hurried into the control room.

Mark and Shala were a good team. It took them only minutes to program the launch. The first phase was to have the roof to the hanger open. It would take ten minutes for it to be fully opened. They set it in motion. Then they began programming the launch coordinates and countdown for launch. They set it at 16 minutes and headed back to the other end of the hanger. Once the others saw them they ran to board the ship. It was much faster than Mark anticipated but he knew the ones on board had to go into cryogenic chambers which would be activated by Shala and Aktal after a few orbits of earth. Then they would blast off to Mara. Suddenly when Mark was not more than half way across the hanger he heard a pop, then a blast, then silence. Aktal yelled out from the still open door of the spacecraft Then George stuck his head out and pointed in the direction of the entrance and yelled out, "Ernie's been shot!" Then George jumped out and sprinted to the entrance.

Mark   had further to go and arrived after George. He saw George standing over Ernie in front of where the vans were parked. There was a guard lying dead on the ground near one of the vans. Ernie was moaning. He was shot just below the chest and it did not look good. Mark pulled George away and told him to hurry back to the ship because it was going to launch. The ceiling to the hanger was now open. George stared at the blood on his hands. He stood up and walked like a zombie towards the door leading to the hanger where Aktal and Shala met him. The two robots stared at Mark and at Ernie. "Go", Mark said to Mr. Kyn's sexual robots. The women turned and took George back to the spacecraft.

Mark stayed with Ernie and administered as much help as he could. Sirens went off outside and inside. Mark lost all track of time and had no concept when the ship would take off. He just hoped all were on board safely and that help would come for Ernie. Mark knelt over his friend holding his head up as he spit blood. Ernie tried to say something but then he just coughed more blood. Mark comforted him the best he could.

"Don't worry Ernie, help is going to be here shortly. You are going to be fine. You are going to make it." Mark muttered through the tears and emotions.

"Take care of my wife and family." Ernie managed to groan through the immense sharp pain. Ernie was fighting it but the world was growing dim. He could feel the darkness coming. Then like a bolt of lightning striking him from inside out he opened his eyes wide and blurted to Mark, "Mark, tell Tom you will take my place." Then Ernie collapsed and slept forever. Next there was a low rumbling, then a deep hum, then a loud whoosh and the inter-galactic vehicle was away on the next journey. Guards crashed through the door and handcuffed Mark. Medics came for Ernie but Mark was certain he did not survive. The guards took Mark away to the brig on the base.

Chapter 15
Crystal Visions

Mark spent the week on the base in a small but comfortable jail cell. It was not enjoyable and they did not allow any outside communication. HIs sense of loss at having his close friend Ernie die and having the others leave made him feel dark, quiet and pessimistic. Every day the guard brought in two or three Military Intelligence experts and they questioned him. He knew eventually his boss, who was the head of the covert project would be coming in to question him, just exactly when he was not sure. He had no idea what was going to happened to him. He was sure Ernie was dead. One of the officers kept asking about Ernie's family and from the line of questioning he deduced Ernie had passed. He had no idea what the Military had told Ernie's wife and he had no idea if he would ever be able to tell her the truth which she deserved.

Habit, made it so Mark counted the days and today was day seven. The first few days Mark refused to reveal but a few basic facts. He wanted to see how much pressure would be put on him and to his surprise it was a lot less than what he thought so on the third day he started to answer more questions but he still limited the answers until his boss arrived. The one thing Mark knew to do was to not ask for an attorney or anyone else. He knew his only chance of walking away from them was to not bring others in. Obviously his boss wanted to know who else knew, other than Ernie, along with why. Mark did not want to be one of those forever imprisoned traitors, he wanted them to think he may have more information or assets of value and that was equal to his freedom. Right now that seemed a big task. He was wearing down and his thoughts were not staying focused. Worse was the fact the three rings of power were broken and Tom Whitecloud he had no idea what happened to him. He chuckled inside and just remembered Ivan with the photos. Mark had to make some decisions and he had to be prepared to make them when his Boss walked in. They obviously knew George had left with the aliens and they also knew Borghx had basically blown himself up.

Larry Fitzpatrick had been Marks' handler in the CIA for over 25 years. They never had what anyone would think of as a close friendship. Soon after Mark had retire, Mr. Fitzpatrick, though also retired, was asked to come out of retirement and be the liaison between the Feds and Mark. Mr. Fitzpatrick was too old to get too mad but now he was beyond mad. His career was over, the President would hang him and he felt he had let down his country. That was the small part of why he was mad, the second part was that 10 Billion US Taxpayers money that was gone in a flash. Yes, the second ship was under construction but that did not make up for the massive loss of time and money. He came in to Marks room with two burly guards. He stood behind the guards in his dark suit and waited until Mark stood up, which Mark did quickly, and then he spoke, "We both realize what you have done. I am sorry you are too stupid to not know there are others involved in this also. By the way moron, we caught Ivan with the photos. We know Borghx is gone. I should have you hung for treason."

"Sir", Mark interrupted.

"I am not done. Then Larry nodded his head to the guard on the right and he swatted Mark upside his head. Mark shriveled back. "I could have you killed right here right now, trust me the people above me would be happy. You know and I know by now we have searched your compound and found nothing extraordinary. So that means it was planned. So to me, knowing you, that means you have something you are willing to trade in exchange for your freedom. What is it? Spit it out because I only have a limited time before I need to talk to those above me."

Mark took a deep breath, he knew he had to negotiate now. He had thought it out beforehand. Give a little and then see if that is enough. Still it was a difficult decision and he was tired from a week of questioning. He knew Larry would start barking at him any second now, and then it dawned on him. A way he get his own ass off the hook, and give something personal to Larry. He almost laughed, but, held back!

"Larry, Yes, they got rid of everything. Borghx blew himself up and he held all the plans to the various technologies. I think it would be best if I could talk to you privately now." Mark said.

Larry looked at the two guards and motioned for them to walk out of the room.

"Ok, Larry I had to tell you this alone. The technology I got from them is for a sexual robot. A female sexual robot companion, not a fighting machine. I guess after a few decades of development they could become fighting machines, I just don't know for sure." Mark said.

"Bullshit, what else do you have? We were promised the full plans to those two robots!" Larry yelled.

"They were all destroyed" Mark replied. "I have what I have. I was lucky to get what I have. I held out this long because I only wanted to tell you. Look Larry, I did my best to protect these aliens because they saved my life at one point, so I helped them with their plan to leave. I was told they were leaving the plans for the robots with you."

"We have nothing and you know it. You know it because you probably set the whole thing up! I know you to well. I know how you operate." Larry stated.

Mark wanted to laugh, it was true, but not true, yet what else could he do. In this lovely circumstance of time he realized he needed to evolve far beyond what Mr. Kyn, or even Borghx for that matter, and surly way beyond his innate patriotism, to what he truly believed was the essence of the three rings of power. His mind was working a mile a minute. He realized he had to offer as little as possible and then he could offer more if they would allow him to go free. He knew if they had already searched the compound they most likely did find some valuable information and now they just wanted to extract everything they could out of him. Mark just didn't want it to turn to torture.

"Sir that is all I have to trade. I will only trade it for my freedom or I will die. The information is in a secure place. Ok, yes, there are a few other tidbits of things, like advanced drone technology, and some other interesting things. It is all I have. My lawyers will fight for whatever interests I have in various corporations but I understand the losses are catastrophic. So bankruptcy is inevitable. You understand, I would have been killed if I did not obey them." Mark said knowing he needed to make Larry feel some little bit of sympathy. He was tired now. Lying was all he could do if he wanted to be free. He wanted to get out. He needed to see Ernie's wife and he wanted to go back to his retreat to see how badly they trashed it out.

Larry had no bad feelings towards Mark other than the fact he ruined his career! "Shut up, Mark. This is your doing and I know it. No one threatened you and you know it. Now look, I know we have not always had the best relationship over the years but we never had to deal with anything like this either. You know as well as I do that with the administration we have in power now there are going to be endless insider hearings. The money is going to have to be accounted for. I have done my homework before I came in here to talk to you. You must understand all your interests in any US or Offshore Corporations must be given up if you want to walk out of here with any deal. You must also know that if the people above me are not satisfied with whatever information regarding new technologies you fork over is not enough you will be endlessly jailed until they can find more. I am your only hope so if I continue to hear more lies then your hope is fading. Now tell me where I can find the information"

Mark knew it was the end of line for him and he had no more cards to play so he told Larry where the safe deposit box was with the flash drives. That was all he could do for now. He would just have to wait and see what happened next. For the next few days he did get visits from other interrogators. Time just passed and he wondered if he had any future at all.

On the fourth day a guard came to the cell and opened it up. He led Mark to the front to the desk. Larry was waiting for him and there was a box on the floor. "Inside the box are a few things from your office. There is an envelope in there with $10,000 cash. Outside is a government jeep and you can take it to your property and gather a few more of your personal items if you want. Your property is being taken over by eminent domain. It has been searched top to bottom and we have decided we want to keep it anyway and maybe look again at a later time. Papers have been filed in court removing you from all of your business interests except for your interest in the fish farm in New Mexico. Ernie's widow is there and probably she would like to have a visit and explanation from you. We told her Ernie died trying to help you thwart a plot by some Soviet agents. That is all she needs to know or anyone else for that matter. My superiors are satisfied for now with the information you have given to us. They have allowed me to determine your fate. Some want you locked up for the rest of your life but I explained to them that you may have been under psychological control or duress. So basically, you are a free man with $10,000 cash and your fish farm. I hope you stay on your fish farm and stay away from me. Oh, yeah just leave the jeep at your property when you get there." Larry turned walked out and left. There was nothing else to say.

Mark stared out at the base from the porch and looked at the jeep in front of him. He was tired and hungry. He looked to where the hanger was and saw a flurry of activity. The roof was now closed. There were so many trucks he couldn't count. He drove straight out the front gate. A few miles down the road he found a restaurant and ate his first decent meal in a few weeks. He had a two beers. It was a country type stop and Mark enjoyed the Americana feeling. He was done. All he had was part of a fish farm. For the first time in his life he thought about God. Maybe there was a God. At least he was out of jail and still alive. It could have been a lot worse. He felt very lucky.

The ring of three was broken but never ended. What is two could someday become three and what is three can become millions! Mark laughed and the waitress scowled at the grungy man sitting in the corner booth. Mark tried to smile at her then he realized what he looked like and stared back. He causally began to eat then after a few seconds he raised his hand. "Bring me another beer!" When he paid he tipped with a hundred dollar bill.

It was a long lonely sad ride back to his retreat. The aliens had been there for many years. There were many memories and most all of them enlightening, compassionate, and enjoyable. Mark wondered if he was being followed but as he kept looking back he saw nothing. Mark believed Larry was honest with him, or he would not have left him with the $10,000 and the fish farm, because his superiors would have wanted to leave Mark with nothing or have him killed.

It had been an ordeal over nearly two weeks and Mark was mentally and physically drained. The food from the dinner helped a lot and Mark knew he had nothing if he did not create some kind of future for himself. Before he realized it he was at the gate going to his property. The main gate was broke. The estate was wide open. As he drove in he saw sheds, well covers, pipes, wiring, and furniture of all kinds strewn on the drive up to the main compound. Half way in Mark stopped his car and looked around at the mess in front of him. Then it dawned on him. Ernie's last words. "Be sure to tell Tom you will take my place." Mark continued to drive into what had been a small paradise and now looked like a bomb had hit it. As he got closer he noticed all the gates were wide open and debris was everywhere. He stopped the jeep and went inside and the inside was worse. He then looked out on the patio where they had the ceremony for Borghx and surprisingly the patio was far less messy, maybe because it was usually always empty. The few tables were still there. Mark went through the patio door and went to one of the tables that overlooked the steep cliff below and sat down. He needed to think.

Mark starred out over the valley below. The view was really one of the reasons he had purchased the property. It was stunning and at a certain time of year the sun set in the far valley below but this was not that time of year and the sun was far from setting. Reality sunk in, and Mark knew he only had limited time on what had been his own property. Mark sat up tall and took a few deep breaths. He was ready to go back inside and scrounge around for some memories then leave when he heard something from the other side of the wall. He trained his ear and listened again. It was as soft voice from the other side of the wall. "Mark, Mark is that you. "Mark, Mark, is that you?"

Mark recognized the voice and went to the side of the wall and leaned over. Sure enough it was Tom Whitecloud, hanging onto a rock that he must have climbed up on before because it was perched fairly high above the canyon wall below. 'Tom, I see you." Mark yelled out from above."

Tom strained his neck and saw Mark above him nearly 15 yards and like an old mountain goat he made his way very carefully up to the wall and pulled himself over.

"My God Tom, at your age, how did you do that?" You are like a human goat!" Mark said as he reached his hand out to Tom and offered for him to sit down.

Tom laughed and sat down to catch his breath. It was not as easy as when he was younger but he stayed in good shape in New Mexico with the natural landscape near Ernie's fish farm.

"Let's go inside and get some food. That's one thing they left plenty of. I have been waiting for you to come back here. I told myself I would wait one month but you came back a lot sooner. I took off the day you left with everyone for the base and hung around town. When you didn't return I got a hotel for the night then headed the next day back here and saw all the vehicles and helicopters, so I went back to town and got a room for a month. I came back every day to check on the place and see if they let you out. Three days ago they abandoned the place. I found a path up and it goes all the way to the patio. It is the back way in so it is safe. I may have left in a day or two, but I am happy I ran into you."

Mark told him the whole story as they went inside and sat down with food and drink. Tom was sad to here Ernie was dead. Tom's eyes went blank for a few seconds and he stopped talking about the government people that were going through the compound. Mark assured Tom that the aliens and George were on their way back to Mara. When Mark told Tom all he had was $10,000 and the jeep, Tom said that was pretty good! He thought Mark was rich! The two of them laughed about the situation even though Ernie's death and the inevitability they had to go to see Ernie's wife was pushing their fate forward.

They decided to spend the night and then drive out in the morning back to New Mexico. Mark had decided he would transfer his interest in the fish farm to Ernie's wife and her brother who had always been there to help her and Ernie. They found a bottle of brandy and sat drinking and talking. Mark was not sure he wanted to bring up the last words of Ernie at this point but he was tired and needed to sleep so he blurted it out to Tom.

Tom stood up. He look startled and scared at the same time. Mark was all Gringo, all Caucasian, and this would be the first time. At least Ernie had some Indian in him, Ernie was Mexican American and Ernie even had some Aztec in his blood.

Mark had nothing in his blood that he knew of, but then again, Mark was Mark, and Borghx liked Mark. Still this was a shock to hear.

Tom remained standing and staring at Mark. Mark was more than half drunk enough to go have a wonderful sleep for the evening after the long crazy day. Mark was not sure what he had unleashed.

Tom walked around in a little circle like he was annoyed then at last sat back down and faced Mark. Mark stared blankly at Tom then Tom took a deep breath. "Look Mark this is something very serious but I will try to explain it to you."

First I think we should probably get away from the house here just in case they have us bugged now. Let's walk down to the little stream. The got up and took some drinks and refreshments with them and headed outside and walked down a small hill where there was a stream flowing and a small clearing where there was a table and some chairs to sit down. Once comfortable Tom began to tell Mark his story.

"When I was 18 years old, the day after my birthday, my Grandfather came by early in the morning and told me he was taking me up to Santa Fe. He would not tell me what for, but I was always close to my Grandfather so I trusted him. It took about two hours to drive to Santa Fe from Socorro. When we got there it was still early so he bought me breakfast and told me we were going to a secret place outside of Santa Fe up in the mountains."

"We were driving up into the mountains. Half way up the road he stopped the car and pulled a note book out of the glove compartment. He handed me the notebook and told me it was his directions and notes of how to get to the place that we were going to. He told me I should add my own notes because it would be important that I know how to return to the place on my own in the future. He seemed very serious so I did take notes. After we parked the car and began to hike it was nearly noon but there was a nice cloud cover so it was not too hot. My Grandpa took his twenty two repeater so I thought maybe we would be hunting for rabbits. I kept asking him if we were going to find some rabbits but he told me to not talk. As we got further down the path it forked off to the right towards the edge of the canyon. It was a steep path. I knew now we were not hunting rabbits. Part way down into the canyon we stopped to rest along an outcrop of rocks. My Grandpa had a bag with some water and cornbread which we ate. I kept asking him where we were going but he would shake his head and just say we will get there soon enough. Just before we started back hiking he turned to me and said, "Ok, sit back down. I am going to tell you this only once and it is very important you always remember it. We are going to a very spiritual place that has many powers. It will not take long from here. There is no reason for you to be scared because this is a place that my own Grandfather took me quite a long time ago. The rule is set in stone and you can only return to this place once. Which means, someone will bring you here and then you will bring someone here once in your lifetime. This is a tradition that has gone unbroken for a lot longer than anyone in our tribe knows and most people in our tribe do not even know that this place exists. You should feel very special. I feel you are very special or I would not have choose you to come with me. I saw myself bringing you here in a dream not long ago, so here we are!"

"I did not know what to say when he told me that. I just felt excited and special. Where was this mystery going to lead? That's all I could think at the time."

"After we started back walking I kept asking questions but my Grandfather laughed and told me to not talk so much or might trip and break my ankle. I was very excited."

"Grandpa.", I asked. "What if the chain is broken?" I knew as soon as I asked, it was a stupid question to ask and really I think I was just too excited, but, either way, after I asked, I expected the whack to my shoulder as my Grandpa turned and hit me in the shoulder as we continued to walk. He never broke stride and I went silent. He then went on calmly to tell me that I had to respect all the traditions and that it was better I did not asked too many questions right now. I couldn't resist and just like the smartass I was I again asked a question. "What is this place for and what is it like there?" I was scared and my Grandpa could see that I was scared so he put his arm out and stop our progress dead in our tracks.

"Look around you, do you even know where you are? Have you been paying attention to the path we have followed? Would you even know how to get back to this place?" He asked me.

I stood very still and looked around. I was not so stupid that I didn't know where I was and how to get in and out of this place. I had observed the path but if my Gramps felt I hadn't I knew better than to talk back to him, so I nodded, that I would be more observant and less talkative. We both looked around then moved back down the path. To make a long story short. We kept hiking and it was longer than I expected, I would say it was a good 8 miles. It was a funny path with big boulders to go around, ridges that were hidden from sight. The reason I am telling you this is that I had chosen Ernie to come with me to this place. It is a magical place. Now I am choosing you. I think we should go soon. It is a place where you will feel and see things far beyond your imagination. I am warning you that it is a long hike but well worth it."

What Mark heard was unexpected but, in a way, welcome. He needed to see Ernie's widow and it would be good to get away. What the place that Tom wanted to take him to was like, he had no clue. It was more important he just get away from all the memories. He told Tom they would take his plane and fly out in the morning.

Socorro

When they arrived in Socorro the weather took a turn to the bad side. A strong spring storm drenched them and the landing was a bit scary for Mark. Normally he may not have risked the landing, but flying out he had mostly avoided the storm so he threw caution to the wind. That was not like him and he knew it. Tom was very upset and promised he would never fly on a small plane again. Mark brushed it off and consoled Tom. They rented a four wheel drive jeep and headed out to Ernie's house. They didn't talk much and Tom said no one had answered the phone when he called from the airport.

It took about 40 minutes to get to the house. When they knocked on the door no one answered. Just as they were getting ready to either leave or break in, Ernie's son Raul came around the side of the house with his fingers to his lips in a gesture of silence. "My Mom doesn't want to see either one of you. She heard a lot of bad things about what happened to my Dad and she blames you. The Feds have already been here and basically said we should avoid contact with you. Look I know my Dad considered you his friends but we are all scared now."

"I understand." Mark said as he reached out his hand to the young man. "We came here to tell you the truth of what happened. Also, to give you this." Mark pulled the packet with the deed to their ranch and other paperwork gifting shares of his corporations to Ernie's family. Raul took the papers.

"I trust you and I do want to hear your story but just not now." Raul said.

"Ok, I will be in touch and if your Mom feels differently I will come and talk with you." Tom nodded and then they both turned and left. There was no use complicating the situation when the emotions were still high.

Tom and Mark spent the night at Tom's trailer. They both drank too much recalling stories of the aliens. After a lazy morning they headed up to Santa Fe. Tom went off with the car to visit a relative and Mark stayed at a nice hotel. The next day they purchased a few supplies then headed up into the mountains. Mark had a notebook and was writing down every twist and turn in each road they took once they drove off the main road. After three hours of driving Tom finally parked and the hike began into the steep mountains. They parked near a bridge along the side of a dry arroyo. It was a more difficult hike than what Mark had expected but he was up to the challenge. The sky was a bit cloudy so it kept the temperature down. The hike seemed to go on for too long and Mark became worried. "Tom, are you sure you know where you are going?" Mark asked

Tom stopped, sat down on rock and put his hands to his head. He was fairly sure where he was going but either way he was not going much further for the day. "We are going to visit someone I know that lives over this ridge. We will go through a ceremony to purify ourselves before we go to the sacred place."

Mark felt a bit relived, he had done enough walking for one day. This was a very remote part of the mountains. He would be happy to rest for the night, purification ceremony or not. "Hey, Tom, I am just your guest. Whatever you say is fine."

They turned off the main path and hiked up a fairly well defined dirt road. At one point it looked like the road could have been driven on in better conditions. Ahead of them near a small hill stood a group of adobe buildings that looked very old and very well built. They were tucked up against the hill and Mark could see they had also tunneled into the hill. It was a small but complex village. To one side down the small valley there were crops with corn dominating the horizon. As they walked closer Tom noticed an old man on a porch. He told Mark to wait as he continued forward to talk to the old man privately. Some village children came up to Mark and sat with him on a cluster of boulders near the edge of the buildings. Mark could sense he should stay away from the buildings. Mark took off his backpack and found some chocolate which he quickly handed out to the children.

Tom did not talk to the man on the porch to long before he casually walked over to where Mark was surrounded by the children. "What's going on Tom?" Mark asked.

"I was just inquiring about Snakeman. It has been awhile since I have been here and he was old then so I wanted to make sure if he was still the one with the powers. He is still up there." Tom said.

Mark had nothing to say. He knew now something serious was going on and it was best to just go with the flow and don't take any big risks. Mark put a piece of chocolate in his mouth and waved goodbye to the kids as he followed Tom down a path off to the side of the village to what appeared to be a looming perfectly flat mesa. After about a mile they came to a much larger arroyo. The path lead down to the bottom of the large gully. There was no water flowing in it now but when it rained they could see the water crept up high on the walls of the rocks. They crossed to the other side and then up a path towards a small hill in the distance. They stopped near the top of the hill and looked back at the tiny village and what was soon to be a very colorful sunset. The sky was a blaze in a multitude of colors and both men stood transfixed on the altering waves of lgiht. The air was still warm from the heat of the day but just as they starting walking down the path again they could feel a gust of cold air rising from the large arroyo behind them. They continued walking in the twilight. Mark followed Tom and Tom seemed to be confident of where they were going. Soon they were at the bottom of the small hill and again there was an arroyo. They cool feel the cool air coming from the arroyo because of the underground water that flowed beneath it.

"We will have to hike for about another hour or so, but the moon will be coming out soon." Tom said as they continued on their journey. Mark said nothing and decide there was no use complaining about the long trek. Tom was older than Mark and that fact alone made Mark feel guilty that he was not in as good of shape as Tom.

"Why do they call this man, Snakeman? Really Tom are you sure he knows we are coming, or maybe he is not even there?" Mark was started to get a bit worried that the long hike was going to be in vain. Plus it was getting dark fairly quickly and they were basically in the wilderness.

"Well, I am not too sure why he is called the Snakeman. I guess it just has to do with his clan. Many Indian tribes associate part of their heritage to an animal spirit, but I am not sure that is why. Some people around here also call him the Keeper of the Hills and others call him, The Keeper of the Gate. The Indians we talked to on the way up here are Navahos and I am fairly certain we are still on their reservation land. Eventually we will leave the reservation land and enter National forest land. " Tom replied as he continued to lead them down the narrow path.

"Well let me guess then." Mark said as he huffed and puffed up a small incline. "He must be some kind of Navajo Medicine man, like you are a Medicine man."

"No, he is not like me. I am pretty much just a normal Medicine man. The Snakeman is a legend. He is a living legend. I am not even sure if anyone knows what tribe he belongs to." Tom said with a bit of humor in his voice. He went on. "What I can tell you is that he lives alone and most people believe he comes from a tribe of Southwest Piute Indians. I think that is just a rumor though. He has been here as long as most people can remember. No one knows his age and he supposedly has never told anyone. He keeps to himself and the knowledge he has is kept in a very small circle of people. As far as I know you will be the first non-Indian person to every meet him. The Council of Medicine Men, to which I belong has a few members that have met him, but we never discuss him. He is the Keeper of the Hills and either he, or someone like him as been here for thousands of years. He has no reason to belong to any council."

"Ok, then what does, Keeper of the Hills mean if he is not the Snakeman? Mark asked a bit sarcastically. Mark was started to regret that he agreed to go on this journey. He could be in Tahiti right now sipping a tropical drink and reminiscing about his experiences over the past few decades, not sweating like a pig hiking in the dark.

Tom could sense Marks frustration but Tom had no mercy for him. Tom knew he was doing the unthinkable in many ways by bring Mark on the journey to such a sacred place, but he had his honor and he would stick to his word because of his vow to Ernie. "Actually Mark, I think you are asking too many questions right now when you should really be concentrating on where we are going and how you will get back if something should happen to me. Anything can happen you know, especially this far out in the wilderness. Very few people have been to where we are going. It is remote, but it is also a very special and beautiful place. It has been guarded in the most secret of traditions for thousands of years amongst the Indians of this region. By the way, to answer one of your other questions. Yes, I am sure the Snakeman knows we are coming! The spirits in nature that are watching us have already told him."

They trekked on and both were getting exhausted so the conversation eased. They reached a flat mesa that looked like a big table in the middle of nowhere. The moonlight was now illuminating their way and it made the landscape appear to be a dark cloud on the horizon. As they entered the mesa area there were five very large granite boulders that glimmered in the subtle moonlight. When they came closer they could see the boulders were massive. They were the size of large houses. There seemed to be a small glow coming from somewhere in the center of the ring of boulders. The path led them around one of the boulders and they saw that the light came from a small kerosene lamp on a little wooden porch of an ancient shelter made of rocks with a wooden roof tucked up against one of the large boulders. Under the lamp they could see in the distance a person sitting on a small wooden bench. Mark wanted to ask if they had finally arrived but his eyes were fixed on the person under the dim light. As they moved closer he could see it was a woman; a very beautiful woman. Then she stood up and motioned and raised her arm with an open hand to greet them. Just then Mark noticed there was another person on the other end of the porch. It was an old man. When they approached the porch the woman leaned down and picked up a bowl with two hands. She moved close to the old man and handed it to him. The old man put the bowl on the bench next to him and stood. He raised his hand to acknowledge Mark and Tom. The woman then stepped silently back inside through the old wooden entrance.

The Snakeman greeted Tom in some Indian language that Mark did not understand. He then sat back down completely ignoring Mark and ate what appeared to be some kind of meat and vegetables from the bowl. He then looked up at Mark as Tom sat on the other bench. Mark felt as if he had slipped through a time warp into some time period far beyond his understanding. Yes, he knew he was tired from the long hike, but tired was not what he felt. He felt more alive than he had ever felt in his life. The simple smile from the Snakeman transformed his thoughts and feelings instantly. He felt very calm. The Spaceman's eyes were black like coal but there was a light that emitting from them that was beyond explanation.

The Snakeman finished eating and put his bowl down beside him on the bench. He stopped speaking to Tom in the Indian tongue and looked at Mark and grinned. Mark could see his teeth were yellowed and old. "I was telling Tom that it has been many years since he has been here to visit his Grandfather." Mark raised his eyebrows. Tom had never mentioned anything about the Snakeman being his Grandfather! Mark wondered why? Then the Snakeman looked at Tom and said, "Now tell me who your friend is?"

"I am sorry Grandfather, this is Mark. He is not the first one I had chosen to come here, but he is the best friend of the man I had picked. Ernie, who was my close friend, died. His last words to Mark were that he wanted Mark to fulfill the quest. I am honoring Ernie's wish." Tom said.

The Snakeman looked back at Mark and stared deep into his eyes with a bit of a frown. Mark wanted to look away but he felt compelled not to. After a few seconds Mark began to feel uncomfortable and he could feel his hands start to sweat even though his body felt cold. Mark knew that was a sign of fear, but there was nothing to fear he thought. Then the Snakeman slowly stood up and approached Mark. He reached out with both of his old wrinkled hands, then as Mark stood up he took Marks hands in his. "I am called the Keeper of the Gate." He said softly but firmly as he continued to stare into Marks eyes. They remained in that position for a few seconds and then they both sat back down. "I have been here for many moons. I am getting very old. Soon there will be another Keeper of the Gate to take my place. I have watched and guarded the passage for as long as I can remember. It has been an honor to protect the secrets on the other side. You and Tom Whitecloud will be the last two to pass under my watch." The Sankeman smiled at Mark and Mark felt like a warm blanket had been wrapped around him. Then he felt the actual blanket and turned to see the woman had come out of the house and was putting a blanket over his shoulders. Mark's eyes met the woman's eyes. It was if they had known each other forever and Mark felt like he was standing naked under a cold waterfall. He shuttered and pulled the blanket around him. The Snakeman continued and the woman silently went back into the small cabin. "Tom has been through the ceremony so he knows what to expect. For you Mark, it may be difficult at first, but this is the way it must be. All that pass beyond must be purified before they enter the gate to the other side."

Mark took a deep breath. Mostly he was now wondering who the beautiful woman was? She was way too young to be the Snakeman's spouse, but one never knows. Mark was familiar with some American Indian cultures and he had visited a reservation near Palm Springs, California once. Mark was not a big believer in spirits, ghosts, angles, demons or any other of those things. He was well aware from his talks with Mr. Kyn and Borghx that the whole concept of an altered state of consciousness was really just a crook of baloney. Drug induced states of consciousness and all the various techniques in Religions, Yoga, and other fields were mainly just physiological responses. Now here he was in the middle of the vast Southwest plateaus with a so called Snakeman! He decided to try and relax and just go with the program. He owed this to Ernie, so he would follow through with it. He knew once he was back in civilization he was going to face inquiries from the government and unending scrutiny for probably the rest of his life. This would be a good break from reality.

The idea of actually going to some sacred Indian location was sort of exciting because he realized now that he was the first, "Whiteman", to do so. He really wanted to ask the Keeper of the Gate a lot of questions but he was very tired, thirsty and hungry. He wondered if Tom felt tired and hungry also. He had to be, Mark thought as he looked over at Tom who sat like a statue. Then the Snakeman laughed as if he had been reading Marks mind. "Don't worry you will do just fine and all of your questions will have answers in due time. For now let's sit here and enjoy the moonlight. My granddaughter, Tarita is preparing some food and drinks for you. She comes here on occasions to stay with me because her mother believes I am getting too old to take care of myself." At that moment Mark realized the woman was the sister of Tom, or at least half-sister. He wondered why the two of them did not greet each other when they first arrived. These Indian cultures were strange, he said to himself.

Rita came from inside with a steaming tray of meat and vegetables. "Hello Tom, hello Mark. I hope the blankets warmed the two of you up." She was attracted to Mark and she knew it instantly. She set the tray down. "I hope you like rattle snake meat?" She said with a smile and a quick wink at Tom. Mark did not notice the wink but he caught on to the joke.

"No really, Mark it is snake meat!" Tom chirped in.

"No it is not snake meat, I can tell you two are trying to kid with me." Mark said smiling at Rita who now sat down next to her Grandfather. "Even if it was, I would probably eat it!" They all laughed together.

They sat and ate. There was also a new bottle of brandy that the Snakeman had opened and everyone had a glass. Rita and Tom talked about relatives and from the conversation Mark learned they had different mothers. After they finished eating Tom and the Snakeman walked out into the moonlight to speak privately with one another and Mark was left alone with Rita on the creaky old wooden porch. "Where are you from Mark?" Rita asked in a soft inquisitive tone. Mark sensed that maybe she was as interested in him as he was in her. He noticed in the moonlight that her eyes were sort of a dark sparkling green so he assumed she was not a full blooded Indian.

"I was born in Los Angeles. I traveled a lot in the past and I try to avoid Los Angeles now if I can. You know, it is just such a crowded place. I have a property about three hours north of Los Angeles. Actually, they are no cities very near where I live. The closest actually town is Lake Isabela. Where are you from Rita?" Mark asked

The electricity between the two of them was palatable and it was obvious they both felt it. Rita answered and at the same time wondered if they would ever go beyond the initial attraction. She hoped he was not married. She did not notice a marriage ring, but past experiences told that was not always a telltale sign. "I grew up here on the Navajo reservation. I don't know if you realize but there are more than a few Navajo reservations here in the Southwest. I have been living in Phoenix for the past eight years. Believe it or not, at my age, I still go to the university there. I am working on my Doctoral dissertation. I enjoy studying. I'm returning to Phoenix in a week or so."

To Rita's surprise and delight Mark moved from the bench he was sitting on across from her to the bench she was sitting on. They sat side by side. "I think the view of the moon is a little better from here." He said with a wry smile.

Rita knew he wanted her and she wanted him. "Yes it is a better view from here." They both leaned in to each other and their shoulders touched.

Meanwhile they could see that Tom and the Snakeman were deeply engaged in a serious conversation. They had taken the bottle of brandy with them and their cups.

"Hey, Tom, do you think we could have a little more that brandy." Mark yelled out.

Tom turned and grinned back at Mark. "Sure, just be careful with my sister! Tom yelled back. He filled his cup and the Snakeman's cup then brought the now more than half empty bottle over to Mark.

"Thanks." Mark said as Rita stood up from the bench and wacked her brother affectionately on the arm as if to let him know he should have never run off with the bottle in the first place.

Meanwhile the Snakeman was staggering back to the porch. "I am going to sleep now. You children enjoy the rest of the evening." He then proceeded past everyone and went inside.

Tom sat down on the bench opposite Mark and Rita and looked back and forth between the two. He had no idea Rita would be here, but he was happy to see her and he was happy that her and Mark were seeming to make a connection. He was not a jealous older brother. Actually he and Rita did not know each other very well because they had been raised in different families. He did know she was always considered the smart one and he the not so smart one. He smiled to himself and continued to stare at Mark and Rita knowing that he was no longer the not so smart one. Everything had changed over the course of their lives. Then a tear started down from the corner of his eye. He remembered Mr. Kyn and Borghx. He missed them and he felt the overwhelming guilt of exposing them to the Council of Indians. He was getting old and he did not have a wife or a family. He hoped that Rita and Mark would at least do more in that regard than him.

"Tom, are you Ok?" Rita stood up and put her arm on his forearm. It took a few seconds for Tom to respond. He was drunk and lost in his thoughts.

Tom took a deep breath, "Yes, yes I am fine. I think I better go lay down. I had a bit too much brandy." Tom stood and went inside with the Snakeman.

Mark looked at Tarita and she smiled back at him. She reached over and took Marks hand. "Come on, let's go for a walk in the moonlight!" She said.

Mark was a bit surprised. He sort of assumed she would not be the assertive type, but it was fine with him. He liked the way her hand felt in his. Just as they were heading out the Snakeman waved at them from a small window. Mark knew he was not alone with the Snakeman's granddaughter.

They walked to a spot outside the ring of boulders. Even though they had just met, they both felt the tinges of fate and thus they felt very comfortable together. The night air was crisp but not that cold. There were millions of stars above them and a full moon to guide them along. The distant sound of a coyote howling at the moon broke the silence and it seemed like music in the Southwest desert. The desert was alive and so were they.

As they strolled along Rita kept turning to the smiling Mark as if she wanted to say something. On about the third time, she stopped and turned to face him. She let go of his hand. "Mark, I did not want to ask you this in front of my Grandfather and really I am just sort of trying to tie things together with you and Tom. Aren't you the person I have seen in the news regarding the government's loss of that inter-galactic vehicle? I mean I don't want to be nosy or anything, but you look just like the man I saw on television?"

Mark was surprised that there had been that much news about what happened. He knew there had been some but he also knew the government tried to keep most of it under wraps. He was sure now that Tarita knew more about Tom than he suspected. It sort of made sense because Tom had been the one who originally exposed the aliens to the Council of Medicine Men. "Yes, that was me you saw. Tell me what is it you heard?"

"Well, I saw on the news that you were the majority stock holder in the company or the corporation that had the contract to build the spaceship and that you were being investigated for possibly sabotaging the project." Rita said.

Mark let out a little chuckle. "Look Rita, trust me, there was no sabotage. It is a very long and complex story. Tom is well aware of most of the details and I am guessing you have not talked with him about it?"

Rita smiled, she really didn't care that much at all either way. She was just curious to know if Mark was the same person she had seen on the news and he had confirmed that. "No, Tom and I do not talk that much."

"Maybe someday I will explain all the details to you if you really want to know. When Tom and I come back from this place we are supposed to visit, if you are still here, we can talk about that some."

"Yes, I will be here!" Rita said emphatically.

They both smiled. Some sparks were starting to fly between the two of them and they both liked the feeling. "Have you ever been to this place that Tom is taking me to?" Mark asked.

"No, I've never been there. Trust me I am lucky to even know that it exists! It is really a well-kept secret even amongst the Indians that live in this area. I believe my Grandfather wishes that I could go, but he has already been there twice. I know my Grandfather sort of wishes now he would have taken me there but there is nothing he can do now. A person can only go there twice in their lifetime. That has been an unbroken rule forever. My Grandfather has told me a few things about the place but always in a vague way, using analogies to various Indian beliefs. Sometimes I have no idea what he is trying to say! I come out here often to visit my Grandfather and look over him. He is getting very old now. I love it out here. The solitude and serenity is unbeatable. I always feel energized when I return home." Rita said.

Rita continued. "I will say from what I have gathered that the history of this place goes back beyond most all of the Indian's history in this era. The Anasazi Indians knew of it, so the history is very old. It goes beyond being even a sacred place, at least this is what I have gathered from my Grandfathers words. It is very well hidden and very well guarded. It is guarded by animals and spirits of animals."

They held hands and walked back into the ring of boulders to the small stone building. They each could feel the attraction between them so they walked without speaking. Mark knew he was embarking on a journey that was special and unexpected. Rita knew she really like Mark and just wanted to be in the moment, feeling the warmth of his hand in hers.

Tom and the Snakeman were inside sound asleep when they returned. There was not much room inside so Rita brought her sleeping bag and some blankets out to the porch. Mark realized how exhausted he was from the long hike. They curled up side by side and with the moonlight illuminating their faces. They smiled at each other and Rita fully expected Mark to kiss her but Marks eyes closed and he was soon sound asleep. As Mark drifted in to a deep sleep he realized he may have at last met the woman of his dreams.

Chapter 16
The Chamber of Dreams

Before dawn the Snakeman and Tom Whitecloud were up preparing the fire for the sweat lodge. When they finished Tom nudged Mark awake. Rita went inside and prepared some food for the men. It was a light breakfast with a lot of water. Tom explained the sweat lodge to Mark. Mark was not too happy about going through this part of his journey but he kept his thoughts to himself.

The sweat lodge was a small stone building barely big enough for the three men. Three small fires were burning around the lodge and a large leather skin of some sort was the door. They had to disrobe and sit naked on a small wooden bench. Tom sat opposite the other two. They were to remain in the lodge until sunset. At first Mark enjoyed it. He had drank plenty of water and he did not mind the mild heat, but as the sun got higher in the sky and as the fires burned down the rocks heated up even more and transferred the heat inside. By noon Mark was ready to leave, but he knew he had to stay. Probably he would have left if not for the fact that Rita came by and shoved two large jugs of water inside. Mark knew if he left he would embarrass himself and look like a weak person. He did not want to appear weak in front of Rita. An hour before sunset Mark felt his energy completely drain out of him. He knew there was not long to go but each second was becoming more and more unbearable. He was sure he was going to feint. The Snakeman opened his eyes and put his hand on top of Marks hand and smiled. "Not long to go, hang in there" He said.

Mark closed his eyes and tried to focus on other things but all he could think about was Tarita's hand with the jugs of water that she had brought earlier. He remembered holding her hand the night before. That is all he could think about. Her soft warm hand holding his, it was engraved in his mind.

The sun finally set. How the Snakeman knew the sun had set Mark would never know. The Snakeman left the sweat lodge followed by Tom and then Mark. When Mark stood outside he felt relieved but very weak. Tom and the Snakeman slowly dressed then headed back to the stone house that was a few hundred yards away. Mark tried to put his cloths on but then he collapsed on the ground. He lay there for a few minutes trying to gather some strength. After a while he was able to dress and he walked slowly back to the house.

Once inside they saw Rita had prepared a nice meal for them. They ate in silence. Mark wanted to talk to Rita but he could tell now was not the time for words. Each time he wanted to say something the Snakeman would look at him and put his finger to his lips to indicate silence. Rita and Mark still exchanged a few smiles. After the meal they sat on the patio outside. There was no brandy this time and the conversation remained light.

Early in the morning Tom woke Mark. Rita had prepared a meal and had packed snacks for them to take with them. The Keeper of the Gate stood on the porch stood on the porch and waved goodbye to them as they headed northeast past the circle of boulders in quest of the secret gate.

They hiked towards the mountains along a narrow trail through a gorge that seemed to appear from nowhere near the edge of the mesa. After a few miles the path they were on seemed to end and in front of them were large boulders that appeared to have been thrust out of the earth like guardians to protect anyone from advancing further. It appeared to Mark that there was absolutely no way to go any further and he was ready to voice his disgust at Tom for bringing them to a dead end. He was sure Tom was lost. Tom seemed to know what Mark was thinking so he turned and smiled at. "Don't worry we are not lost I know where we are going!" Tom smiled like a small child that was happy to have found a piece of candy. They sat down and ate some of their snacks. Tom began to share his experiences from the first time he had come to this place. Mark listened in awe, not sure to believe him or not.

Soon enough they were back up again and Tom led Mark around more boulders. There were places where the invisible trail became so narrow that they had to go single file and squeeze sideways to get through. After sometime Mark believed again that Tom was lost. They had been slithering around the large boulders for at least 20 minutes or so. Mark could hear water flowing alongside of them near the canyon but on occasions the sound stopped as the water must have flowed underground. They made a sharp turn as they headed higher up in the canyon through the boulders. After a short distance they heard the sound of the water again and as they once again squeezed through a narrow opening directly in front of them was magnificent waterfall that dropped into the gorge below. The water made a shimmering veil and dropped down to a large dark pool. They were standing on the edge of a cliff looking at the waterfall in front of them and the bubbling pool below them. They could go no further. There was no way to keep going in any direction. They stopped and Tom turned to Mark and said, "We're here." Mark almost laughed.

"What do you mean we're here? There is nothing here but a bunch of rocks!" Mark was not very happy and would have much rather preferred to be back at the house with Rita!"

Tom laughed out loud then put his back pack down and sat on the grass that was shimmering from the mist of the water. "Come on, you need to help me from now on."

Mark sat down next to him and stared at the amazing view in front of him. "Wow, this really is a beautiful place."

Tom replied, "Yes it is beautiful, but we have a bit further to go. You will be amazed! We have to leave our back backs here."

Mark assumed they had reached their final destination because it had been so difficult to find the place and it was so incredible, but he was wrong. They lay on their backs on the grass resting and bathing in the soft mist from the waterfall. As he stared up at the deep blue sky Mark again thought of Rita. He felt very peaceful. Tom explained the next part of the journey. Mark listened and asked no questions. He was committed now. He was committed to whatever the future brought his way. Rita's eyes shined through his mind and he felt very content.

They stripped down to their underwear and Tom lead the way towards the waterfall. They climbed some rocks on the side of the waterfall. There ancient handholds in the rocks and they climbed nearly straight up vertical. Some of the rocks had a slimy moss but not a lot of it. It was not too difficult to make your way up but they knew if they slipped they would fall to the jagged rocks below. As they neared the top there appeared to be a ridge. Tom climbed over the ridge and Mark followed.

There was a small cave and water from the waterfall was gently seeping in towards the rear of the cave. There was not much room to move around the edge of the small pond. There was nothing in the cave and it was small also. They sat on the edge of the pond with their feet dangling in the cool water. They could feel the current of the water flowing into the pond. It swirled in a small vortex.

"On three, Ok? Tom said.

"One more minute, I need to catch my breath." Mark replied.

"Don't worry it is not too far once you get in. Oh, I forgot to tell you that there are hand holds on both sides similar to the ones on the rocks as we climbed up here. You can use them to pull yourself along if you need to." Tom said.

"You know Tom, this is really crazy. Has anyone ever died doing this?" Mark asked.

"Oh sure, I don't know exactly how many. But I do know from Snakeman that if you do die, or if I die, the rule of only coming to the place twice still applies." Tom said.

"What if we both die?" Mark asked.

"Oh, I never asked him about that!" Tom said and then he started laughing, so Mark joined in and laughed also even though they both knew it was not funny and really a morbid thought.

"Ok, have you rested enough?" Tom asked.

"I guess so, it is now or never. You are going first though." Mark said.

"Yes, I am going first. One, two, three." Tom turned and grinned at Mark then rolled forward into the dark water and disappeared below the surface.

Mark hesitated, he remembered the instructions from Tom earlier to take a big breath and to keep moving forward no matter what. Once in there would not be enough room to turn around and go back. For a second he thought about just skipping the whole experience, but he had come this far so he figured he should follow through with it. A glimmer of a thought creeped into his mind but he couldn't pinpoint what it was. Then he pushed himself off the side of the pond into the vortex of water.

At first he didn't have to do much as the flow of the water pushed him along, but then he realized he probably was not moving fast enough. He couldn't see anything but darkness. He found the hand holds on the side of the water filled tunnel and pulled himself along. His lungs started to burn. He wasn't sure how much further he had to go. The slimy handholds were cold to his touch.

After about 20 seconds of holding his breath and pulling himself along he no longer cared if he made it to the end or not. He was going forward no matter what and he couldn't panic. Then like a flash of light from camera a dream he had as a child surfaced from his subconscious. The dream was like looking in a mirror and he recalled every detail of it. It was the same dream he had recalled on the day he went down the platform to meet the aliens for the same time. His lungs burned but he kept moving forward. Then at the last instant when he felt he would give up and suck in a lung full of murky water the tunnel shifted upwards and he thrust himself up through the surface of the water into another small pond. He blinked his eyes and there was Tom standing in front of him on the edge of the small opening with an ear to ear grin.

"Mark, I was getting worried. I was wondering why it took you so long." Tom blurted out.

Mark held on at the edge of the pool gasping for air. He didn't have the strength to pull himself out of the water so Tom reached out his hand and pulled Mark up to the cold stone floor. Mark lay on his back and peered up at small rays of sunlight filtering in from the ceiling of the cave high above. After a few minutes Mark sat up and noticed they were now in another cave a bit larger than the first one that was under the waterfall.

Mark recovered quickly and realized this was not the final destination when Tom stood and said, "Come on, follow me. We have a bit further to go." Tom was obviously excited. He seemed like a little kid at Christmas. Mark was too exhausted to feel any enthusiasm.

Tom led the way towards one side of the cave where there was a narrow opening in the sheer granite wall. They had to crawl on their knees into the passage, but for Mark at least he was no longer in water and he could see a light at the end of the tunnel which was not too far ahead. When they emerged from the tunnel, Marks mouth dropped.

Mark stood up and peered around. He knew for sure this was not something humans had built and it now dawned on him that obviously Mr. Kyn, Borghx and the other Marans were not the first aliens to visit earth. He had sort of guessed that, but it was never a subject he discussed with Mr. Kyn or Borghx. It was never a subject he had a lot of interest in. Now though, Tom

Whitecloud, The Snakeman, Rita, Ernie, and all the others came to his thoughts. He had always thought he was the smartest among everyone, the leader, the one with the clearest insights, but now that ended in one brilliant flash of revelation.

The room was magnificent and every detail was beyond what any human hand could have created. There was a similarity to the underground domes that the Marans along with their robots had built but there was also a uniqueness to this underground chamber. This was not built as a dwelling as it was too small compared to the shelters the Marans had built. It was a fairly large room, Maybe 40 yards across but it was nearly empty. Light came in from the ceiling which was at least 50 yards above them and also emanated from small clear glass or crystal windows in the walls. The floor and walls were ornate with inlayed silver and gold patterns. The walls were mostly pale blue or white made form a polished smooth stone and the floor was black obsidian. Many of the patterns reminded Mark of Native American geometrical patterns used on their pottery, walls, cloths, and a host of other objects. Some of the patterns had a crystal at their center. The crystals were of a variety of colors and seemed to have a soft glow to them.

Tom walked like he was walking in a church in the middle of the sermon. He headed towards the center of the room and motioned for Mark to follow him. There appeared to be a deep blue circle in the center of the room. As they approached it began to change colors to a dark lavender. Then Mark almost jumped when they reached the dark area in the center of the floor as a plume of water emerged from the spot. It was actually another pool of water and the plume turned into a gentle lavender fountain. The pool was maybe 10 yards across and because of the dark obsidian floor he had not noticed that it was there and probably if Tom had not guided him to the spot he would not have noticed it at all. Then incredibly at the apex of the fountain a crystal ball appeared and started to glow, first pink, then red, then purple. The fountain subsided and amazingly the crystal ball remained suspended in midair. It was just a bit larger than a man's head. There had to be some force keeping it floating above the fountain. As they both stared with their eyes wide open, Tom turned to Mark and whispered for him to remain very still.

The crystal ball began now to gradually spin and a rainbow of colors which were either reflecting the light from the ceiling above and/or from within the crystal emitted a hypnotizing light show. Then out of the water gradually emerged five black cylinders and on top of each one was a slightly smaller crystal ball. They emitted a pale blue light. It reminded Mark of Borghx's skin and he thought there had to be some connection, but his mind was not in an analytical state and the thought quickly evaporated. When the cylinders reached about five feet in height they stopped and then all of a sudden the cylinders dropped back into the water without a splash and the crystals remained suspended in midair just as the larger crystal was also suspended in midair. Both Mark and Tom felt their skin tingle.

"Before we go further I am required by the traditions passed down to me to explain a few concepts to you, Mark." Tom had reached over and put his hand on Mark's shoulder. Mark was lost in the moment. Tom gently tugged at the astonished Mark and motioned for him to back away from the pond and sit down. They sat on the inlayed black obsidian floor about ten yards from the pond with the glowing and spinning globes. "Mark, it is very important that you remember the things that I am going to tell you because when you return you must pass them on to the person you decide to bring here. First and probably at some point it has crossed your mind that it must be nearly impossible for this chain of visitors to go unbroken because at some point in time one of the people that came here for their first time would die. The Gate Keeper is well aware of that fact and if a certain length of time passes, at his discretion he picks someone else to replace the person that died, whether that person has died or not. Trust me, most the time the Gate Keeper knows what happens to the people that come here."

Tom continued, "What is important is that you remember the general context of what I am going to tell you and not my exact words. There is no concept of time here. You can interrupt that however you like. For most of us southwestern Indians, that is not a hard concept to understand. The vast majority of tribes in this area lack even verb tenses. The result is no conception of time. The closest a few have to a sense of time are two words; one meaning "sooner" and another meaning "later." The concept that time does not exist is even more apparent where we are now. To digress a bit, you know that when I met the Marans and Borghx, I was considered by many to be, "slow." I barely made it through High School and did not discover that I was Dyslectic until well into my twenties. Borghx helped me to regain my confidence and to expand my learning. My lineage allowed me to join the Council of Medicine Men more than anything else. Most of the men on the council have been here. We know that aliens have been to earth most likely numerous times in the past and for a variety of reasons. I never discussed this place with Borghx or Mr. Kyn, but I am fairly certain they knew of its existence."

Mark was listening very intently. He, as many others, had very much miss-judged Tom Whitecloud and now he regretted it. Tom paused for a few seconds and recognized the feeling of regret Mark had so he smiled inside. It meant little to Tom how others viewed him because he was confident and had already chosen his destiny. "Look Mark, I think it is important for you to understand why the council decided to go public with their knowledge of Mr. Kyn, Borghx and the others. I understand that was a major turning point in your life and led you to this moment. It also led to the death our friend Ernie, so I should explain more clearly to you the circumstances. As I stated before, we on the council have always been aware that aliens have been to earth. It is obviously possible other aliens are on earth at this moment. That I do not know. What we in the council knew was that the mission of Borghx and Mr. Kyn was a very specific one and that mission needed to succeed so that our Mother Earth would not die in a nuclear holocaust someday. We debated the issue for a long time on the council and we still planned to discuss the issue with Borghx and Mr. Kyn, but, unfortunately there was a reporter outside our meeting and the word was leaked out that the council knew the whereabouts of aliens. The US Security agencies picked up on that information before we could do anything about it. So even if our goal was just and our intent was in accord with Borghx's mission, once the leak was out; well you know the rest of the story. Thanks to your compassion and devotion, along with that of your friends, it appears most things have worked out pretty well." Tom paused and Mark nodded his head to show he at last understood what George and Ernie maybe never did understand.

"The last thing I have to tell you is that when we return to the pool and look at the crystal balls that are suspended, you must choose one and only one to focus your attention on. This is what we call the cavern of dreams and if you keep looking from ball to ball you will lose your mind. Seriously, I mean you will completely lose your mind. The same goes for the ball in the center. You cannot just stare at or focus on that one for any length of time or you will lose your mind. You will leave here and not even have a clue who you are or where you have been. Don't ask me how or why this place exists because I am not sure anyone that has been here really knows the reason. What we do know is that it is the cavern of dreams. If you allow your free will to guide your choice of which ball to stare into, you will see your future, you will understand everything that has happened to you in your life to this point in time and your view of reality will forever be changed."

"What if we both choose the same ball?" Mark asked

"Don't worry, we won't." Tom replied.

"How do you know that?" Mark asked.

"I don't really, but I have never heard of that happening and I am not willing to experiment. Plus, I will go first and choose and then you can follow a few minutes after me."

"Fair enough. I guess I am ready." Mark said as he was now anxious to see how he would be affected." He glanced over to where the balls were slowly spinning and at the ball in the center that was now emitted a soft green light.

Tom walked over first and sat on a small black obsidian cylinder that Mark had not noticed that had come out of the floor in front of the orb. Tom had not expressed to Mark what had happened the first time he came to the chamber of dreams. He had seen the Indian Council of which he became a member. He did not believe his vision and made no attempt to act on it until he met the aliens. Only then did he realize his vision had been true. This time he was in a more peaceful state of mind.

He saw an old man with long grey hair, it was the Snakeman. As he peered more deeply into the crystal orb he realized he was seeing an older version of himself. He had become the Keeper of the Gate. Tom smiled. He likee that future. There was also a beautiful woman with him. She was younger than him but she also held a child. It was his child. It was a boy. The vision was very clear and very fulfilling. For a brief instant Tom thought of staying longer and knowing more because this would be the last time he would come to this place, but quickly he decided against staying longer. He had seen a vision of peace for himself and a happy life, there was no reason to linger so he forced his eyes away from the globe and saw now that Mark had chosen one of the globes on the opposite side of him. Mark looked like a statue frozen in place. Marks eyes were nearly as big as the globes.

The very first thing Mark saw when he stared into the globe was an extremely large and odd room. The room was very lavish. There were intricate inlays on the walls with bright gemstones sparkling everywhere he looked. He began to walk through the room and he saw a circular door. He decided to walk through the room and go to the door. He pulled the door open and entered into another room. Almost immediately there were two small very mechanical looking robots that motioned him to follow. The robots seemed to be made of glass. He could see right through them. They led him down a passage off to the side of the room into yet another room.

Seated in the center of the room in what seemed like oversized chairs at an oversized dark red stone table inlayed with other types of colored stones were the aliens! It was Mr. Kyn, Kafta, Jacon, Shala, Aktal and his old friend George! They all stood and motioned for him to sit down, so he sat down. Then they sat back down continuning their eating, drinking and loud conversations seemingly ignoring him. George looked very young and very happy. He had never seen George look that way before. Then he noticed beside George was a small boy, it had to be Georges son. The boy smiled at him and he smiled back. Then as if by magic, Tarita appeared standing next to him. She had her hand on his shoulder. Mark turned and looked into her eyes and wanted to kiss her. She was wearing a sheer silken white robe. Her eyes sparkled with a strange light and it made him fall madly in love with her.

He kept staring into Tarita's eyes and before he realized what was happening the two of them were rising above the room. They were outside in the sky and an eagle was flying beside them. They were below the marshmallow clouds but they were flying above the land below. Then their flight slowed down and they saw there was a hidden valley with a crystal blue stream below them. Then Mark realized it was only a spiritual flight and he was back in his body, human again. He and Tarita were lying naked near the stream, kissing, and embracing on a grassy knoll. A soft light circled above them reflecting their inner cosmos.

Instinctively Mark closed his eyes and tried to hold on to the vision. When he opened them Tom was standing by his side and pulling him away from the pond. All of the globes had descended back into the pool of water and now the water seemed to be boiling. Mark started to tear up. He looked away from the pond, he backed away from Tom and collapsed to the hard stone floor weeping like baby. He felt lost but happy. He had no idea where he was and he was not sure if he was dreaming or awake. He had never experienced those two emotions at the same time and it overwhelmed him. He recalled everything important that had happened to him so far in his life and he felt regrets, maybe too many regrets, maybe it was those thoughts that made him weep even more. He didn't cry for long though, because his macho American man side kicked in and he realized Tom Whitecloud was standing over him so put his hand up as if to indicate he was going to be fine. Then he stood up and grinned at Tom, "I guess I just got a little emotionally overwhelmed. Hopefully I did not stare into that globe too long. The visions or dreams, whatever you want to call it brought out a lot of feelings I never knew I had. How long do you think we have been here? Is there more to see or do? I am not sure I can handle any more of this place. I am fairly certain this place was constructed by Borghx's people. I think it is some kind of power center that tries to have an influence on the human race in a good way of course. Maybe that is the reason it is so secret."

Tom nodded in agreement, "I think we need to get going now. It is near dawn. We have been here longer than both of us realize."

Tom led them to a far corner of the chamber where there was a large slab of dark blue granite standing alone against the wall. "Come on Mark you need to help me push this." So they both pushed one end of the large stone slab and it slowly revealed an opening into another tunnel. After they entered the tunnel the slab closed in back of them. They crawled on their hands and knees for about thirty yards and came to ledge that opened up to the river below them. It was a calm part of the river but there was no way down other than to leap into the water. It was only about 30 feet down and Tom went first. Mark followed him into the cold water. They swam to the shore and then Tom led them up a path to where they had left their cloths and backpacks. They dressed, ate and rested for an hour in the warm morning sun.

The journey back seemed to go twice as fast. They talked very little. Mark noticed that many different birds would swoop down near them and there were two eagles high in the sky that seemed to follow them the whole way back.

When they reached the Snakeman's place it was late in the afternoon. Tarita came running out and went straight into Mark's arms giving him a warm welcoming hug. "I had the most incredible dream last night!" She whispered into his ear. They went arm and arm back to Snakeman's porch and as they stepped onto the porch another Indian woman appeared from inside and smiled at them.

Snakeman looked at Tom, "This is my niece, Tanya." Tom and Tanya smiled at each other. Tom knew this was the woman he saw in his dream and his future wife. Time seemed to stand still with a glow that enveloped all of them.

The two men bathed and cleaned themselves from the journey. Even though they had not slept now for a day and a half neither one of them was tired. Food was prepared and they ate their first hot meal in what seemed like forever. They sat around on the porch sharing stories as the sun sunk low onto the horizon.

Snakeman brought out a bottle of his brandy and they shared some drinks as the sun set in the West off to their left behind some large boulders that were part of the ring of boulders. As the sky darkened a full moon appeared on the opposite side. The night air was crisp and clear. The moon rose above the silhouetted dark mountains and the Snakeman grew very silent. He closed his eyes almost as if he was going to sleep and let the others converse. After some time he opened his eyes and fixed them on the rising moon. After a half an hour or so he rose up from his chair and put one hand in the air motioning to the others that he had something important to say.

"I have known for some time that Tom Whitecloud would become my successor here. He will become the next Keeper of the Gate. I have been here many years watching over the passage to the Cavern of Dreams. There have only been a few instances of outsiders trying to seek the path and I was able to send them in another direction with no harm. The secret has been kept for longer than any of us know." He then sat back down and took a long deep breath. Maybe he was feeling nostalgic for his younger years or maybe he was at last relived that he would move on with what remained of his elderly life. The others knew he had more to say.

"I looked for many years to see the sign of a successor coming here and now I know Tom is my successor. I am happy he returned with Mark and fulfilled his path." Then the Snakeman stood again and raised his hand as he had done earlier. "I can feel the warmth of this moon in my heart. Come! Come! We must all go now to view the final sign. It is a rare and magnificent sign that we will all take the path to our final destiny starting tonight."

How old the Snakeman was, no one really knew. Tarita had told Mark that he was her Grandfather, but Mark knew that could mean her Great Grandfather, but it really didn't matter now. The old man hopped from the porch like he was a teenager. "Come. Follow me. We must go now." He said as he scurried off in the direction of the looming full moon. The others followed. They were clueless to what he was saying or where he was leading them, but they followed.

Even though his body was old and frail he walked quickly with a purpose. He led them pass the circle of boulders onto the flat mesa. After a few minutes the mesa opened into a depression. It was a large crater maybe the size of a football field and it was not noticeable until you were almost at the edge of it.

He slowed his walk and headed towards the center of the crater almost as if he was stalking an elusive prey. Then he stopped near the center and turned to the others. They were all staring at a large branching tall cactus. The cactus was alone with no other vegetation near it. It was taller than a man but in a way it looked like a man. The Snake man whispered for them to sit around the cactus in a circle and to be very silent so they followed his directions. There was a single tightly closed long flower at the top of the cactus. It was not open and it was at least a foot and a half long. The Snakeman sat so the flower was silhouetted against the full moon in the background.

They waited and watched. The Keeper of the Gate began to chant in a soft rhythmic voice. The air became very still and there seemed to be a radiant heat coming up from the earth.

Very slowly, like a person waking from a beautiful dream, the flower began to open. It was a large and radiant white flower. It pointed towards the full moon. The Snakeman stopped his chant and told the others that the flower only bloomed on this cactus one night during a full moon every seven years. It was a very rare event. Tarita held Marks hand. Tanya snuggled close to Tom. Somewhere in the distance a night bird began to sing breaking the silence of the moonlit night.

The End

Made in the USA
San Bernardino, CA
14 August 2017